Lesson in Red

ALSO BY MARIA HUMMEL

Still Lives

Motherland

House and Fire

Wilderness Run

LESSON IN RED

A Novel

Maria Hummel

COUNTERPOINT
Berkeley, California

Lesson in Red

First hardcover edition: 2021

Library of Congress Cataloging-in-Publication Data

Names: Hummel, Maria, author.
Title: Lesson in red : a novel / Maria Hummel.
Description: First hardcover edition. | Berkeley, California : Counterpoint, 2021.
Identifiers: LCCN 2020029463 | ISBN 9781640094314 (hardcover) | ISBN 9781640094321 (ebook)
Subjects: GSAFD: Mystery fiction.
Classification: LCC PS3608.U46 L47 2021 | DDC 813/.6—dc23
LC record available at https://lccn.loc.gov/2020029463

Jacket design by Jaya Miceli
Book design by Jordan Koluch

COUNTERPOINT
2560 Ninth Street, Suite 318
Berkeley, CA 94710
www.counterpointpress.com

Printed in the United States of America

10 9 8 7 6 5 4 3 2 1

for Margaret Parmelee Hummel

There is a wonderful kidnapped hunted raped and betrayed girl
In fairy tales. She has a name, but the vowels and subjects
Around can't be switched to fit.

She wants to escape but letters won't let her.

She never thinks about darkness or dying because they're natural
And don't require thought.

She carries her darkness everywhere.
What is not natural

Is being here an utter stranger.
And flight being no metaphor.

—FANNY HOWE, from "The Definitions"

Cast of Characters

The Rocque Museum

Maggie Richter, copy editor
Yegina Nguyen, exhibitions manager
Janis Rocque, founder and chief donor
Hiro Isami, grant writer, Yegina's boyfriend
Dee Rager, crew manager, Janis's girlfriend
Lynne Feldman, chief curator
Phil and Spike Dingman, graphic designers, twins
Bas Tarrant, museum director

The Westing Gallery

Nelson de Wilde, gallerist
Hal Giroux, LAAC MFA director
Pearson Winters, former LAAC student

Layla Goetz-Middleton, LAAC student
Erik Reidl, LAAC student
Zania de Wilde, LAAC student, Nelson's daughter

The Investigations

Brenae Brasil, LAAC student, deceased
Ray Hendricks, private investigator
Calvin Teicher, art history scholar, half brother of Ray, deceased
Alicia Ruiz, LAPD detective
Davi Brasil, musician, brother of Brenae
Nancy and Fernando Brasil, parents of Brenae
Jay Eastman, journalist, Maggie's former boss
Nikki Bolio, Maggie and Jay's informant, deceased

Art World

Steve Goetz, collector, father of Layla
Kim Lord, artist, deceased
James Compton, 1990s artist and organizer, deceased

Lesson in Red

1

SOON AFTER I MOVED TO Los Angeles to start a new life, I went to an anniversary screening of *Dr. Zhivago* in the dark, ornate theater where it had once premiered. Afterward, the art director took the stage to tell some stories about the filmmaking.

"Remember the scene on the moving train," he said, "where the peasant woman runs and leaps into the speeding car? She's wearing all that heavy wool, and she almost doesn't make it up through the doors in time."

That was because the actress had to do the jump twice, weeks apart. "The first time she tried, she slipped, and the train badly smashed her legs," the art director said, nodding at the gasps in the audience. So the woman had to heal, and then hurl herself again. The second time, she succeeded. "Her sacrifice was a sign of everyone's devotion to the movie," he marveled. "She caught her train, and the scene was saved."

Yet when they cut the film together, he added, they spliced in the footage from the first take, when the woman knows she won't make it. You can watch the fear flash and deepen in her face. "You hear her scream," he said. "The scream is real."

I could have told this story when people in my Vermont hometown asked me what L.A. was like. But I didn't. *Sunny. Crowded,* I replied instead. *I saw some movie stars. I miss the fish tacos.* I said these things, because it was easier to offer up what my rural neighbors expected. To let them conclude I was over the city, and back in Vermont for good. They laughed and let me alone, relieved to have their convictions confirmed. If anyone probed deeper, I talked about my job at the art museum and my Hollywood bungalow, but the tales were flat and they had no endings, because I couldn't say the truth. I lost a love in L.A. I almost died there. And hardest of all: For one brief hour, I was certain I had all the clues to save a missing woman, a brilliant and generous artist, probably a genius. And then someone told me she was already dead, murdered and abandoned in a shallow grave.

I did miss L.A., though. I missed it in pieces. Hiking the steep, sunny sides of Runyon Canyon. Eating frozen rosewater topped with saffron ice cream. Ducking into dim bars in Echo Park, loud guitars blistering in my ears. I even missed the rush-hour river on the 101, how it made me stay late downtown for happy hours on hotel rooftops, until the dazed afternoons grew cool and sharper with darkness, under heat lamps and towering skyscrapers. And I'd had good friends in L.A., women, mostly, also living on the sliding edge of our late twenties, torn between who our mothers had been and the career divas we were told we could become. Together, we'd catch our reflections in long windows, those slim, agile strangers gliding to the next block.

But when I thought about my last month in Los Angeles, of the night I had driven across the city, mad with fear, and climbed into my ex's empty bed and put on his missing girlfriend's clothes, it made me curl into a tight ball inside. Who was that Maggie, and how had she become so unhinged, so obsessed and reckless? I didn't want to meet her gaze in the mirror. Yet I knew her well. That Maggie had been inside me for a long time, ever since a freezing spring years ago, when a young woman's body had washed up on a Vermont lakeshore. The third day I was home, I drove past the bay where my source had been murdered, and my neck ached all the way down to my fingertips, as if I had been holding myself rigid for hours.

One cool night in May, not long after, I found myself in the same bed where I had slept as a teenager, tossing, awake. I had to face down that other Maggie, and I wasn't sure I was strong enough to confront her alone, so far away. At three in the morning, I rose and went to my parents' study, quietly closing the door to cover the whistle of their dial-up modem. My fingers typed an online classified ad for my Hollywood courtyard bungalow, offering it as a cheap sublet until September. By morning, I had fifty applicants. At least ten seemed polite, reliable, and incredibly desperate. *I drove by your bungalow and it's so cute. It looks lonely, too. I'll take great care of it.* The more letters I read, the more the apartment slipped from me, and my return to Los Angeles as well. I'd had my shot at L.A. Maybe it was time to give someone else a chance. Maybe I wasn't cut out for the city on my own; I had only ventured there because my ex had accompanied me. The next day, I sublet my bungalow to a couple who were uprooting from Boston and wanted a soft landing. He was a TV editor; she was a private-school history teacher. They had both gone to Ivy League schools, and one of their references was from a modestly famous writer, who adored them and teasingly chastised me for luring them away.

The couple knew that I intended to come back in the fall, but could they have the place until January 1? *We know it's asking a lot, but it would make things so much easier for us.*

Let me think about it, I wrote back. And the next day, heart pounding, I said yes.

I told my parents and best friend, Yegina, about the sublet but not the extension. As long as I didn't acknowledge it aloud, my bungalow was still mine, and I could return to it and to my job when my medical leave concluded at the end of September. At the same time, I left open the possibility that I would not fly west, and that the Rocque Museum would have to fire me. In truth, I dreaded either future: staying in Vermont with my parents, or rebuilding my life in Los Angeles. Instead, I liked to imagine the history teacher, perched on my yellow couch, delighting in the avocado tree on the patio. She might even start gardening a little, setting out terra-cotta pots of basil and cherry tomatoes, glorying in her first California sunshine.

I talked to Yegina once or twice a week that summer, catching up on museum gossip and relating my mother's perplexingly animated engagement with my hometown's solid waste committee. We laughed a lot and kept things light. Still, it felt like someone was laying down more miles between us every time we spoke. When Yegina asked me one warm August day when I was returning, I said the same thing I'd always said: late September. But still I hadn't bought a ticket. I didn't name a date.

"*Still Lives* is closing September 15," she informed me. "We had a big debate about extending the dates, because it's still drawing a lot of visitors. But Janis wants us to move on. She says we're not in the business of 'titillating tourists.'"

I laughed at Yegina's imitation of our museum leader's deep, brusque voice, but it was hard to imagine our crew taking down the paintings of murdered women, hanging them on racks in our crowded storage room, shrouded by cloth. All those panicked, lovely, and shuttered expressions, all those Kims looking out from the horror of their deaths, soon to be locked away.

"I thought, maybe, *Still Lives* was one of the reasons you haven't come back," Yegina said tentatively. "It's been hard for everyone at the museum. Every day the visitors come to see it, we have to keep reliving what happened. But you won't have to, if you return after the fifteenth."

"I sublet my place till New Year's," I admitted.

There was a pause as the news sank in.

"But your job," Yegina said. "The designers are already falling apart. The museum can't extend your leave until 2004."

"I know they can't." I told her how happy the Ivy League couple seemed, how grateful, how eminently successful. He'd landed a position with Universal. She was applying for a PhD at UCLA. They were thrilled by my bungalow's location and hoped to find a place exactly like it. Hint, hint.

"So you're quitting the Rocque," Yegina said.

"No. Not yet, anyway."

"Please don't tell me you're abandoning your whole life here to make a couple of snobby strangers happy."

"I'm not," I said. "But I have to practice letting go for real. I have to try it out. So if I go back to California, it's for the right reasons."

It was hard to convince Yegina that a Hollywood bungalow rented below today's market value wasn't reason enough, but we ended up riffing happily together over the ridiculousness of California real estate. I was relieved that she finally knew the whole truth. She, too, seemed lightened by my honesty, though her voice hollowed when we said good-bye. So did mine.

I hung the phone on its hook, made small talk with my mother, and ate a fresh tomato sandwich. Then I wandered to the creek to watch where a tributary came in, thinking about the scientist who claimed that time could branch, that it could contain two futures at once. All I'd ever seen was the opposite: two rivers blending into one, then another joining from elsewhere, the current deeper, mightier. One stream formed from many: that was time for me. And the present, my present, held multiple, powerful pasts.

"You look stronger every day," my mother commented to me when I came in, muddy and mosquito bitten. She stood at our kitchen counter, graying blond hair lit by sun, her fists deep in bread dough. "Does your side still hurt a lot?"

"No," I said, flipping through the mail, letters and bills, none of them for me.

"There's a cider festival this weekend in town," she said. "Might be fun."

I didn't want to go to a cider festival in town, but I knew that saying this aloud would come out wrong. "I do feel stronger," I told her sincerely. "I'm grateful for all you've done for me."

My mother gathered the edges of the dough, thumped it, and pushed into it again.

"We're glad to have you home," she said. "Does it feel like home?"

"Sometimes." My voice caught in my throat. "It feels familiar."

"You still miss California," she said.

I nodded.

"Do you miss someone in particular?" She kept her eyes on her kneading, but her voice circled me gently.

"No," I said. I wasn't lying. The same person had kept materializing in my mind that day, but we weren't friends. I didn't miss her. I had no right, no claim of personal relationship. Instead, Janis Rocque was an icon to me, brimming with power and influence. Yet we'd struck up an odd correspondence over the summer, and her last message, this morning, was the most strange and compelling of all.

"How can I help out today?" I asked to distract myself. "Give me a job."

My mother stopped kneading and regarded me. I could tell she wanted to probe more, but I kept my expression blank and friendly, and she gave in. "You could pick up the drops," she said, gesturing out the window with a floury hand. "Around the pear tree. I can't keep up with them."

BUCKET BESIDE ME, I GATHERED the pears that had fallen from the backyard tree, reaching carefully to avoid the bees that drank themselves silly on the sun-fermented fruit. As the green orbs piled up, I thought about Janis. At Rocque planning meetings, Janis always sat erect, with her feet crossed in practical black flats. The suits she wore—navy or gray, and never a skirt—seemed designed to erase any impressions her body might deliver, and emphasized instead her fierce, ageless face. Her nose was long but shapely, her hair swept forward over a high forehead, and her gaze had the depth of a cauldron. Her alto voice cut through chatter and commanded silence. No one knew what would come out of her mouth: rousing praise or a precise and painful rebuke; art-world gossip; imperious pronouncements, sometimes wise, "We don't look at great art and think *That's beautiful*; we think *That's true*," sometimes bizarrely regionalist, "San Francisco is for gamers and toadies." But Janis wasn't a performer. She only talked when necessary. Her dark head cocked to listen to our curators, and bent, frowning over some new report on the Rocque's depressing finances. She nodded when new staff members spoke up, encouraging them. She steered the museum through the entire *Still Lives* crisis with firm kindness, transforming my fears at incurring her disapproval into an abiding yearning to impress her.

Back in July, Janis had sent an inquiry into my health, and a request. *I know you are off duty these days, but I need the right person to write about Kim Lord. When* Still Lives *comes down, two of her paintings will be installed in our permanent collection. We need a good wall text to go with them. Nothing sensational, but the facts must be there.*

I labored over the assignment for three days and sent Janis the results. She quibbled with a line and then wanted more, and soon we found ourselves in a correspondence that ranged beyond the text to what had happened to us at the museum when Kim was murdered by another Rocque employee, and a rich collector confessed to rigging the artist's career. In person, Janis would never have opened up so much to me. I was sure of it. But something about my distance and my injury complicated her usual conduct with personnel. She'd seen me carried, bleeding, away from her property. She knew what I'd done. She felt sympathy for me, and she needed to make sense of the tragedy with someone who wasn't at the museum, walking among all her shocked and hurting staff.

Yesterday, Janis sent me a new message: terse, a few lines. She said she was glad that I was returning soon, and she wanted to know if I had gone to Los Angeles Art College and knew anyone there.

No, I wrote back. *I have not gone to LAAC or any art school. I am not an artist or hoping to be, though I love writing about art. I once worked for Jay Eastman, and he told me that "you know that you've found your subject when it changes how you see the world."* Mentioning Eastman was a little brag. I knew Janis would recognize the name of the famous reporter.

I'm flattered to be asked, though, I went on. To be a graduate of LAAC was, I knew, to be an inductee into one of the most selective art circles in L.A. The small school in nearby Valdivia had produced a long list of stars, from all the way back into the eighties. *Our designers at the Rocque went to LAAC, and they have told me terrific stories of the place.*

Why? I added. And then I erased the word. It sounded so bold. I wrote it again, a different way. *Why are you curious?* Erased that, too.

Let me know if I can be of any help, I typed finally, and left it at that.

Janis responded this morning.

Maybe you can, she wrote. *There's a tragic story involving LAAC, and someone discreet needs to tell it. Let me know when you're back.*

2

"ARE YOU GETTING ENOUGH AIR back there?" Yegina said, twisting to check on me for the fifth time since we'd left her house in Silver Lake. Huge round sunglasses obscured her eyes.

"If you can call what we breathe air," I said agreeably.

Air wasn't my problem in the cramped back seat of my best friend's yellow Mazda. It was leg room. Yegina and her boyfriend, Hiro, had packed as if they had been evacuating Paris instead of spending a night in the desert outside Twentynine Palms, looking at new art installations. Duffel bags bulged beside me, their zippers straining. Grocery sacks filled with snacks and drinks enough for twenty. And I knew that a large canvas tote held Yegina's snowy comforter. She couldn't sleep under hotel duvets. Most hotels washed their coverlets only a couple of times a year, she had informed me once, a statistic I could have guessed at, but then we all have obvious facts we like to ignore.

Hiro was in the passenger seat, flipping through her CDs and murmuring at their names. He had been doing this for nearly thirty minutes, which suggested two things to me. First, Hiro had a distinctive capacity to marvel over things before he chose them, and, second, he was dreading the actual songs. So was I. Yegina favored nineties hardcore, the more caustic the better. The harsh chords made something spring loose inside her, and her head would bob, her chin would jut, her black hair falling in her eyes. Suddenly, late-twenties, business-casual Yegina rewound to her rebellious teen years, when she would sneak out of her house in leather pants and steel-toed boots to jump into mosh pits at a bowling-alley punk club in Highland Park. Instead of progressing past this musical phase like the rest of the sane adult world, Yegina had become an obsessive collector of its history.

"The Mormons," Hiro said, pondering one disc. "Are they really Mormons?"

It was a dumb question in a way, an easy setup for a snappy comeback from my quick-witted best friend, but Yegina smiled at him. Hiro had a shy, sincere manner that made him difficult to mock, and the two of them had become very close in the months that I'd been gone. Wedged in the back seat next to their heaps of possessions, I felt my imposition more than ever. I was grateful for their friendship and for the ride to Wonder Valley, but I chafed at being a third wheel.

"You sure you want us to just drop you off?" Yegina said, as if she sensed my feelings.

I nodded. "There's only a couple of scheduled screenings. I don't want to miss them."

"We could stay for the first one, couldn't we?" Yegina said to Hiro. "It's Brenae Brasil."

"Um," he said. It was clear the name didn't register. "My cousin said six o'clock."

There was a silence.

"Okay, that's a no. Let's keep it simple," Yegina said to me. "We'll take your bag to your hotel for you. If we see you tonight, we see you. I hope we see you. If not, we'll swing by at noon tomorrow for the ride back."

Our plans weren't simple, but they were pure Yegina, well intentioned and multitasked. They were going to dinner at Hiro's cousin's house in Twentynine Palms, then visiting some of the art pieces on the festival's extensive map before checking in at their hotel. I was meeting Janis Rocque and her girlfriend, Dee Rager, at The Oasis to watch a screening. I would get a ride with them to their hotel, where I had a room, too. Tomorrow, I would carpool home with Yegina and Hiro. I had no car, iffy reception on my cheap phone, and a giant desert to get lost in, but I had my friends.

I hoped I had my friends.

That moment would have been a good time to admit that my reception was weak and I hadn't heard from Dee, but I didn't want Yegina to worry about me. She had a wealthy cousin to impress, and I would finally learn more about Janis's summons. I'd come back to the Rocque in time to see *Still Lives* close. I'd stood at the edge of the galleries as Dee and her crew maneuvered the paintings off the walls, silently, without their usual chatter and ribbing. The still life, the largest canvas, was last. It was also the only artwork without Kim Lord's face in it, and I could regard it without losing my breath. I let my eyes ride over the painted notebook, the bloodstained screwdriver, and the split white apple, promising myself not to forget Kim's fearlessness and generosity.

I'd also returned to a map on my office desk. From Janis. The map advertised a Joshua Tree art festival the third weekend in October, with Brenae Brasil's screening circled on it. *Dee and I are going to this,* said a note beside it. *Could you meet us there? We'll get you a room at the Major Motel. I want you to see it, and then we'll talk in detail.* Janis was away on a collecting vacation in China and Japan, but she'd be back the next month. The festival would give me a chance to see dozens of new art installations on remote desert properties, and the Major Motel was an exorbitant desert getaway, the kind that rock stars stayed in. The invitation flattered me, but my gut squeezed at what I had really committed myself to. I knew who Brenae Brasil was:

an LAAC student who'd shot herself in her studio early last spring, right around the time we were planning the *Still Lives* gala.

Brenae Brasil's name, underlined by Janis in heavy black pen, clanged like a warning now. *Don't get involved in this.*

But I was already involved. Without Janis's promise of a story for me, I wouldn't be back in L.A. I'd be home, adding a wool hat and gloves to my warm autumn jacket. I'd be applying for a communications job at the local university. Janis had told me just enough to hook me: she had inside knowledge that Brenae's death was more complicated than it seemed, and that the culture of the school needed investigating. *I know what happened on my property, and what secret you kept,* she wrote to me. *This situation is very delicate, and whoever looks into it must (1) know the art world and (2) use discretion about when to go public. You'd be paid well. I can tell you more when we meet.*

So I'd hugged both my parents hard when I told them I was moving back, and I'd found a month-to-month sublet in Marina del Rey with aggressively bland decor. Though it was a safe location, it wasn't home like my bungalow. And work wasn't the same place, either. My boss, Jayme, had quit and moved to Hawaii, and the twin designers had new girlfriends and were disappointingly absent and self-absorbed. The Rocque social life had moved on from rooftop hotel bars to a downtown dive coated with dust so vintage that it could be River Phoenix's sloughed-off skin from the early nineties. With my old pals, I went through the motions of drinking and dancing and grousing about work. I had a one-night stand with an art installer in town for the weekend. He was ten years older than me, wiry, British, funny, and adept at charmingly harmless seduction. I enjoyed myself, but it all seemed to take too long and be over too soon.

Still, the temporary fling was preferable to the Yegina-Hiro dynamic—their overpacked car, the portentous meeting with the relatives, all the pressures of being in love longer than the first few dizzy months. I was happy for my friend, but I wondered if she was happy for herself.

"I hope I see you tonight, too," I said to Yegina. I wanted to hear how it went.

HOURS LATER, AFTER YEGINA'S HARDCORE had given us all migraines and we'd traded for a dull hangover of Hiro's Dvořák selections, we inched through the busy strips of Yucca Valley and Joshua Tree. Beyond them, the nowhere gained on us fast. Rocks and scrabble and mountain peaks lined the distance. A long, loping sky unfolded. The sun was setting when we reached Wonder Valley, which was first defined by nothingness on either side of the road. Then we passed car after car parked on the right, and a large sign sprang up, dark letters on white paint, framed by unfinished wood: THE OASIS BAR AND RESTAURANT. A crude mask-like face gazed out from the sign's center. The lot was so choked with dusty, dented trucks that it resembled a junkyard. Behind it squatted a one-story cinder-block building, beer signs glowing, and behind that, some kind of stage and a giant movie screen, flickering with the black-and-white image of a gun stuck in the back of a woman's tight jeans. Her behind was the size and shape of a shack, the gun handle its crooked chimney.

"Is that—" said Yegina.

"I think so," I said. The sight of Brenae Brasil made me cold.

Immediately we were back in the open desert, flanked by another line of parked cars. Yegina's tires spun in the sand as we turned to loop back.

"She looks so young," she said.

So young, so sexy, and so dangerous. Another dead girl reversed to life again by her beautiful image.

According to a Valdivia newspaper article, Brenae Brasil had killed herself in her LAAC studio one night with the gun she had been using on-screen. She'd been found dead a couple of days later. That was the official take on it.

Official takes didn't sit well with me anymore. Maybe Brenae hadn't ended her life. Maybe someone had ended it for her. Gun suicides are easy to fake. There was more to discover, I was sure, but I had resisted the itch to dig further. Let Janis make her case to me first.

"Thanks for the ride," I said lightly, trying to suppress my dread. Now that I'd arrived, I wanted to turn around. I wanted to crash the dinner with the rich cousin.

Yegina caught sight of my face and slowed to a stop beside a big black truck. "You're sure Janis and Dee are coming? We could go in with you for a few minutes."

Hiro blinked and took a breath. They were already almost late for dinner. "Sure," he said.

"Just a few," Yegina said to him, and he nodded.

The pity in both my friends' faces gave me resolve.

"No need. I just got a voicemail," I lied, holding up my phone. "They're already inside. Can you imagine how uncomfortable Janis is?" Janis hated to expose her personal life; it had taken her months to see how this hurt Dee, but now the two made appearances together as a couple from time to time. "I've got to go," I added, leaping out. "She's probably going to last about five more minutes."

The sound of Yegina's worried laugh broke as I slammed my door and headed through the dust to the bar.

IN THE FIRST ROOM AT The Oasis, two men leaned beside a pool table that looked like it had barely survived a sandstorm. They glanced at me, then back at their game. Customers clogged every inch of the wooden counter beyond. Skinny female hipsters in embroidered T-shirts shoved up against bleach-haired lady smokers giving them the stink-eye. The clamor was intense, but no one seemed to be talking to one another, just shouting in the general direction of the liquor bottles about whether or not our new celebrity governor was going to keep any of his campaign promises.

I was thirsty, but the wait would be long, so I went to look for Janis and Dee. I threaded my way to the next room, scanning the crowd. There were no short, intense middle-aged women and their fey British girlfriends. Battered road signs hung from the walls, larger than life. NO RIGHT TURN. BINGO! FRI & SAT. The air thickened with every step, growing layers of smoke, beer, sweat, and the dreamy cellophane aura of ambition that follows all the young people who move to L.A. Beyond: another cavern, this one full of booths, each stuffed with customers, elbow to elbow, holding clear and golden drinks. I smiled to myself at the scene and found a small corner of space beside a giant black papier-mâché cat. It wore a red velvet robe. An empress cat. I liked it immediately. It reminded me of Janis.

All of us at the Rocque had our stories about Janis's regal benevolence. How she measured each of us with her alert gaze. She made sure our benefits were top-notch, despite the cost to the budget. She loved having company for Dodgers games and slipped surprise tickets into people's mailboxes. She knew everyone's name and their problems, and in late afternoons, usually before a new exhibition was to open, she wandered the museum corridors, finding an office and sailing in. She would begin her prying by asking about the art on view. She wanted to hear true opinions, and to argue them down victoriously. And then she wanted gossip. What did you hear about Brent, the crew leader, and his ill wife? "He carries great personal burdens, you know. Great burdens," Janis would say, dangling the opportunity for her listener to contribute. "This can't go beyond this room," she would add, stern but cozy with you. She rarely maligned anyone, but she dug and ferreted and delighted over nuggets of personal information from people, the more famous and powerful the better. Confidentiality was a promise that you knew that Janis herself would betray as soon she drifted to the next office, yet to be blessed with her attention meant you belonged at the Rocque and she cherished you. I'd come 150 miles to prove myself to her, and she wasn't even here.

The empress cat was too short to hide behind for long, but its raised paw aimed out the door to a trellised yard. I was just about to follow its directive when I felt someone's eyes. I looked back to the bar and froze.

Slouched in the half-light, bearded, with a sky-blue trucker cap pulled low and his face fixed in a dopey, roamed-out expression, he almost fooled me. But there was no mistaking that gaze, the way it sharpened so slowly I used to think he was half-awake. And there was no mistaking the swift, dexterous way he moved. My chest started ramming so hard it hurt. Before I could step forward, he pushed back from the bar and vanished around the corner, out of sight.

I hadn't seen Ray Hendricks since the L.A. hospital room where he told me to lie to the police about an attempt on my life. In the months that had passed since, he'd made no contact with me except for one letter, and I'd assumed he had gone back to North Carolina. From time to time, I searched his name online, but if he'd returned to his special agent job busting meth labs in the Appalachian Mountains, the media was not reporting it. What was he doing in Wonder Valley? Seeing him summoned a wave of memories: Ray at my museum's press conference, handing me my butterfly earring; Ray at the bar, grimly telling me Kim Lord was dead; Ray leaping into a pit of broken glass to rescue me; Ray's bandaged hand on mine in the hospital room. How many times had I turned those memories over in my mind, wanting to believe they had meant something? And yet here he was now, in the flesh, walking away without the slightest acknowledgment. My recollections seemed oversize and ludicrous.

After several people pushed past me, dazed and motionless, I slipped outside to compose myself. As soon as I passed through the door, a hand grabbed my wrist and tugged me along the rough adobe wall, into the dark. I knew it was Ray before I saw his low cap and beard. But still his appearance shocked me. Sculpted by shadows, his face looked hawk-like, predatory. He also looked—strangely—afraid.

"Janis and Dee can't make it tonight," he said quietly, still holding my wrist. "But your room is booked, and I can get you a cab there—"

"Why couldn't they come?" I said. "Why are you here?"

Ray jerked his head toward the giant projection, which was flickering to black. The screening was about to begin. "I'll explain later." He paused. "You don't know me tonight, though, okay? I'll find you. Don't look for me."

I'd missed Ray's voice, the mellowing timbre that inflected his words. But I didn't want him to see that. I wasn't there for him.

"I won't." I pulled at my trapped wrist, and Ray stared at it, as if he didn't know it was in his grip. His thumb gently stroked my inner arm, then he let go and strode away, adjusting his cap.

On the screen, the word PACKING appeared, accompanied by a groan of music, and everyone started streaming from the bar to watch. The crowd pushed me closer to the screen, closer to where Ray was standing, behind a clump of . . . grad students? Young art collectors? Two men, two women, all in their twenties, a tight-knit collective. Ray had his head angled toward the screen, but I could tell he was watching them. Why? They didn't appear menacing, just shoddy in an expensive way. Rich kids trying to slum with their low-slung jeans and layered shirts. Or maybe I was judging them too fast. The bald guy wore shorts and orthotic sneakers. The redhead had her own look, like a teenager who'd dressed herself from a flea market, but her hair glowed with the luster of salon-grade shampoo, and no one did makeup like that unless they'd been trained by Hollywood. She seemed familiar, too, though I didn't know why.

A stern female voice intoned, "Welcome to the first public screening of a landmark film by an artist who died too young."

My goodness, Lynne Feldman was present. And speaking to this crowd. I'd always set great store by my chief curator's tastes, which were as sharp and surprising as a Japanese pickled plum. So I was curious to see her endorse a mere grad student, albeit a grad student of world-renowned LAAC.

The screen popped and there they stood, Lynne the curator in her usual dark suit and scarlet mouth, silhouetted before Brenae Brasil, huge, facing forward now, every detail of her physique magnified. There was the young artist's curly black hair, lifted by a headband, there her dark brows and full cheeks, her muscular body clad in T-shirt and jeans. Frozen, illuminated, and enlarged like this, Brenae Brasil had the air of an idol. She glowed. She symbolized. It was hard to imagine the real person behind the image, a twenty-two-year-old woman with private thoughts and fears, alone in her studio.

Lynne lifted the mic. "Tonight, we get to see one of the last projects Brenae Brasil completed before she died, a film that documents the week Brasil spent carrying a loaded gun on her person, twenty-four hours a day, to campus, to the grocery store, to the bathroom, to meals, to bed. A loaded gun," Lynne repeated. "A female body connected to violence and self-defense, twenty-four hours a day, in public as well as in its most intimate moments. Critics"—Lynne paused and raised an eyebrow—"among them, me, have already nominated *Packing* for several awards, including . . ." She plunged into a jungle of complicated accolades that few people care about other than the ones pining to receive them.

Scattered claps and cheers greeted her remarks. Ray's foursome was whispering together. The redhead looked coolly angry, then blank.

The video opened on a woman at a breakfast table eating cereal with the barrel of her gun. The scene unfolded so slowly it was almost obscene: Brenae held the handle, dipped the gun's tip into the flakes and milk, lifted them, slopping and dripping. She sucked the tip with her lips. Then over again. The gun in her fist, her jaw grinding. Milk dribbled down her chin, white and glistening.

"It can't be loaded," someone beside me muttered, and someone else insisted it was. Brenae had had other students check her gun throughout the day.

As Brenae Brasil drove around L.A. with the weapon on her lap, shopped for mangoes with the gun tucked in the back of her pants, and brushed her teeth with the red toothbrush stuck in the barrel, her comic charisma overtook the screen. Her slow gestures made every action seem full of wonder and newness, as if she were just noticing for the first time the gun in her fist, the curves of metal, the drips of milk. When she walked, she strolled. She cupped the mangoes in her palms and sniffed them. She dozed on her bed with a little half smile, the gun on her pillow, her fingers brushing the barrel. She had elegant, tapered hands.

Despite the violence implied in every frame, I couldn't imagine this woman wanting to die. Art schools in the United States welcomed more than ten thousand hopeful MFA students a year, and only a few dozen would make any international waves before they graduated. According to Lynne's remarks, Brenae had already been hailed by one critic as "the next generation's Marina Abramović" for her inclusion in a notable world-traveling group show. With two or three more breakthrough moments, she might have launched a major solo career.

I looked at the faces of the crowd and registered awe and sadness at the video, as well as flickers of frustration and regret. Ray's foursome had sunk into impassive silence.

The movie ended with Brenae in bed, cradling the gun next to her cheek. As the screen went black, the crowd clapped and burst into conversation again, but in the fresh dark, their voices sounded restless. People began milling around, blocking my view of Ray. I wanted to see his face, his reaction. I pushed my way through so fast that a girl hissed to her friend, "There's waaaay too many L.A. bitches here." When I reached the place Ray had been standing, he was gone. The foursome he had been observing had vanished, too. The space seemed scrubbed of any evidence of them, the ground scattered with cigarette butts and crumpled maps to the other installation sites. I picked up the maps, refolded them, and set them on a nearby table. A band started jangling on the stage.

"How do you get a drink here?" said a voice. It was Lynne Feldman, alone, her expression befuddled. In this laid-back atmosphere, my chief curator's hair looked too groomed and her lips too painted, her all-black getup an overdone urban armor. If this were a West Side party for already famous artists, Lynne would simply wait like a beacon and let the party come to her, but this was a young East Side crowd and they were too intimidated to approach. The official gatekeeper of the Rocque Museum! Lynne Feldman was a goal for them, not a living person.

"Did you get a drink yet?" she said when I didn't answer.

"No. It's so crowded." I wondered if Lynne would know why Janis Rocque hadn't come tonight. "I still haven't managed it."

"Well," said Lynne, with an unnervingly chummy grin. "Neither of us would survive long in the desert, would we?"

I smiled obligingly, scanning the festivalgoers. Everyone was draining back inside. I heard a few cars start up, people heading out to see other installations nearby. Should I go to the parking lot, too?

"The screening must have interested you. Weren't you an LAAC student?" Lynne persisted.

"No, I wasn't," I said, less surprised by Lynne's ignorance than by the fact she had asked me a question at all. Lynne rarely cared what anyone else thought. Critical opinions were her territory alone. And tonight, her critical opinion had puzzled me. I decided to press her. "But I was impressed by the film," I said, "and I was touched by what you said about Brenae Brasil. Any young artist would have been very grateful for that kind of support."

Lynne blinked. "I'm glad you heard that," she said. "Her own institution would like to brush her under the rug. You know, Hal Giroux declined to do the introduction."

Hal Giroux was the director of Brenae's graduate program. I understood why Brenae's peers might be jealous of her, but her director? Wouldn't LAAC love their star? I asked Lynne.

She shrugged. "Let's just say I heard that Brenae was about to make a very public criticism of their culture for women and minorities. I can't tell you more than that, because I really don't know. But Brenae was right, and I'm tired of what happens there." Defeat did not sync well with Lynne's usual proud composure, and after a wobbly moment, she steeled her shoulders. “I may brave it. I may just go to my hotel,” she muttered in the direction of the bar.

“Same,” I said, but the dread I’d been feeling all night had transformed into something else. Anger? No, the sensation was too hardened and familiar: here we were, two women, talking about another female victim, talking about our exhaustion with it, and then letting it go.

“I hate to ask this,” I said, “but have you heard anything about why she committed suicide?”

Lynne nodded and waved to someone over my shoulder, her face springing back to its usual forceful, enterprising expression. I followed her gaze to the doorway inside and saw the taut smile of Nelson de Wilde, the well-known gallery owner who was no doubt scouting for new talent this weekend. “I have to speak to Nelson,” she said, then swiveled back, as if my query had just registered. “Why? I heard she went off her antidepressants,” she said. “I heard she was isolated. I heard she was blocked, or she wasn’t that talented after all, and the pressure was eating her up. But why does anyone do the unthinkable?” She sighed. “Because they can’t imagine living another day.”

3

WHILE I POUNDED TWO LONELY gin and tonics in quick succession, I reviewed my situation. I wasn't a total outcast at The Oasis. I could find someone with Rocque connections to chat with, and I could blend in, with my faded jeans and my navy shirt with its cleverly jagged hem. But to do so would mean giving up my freedom to spy on people, and I'd lost my taste for small talk. So I wedged myself into a little corner alone and watched the pool game.

Two men circled the table, intent, not caring when their sticks jabbed strangers. Only when the bar's lone waitress passed did they pause, their eyes downcast, as if they had been reprimanded before. And they played with speed, the shots sure, the balls reeling into holes. Blurs of color, clacks and knocks. Fast games. I counted three, four, before I realized the same man kept winning. He was the smaller of the two, bent at the shoulders, with an unhealthy leanness to his face. It was possible that he was far older than his spry body let on. The other man was looser, floppier, with long, dirty-blond hair, a soft gut, a casual slump when he wasn't shooting. When he did take aim, he tensed like a hornet, and his strokes stung. The balls obeyed him completely. But the older man always triumphed. He won by strategy. He won by patience. An eight ball almost tipped into a pocket. A striped ball blocking a solid. A cue ball impossible not to scratch.

By the fifth game, the loser was starting to mutter, his sneakers punching the ground. His confidence was fading, too, and he muffed the first break, the balls barely spinning apart. The winner noticed me staring and leered. The expression turned him ancient, lizard-like, and nasty.

I turned away and wandered outside to the parking lot again. No Janis, no Dee. No Ray. Lynne must have left for her hotel. The screen that showed Brenae Brasil's video was still there, but it was now unlit and looked more like a wall with no building behind it, one of those facades on western film sets. The desert sky seemed bigger and darker, chaotic with stars.

Unsure what I was waiting for, and still unwilling to leave, I stood in line for the steamy, disgusting bathroom, hurried through my time in the stall, and washed my hands. The mirror was too spotted and warped to show my face. I bought another gin and tonic, but I had lost the thirst for booze and boldly took up my roost near the pool table and sucked on the ice. I ignored the victor's lewd glance. I could stand where I wanted.

An hour had passed now, and the crowd was thick and loud. Everyone who was going to make the drive from L.A. had made it, and their numbers overwhelmed the locals, scattering them to small atolls of denim and middle age at the bar. In the packed booths, where the students and hipsters reigned, chatter replaced argument, and young bodies slurred to single glossy, laughing creatures. I heard the name Brenae Brasil more than any other, although dozens of up-and-coming artists were showing at sites nearby. I envisioned her among them. The dark-haired, muscular twenty-two-year-old on the video looked the part, but somehow I couldn't see her happily squashed in with the others. She seemed too serious, too impatient for success to participate in this rowdy field trip from the metropolis.

Something flew past my head and hit the wall beside me. A thud, then shattering. It took me a second to understand that the projectile was a bottle of beer from the hand of the blond pool player, who'd thrown it toward his opponent, who'd ducked. I froze as they began to fight, fists on ribs, then slapping and grappling as the younger, larger man tried to pick up his opponent by the shirt and shove him down. Shrieks filled the air and a mob pushed backward, out of the way of the fight. The bartender charged out, elbowing the bystanders, yelling, "Break it up, break it up!" Glass fell from my hair and tumbled to the ground, and I smelled the sour odor of beer.

The older man tripped his opponent and flung him back on the pool table, his lean face carved by a smile, as if all along this fight was what he'd been playing for. He took a yellow-striped pool ball, raised it in his fist, and smashed it down on the other man's nose, then abruptly dropped him, hands soaked in blood, and strode toward The Oasis door, which was just beyond me and the broken glass.

I was one of the people who screamed, though I couldn't recall opening my mouth. I knew it because I heard my voice. I backed toward the doorway. The lean-faced man shouldered past me, leered again, and with one quick snaking hand grabbed my left breast hard, and twisted, before stepping around me and slipping out the threshold. After another minute, his truck roared out of the lot, large and black.

By the time my own shock broke, the entire bar had burst into motion. The bartender blotted the injured man's face with a towel and gently rolled him to his feet. The waitress got on the phone, calling an ambulance or the police or both. No one seemed to have noticed the groping, or if they had, they didn't know what to say. I found myself standing in a circle of space, utterly alone. My breast and nipple throbbed. I pulled my wrinkled shirt flat, then stumbled away from my place on the wall and headed for the bathroom again. But the line was too long, and I couldn't stand still and wait.

For the next several minutes I let the milling crowd shoulder me around the room, moving into one gap, then out to another. If people stared, I fixed my face with the look of expectation, as if I spotted someone across the way whom I couldn't quite reach. The injured pool player staggered outside, holding his blood-soaked face. His groans were raw and guttural.

When the bartender returned to the bar, I wormed a path to him to ask if there were any taxis to Twentynine Palms. I tried to keep the choke from my voice, but it came through anyway.

"You ready to go, honey?" the bartender said, pausing with a tumbler of ice in one hand, a bottle of vodka in the other. "I'll phone a guy right now. He charges thirty bucks. Fifty if it's after midnight."

I felt a neighboring woman's sympathetic eyes on me. She was at least ten years older than me, with a low-cut shirt and thinning blond hair that she teased forward toward her face. A permanent tan roughened and speckled her cleavage. "Whoever he is, he's not worth waiting for," she murmured.

"Thanks," I half yelled to the bartender. "I can't find my friends."

The cab ride smelled of pipe tobacco, my driver silent and incurious but not unfriendly. He waited until I entered the hotel before driving off. An e-mail message from Dee popped up in my laptop inbox when I connected to the internet in my large, serene room: *So sorry, Maggie, but by now you know we couldn't make it. Janis will find you at work on Monday and explain. Hope you have an amazing time. Get room service!*

I saw the screening, I wrote back. *Intense.*

She didn't reply.

For all her warmth and charm, Dee was a private person, a keeper of secrets, or she couldn't have stayed with Janis. Whatever Janis wanted to tell me about Brenae Brasil would wait until Janis was ready, but I chafed at her secrecy after the night I'd had. I'd thought there was a mutual trust between us, from our confidences this summer. I'd come all this way. I paced the expensive room, unable to sit down. The rug was soft and deep on my bare feet; a long mirror, framed in dark wood, reshaped my figure, taller, slimmer. Inside, however, I felt raw and scraped and determined, a wintry version of me. I'd returned to L.A. because of the offer Janis had dangled—but now I wondered what I was signing up for. Janis wasn't an editor. She was a rich, influential woman, used to getting her way. Say there was a real story behind Brenae's death; would it be my story, or my benefactor's? What power would I have to shape my reporting, to pitch magazines? I slumped down on a chair by the empty desk. The room got small. The air tasted clean but close. In the silence, I didn't know what I was listening for. Cars on the road outside? The accommodations were too pricey for that. But the presence of the road—that I heard, not as a noise, but as a lapse in the night's total stillness.

Kim Lord's paintings had taught me one thing: women died violent deaths all the time, in agonized and humiliating ways, and you shouldn't publicize any one of their severed lives unless you searched inside yourself and questioned why.

I rose, soaped and rinsed my body twice in the sparkling white bathtub, drank two glasses of water to avoid a hangover, and crawled into the dead center of the soft, smooth king, unable to touch any of the edges. The distance felt good, but I got up anyway, checked the door's lock for a third time, then switched off the light.

I woke up an hour later, completely alert, my heart racing, as if someone had shouted in my ear. I clicked on the light, but the room was empty and quiet. I turned off the lamp again and closed my eyes. I couldn't sleep. In my mind's eye, I saw the gun touching Brenae's lips. The milk dribbling from her chin. The footage had been so tender and lush. So deliberate. Who had been holding the camera? It had to have been someone she trusted.

Eventually, tired of lying there sleepless, I got up and tidied the room, hanging the towels, zipping away my makeup, folding the evening's clothes. It was only then that I noticed the faint stain on the front of my navy shirt. In the bathroom's fluorescent glow: dark smudges from the man's hand. I threw the shirt in the sink and turned on the faucet, squeezing and rubbing until the water ran rusty, then clear. Then I squeezed the cloth and hung it, dripping.

4

BRENAE BRASIL HAD BEEN RAISED in a small town in the Central Valley, the long swath of premier agricultural land off the highway between San Francisco and Los Angeles. Her father was an assistant manager at a dairy farm that had been owned by his extended Portuguese-American family for three generations. Her mother was Italian-Chinese-Irish and worked as a clerk for an auto parts store. Brenae had three brothers: one a farmer, one a musician, the other likely headed to jail for dealing meth. None of them had commented on her death in the press last spring, but her high school English teacher had called Brenae one of the "most brilliant and definitely most provocative" students she'd ever had.

Brenae had gotten a scholarship to USC for premed, then switched majors to art after she won a student award for a video she made of her campout in a foreclosed home in South Central. Her junior year, she'd taped her mouth and eyes shut and filmed herself trying to swim the length of a swimming pool. She named the work *First-Generation College Student*. It turned into a series: Brenae folding herself tightly inside a cardboard box from the university bookstore, shifting and squishing her body until she could close the lid. Brenae with ten mugs of beer lined up in front of her, their bottoms taped with her course names, drinking one after another slower and slower, collapsing on the table before she finished the sixth. With another full scholarship offer, she'd rocketed straight to Los Angeles Art College for her master's degree. This past March, little more than halfway through her first year, she had lain down on the mattress in her studio, put a pillow over her head, and shot herself. The police dated her death to sometime in the early morning. Two people had heard a loud popping noise then. The police found a suicide note, a bottle of sleeping pills, evidence of temazepam in her system. The gun was hers.

The official news stories were fewer than I'd expected: one short piece in the *L.A. Times*, one in the *Valdivia Star*, and several posts by art bloggers. There had been a quick school memorial, but by now the next class had arrived at LAAC, replacing Brenae, filling the studios with their own ideals, ironies, and micromanaged playlists.

And yet.

And yet her story was not entirely over. *Packing* would tour in a couple of big traveling exhibitions and get press for another year or two. A gallerist or curator might even take interest in Brenae's undergraduate films, but eventually, with no new work, she would become an anecdote of LAAC and its pressures: *An artist tragically killed herself in her first year.* Then a legend: *Didn't some girl shoot herself in this building?* And finally, a ghost: *Did you hear that noise last night? I'm so creeped out.*

On Monday morning, Janis's dark blue Lexus arrived outside the Rocque and pulled to a stop beside a wall banner for our next exhibition, a cool, arid show about California light and California architects. For a moment, I recalled the old *Still Lives* banner, the sickening flash of Kim Lord's smile in her self-portrait as murder victim Roseann Quinn. Then I stuffed it away. I walked slowly to the car and got in.

"Café Francesca," Janis Rocque told her driver, and he peeled out into traffic, pinning me to the leather seat beside her.

"I love Café Francesca," I said, surprised. The two-story café sat like a stranded French ship in the old theater district, serving up sandwiches, salads, Gypsy guitar music, and real Parisian waiters that scorned and flirted with you with equal charm. But it was a far drive from Janis's Bel Air estate, and not the kind of place that attracted multimillionaires.

"Do you?" said Janis. "You seem shocked we're going there."

"I'm shocked that we're finally talking," I said truthfully. "It was a strange weekend."

She grunted. "I'm sorry we didn't make it to the desert. It wasn't my choice," she said, sounding genuinely contrite, and for a moment I thought she would explain why, but she blinked, and her voice changed back to the old brisk Janis. "You said you got a chance to see her work."

"I did," I said.

"And you were impressed by it."

When Janis had written to me yesterday, asking about the trip and inviting me to lunch, I had given her a brief summary of my impressions.

"She had talent," I said.

"Talent," Janis muttered. "Talent is like salmon eggs, Maggie. You mean you think she had the potential to do great work, but you aren't sure."

I knew Janis's combative tone was a test and not a judgment. "I mean she had real presence on-screen," I clarified. "A magnetism. You can't fake that. But it would all depend on what she did next."

She propped her head on the window, but her attention was still on my face. "You spend much time in galleries?"

"I try to go down there once a week," I said. "Dee and the crew do terrific work."

"Not our galleries," she said. "Commercial galleries. Blum & Poe. LACE. You ever want to be a gallerina?"

She said the last word, *gallerina*, with a slightly mocking tone. The term carried both the spite and the admiration that people (well, yes, including me) had for the beautiful, cool young women who often operated as gatekeepers to the upscale art showrooms.

"Not really," I said, puzzled. "I don't do that well with rich people."

My voice crumpled as I realized my gaffe, but Janis chuckled. "No kidding," she said, then held up her hand when I tried to apologize. Her driver sped down the hill and turned right on Olive, neatly threading past a man pushing an ice cream cart stickered with images of ice pops and cones. "I'll let you hear everything from Ray first."

I kept myself from reacting at Ray's name, but Janis had sunk into her seat, shutting her eyes. Without her stern, bright gaze, she looked older, frailer than fifty-three. The veins stood out in her neck and hands. It seemed unfair to observe her this way, stripped of her usual armor, and yet I had the odd feeling she wanted me to see it, her tiredness, and that this was a message, too.

A few more blocks, and the corporate skyscrapers of Bunker Hill receded behind us. Janis would have been a young child when the city razed hundreds of the hill's "blighted" Victorian mansions and relocated thousands of its residents to erect the face of L.A.'s new downtown. She would have come of age in the decades-long fiasco that followed: housing towers on the summit with sixty percent occupancy, while in the hill's shadow the simultaneous demolition of Skid Row hotels and sharp increase of homeless Vietnam vets and the mentally ill led to the rise of permanent tent cities in the street. In her twenties, Janis had watched her father campaign to convert a former police-car garage into a contemporary art museum, and when he died young, she had carried on his vision and made it hers. She fought the late-eighties culture battles with the Rocque's epic exhibition *Indecency*, showing every artist decried as "offensive" by a powerful U.S. senator. She paved the way for the country's first major Chicano art retrospective, financed the nineties' whimsical displays of dirty dinner dishes and sea creatures in formaldehyde, and led the Rocque into the twenty-first century with *Still Lives*. No wonder she was weary.

Now the faded glamour of the old theater district sprang up around us. In the building's first stories, red-and-yellow sale signs advertised knock-off watches and jewelry. Grand windows and porticos vaulted above them, blackened by smog and crusted with pigeon droppings. Yegina had told me these blocks were filled with illegal garment sweatshops, but if people really were working upstairs, they didn't come near the dusty panes. The upper stories projected emptiness and ruin. The only life was at the street level: a pop-up Pentecostal church, vendors of cheap, glittering luxuries. A bridal and tuxedo store spilled to the sidewalk with poufy pastel shirts and dresses, but even it looked less vibrant than impulsive, as if the storefront could fold up tomorrow and disappear.

Janis opened her eyes. "Dee wants a tux from that place," she observed, staring out the window.

"She'd look fantastic in one," I said. With Dee's choppy blond hair and lean form, she could pretty much wear any garment and make it seem cool and carefree. "Maybe for her show next week," I added.

Dee was in an "ethereal punk" band and had invited me and Yegina to their upcoming gig. I was pretty sure her style would outstrip her musical ability, and very sure that we would love it anyway. That was the Dee effect, and she still cast it, even through the hardship of keeping her crew together after they'd found out the whole story of Kim Lord's death.

"Maybe," said Janis, brightening for the first time as she gazed at the tuxes. A gift for Dee. It was touching how much Janis liked being generous.

The car slowed; we were outside Café Francesca. The restaurant occupied both floors of a narrow brick building where two streets arrowed together. Downstairs and upstairs patios extended in tiers, each girded by a delicate, white wrought-iron rail and shaded by red umbrellas. The food was delicious, and usually a little beyond my budget.

Janis Rocque leaped out. "We're late," she said. I hurried after her upstairs through the creamy yellow rooms of the restaurant and out to the top deck, where couples were sitting, holding menus. It took me a moment to register one couple in particular: They sat at a four-top, talking intently. Ray's back was to me, leaning forward in a navy button-down, but the instant we arrived, he twisted as if someone had called his name. His blue eyes caught mine, then looked away. The woman with him had black hair combed down to her shoulders and wore a pale purple suit that hugged her curves. Detective Alicia Ruiz had the same thick eyebrows and calm, receptive face, but she appeared different and, frankly, much lovelier than when I'd last seen her. New uniform? Or was this her day off?

They both rose when they saw Janis. She motioned them down, pulled out a chair, and gestured for me to sit. I obeyed reluctantly, perching on the spindly, white metal seat pounded into the shape of grape clusters.

"Here we are," Janis announced, still standing. "I believe you both know Maggie Richter."

Ray and the detective exchanged a look, and the detective's fist curled on the table, as if she were steeling herself to say something.

"Nice to see you again," Detective Ruiz said to me.

I nodded. I had been expecting to see Ray, but not Ray and a police detective. Especially not this detective. I knew that she was sharp, and I also knew I had lied to her last spring during the Kim Lord case. Was this an actual criminal investigation? It couldn't be. Police and journalists didn't usually mix well—a police presence could threaten relationships with vulnerable sources, and journalists could make a PR nightmare for cops. "You look well," I told her.

Then I allowed myself a glance at Ray, who was wearing one of his blank courteous looks. The beard and cap were gone, and his brown hair had been cropped close to his head. He looked thinner somehow, more careworn. He rose and held out his hand, greeting me, his voice even, palm warm and dry, but when we touched, I saw tension jump in his face.

"Maggie has generously agreed to come here without knowing very much about this affair," Janis said, sitting down. "Ray and Alicia are here to give you the details and explain the legal parameters of what I want you to do."

What I want you to do. The ownership in that statement did not escape me. No other potential reporters had been vetted, I felt certain now, because Janis could not oversee them the way she intended to oversee me. And yet there was a heaviness in her tone that distracted me, as if beneath her usual clear directives some dark emotion was dragging at her.

A waiter appeared at the table with an inquiring look. Detective Ruiz checked her watch. "Water's fine," she muttered.

"Let's order everything now. We need to eat," commanded Janis. "Croque Monsieur is ham and cheese. Madame adds an egg." She tapped at Ray's menu. "Madame is too rich if you ask me. But you do what you want."

"Sounds great," Ray said to Janis. "You choose for me." He handed her his menu.

Detective Ruiz rubbed her forehead with a manicured finger. "Why don't you order for all of us. If that's okay with Maggie," she said, then added without waiting, "Light on the garlic; I've got meetings all afternoon."

I shrugged my agreement. There was some battle being waged, but I wasn't going to engage with it until I understood what it was. Janis rattled off what sounded like seven courses, the waiter left, and a silence fell. The morning haze had burned off, and the patio was blinding. Across the street, a couple of mothers with small children entered a Pentecostal church, its red marquee letters blazing, JESUCRISTO ES EL SEÑOR.

Janis began, "Let me first say that you would be paid well for your time, and that I can't have any gossip about this, regardless. Not to anyone."

"I understand," I said, and then my heart sank, though I didn't know why. Janis gripped the table, as if momentarily unsteady, and then released it. She sighed.

"You brought the DVD?" she asked Ray.

He looked confused by her question but nodded.

"Give it to me," she said.

She held up the silver disc in its sleeve, shining it at me.

"For a variety of reasons, some quite alarming, I had to fire my personal assistant of ten years in July," Janis said. "My new assistant found an entire closet full of mail that had never been touched, mostly pleas for my appearance at openings I could never attend. Among them was a package with this video and a note." Janis paused. "Brenae Brasil sent it to me before she died." She examined me. "You want to know why you're here. I believe that something systemic is wrong with that school—something you'll see on this video—and it led to Brenae Brasil's suicide. I want that uncovered. The artist asked for my help, and I didn't give it in time. I want to remedy that now, as best I can."

So many questions flew into my head, I didn't know which one to pick. The odd mix of sympathy and frustration on Detective Ruiz's face made me choose.

"Brenae Brasil," I repeated. "But her death was investigated already last spring. By you?" I asked the detective.

"By LASD, not LAPD," the detective said to me. "It happened in Valdivia, so it was a county job. But yes, it was thoroughly investigated."

"And there's no doubt it was a suicide?"

"There's always doubt. But very little this time." Her phone buzzed. She glanced at it and turned it off, stuffing it in her pocket. "First, I just want to interject, with all due respect to you, not knowing what the hell this is all about, that everything we say is confidential from here on out."

"Okay," I said. "Except—"

"Completely confidential," the detective said again in a firm tone.

"Got it," I said.

"In the early morning of March 13, Brenae took some sleeping pills, put a pillow over her head, and shot herself," said the detective. "The college discovered her body when she didn't show up for her job at the campus Super Shop. She was also off her depression medication, had been doing poorly in classes, and had recently lost her funding for her second year. There was a note on her laptop that said, *Watch me.*"

"No funding for her second year," I said. "Really?" According to Lynne's introduction the other night, Brenae had come to LAAC on a full two-year scholarship. If Brenae had stayed on without her scholarship, she would have owed the school tens of thousands of dollars. If she'd left, no degree. It was a terrifying position to put a student in. Even a cruel one. "But I thought she was a star."

"She was at odds with the school," said Janis. "As you'll see."

"LASD knew there were two other films made by Brenae Brasil in the months before she died, both of which she submitted to Hal Giroux," Detective Ruiz said to me, "but no copies have been found. Giroux denies ever possessing any. He says he watched them on her laptop in his office when they met about Brenae's academic probation. There are no files of either on her hard drive. In fact, it appears that her laptop was tampered with after her death."

"This, we think, is one of the films," said Janis.

Ray inserted the disc into his open laptop and aimed the screen at me. It was hard to see the footage in the bright light. A title card said LESSON IN RED in bold white letters, and then a camera showed a couple on a mattress on a bare floor, a blanket covering them. The man was on top, and his rhythmic motions underneath the blanket suggested sex. The woman's eyes, Brenae's eyes, were blank, her mouth slack. The man's head had been blurred out by editing, emphasizing the thrust of his hips. The blanket wrinkled and shuddered, slipping down, exposing one of Brenae's breasts. A toneless female voice spoke over the images:

He comes.
He asks me.
I say yes.
What can I say?

What will happen if I say no?
Where will I go?

The three questions repeated over and over, louder and louder, building like Ravel's *Boléro.* As they did, a red tone crept over the scene, deepening and darkening until it blotted out the figures on the screen.

Unlike the sensual and almost glamorous tone of *Packing*, this video was gritty, dull, and excruciating. Limbs and heads, the jolting rhythm of sex. A bad taste flooded my mouth. When I looked down at my hands, I saw that they were fisted, my thighs pressed tight together.

"It's horrifying to watch, isn't it?" said Janis, her eyes on me. "Imagine making it. Showing it."

"I was," I said.

"It appears to be Brenae's. Obviously, the footage includes her, and the voice matches hers as well," the detective said. "Though anyone could have sent it to Janis."

"What did Hal Giroux say about it?" I asked.

Janis's voice was low, almost tender. "Maggie, it's my belief that Brenae's suicide may be tied to Hal Giroux himself," she said. "That's why this has to be done so carefully."

Hal Giroux. His name flowed like water through the history of the L.A. art world. He was the longtime director of the graduate program at LAAC, the launcher of dozens, maybe hundreds, of important careers. There was no love lost between him and Janis, but we showed his rising artists regularly at the Rocque.

"Here's the note that came with the artwork," said Janis, holding out a photocopy of a handwritten letter, the letters tense and clear.

Dear Ms. Rocque:

I have long been an admirer of you and your museum, and it was such a pleasure to meet you at the Chavez opening. I would be honored to invite

you to my studio, but my college has become a hostile environment for me. Please view this example of my work, and perhaps we could arrange to meet elsewhere. I desperately need your help, and hope you will reply soon.
—Brenae Brasil

"I honestly don't remember meeting her," muttered Janis. "Some of those East Side openings are like heat waves in a sardine can, and I greet strangers as a way of fleeing."

"How do we know it's Brenae's handwriting?" I asked.

"It matches samples from her apartment," said the detective.

The last words in Brenae's note sounded so vulnerable. "I wonder what help she wanted," I said.

"I have been wondering that, too, ever since the moment I read it," said Janis.

The sun had shifted again in the sky, falling on my end of the table like a brilliant wall.

"But how do you think Hal Giroux was involved?" I blinked through the light at Ray.

Instead of answering, he gestured to a waiter passing. "Can we move that umbrella over a little?"

We all waited while the waiter dragged a second umbrella closer to us. Cool shade poured over me.

"Someone deleted two files on her laptop after she died, judging by the medical examiner's determined time of death," he said. "In fact, not just deleted, but shredded. That means someone found her body and then made sure they got rid of this"—he held up the DVD—"and one other file. LASD ran into a dead end there, despite some rigorous attempts."

A gunshot in the heart of LAAC. Files shredded. A paltry memorial. The death and its response didn't match up.

"Out of curiosity," I said, "what was Brenae wearing when she was found?"

I saw the detective exchange looks with Ray.

"She wasn't wearing clothes," the detective said reluctantly.

"None?"

"Not a stitch."

This surprised me, and then it didn't.

"Why do you ask?" said Ray, intent on me.

"She grew up in a Luso-American farming community. Catholic and conservative," I said. "Suicide is a violation of Catholic doctrine. To strip yourself naked, too—for a young woman, unmarried . . . I know this is the twenty-first century, but it's still a huge statement." Or maybe it wasn't Brenae's statement. It was someone else's. Someone who wanted her not just dead but shamed as well.

The detective shifted; she hadn't expected me to come prepared.

"Out of respect for the family," she said, her words freighted with judgment, "we don't always release details."

There it was. The battle between Alicia Ruiz and Janis: involving Ray meant that the investigation stayed an investigation, but involving me meant that it could become a public story. Open, exposing, and potentially out of control.

"So what do you need me for?" I said.

No one spoke up immediately, and in their silence I heard the clatter of the restaurant, the whoosh of cars passing below.

"It's a bit unusual," said Janis. "Go ahead, Ray."

Ray seemed to hold a brief consultation with his knuckles, and then nodded.

"Having a person on the inside can be an effective investigation strategy in sensitive communities," he said. "People won't let their guard down with known investigators, but the fact of an investigation often stirs them to talk to one another. An inside informant can glean a lot of information." He paused. "Tomorrow Hal Giroux's crew starts building his next show at the Westing Gallery. His crew—all four of them—are current or former LAAC students, and they were once close with Brenae. They may have insights into what went on at LAAC. I've approached them on Janis's behalf, and they are willing to be interviewed. But meanwhile, we wanted to have someone observe them, too. Janis has worked out a deal with the Westing owner. For someone to work at the gallery and listen in. While they build Hal's show."

"You," said Janis. "They know they're talking to a private investigator when they talk to Ray," said Janis. "But they won't know they are also being watched by a second one during the day."

"In other words, you would act as the Westing's gallerina, but you would be an informant, too," the detective said. "Eyes and ears for Ray's investigation."

My mind lodged on the last words. *Ray's investigation.* Me assisting him. Not my story and not my reporting. Detective Ruiz didn't see me as an equal in this, not Maggie the copy editor at the Rocque. And why would she? I glanced at Janis, waiting for her to interject, to insist I'd actually be gathering information for my own project—a pitch, an article, maybe even a series of articles. But Janis remained silent, holding the DVD case, staring down into the silver disc. She was going to defer to the detective's perspective. Cautious inquiry now. Story later. Maybe.

My face and neck went hot, like the full sun was still pouring over them, but I kept my voice cool.

"The police aren't interested in this?" I asked the detective.

She shook her head. "They—I don't see any evidence of criminal activity." Now she sounded like she was weighing her words. "I'm actually here as a favor. To make absolutely sure Janis's operation stays legal."

Ray spoke then, his voice low. "There is some kind of cover-up here. I've been digging into this, and it's clear we won't get the full facts by going after them directly." His blue eyes finally met mine.

I felt the force of his attention now, and it was full of warning. *Let the dead go.*

Janis pursed her lips and folded the photocopy of Brenae's pleading note. Brenae's eyes had looked so glassy and lost in the video. The voice-over had implied her lover's power over her. *Lesson in Red.* The title suggested a teacher, a school. Her position suggested she was being fucked.

The sun was moving again, its wilting heat climbing my spine. The lunch crowds were filling in, mostly business and lawyer types from Bunker Hill, their conversation loud and self-important. For a moment it seemed like every man around me was looming, in a full suit, and every woman nodding, gazing up at him in some slip of a dress, her bare shoulders exposed. At the same time, I knew it was a mirage. That it was just what my mood made me see.

"The regular gallerina there is taking some time off," Janis said, "so you can tell people you're a temp. Nelson de Wilde has promised to cover any major client questions himself. He was a big fan of Brenae's, and he's on board with this."

Nelson de Wilde. Hearing his name conjured an instant vision of the last time I'd seen him, in the crowd at The Oasis, a silver-headed man with a cunning, youthful expression and a tan so deep it looked like the sun had soaked beyond his skin, into his blood. He was the powerful gallerist who had once represented Kim Lord and had probably let a greedy collector rig her growing reputation. Maybe he was trying to make up for past failures. Maybe Janis had made him an offer he couldn't refuse.

Now the three of them were watching me, waiting for my response. They wanted me to play gallerina while the students built their director's show. They wanted me to eavesdrop on twentysomethings while I pretended to call clients and process purchases.

Janis cleared her throat. "May I add one more thing?" she said and named an expensive boutique on the West Side. "You can charge a couple of good suits in my name there. I'll call them," she said. "I'll get you out of your day job, of course. And as I said, you'll be paid well, by me."

"There isn't anyone else who can do this?" I said.

I knew there had to be, and this fact made me more reluctant than anything.

Ray folded one hand over the other, a gesture that reminded me of my father when he was caving in to some irrational request of my mother's.

Detective Ruiz said, "Assuredly. I've personally suggested some other investigators—"

"But I personally don't trust them," Janis Rocque broke in. "Maggie knows this world. She's smart and discreet. She worked for Jay Eastman. Her credentials add up. And we're out of time. The installation begins tomorrow, and one of the assistants is talking about moving to New York. This may be the last stretch that they're all together. So are you in?"

"Don't let her rush you," said Detective Ruiz. "You can take a few moments."

Ray said nothing and kept his eyes on the table, his expression blank. I could feel the others watching me, but I studied him anyway, the subtle lines in his forehead, the slight hunch in his shoulders. I remembered him standing against the crumbly wall of The Oasis, gripping my arm. The fear in his face. I'd never seen it before. *You don't know me, though, okay?* Something had made him afraid. And deep down I knew: that fear was why Ray was back in L.A.

A shadow fell over me, and Ray raised his head; he was gazing behind me, eyes widening. It was our food—three huge trays of fries and sandwiches and salads riding on the shoulders of three waiters, all of them sweating in the white sunlight.

"Dear God," said Janis Rocque. "It's not all supposed to come at once."

It wasn't all supposed to come at once, what you wanted, what hurt you, and what made you want to risk everything, but sometimes it did.

"I'm sorry," I said. "I don't think I can help you."

5

I'D SAID NO TO THEM, and I'd left the café without eating lunch because what more was there to say? Janis wouldn't look at me. When she told her driver to call me a cab back to the museum, her low voice dropped another octave, as if her throat had opened to a bottomless pit. The detective seemed relieved, Ray inscrutable. I hadn't given them a reason, because I didn't want to tell Janis that it violated a central principle of my journalistic training to deceive people into yielding up their stories, and though I respected Ray, joining his investigation would not benefit me in the slightest. In fact, for my own sanity, I refused to involve myself in another woman's violent death.

On my way home in my own car, I called Yegina and left a message. She was on a plane to a conference in D.C. At our director's behest, she'd started traveling a lot for the museum, speaking on panels, courting international donors. She came to work now with crisp ruffled blouses, a razored bob, and a new polished attitude that was hard for anyone to say no to. She was climbing, career-wise, and would be intensely interested in the potential downfall of Hal Giroux.

Regardless of what Janis and her team found, Hal had to be reaching the end of his tenure as director of LAAC's star-studded MFA program. A show at the Westing Gallery in Venice might be seen as a nostalgic return for Hal, who'd cut his teeth there in the 1960s, in the assemblage and Finish Fetish studios scattered among the oil derricks. Venice was Hal's origin story, written in sultry beach air and the smell of molded plastic.

But a show at the Westing was still a gallery show. It was not a museum show. It was the rock-band equivalent of selling out a small auditorium instead of a stadium.

I had seen Hal often at openings. He was a small man with a beard and glistening brown eyes, his attire neither formal nor sloppy, neither youthful nor old. He wore suit jackets and belted jeans or cords, and rumpled denim button-downs with an open collar. He spoke to most young people in benevolent but scolding tones, as if we were all beautiful children trespassing in his garden. Very few protégés he took seriously. Those, I've been told, he saturated with approval and a demanding exactitude so intense that they invariably transformed into stars.

In his first decades at LAAC, Hal had revolutionized the L.A. art scene by adopting and rearing the scruffy outliers who didn't fit with the Venice studios' frenzy for surfaces or with the fine-art standards of the stuffier city schools. Many of Hal's students had been male performance artists: showy, good-looking, confrontational guys who used their bodies as art, burying themselves alive or rolling around New York inside oil drums. Others had painted, but rarely with paint, or had made video art when video was still new. Hal's support had launched numerous careers. As his early students thrived, so did Hal, commanding major retrospectives in London and New York for interactive installations that walked the line between silliness and horror. His 1981 artwork *Showers* got frequent mentions in textbooks. We showed it at the Rocque once; it was hellish to install—a darkened gallery with four flowing, curtained showers that drained beneath the floor and sent the water up through the heads again. Each illuminated shower hid a silhouetted human figure inside. Beneath the rush of the water, three of the silhouettes sang the same steady, wordless song in harmony. The fourth screamed it. The room's eerie noise shifted between pleasure and violent discord. It was Gregorian chant, the showers like giant altar candles. It was also *Psycho*. Visitors loved it.

But something had slipped for Hal in the past ten years. He was approaching sixty, his shoulders had begun to hunch, and he kept resisting the same premodern convention that art was a made thing, instead of the *idea of making* in the mind of the artist. Everyone knew Hal commandeered his most talented students and alumni to build his installations, and then took credit for their skills. In the seventies, this was an upstart move, but now it looked like indentured servitude. Meanwhile, a mounting number of women and people of color at LAAC had started to complain about the masculine, bravado-puffed ethos of the school, claiming that its scholarships and grants always went to the same kind of white male.

No one had ever claimed sexual harassment, though. In all my encounters with Hal, I'd never seen him touch anyone, not even in greeting. He simply didn't breach the gap between bodies. He materialized right next to people, but he was short and his arms stayed glued to his sides. He popped up, exchanged cutting banter, then vanished and popped up elsewhere.

"He's like a social whack-a-mole," Yegina had muttered to me one night. "Where's my hammer."

Yegina hated Hal because Janis Rocque had hated Hal for decades. The two had started as pals, young groundbreakers with common goals—Janis downtown and Hal in Valdivia. In 1976, shortly after Janis had signed off on a major gift to LAAC, a group of the college's women artists had transformed every room in an old East L.A. mansion—from kitchen to bathroom to bedroom—into a bower of feminist art. It was called *Womb/House*. Thousands had come to view it, elevating LAAC to a media phenomenon: the new West Coast art school that was suddenly outshining New York. Janis asked Hal to use her donation toward buying *Womb/House* so that the college could own it in perpetuity, but Hal refused, saying he had already earmarked her funds for general operating costs. She could give more if she wanted. Janis said fat chance. The installation had been dismantled and lost to time, and a new enmity had sprung up in the L.A. art world. Ever since, Janis and Hal had clashed over the city's creative future. Personally, I thought the contemporary art scene had largely benefited from the war between them, two titans, each equally mighty. And yet. I couldn't erase Brenae's staring face, her voice-over, from my mind.

As I crept west on the crowded freeway, my phone vibrated. I let it go to voicemail and then pressed speaker to hear the message. It was my friend Kaye, who'd become a birthing doula for Hollywood royalty. At a party at Kaye's last week, I'd struck up a conversation with an up-and-coming actress. The actress was an intense person, allergic to chatter and self-help advice, and had ended up bored and adrift in a corner of the patio, staring at her wineglass. I knew that she was about to play Françoise Gilot in a play on Broadway, and I knew about Gilot, a painter who had become Picasso's lover when she was twenty-seven and he was sixty-one. We'd talked for an hour, and then I'd given her my number and told her to call if she ever wanted me to pitch a profile on her.

Kaye's excited voice made me nearly swerve into someone's white Jeep. *She wants an interview tomorrow. Noon?*

A wave of stubborn pride washed through me. I could sell a profile on the actress in a heartbeat, to any number of publications. She was on her way to becoming a major star. This was the kind of uncomplicated, sure-to-succeed opportunity that never happened to me.

Now it was happening. I took the freeway exit for the boutique that Janis had named earlier, parked, and returned Kaye's call. "Yes, please," I said. "How'd you do it?"

"I didn't! She called me. She really liked you."

"But I owe you anyway." I tried unsuccessfully to thank Kaye for several minutes, and then told her I needed to go. If I didn't enter the boutique soon, in the flush of my victory, I'd get practical and self-deprecating and change my mind. The rumble and rush of the city rose around me as I slid out of the car, conscious of my sandals on the sidewalk, the steps to my next career. As much as I loved the Rocque, as bad as I felt for Brenae Brasil, I needed this chance. And I needed the right suit, the Tom Wolfe suit, the Gay Talese suit, the snappy, refined costume that said you knew what you were doing, that people paid you well to tell their stories.

My reflection rose across the window of the boutique, my eager face layering over the immobile features of the mannequins. No living person could lean back at their angles, but their clothes were gorgeous. Even through the storefront glass, the cut and the fabric made a laughingstock of ordinary brands.

I stepped inside, breathing in the sharp, clean air. It tasted as if someone had polished it, lovingly, molecule by molecule. The racks were few, and the eyes of the clerks roved over me, their smiles judging. They were twenty percent prettier than the prettiest girl I'd known in high school, and almost twice as old. I stepped toward the suits. My hands flicked through a couple of unmarked ones before a clerk appeared behind my shoulder.

"We usually find options for you," she said smoothly. "You like this style?"

I said yes and meekly gave her my size. She nodded as if she already knew it and pointed to a dressing room. There were no price tags, and apparently there was no private shopping. I chose a curtained room with a velvet couch, and there I sat, cradling my car keys, heart racing, wondering how much the garments really cost here. It didn't matter. It couldn't matter. I had to be impressive tomorrow.

Beyond the curtain, shadowy forms moved to and fro across the vaulting space of the boutique. I heard the soft jangle of hangers.

"Try these," said a voice, and a pink-manicured claw extended three suits through the opening. I took them. They weighed so little. The soft, melty fabric of the first—olive green—glided against my knuckles. I opened the jacket, button by button, the plastic slipping against the threaded hole. The pants were on when my phone vibrated. Yegina.

"So?" she said in my ear. "How did it go at lunch?"

"Hang on," I said, zipping. "Guess who I'm meeting tomorrow for an interview?"

"Way to go!" Yegina said when I told her the name. "That's incredible."

"I know. Hold on again," I said and pulled on the suit jacket. The ensemble fit perfectly. It hugged my shoulders, my waist, my hips. It defined me. I stared at my smooth, elegant self.

"Where are you?" said Yegina's voice.

The clerk, sounding very close, said, "How are things?"

"Wonderful," I said. "I've just tried on the green one, but you got the right size."

"You're shopping? You?" said Yegina.

I named the boutique.

"Damn," said Yegina. "But what about the meeting with Janis?"

I told her in my quietest tones about what I'd learned at Café Francesca. "I said no. It's not the right opportunity for me."

I waited for a plethora of questions, but instead Yegina went silent. "You said no to Janis?" she said after a moment. "She was offering you paid time off and free designer suits to do her a little favor."

If I revered Janis, then Yegina worshipped her. But still. There was something extra in her voice. A thin wire of anxiety that I'd never heard before.

"It's more than a favor, and I'm not the right person for it," I said. "And now I have this interview tomorrow anyway." I told her how easily the actress and I had fallen into conversation, how much there was to discuss about her next role, but as I was speaking, I saw Brenae on the bed, her slack mouth jiggling as the man thrust into her. Goosebumps rose on my arms, and the suit suddenly felt slick and heavy.

The clerk's shadow passed beyond the curtain. "Let me know what else I can find for you," she said.

I undressed clumsily, still holding the phone. "I will."

"I want to see the play," said Yegina. "Maybe if you sell the story, we could fly to New York and get tickets. Just us two."

"It's a deal," I promised, wondering why she still sounded upset. Was her family okay? Fine. Hiro? Great. He was flying to D.C. to meet her. I asked her what question she thought was most important for me to pose to the actress.

"Why don't you ask her what her dream role is?" she said. "That says a lot about a person. Even if they don't know."

"Should I really buy this?" I said, transfixed by the olive suit. "Should I try it on again to make sure?"

"Of course you should," said Yegina. "And try it on again at home."

Only on the drive back did I wonder what my own dream role was, and if Yegina had meant for me to turn the question on myself.

IT WAS BARELY THREE O'CLOCK when I pulled up to my sublet in Marina del Rey. My new digs—a one-bedroom flat in a noxiously pink adobe complex with a carport underneath—had the distinction of being available, safe, expensive, and utterly forgettable. I'd found the place after a week of examining worse options—hot little boxes with kitchenettes in Mid-Wilshire high-rises, a top-floor Hollywood apartment with a leering landlord named Don who was a locksmith by trade and lived right below. After extracting myself from Don's sweaty handshake, I drove past my old bungalow and stared at the blooming bougainvillea beside my stoop, waiting for the Ivy League couple to come out. They didn't, though once I saw a shadow cross the glass. Clearly, they were happy inside. Silver Lake and Echo Park were total busts for me; every time I made an offer, I was beat out the same day by a trust funder with freshly inked arms and their dad's cash.

So I started scouring farther on the West Side, into the boring grids and bland, agreeable, beach-adjacent wealth scorned by many of my Rocque friends. The sea layer cooled the heat the closer I got to the Pacific, and my temporary home's location on the rim of Venice's posh single-family homes meant that there was only a wall and a gate surrounding the property, and not bars on the windows. At night, I could hear someone's kid practicing trumpet. It reminded me that once, a long time ago, I'd lived among families.

When I got out of my car, I tasted dust and the flat, stale air of a city that needed a storm to freshen it. No rain for months. Even the West Side was slowly baking to dusty, pastel kindling. A week ago, the smog was so thick downtown that the morning light had turned as orange-gold as evening, and when I'd strolled up the steps to the museum at nine, I'd had the odd feeling that the day was done and I ought to be heading home. Today was the opposite. I was home already, and I wished I was still at work. The afternoon had left me jittery and I didn't want quiet and isolation, but here I was.

The olive-green suit floated like a wing behind me as I took the stairs to my second-floor flat. The suit cost a whole paycheck and a half. But I would look better than I ever had before in L.A., and I needed that.

I unlocked the door to my hodgepodge decor. A plush blue sofa plumped beside a knockoff Eames dining room set. Lamps jutted in corners like twin rockets. Black-and-white photos of empty sidewalks hung on the wall. The sunlight in the apartment made the least effort and offered the most comfort—the long windows boasted no view but a busy street, yet they cast a lovely glow across the rooms. The woman who had sublet the place to me was a single, globetrotting airline food consultant who was gone for long stretches. She was groomed to the last cuticle and name-dropped her visits to international cities with a determined pleasure. And yet there were three dressers in the bedroom, a lot of expensive matching dishes tucked away in a closet box, and it was clear she'd owned a cat—the sofa was scratched. I wondered if she'd had a different life once.

I grabbed my stack of notes and sat down on the couch to page through them. In a few days, the actress was going to New York to play the real, still-living Françoise Gilot in a Broadway production of Pablo Picasso's life. At age sixty-one, in Nazi-occupied Paris, Picasso had wandered up to two attractive young women sitting at a café table and offered them cherries. One of them, Françoise Gilot, was an emerging painter with a gallery show. Gilot had a luminous face—a long nose, dark eyebrows, and lush dark hair—and an intellectual and emotional fearlessness that drew Picasso to her, and she to him. They became confidants, then lovers, and later Gilot became the mother to two of his children. She also famously dumped Picasso in 1953.

In one of my fantasies, the actress and I would eat our requisite salads with dainty sides of grilled cheese and share our secret, abiding love for Gilot. Centuries of Western Civilization have seen many female beauties, geniuses, and queens, but only the most powerful, lovely, or prolific have made it into history books. Gilot happened to be all of the above, and she carved her own path despite Picasso's vindictive attempts to squash her career. "If you attempt to take a step outside my reality . . . you're headed straight for the desert," he said when she told him she was leaving him. "And if you go, that's exactly what I wish for you."

Lying on the couch, I lingered over a splendid photo of Gilot and Picasso on the beach in Antibes in 1946, early in their relationship. She walks ahead of him, beaming, in a straw hat, a narrow-waisted beach dress, a necklace of chunky white shells. Her arms swing, her head is thrown back, her hair falls to her shoulders. Behind her follows Picasso, hoisting an enormous umbrella, its white fringe shining in the sun. Picasso, too, wears a smile, but the lines of his aging face make it a frowning smile, his eyes darkened with dread.

That Antibes beach photo and I had a long history. I'd once had it posted on my wall at college. I'd hung it in honor of a mentor whom I'd loved desperately, and without return.

Teague had been my TA. At the ancient age of twenty-five, he had presided over my discussion section for a European art history class. A tense, short, muscular guy with red hair and a flat gaze, Teague had been prone to wearing the same jeans and ratty canvas sneakers daily, while his shirts shifted radically between obscure heavy metal bands and uniforms from the many blue-collar jobs he'd worked. His voice was low, rich, and emphatic. When I closed my eyes to think about him at night, I never saw Teague; instead, his voice came to me, its mutters and rejoinders, the way it goaded me to think harder, think harder.

There's more here, Maggie. Whenever Teague said those words, I felt the sharp prick of my own insufficiency. Naturally I wrote my paper on Françoise Gilot. Teague praised it warmly. In our last class, I told him I was thinking of getting an art history degree, maybe specializing in postwar Paris.

"Why?" Teague said. "What are you, Maggie, a freshman?"

I nodded, stung by the scorn in his deep, brutal voice.

He scrunched his nose and sighed. "Gilot isn't an end. She's a means. She's a reason to engage in your world. This world. Here. Right now. Don't lock yourself away for her sake."

It hadn't occurred to me then that Teague had been probably talking himself out of his PhD, and soon another blue-collar T-shirt would be added to his rotating collection. At the time, I'd merely assumed he'd seen through my transparent attempt to appeal to him. I'd thrown the Gilot essay in a drawer and ripped down the photo, never to think about them again until a couple of weeks ago, when Kaye had brought up the actress and her new role.

Sitting there, holding Gilot's smiling, tilted face, my own young, raw longings came flooding back. I had loved her book and her work, but I had listened to Teague's advice. I'd studied journalism. I'd paid attention to this world. My world. It had led me to Jay Eastman, his book on the drug trade in Vermont, and then the murder of Nikki Bolio, and a lot of running away, until I entwined myself in Kim Lord's case last spring so deeply that I almost didn't get out. The one thing I should avoid now was studying another woman's death. I knew that. I knew it like I knew the sound of my own name.

"I'm glad I said no," I said aloud to the photos of sidewalks on the wall. My voice was loud and hollow, as if having no listener had punched a hole in every word.

But then I tried to picture a pretty, ineffectual not-me sitting in the gallery, talking to Ray afterward, and I thought about Gilot and how she refused to be afraid. She didn't scare at the judgment of her friends and family. She didn't fear Picasso. She didn't care if the world rejected her for leaving him. She made her own brave choices.

I slid the Gilot picture to the bottom of the stack, made a mushroom barley soup, and dug around for a Jane Austen novel to read while I spooned up the broth. At twilight, I unlocked my front door, checked the empty street, locked the door again, tugged the handle, went to each window to verify each bolt, and pulled the shades low, as I had done every night since I'd moved in. Then I read more until I dozed, trying to block out the memory of Brenae Brasil's eyes in the video, how they winced, went blank again, winced, went blank.

6

THE BUZZER WOKE ME, AND I lurched up from the couch, hair matted to my cheek like seaweed. Fumbled with a lamp. It was eight thirty at night. Not too late for a mistaken food delivery.

I pressed the intercom. "Hello?"

"Maggie." A man's voice, flattened by the speaker. I couldn't place it. Then I could. But how did Ray know my address?

"I need your opinion on something." His words sounded hasty. "Just tonight, I swear. Come with me. You'd be doing me a favor."

I hesitated. I didn't want to go anywhere with Ray. Or rather, I wanted to go exactly nowhere with him. Ray was a where I was successfully avoiding.

"It has to do with the Rocque," he said. "It's important."

What could Ray know about the Rocque that I didn't? I asked him.

"I'd rather not shout it on the street."

"Fine," I said. One night. "I'll be down in ten minutes."

THE AIR WAS COOL AND dry when I emerged, the sky rubbed orange by thousands of lights, the wind carrying a slight tinge of smoke. I hadn't been out after dark since the trip to Wonder Valley, and instantly missed the nocturnal openness and possibility of the desert. I missed the way the band's chords seemed to touch the horizon. Here, every noise layered upon another noise: loud horn, tire screech, the creak of the car door that Ray opened for me.

I'd resisted fixing myself up for him, and wore minimal lipstick, a T-shirt, and jeans. Ray slid in next to me, also dressed casually. I tried not to observe the way his bare bicep swelled out his T-shirt sleeve when he switched gears. He didn't look me over either, except once, to make sure my feet were in before he shut my door. There was some discordant song in another language playing on the stereo, and Ray turned it low.

"Where are we going?" I asked.

Ray named a club in West Hollywood. "Brenae's brother is in a band. I was hoping we could catch him on a break between sets. He blames LAAC for her death."

"I'm not participating in this, though."

"I know." He sounded guilty or nervous, I wasn't sure which. "I just need your advice on something."

I wasn't sure how giving advice constituted not participating, but I didn't object to hearing some music. I'd been to the club a few times, for bigger shows. If its fifty years of performances could have been recorded by its wooden walls, it would have been a World Heritage Site for musicologists. Elton John. Joni Mitchell. Guns N' Roses. Already I could sense its dank, vaulting interior, the glow on the drums, the dark headstones of the amps.

"You doing all right?" Ray said as we nudged east on Venice.

Was I supposed to answer that truthfully or not?

"I'm here," I said. "Keeping busy."

He glanced at me. "You were asleep at eight. You've got a couch-pillow line on your face."

"It's a big couch," I grumbled. "It takes up half the apartment."

Ray smiled at this, then shot into a gap. He had impeccable reflexes in traffic. He was also the kind of driver who hawked his mirrors, minding the road behind him as obsessively as the one before, scowling at tailgaters, and flashing his brakes. It amused me to watch him.

"What?" Ray said, looking over.

"Nothing."

"You know any recent LAAC grads through the Rocque?" he said. "I mean someone who could be discreet."

"Some," I said, thinking of several coworkers. "I can give you their names."

"Much obliged," he said.

"Was that it?" I said, my hand on the door handle. I obviously wasn't getting out, but I wanted to give the hint. "The advice you needed?"

"No, it's not," he said. The headlights of an oncoming car illuminated his face, and he looked suddenly skinned by the glare: stark and pale.

"What then?" I said.

"There's something you should know about Janis," said Ray.

My memory rewound to the meeting at the café, Janis's hesitation, the drop in her voice, and her and Dee's sudden, inexplicable absence in Wonder Valley. "Is something wrong with her?"

He glanced over at me, his mouth grim.

It was hard to form the words again. "What's wrong with her?"

"She has breast cancer," he said. "Stage two. But it's been aggressive."

My whole body went icy and rigid. I stared at the glove compartment, the light scratches on the gleaming black vinyl. Its little silver lock. It was as far as I could look.

"I didn't figure I'd be the one to tell you," he added, sounding genuinely sorry. "But if you didn't know . . . The thing is, she didn't expect you to say no today."

"Who else has heard this?" I said.

"Just a few people," said Ray. "Dee, Bas. Me and Alicia."

"Yegina," I said. Yegina knew. On the phone, she'd sounded like she was already grieving. Of course she was.

"Probably," agreed Ray. "Not much escapes her."

"I can't believe it," I said, even though all the way back in Wonder Valley, when I'd seen Ray's face for the first time, I'd known something was off.

What did Janis matter to him? He talked of her like an old friend.

What did Janis matter to me? It wasn't just me; it was us. The museum. Her approval, her leadership—how could I calculate how much we all lived for it at the Rocque? Janis was our brave, intelligent, idiosyncratic presence in L.A. She was every exhibition we'd ever had.

"You ever dig into the Rocque's history?" Ray said.

"I wrote a short book on it a couple of years ago for our twentieth anniversary."

"Who owns the land that the building is on?"

"Well, that's one of the great things about it," I said, puzzled by the question. "The city rents it to us for ten dollars a year. Janis's father paid for the construction costs, but without the city giving him the land, the museum would not exist."

He nodded. "Any idea when the lease runs out?"

"Oh, every ten years or so, but they always renew it." Suddenly I realized what he was implying. "Why? The city's not renewing it?"

"I don't know," said Ray. "But for the life of me, I couldn't figure out why a possibly terminally ill woman was so hellbent on taking down Hal Giroux, until I was talking with another collector about . . ."

Ray kept speaking, but I stopped listening. The words *terminally ill* dug a fresh hole in me. I'd just seen Janis today. She hadn't looked ill, but she had looked exhausted.

". . . and how he's been backed by a couple of key collectors quietly looking for seed money to build a big new contemporary art museum downtown."

"Downtown," I said, slow to process what Ray was saying.

Hal Giroux wanted to build a museum that would supplant the Rocque.

"Your CFO ever give reports on your building, how much renovations would cost?" said Ray.

There had been reports. For years. The Rocque building was old by L.A. standards and would need further retrofitting for earthquakes. We just kept vainly hoping that increased donorship and numbers at the box office would boost us to a bigger budget. But a competitor in the same neighborhood could destroy us.

"Janis wants dirt on Hal, and she thinks it's there. I honestly don't know if she's right, Maggie"—he cocked his head—"but I can tell you that I've looked into the scholarship recipients in visual arts for the past ten years, and eighty percent are male. Hal Giroux brings in the biggest funders to the college, and they must let him divide the spoils how he wants."

"Why didn't she tell me today?" I said, though I knew why.

"I assumed she would," he said. "I guess she chickened out. Can't blame her."

I didn't know what to say. The idea of Janis seriously ill or dying trumped every other thought I had.

"I know," said Ray quietly. "It hurts."

After a moment, he turned up the volume on the stereo. A mournful, soulful singer filled the small box of space around us, her foreign words punctuated by quick, harsh strings. Her voice was unbearably sad. We sat shoulder to shoulder for the whole song, staring at the ghostly windshield and beyond it, into the glittering pattern of red lights on the 405. When the music ended, my heart felt like it had been pummeled.

"Is this what you're taking us to hear tonight?" My throat was hoarse.

Ray ducked his head. "No, that's real fado."

I didn't know what fado was. "I don't think I can go to a club right now, Ray."

Ray sighed.

"You think *I* don't care how Janis feels?" he said. "She has her heart set on this whole thing: me investigating in my way, you gathering research for a pitch, everyone working together to find all the angles—"

"She didn't say that at all," I said. "That's not the picture I got."

"Well, she meant it."

"No, you mean it," I said. "That's different. You're her contractor; I'm her employee. That's how she saw my role. I'd take directions from you. I wouldn't be surprised if I was supposed to fetch you your coffee." This was going too far, especially after the news, and my mouth went sour, but Ray didn't contradict me or say anything further. He inched us along the freeway, alert for gaps. I wasn't sure if I was grateful to him or not.

"I'll get the first exit," he said. "Take you home."

I didn't want to be home, alone in the woman's mismatched apartment, with its air of desertion. "It's all right," I said. "I'm not doing the gallerina thing. But I'll go with you tonight."

THE MURKY SPOTLIGHT LOVED DAVI Brasil. He had a soulful gaze and dark curls, a wide frame that might grow pudgy with age but was underfed now and poked out his clothes in sharp angles. His hip bones held up his trousers; his rib cage jutted against his white tank top. His songs were not hoarse and wrenching, not like what Ray had just played for me, but their pleasant pop cousin. And the way he carried his voice, the way he commanded center stage, he seemed like a star. Another star from the same Brasil family. I wondered what their parents were like.

Ray stood beside me, sipping at his usual grapefruit juice. I ordered a cola to stay awake. I finished it in three cloying swallows. Then we watched. Ray seemed content to listen to the band, though he sometimes glanced around to measure the crowd, which was filling the club's first floor but not its balconies, and the merch table, stacked with T-shirts no one was buying. Davi was still building his fan base. Someone was taking a risk on him.

Whatever Ray was thinking now, I suspected he wouldn't tell me. This was how it would have been, working with him. My interview with the actress tomorrow—what a simple affair by comparison. It would be my own gig, start to finish. The actress would want the publicity, and so she would give me what I needed. Gilot would be with us in spirit, bringing the luster of a life well lived. There would be a tasty lunch, sparkling water with a twist of lime. Our common enterprise as clear as sunlight.

Davi had three bandmates, all guitarists, and they didn't stop strumming until the oldest one set down his instrument with a definitive *thunk* at the end of a long song. Heavyset and bearded, he rose first, swabbing his sweaty forehead with a handkerchief, and then headed backstage. Davi and the others waited through most of their applause before following.

"Now," Ray said and grabbed my elbow, steering me toward the back of the stage, where a muscular bald man blocked the narrow corridor beyond. Ray gave a nod to the man, who blinked but did not stop us from edging past him and heading down the paneled hall to a door. I looked at Ray, and he gave a little shrug, as if to say, *What did you expect? I know what I'm doing.*

Ray made one sharp knock, and after a moment the bearded bandmate poked his head out.

"Naw, man, no," he said, waving Ray off. "Come back after."

"Can't do that," Ray said. "We need to talk to him now."

The bearded guy retreated, and he said something to Davi in rapid Portuguese. Davi's retort was loud, and they argued for a while. Finally, the bandmate heaved a sigh and turned away, leaving the door unguarded. Ray pushed in, and I followed.

The four men sat on stools in a room with scratched purple walls and a mirror topped by a track of glowing bulbs. They stared at us, their faces and shirts soaked in sweat. Davi was clearly the youngest, and he wore the most suspicious expression, almost a sneer.

"We're on break," he said. "Can't this wait?"

"I've got an early bedtime," said Ray. Suddenly he looked colder and sterner than usual, more of a prototypical cop. His southern accent was stronger, too. "As I told your colleague here, I've been hired by someone who wants to find out the truth of what happened to your sister. I have a few short questions."

Davi cracked a can of beer and scowled at the foam rising through the hole.

"When did you last see her?" said Ray.

"The week before she died," Davi said.

"Which day?"

"I don't know. Saturday. She came to one of my sets." He pounded half the beer, then tossed it in a nearby trash. "This stuff tastes like dung. We got anything better?"

"Harder," said his bandmate, pulling out a clear bottle.

I watched Ray witness the exchange. He seemed to be measuring something in Davi, who up close resembled his sister more than he did onstage. They had the same dark brows and slightly short chin. Davi grabbed the bottle, unscrewed the cap, sniffed it, and handed it back. "That crap will ruin my voice," he said. "Get us something from the bar. Top shelf."

His bandmate looked peeved by the request, but he stalked from the room.

"Anything else?" Davi said to Ray with exaggerated slowness.

"Did you notice anything different about her the last time you saw her?"

"She seemed . . ." Davi paused. "Restless, I guess. Nervous. She dropped her beer, and my sister was not the clumsy type."

"Did she ask you about the money you owed her?"

The other two men did not look surprised at this, but I saw something slam behind Davi's eyes. "What are you saying?"

"You owed her four grand. There's a bank record of a check that she wrote to you. Just as she was about to lose all her funding at her school."

Davi blinked. "How do you know I didn't pay her back in cash?"

Ray just stood there and folded his arms. I didn't understand his attitude. His posture. I would have thought he'd be polite to Davi, someone who'd lost his sister so violently. I would have thought he'd be thankful for any information he could give. Then I felt naïve for assuming all this.

"Listen," Davi said, "I never touched a hair on my sister's head. The cops say she killed herself. You're meowing up the wrong fucking tree—"

"I agree," said Ray in the same tough tone. "So what's the right tree, Davi?"

His sudden change in tack disarmed Davi, who shut his mouth and shook his head.

"Get out," said the bearded man, halfheartedly. "You asked enough questions."

"You must have an idea," said Ray.

Davi frowned. "She left us years ago, you know? She didn't lose touch, but she always had different tastes and you could see her nose up, judging everything. So most hometown people just left her alone. I didn't know her crowd at college. I never met any of them, not at USC, not at LAAC. But she was happy, she was practically flying, until late last fall, and something happened. She told me it was a breakup of a relationship that never should have been. But she didn't say who." He picked up his empty guitar case and ran a hand over the black velvet interior. He seemed inclined to say more. Then he shut the case and set it down again. "And then she was just crazy depressed. Again. I heard she stopped her meds, too." His brow furrowed. "You must have your own idea."

"I've got too many ideas," said Ray. "But thank you for yours. Great set."

Davi didn't acknowledge the compliment. He was gazing at me. "Did you know Brenae?"

I glanced at Ray. Should I lie? He gave no sign either way. He was studying the open guitar case.

"No," I said, clearing my throat. "I saw her videos. Did you shoot them?"

Davi wore a quizzical expression.

"It had to have been someone she knew well," I said, feeling Ray's eyes on me. "She seemed so comfortable. Also, it was someone talented." I paused, lingering over the phrase. "I loved your set, too."

"No, I didn't shoot her movies." Davi turned back to the guitar case, his voice husky.

"We got to do our set list, Dav," growled one of the bandmates.

"Thank you for your time," Ray said to Davi, then nodded at me.

When I followed him out the door, I heard Davi say, "I paid Brenae back. Not all of it, but some. I was going to pay it all."

"DID YOU THINK HE HAD something to do with her suicide?" I asked as Ray drove me home.

"As much as anyone," said Ray. "I was curious what he knew about LAAC. And her funding."

"I don't think he knew that she'd lost it."

"Me neither. Or that she was behind on rent. LASD found an eviction notice in her mail. She was broke."

Ray's tense, tough air had disappeared. He was a different man now, slouched in his seat, steering with one hand at the top of the wheel. The hair at his temples was damp with sweat.

"Why did you talk to him like that?" I said.

"Like what?"

"Like a . . . cop," I said, wishing I had a different word.

"What do you think I am?" Ray said. The streetlights made panels of his face. "You think if I went in there like his buddy he would open up to me? People like Davi hate cops. He doesn't have a record, but their older brother does. He was in and out of juvenile detention for years. I go in there like I'm Davi's pal, like I'm sorry for his loss, and even if I am really genuinely sorry his sister is dead, he'll shut down. He's trained himself to be guarded against assholes like me since he was a kid. He'll think I have something on him, and he'll shut down just in case I do." He looked over. "You didn't like it, right?" He shrugged. "That's the point. It's not about being liked. It's about getting what you need, then getting out of people's lives."

It was a long speech for Ray, and when it was done, the silence in the car felt thick and deep. It hadn't occurred to me that he didn't want this gig, either. Or did he? Why was he here, back in L.A.? It couldn't be only for Janis. Ray had to have some lead on his own brother's homicide, which had happened last winter, a mystery that had first driven him to California. I longed to ask, but there was something fragile in his speech, despite the direct way he had delivered it—I didn't want to push him to confess anything to me now. The night had been full enough.

We passed a small, glass-fronted burger joint with a sign in red cursive: MO MEATTY MEATBURGERS! My ex and I used to read it aloud whenever we passed. It seemed so L.A.: the flamboyant, if slightly incorrect, overstatement. But we'd never stopped there to eat. For the first time, I wondered why. What were we afraid of?

"You asked a great question. One that I hadn't thought through," Ray added in his usual neutral, courtly tone. "I need to find out who filmed *Packing*. I don't remember seeing credits, do you?"

"No," I said. "Maybe that's the relationship Davi was talking about, though."

"Maybe." His hand tensed on the wheel. The fado singer was still playing low, her voice distant and sorrowful. We slowed in a line of traffic for a stoplight. The smell of spicy fried meat seeped through the windows, and we passed steam and smoke first, then a man cooking sausages on an open grill by the sidewalk, his spatula waving through the air. My stomach growled.

"You hungry?" Ray said. He sounded hungry, too. Or lonely. For a moment I felt a tug for him, for Ray as a man and not as a colleague or an adversary. The old tug, the one I'd felt months ago in the hospital when he put his hand over mine. But I shook it away.

"I've got to turn in," I said, sighing, "if I'm going to pull off being a gallerina tomorrow. And I will have to leave for lunch. Two or three hours."

A stillness fell over Ray. "You sure?" he said after a moment.

"I have an important interview," I said. "I'm not missing it."

"No, I mean about the other. Filling in at the gallery."

He turned onto the broad boulevard that led to my apartment, but even with his hands moving on the wheel he gave the impression of utter absorption, as if he were listening to something I couldn't hear.

"Sure as I ever will be," I said. I wasn't certain when I had decided this—maybe after watching Davi's face go dark with grief—but it was for Janis and for the Rocque that I was doing it. If my listening in on a few students gossiping about their director would give her peace of mind about our museum's future, then what did one week matter to me? I would leverage my interview with the actress toward more writing gigs. I would pave my own way.

Ray waited for a moment, then nodded. "We should meet early tomorrow so I can brief you on the crew." He named a café near the gallery. "Case report's in the door there beside you. Terrific bedtime reading, if you want."

So he *had* been certain that he would convince me tonight. The music. The meeting place tomorrow picked out. The case file in the door. I had been manipulated like Davi into giving Ray the answer he wanted.

"Thanks," I said stiffly, lifting the thick folder from the pocket.

He pulled up at the curb. I opened my door as soon as the car stopped. "Good night," I said.

"You don't want to act like you're playing a part," Ray said suddenly. "People can always tell when you're playing a part."

I held the handle, waiting.

"I mean tonight, you asked the right question. A smart question. But Davi could tell you were trying to play him, flattering him like that," Ray said, wearing a slight frown. "He didn't mind, but he could tell. Someone else might distrust you, and you'd lose the setup right there."

I tried to remember what expression I'd worn in the bar's back room, how I had been standing when I'd spoken to Davi. Then I saw myself crossing my arms, leaning on one leg, my hip cocked. Had I done that? Had I really pouted and looked out at Davi from lowered eyes? Ray was right. The body language wasn't me. "So how should I act?" I said.

"Like yourself. But yourself as the gallerina," said Ray. He waved his hand and looked over his shoulder, as if he saw someone quickly driving up on us. "You know. Sweet. Brainy," he said to his window.

It took me a few seconds, but I swallowed all the mixed feelings this summary raised in me.

I said, "See you in the morning."

The woman was still singing low when I exited the car. I closed the door on her voice, and on Ray sneaking a last glance at me, a slight puzzlement in his eyes, as if he wasn't certain who I'd become. Then he gave me a polite nod, and we parted.

SAFELY INSIDE, I PUT THE file down and took a bath. The bathtub had been a selling point for the sublet—deep and spacious for a boxy apartment and its generic little bathroom—and when I sank into it and closed my eyes, I felt like I understood why the woman kept this place, even as she fled it. It was reassuring to possess your own small retreat in this massive city, to have one spot that was quiet and yours alone. I didn't read. I just soaked in hot water, sweating, the tub so full I could almost float. My mind drifted over memories of Janis: Telling Bas off in his office. Standing at the podium in the museum auditorium, delivering the news of Kim Lord's disappearance. Holding Dee's hand at a Rocque exhibition opening, the first time she'd publicly acknowledged their relationship. She'd looked defiant, happy, and supremely uncomfortable. For all her fame and influence, Janis hated the spotlight. She hated any notice at all. I couldn't imagine how much she despised her body becoming public through her disease, her weekly face-offs with oncologists and technicians.

After I toweled dry and dressed in my softest pajamas, I circled the death report a few times, making tea, a piece of buttered toast. Just as I was about to pick up the file, my stomach churned and I decided I couldn't read it or I would never sleep. I still wasn't sure I could bear getting tied up in the sadness of Brenae's story.

And the sadness was, unfortunately, beside the point. No matter what had happened to Brenae, her story was a pawn in Janis's game. Janis's real goal was to keep her own strong hand in shaping downtown culture. If L.A. in the sixties and seventies had had the best parties, and the eighties and nineties massive riots and earthquake devastation, then our moment now was about spending the future, building the new cosmopolis from the center outward. We were two years post 9/11, and American cities were precious, necessary, ours. Everyone rich enough in L.A. craved a building project; even famous actors and pop stars asked our museum director for introductions to the architects showing their designs at the Rocque. Drugs, sex, and high-end vacations were all fine and good, but renovating a loft building off Broadway, or opening a dark-paneled Sixth Street speakeasy—now that was a lucky life. Janis wanted her own vision to endure in this urban frontier frenzy, and who could blame her? For decades, the Rocque had been *the* reason to visit its block on weekends, when the surrounding skyscrapers had emptied themselves of their bankers and lawyers and the only open restaurant served the same Thai chicken pizza you could get in Hemet. Now Janis's nemesis threatened to sail in and claim the same turf she'd fought so hard for. She would find a reason to stop him. But Brenae wasn't a reason. She was a person. I looked over at the closed file, the thick stack of papers inside. *I desperately need your help.* I turned away, crawled into bed, and closed my eyes.

AN HOUR LATER, I FOUND I couldn't sleep, so I got up and wrote to my mother. Whenever I didn't want to update my mother on my life, I told her about what I was reading. I presumed that we both found this a reassuring practice. In her mind, as long as I was reading books, I must be staying home at night and I had not fallen off a cliff into despondency or self-destructive behavior; in my mind, as long as Mom was there to listen to my thoughts, they actually mattered.

Tonight, I wrote about the wonderful book I'd read that summer on James Compton, a lost figure in the 1990s British art scene. Brilliant, blond, brash, upper crust, and frequently spotted in an immaculate white suit, Compton had been the brief Warhol of his tribe. He was the first to open a gallery in Shoreditch, one of London's derelict warehouse districts, and it soon became a hub for a loose confederation of young artists. He organized a street fair with kissing booths, clowns, and drawings for sale, all staffed by young names who became art-world legends within five years. He also smoked crack, held a cake knife to his throat at his birthday party, and was rumored to have connections with a Turkish crime family. Within five years, he'd died, the victim of an ether overdose. The funeral for Compton was huge, but since then—without his powerful personality and showmanship—his name had ebbed.

I told my mother that reading about Compton had made me sad for him, but that the writer's eloquent praise of his achievements took that sadness and added something, the way the second note of a chord takes a lonely, simple sound and makes it lovely and full. When I finished the book, I felt bereft, partly because Compton had died at twenty-eight and there was so much he could have done, and partly because the text's warm, edifying voice had finished talking to me.

I didn't say that the book was not a book, but a thesis. I didn't say that the author was Calvin Teicher, Ray's half brother, or that he was also dead, found in a Boyle Heights hotel about a year ago, beaten and floating facedown in a bathtub, the shower running, the drain closed. His death not from blows, but from water in his lungs. The investigation inconclusive.

Calvin's murderer still free. I didn't believe Ray was back in L.A. only for Janis Rocque, or that, deep down, he really cared what had happened to Brenae Brasil. He must have some new insight into his brother's case, and he would be chewing on it the whole time we worked together. You don't want to act like you're playing a part. People can always tell.

Interview with Hal Giroux

March 16, 2003
LAAC
Detective Strick

Tell me how long and in what context you knew Brenae Brasil.
She was one of my star students in the fall. She came in blazing, straight from undergraduate. I hired her to work on my crew, and she assisted in building my London show. I was also the chair of her review committee.

So exactly how many months did you know her?
August to March. Seven or eight months.

You'd never met her before she was a student at LAAC?
No.

Did your relationship to Brenae change over the course of those months?
My relationship to all of my students is fairly constant. I expect the best of them.

What made you hire her to work on your crew?
I thought she was talented. I wanted to give her a chance.

Did Brenae do her best, in your mind?
I don't think Brenae was ready for the intensity of graduate school. Her second semester was a total disaster. She barely attended any classes. She was showing up to places clearly under the influence—

How so?
Slurring and stumbling.

What "places" are you referring to?
Open studios, presentations. LAAC social gatherings mostly.

Was she the only student to show up to social events inebriated?
Of course not. I brought it up because you asked what changed. She changed.

Tell me about your probationary meeting on March 5, 2003.
I meet with all my students at the end of their first year to have a preliminary talk about their graduation show. In Brenae's case, we met early because I was worried about her career at LAAC. She hadn't produced anything since the fall, and she was likely to flunk her classes. Her future funding had been suspended because her performance was so poor. Frankly, I thought she ought to put school on hiatus and come back and finish the degree when she felt well again. I told her so. I promised her a place.

She refused and insisted that she had in fact produced some work and she wanted to show it to me.

What work?

There were two videos. One was quite long, but I watched the whole thing. It was footage she'd taken over the past year at openings and parties, of people walking away to their cars. That's all it was. The parties breaking up.

I didn't think much of it. It had none of Brenae's usual verve. She wasn't starring in it. That was a big problem. The other problem is that students think their social lives are more interesting than they are.

What was in the second video?

The other video showed Brenae engaged in a sexual act with an unidentified male. She'd put together a voice-over that implied that he was forcing her. That shocked me. Then she told me that as part of her graduation project, she wanted to project it on a wall in our main building. She thought this was a daring idea, a confrontation of sexual politics at LAAC, and she didn't see any of its complications for her, for the school, for whoever her sexual partner was. I told her that was impossible.

Do you know who it was?

No. The man's head was blurred out.

No guesses? You must have guessed.

None.

And she didn't tell you?

No.

Why didn't you ask?

I did. I asked Brenae if she wanted to initiate formal sexual harassment proceedings with the college. She said that "a specific perpetrator, a specific victim" wasn't the point. I remember those were her exact words. I told her that no one would see a symbol when they saw that footage. They would see a man. And they would see her. And she could get sued. I don't think she anticipated how much damage she could do to herself.

Did you discuss these videos with anyone?
No. I told her that her best route was to take time off. I told her that procedures were always in place for her to lodge a formal complaint, and I gave her the names of dedicated staff who could help her with her personal crisis and with transitioning to taking a leave from LAAC. We have a great mental health team here at LAAC.

The videos you describe are missing. The files erased from her hard drive. What do you think happened to them?
Maybe she erased them herself. I never tell students to destroy their work, although sometimes that's exactly the remedy they need. But I don't coddle them, either. I was devastated when I heard she ended her life. I believed in her talent and vision. But I wouldn't have been doing her any favors paying her another year to burn bridges at LAAC. You have to launch from this place with success and momentum, or you can't make the leaps you need to.

The videos were erased after her death. How is that possible, in your mind?
It's not. I asked our staff to do a welfare check and they found her, and I promptly called the police. The studio was under lock and key that whole time. No one could have tampered with her laptop.

What if someone entered the studio after her death, erased the files, and then locked the door again and walked away?
That's an insidious claim. Wouldn't there be evidence? Fingerprints?

Who has keys to the studio?
The student. And custodial has a set. That's it.

Where do the custodians keep them?
I don't know actually. Their office somewhere, I suppose. You can ask.

So it's technically possible that someone lifted the key, unlocked the studio, erased the files, and replaced the key.
Sure. It sounds like an awful lot of trouble for a couple of student films, though. Isn't it more likely that you have the dates and times wrong and that Brenae erased them herself?

Let's go back to your last meeting with Brenae. You didn't think the subject of the second video merited further investigation on your part.
As I've said twice now, I asked Brenae if she wanted to initiate formal sexual harassment proceedings with the college. She said only after she projected the video on a wall on campus. I said no deal. Students rarely consider the legal implications of what they do, but I have to. Our program can't survive expensive public lawsuits.

What measures did the school take to make sure that students don't carry firearms to campus?
We don't allow firearms. I heard of Brenae's *Packing* project about halfway through the week she was making it. I contacted her immediately and told her that she could never bring the weapon to campus or it would be confiscated and she would be suspended. She agreed, in writing. I can have my assistant show you the contract. I asked her once what she did with the gun after she completed the project, and she told me she'd sold it back to the gun dealer. I had no idea she stored it in her studio until she shot herself.

When did you learn of her death?
The day my staff discovered her. I won't forget that day for a long time. The school has been very impacted by her loss. Very impacted.

She may have been in her studio for an entire day and night before she shot herself. Do you find it unusual that no one would notice this?
Our student artists often retreat to get their work done. Frankly, they like to binge on isolation. It's part of their process. So, no, it would not come off as unusual.

She wrote "Watch me" in a note on her laptop. What does that mean to you?
I don't know. It sounds like a dare. The language. It's provocative.

You don't think it's in reference to the erased files or to the sexual situation she revealed on one of them?
Brenae made some fine artworks in her life. Maybe she wanted people to watch them all.

Do you have any further thoughts about Brenae Brasil that you would like to share?
My heart goes out to her family. I'm very sorry for their loss. And I'm very sorry for ours.

7

INSIDE THE CASE FILE THE next morning, I half expected to find lurid photographs of Brenae's dead body, like I'd seen from TV crime shows, but if there had been photos, our source hadn't included them. Instead, I encountered pages and pages of forms in a tiny font. Dates, times, locations, numbers. A lot of numbers. Even the paramedics who'd been called to her studio had had numbers assigned to them.

The file's chronology followed the detectives from the moment they were given the case to the moment they made their conclusions, noting the reports, interviews, and tips that came to them along the way. Brenae's suicide boiled down to a series of steps and calculations, her fate and character reconstructed in hindsight. A twenty-two-year-old woman. A woman mostly estranged from her family, except for her musician brother. A student who, according to one witness, "had a talent for controversy." A student who had been given the world last spring with a rare full scholarship to LAAC, and who had gone from exceeding her professors' expectations to missing weeks of classes and failing to turn in assignments.

The interview with Hal Giroux halted me for a while. He didn't sound like a man covering up his own guilt. But what about the guilt of someone else? Why wouldn't he look harder into the situation that Brenae presented to him, instead of essentially cutting her off? Wasn't that his job as director of his program? There were interviews with other professors as well, including a female instructor who claimed she'd brought Brenae's lapses to Hal's attention, and that Brenae had started catching up on her missed work before she shot herself. "She was digging herself out, but I think when she realized she was going to finish the year with Bs and Cs, she just gave up," the instructor reflected. "She could only be a star or a failure, and nothing in between."

The file's forensic information I found overwhelming and hard to read. Brenae's wounds were numbered, and there was only one that mattered: the shot that killed her. Otherwise, she'd had two small bruises, one on her right ankle and one on her left thigh. No signs of any sexual penetration. I didn't understand all the abbreviations, but the medical examiner's report indicated temazepam in her bloodstream—which I already knew about from the newspaper accounts—and described the trajectory of the bullet from under her chin through the top of her skull. Time of death was somewhere between midnight and 4:00 a.m., the day before she was found. The gun had only her fingerprints on it.

Two students—reluctant to admit they'd been sleeping together in one of their studios—confirmed a loud noise in the early hours of Thursday morning, though they didn't suspect it was a gun firing. "It sounded like a pop," said one student. "We thought someone was setting off fireworks."

The property and evidence report cataloged objects in Brenae's studio, from crumpled tissues in the wastebasket to a metal safe to her bloody pillow.

Her phone records revealed little. Brenae's landline and prepaid cell had few calls out, mostly to her brother Davi in her last month. Her only registered e-mail was the school e-mail address, and here, too, she had minimal interactions beyond setting up meetings and responding (or not responding) to assignments. Her laptop held more clues. A Friendster page surfaced. Brenae had 111 friends and posted stills from her videos. Three were from her *After-Parties* video. The stills showed clusters of mostly young, hip people in the light-soaked L.A. night. But *After-Parties* wasn't in the contents of her hard drive. Nor was *Lesson in Red.* In fact, as the interview with Hal had disclosed, it appeared as if someone had gotten to her computer twenty-four hours before she was found and erased and shredded some data. Most people think if they erase a file, it's deleted from a computer, but actually only the pathway is deleted, not the data. It takes effort and software to shred. It takes a person so anxious to hide something, they will make sure it is gone. Computer forensics identified the time it was done: Thursday at 8:00 p.m. According to the coroner, Brenae died in the early morning hours on Thursday. She was found on Friday.

The report contained so much information, it would take me many more hours to pore over it all. And yet a team of qualified professionals had scoured Brenae's existence for why she died, and they'd come up with one clear conclusion: she planned her own exit, and she took it alone. I don't know why this depressed me the most. Murder wouldn't have been better, but someone else's jealousy or rage was easier to swallow than Brenae's abject despair.

An hour before I was supposed to meet Ray, I put down the case file, showered, pulled on the suit, smoothed my hair back into a clip, and stepped to the mirror. My lower half was as sleek as a seal, but I didn't know what to do about my obtrusively wholesome, sincere face. Eye makeup wouldn't help; it tended to turn me into a sad clown. It was too late to sculpt my brows to arched lines. Darker lipstick would have to do. I swiped my mouth. Too red. Blood red. I cleaned it off and put on a lighter shade. Fake pink. Garish. I scoured my lips with a tissue. Darker again. Berry brown. A Gorgon's mouth. I rubbed it off. Went for a gloss, smearing a little too hard. The glisten sickened me. I pushed myself away from the mirror and opened the bathroom window, taking gulping breaths. Even without grisly crime photos, the facts were enough. I saw Brenae lying on that mattress, her head an exploded nest of blood.

The air carried the faintest tang of the ocean. I pressed my cheek to the window screen, willing myself to focus on what today was really about: interviewing the talented young actress who would play Françoise Gilot. The rest was simply a favor to Janis. When my pulse had settled, I fixed my lips up with a dulled garnet color, grabbed my notes, and headed down the stairs to the carport. Warm morning sun kissed my face and hair. I'd always loved the early hours of the Southern California day. They made me feel ageless and light. When I reached my car, I hesitated. A little stroll might help me now. It was only eight blocks to the gallery, twelve to the coffee shop. A long walk, but there was a breeze. I started striding.

For the first five glorious minutes, I imagined my day as gallerina, as Hollywood interviewer. Then the haze began to burn off, and even behind my sunglasses I could feel the city blocks heating up. Every window glared. I started to sweat and veered off the big boulevard for the smaller streets. Mistake. There was little shade in the manicured neighborhoods. Lawns were dotted with green hedges and dwarf trees. Small white signs indicated vigorous security surveillance. *Wealth is here,* they announced, as if anyone needed reminding.

Sweat trickled in my eyes. I tripped on a fallen palm frond and tweaked my ankle, staggering. I almost turned around. But no one had seen. No one was walking outside but me, and I ducked my head and kept going.

Several more turns, and I arrived at the main commercial boulevard. The buildings grew spotless windows and cursive signs, showcasing the delights inside, an organic juicery, sushi, New Age books, small-batch ice cream. I'd pass the gallery in three blocks. Two blocks. One. Rush-hour exhaust filled my mouth. There was Hal's name printed on the glass and, beyond, the unlit emptiness of the white cube. Wait, no. I spotted shadows, then figures. Three of the four young people from the desert were there: the redheaded woman and the two guys. They were already inside, already talking. I sped up, my stomach sinking. I had finally recognized the redhead.

Earlier this year, I'd seen pictures of her online, smiling with her horrible father, the rich, overbearing collector who'd secretly tried to rig Kim Lord's career and one of Ray's principal suspects in the violent death of his brother.

She was Layla Goetz-Middleton.

8

AFTER I FIXED MY DAMP hairline as best I could in the coffee shop window, I tugged my suit straight and entered. Ray was at a table, flipping through the city's free weekly paper, a smart publication that supported itself mostly with thinly veiled prostitution ads. I wondered how the arts editor would respond to an exposé about a suicide and sexual harassment at LAAC. I could see Brenae's face on the weekly's cover, staring out, her thick hair like a halo. But not my own byline.

Ray rose from his seat as I approached. He looked like he might be wearing the same T-shirt and jeans as last night, a suit jacket thrown over them, and his eye sockets were dark from lack of sleep.

As we waited in line together, he told me that Detective Ruiz was also on her way, but her one-year-old had dropped her cell phone in the toilet that morning and she was stopping to get a new one. I heard my shocked laugh, and expressions of sympathy and pity, but inside I was thinking, *She's a mom? How could I not know?* Ray seemed unsurprised, entertained even. It struck me again that they seemed to know each other well. Better than professionals engaged in the same task. Like friends. Or more than friends.

We both ordered large plain coffees, and I noted with some amusement that Ray seemed to approve of this spartan choice. Paper cups slid warm into our hands. "I want it noted that I'm fetching you your coffee," Ray said, brandishing a credit card. "Long day ahead of us."

"The students are already there," I said as we sat down. "They didn't spot me," I added, noting his alarmed look. "But I saw Layla. It's his daughter, isn't it? Layla Goetz-Middleton?"

Ray nodded, taking a sip of his coffee. "Funny how we always skip the small talk."

"Funny that she's involved in this and that you didn't mention her yesterday," I said.

When artist Kim Lord went missing on the opening night of her Rocque exhibition in April, Ray and I ended up independently following the same dead-end lead, to a rich collector named Steve Goetz. Goetz had spent the better part of two decades trying to rig Kim Lord's value in the art market by buying and rebuying her artworks under different identities. He considered it a conceptual experiment, demonstrating the power of the collector to fix an artist's worth. But when Kim was murdered, Janis had strong-armed Goetz into selling most of the paintings to the Rocque's collection, and the collector's manipulations had never reached the public.

Still, Goetz had frightened me when I met him at his gallery last spring. I remembered his coldness and his pride. And I remembered Ray's hostility toward him, too.

"You seemed suspicious of him, even after . . ." I didn't finish.

"You really all healed up?" Ray said, his blue eyes examining me.

His concern for my physical health seemed genuine. Also spontaneous, as if he hadn't thought to ask before now. Not last night, not at Café Francesca, not in Wonder Valley.

"I guess I'm 'healed up,'" I said, unsettled. "Why?"

"You've got this expression now."

I stared at him quizzically.

"I don't know how to explain it." He sighed, running a hand through his hair. "Like parts of you are tensed to fight."

My ribs felt tight. "I'm fine," I muttered.

"Thank God," said a voice behind us, and then a chair pulled back and the detective slumped down beside us. This morning, she looked like yet another person. She was wearing another pressed pastel suit, but her eyes were wild, her hair mussed. "I can't deal with another . . ." She paused, absorbing the posh coffee-scented air. "I need the rest of this morning to be crisis-free," she said in a smoother, more professional tone. "Now that we're all here . . ." She focused harder on me and gaped. "Jesus. Did you freaking jog here?"

"I walked," I said.

"You're burning up," she said. "I'm getting you an ice water."

She bounded up from her chair and stood in the coffee line, smoothing her own hair and casting suspicious glances back at me.

I shrugged, then stripped off my jacket, keeping my face blank. But the air-conditioned room stung my bare arms and shoulders; the black tank top I wore was silky and thin, and I hadn't expected to be undressing down to it, especially not in front of Ray. He had the good manners to look elsewhere. I understood Detective Ruiz's reaction: Why would I take a stupid walk and ruin a look that had cost me more than a grand? To feel young and free? To insist I wasn't caged by this city? Neither was true. It was Brenae. I'd wanted to distract myself from my corrosive anger at her case. I hadn't succeeded.

"Hey." Ray leaned in. I smelled coffee and, beneath it, the scent of his skin and hair, which was dry and sweet, almost straw-like. "Two things. One, you are not the reason Alicia's spazzing out now. Two, I am as interested in Steve Goetz as I am in my left toenail. Okay?"

"That doesn't make sense," I said.

"It's true," he said.

"I mean about the toenail," I said, and wished I hadn't because something had been shifting in his face and I'd caught a glimpse of the same fear that I'd seen on the night in Wonder Valley. But now it abruptly vanished.

"What?" he said.

"A left toenail isn't a thing."

"Not to a literalist Yankee, no," he said.

"Literalism isn't regional," I said.

"Being a Yankee is." A smirk tugged at his mouth. "You got some Yankeeness rubbed back on you when you went home."

"How would you know?"

"It's all over your voice." He was gleaming with good humor now.

"That doesn't make any sense, either."

"Of course not." He leaned back. "But I knew a pointless argument would cheer you up."

"You really ready to do this?" Detective Ruiz said as she slid my ice water to me. Her tone was apologetic, but her face remained dubious. "I hope so. I can't handle more 'emergency meetings' with Janis. I want to be done."

I told the detective I would work the week at the Westing and then we could reevaluate to see what information Ray and I had. "I have a freelance assignment that I'm also—" I started to say, wanting to name-drop the actress.

But the detective was already launching into an explanation about eavesdropping and wiretapping, and how neither Ray nor I could use a mic to record other people's conversations unless an official felony law enforcement case was involved. I would not use any devices unless I got her permission.

"Okay?" she said.

I nodded. Ray nodded. Then Ray told me about the people I'd be observing. He described a close-knit group that had traveled to London last fall to premiere Hal's Westing show: two men, Pearson Winters and Erik Reidl, and three women, Layla Goetz-Middleton, Zania de Wilde, and Brenae Brasil. A few significant facts lodged with me: Layla and Erik had been a romantic couple on and off for a year. Pearson had had a prior felony: an assault on another man. Zania was the gallerist's daughter. All four were willing to talk with Ray today.

"Any questions?" he concluded. "The interviews start at four o'clock."

"Does Hal know they're participating?" I asked.

"No," said Ray.

"Do you think any of them know about the video, or why it was erased?"

"Not sure. We'll find out what we can," said Ray. "I'm going to show it to each of them."

I tried to imagine the students' reactions when Ray approached them. They must have been wounded by Brenae's death, or they wouldn't have agreed. I wondered what they'd think of being spied on. I didn't feel sorry for them, but I wished they understood the stakes of what they'd see and might say.

"Are we good?" the detective said, looking at Ray. "I have a mountain of paperwork at the office."

Before Ray could speak, her phone buzzed and she looked at the number. "Janis." She sighed. "Didn't you tell her to call you from now on?" she asked Ray.

He shrugged. "Yeah, but the problem is, she likes you better."

She answered the phone and then handed it to me. "Last instructions," she said.

I took it gingerly and said hello.

"Maggie," said Janis. "Good. I explained to Bas that you were doing some important freelance work for my foundation and that this shouldn't count as vacation days. You ready? Ray thinks the world of you, you know, and you'll make the right team for this. It's delicate. Hal's not an evil man. He's done a lot of good." She sounded frail suddenly. "And this woman deserved better. You need to help me make sure people are held accountable. Okay?"

I faltered at saying what was really on my mind: *I'm sorry.* "I will," I said.

"It's almost nine thirty," she said. "You better get going."

9

I ENTERED THE GALLERY WITH the keys Ray had given me and headed for the desk where I'd been told to sit. Layla Goetz-Middleton was gone. Only the two men were left in the space. Pearson was sitting on a stool. Erik was squatting, his heels lightly raised, picking through piles of used shoes: sneakers, sandals, penny loafers, boots—some polished, some bent and stained, some missing laces. The room smelled faintly of canvas, leather, and old sweat. Spools of wire were piled against the wall.

"This same crew has built Hal's shows for the past two years," Ray had told us at the coffee shop. "It's a coveted role, apparently, as they go with him expense-free when his shows travel, and former crew members have moved on to star careers."

Pearson was a devoted LAAC alum and the secret sauce to Hal's shows since 1996—whatever Hal envisioned, Pearson executed. He lived alone in North Hollywood, working intermittently on lighting for movie productions, then accompanying Hal's shows on the road to make sure they were installed correctly. Pearson had a sturdy, capable look—all his limbs were large for his frame—even so, his head seemed over-big, and shiny, lacking any hair to cap it. He wore a blank, placid expression, as if he were processing a very slow thought.

If Pearson was the organizing genius, Erik was the craftsman, a native of Vienna who had come to L.A. five years ago, first USC, then LAAC, where he'd quickly become a favorite of Hal's. Erik had grown up in American international schools; he wanted to stay in this country for good. He was taking an extra semester to finish his graduation project: *Bull*, a herd of fifteen-foot-tall animals made from silver-blue cans of Red Bull. Rumor had it that Steve Goetz had already bought *Bull*, unfinished, for a large price tag, and other collectors were clamoring for more work. Erik was the physical opposite of Pearson—curly-headed, small, lithe, in constant motion. Yet he, too, seemed to have studied the art of expressionlessness, and I couldn't get a read on how either felt about the installation.

"Color? Texture? Shape?" said Erik, tossing a high-heeled red pump. "What are we supposed to go on?"

"Hal gave us his key." Pearson turned to me. "In case you were worrying."

I greeted him and introduced myself as Mary. "Temporary replacement," I added.

"I need a temp replacement." Erik shook his head at a strappy white sandal, chucked it. It clunked a wall.

"How many shoes are there?" I said.

"Less than half of what we need," said Erik glumly.

"Direction," Pearson said to Erik. "This space is loftier than London, but we still need to build from the ground up."

If Erik, the native Austrian, had surprisingly no accent except a slight Californian uplift, Pearson's voice carried a faint impression of the nasal vowels and burred *r* sounds that I recognized from my own childhood in the Northeast. A rural working-class inflection, just a smidge of it, but recognizable. An odd inflection for someone with such a pretentious name. Pearson Winters.

"We should start with the nave," Pearson added.

"That high?" Erik tipped his head to the gallery's twenty-foot ceiling, his curly hair falling back. "Layla won't do ladders."

"Layla doesn't have to," Pearson said, then turned to me. "Anything you need from us?"

"No." It was time for me to act like I had a job to do. I walked toward the gallery desk. "Keep on with your knavery."

They looked startled at my pun. No doubt I came off as stuffy and middle-aged, with my suit and heels, even though Pearson was older than me. They were both wearing T-shirts and jeans—the loose, faded, but expensive kind that emitted a scripted nonchalance. Their shoes gave away their fashion origins. Erik was the surfer, slapping around on canvas shoes, and Pearson the post-punk strutter in leather boots. They seemed comfortable together. And yet did I detect a small tension about Layla radiating through their banter?

I sat down at the chrome desk and turned on the computer, typed the temporary login and password I'd been given. It led me to something like a library page, only the internet available, the home page the gallery's website. No inbox. No gallery files. No price lists. What should I pretend to do now? Not for the first time, I wondered why Nelson de Wilde had approved of this plan. Janis said he owed her, but still. I was spying on the crew of one of his artists, a prominent figure who could connect him to many rising future stars.

After a moment, Erik called after me. "Does your agency employ serfs? We need about thirty."

"The serfs are all working on the latest Michael Bay movie," I called back, and regretted it, because again the response was silence. Mystified silence? Social condemnation? I should be acting more formal. Driven. A gallerina was polished. She was ambitious. She was overqualified, with an impressive art history degree and letters of reference from prominent collectors. She dreamed . . . of what? Of learning the business here so that she could go work at Catesby's or another auction house, so that she could go into consulting. Mostly she dreamed of building her own modest collection. An artist sought meaning. A curator sought significance. The gallerina sought taste. The longer and harder she worked, the more she looked the part, the more she became an arbiter of what others should own.

I hadn't seen too many gallerinas at the Rocque, but sometimes a female intern left the museum for that path. Invariably she had been born wealthy, had a real collector in the family, and possessed some flawless physical trait: her skin, her hair, her figure. The gallery side of the art world, where the deals were made, would pull her like a magnet from the museum side, because she enjoyed the commerce and because she could become the living representation of the formality of those white cubes—austere and classical, splashed by well-chosen color.

Now that I was here, I could see the attraction of the gallerina life. My new suit made me feel like the air around me parted differently, that my waist and hips formed a perfect contour, and my shoulders lanced above my breasts, strong as a man's, but finer. If only the garment worked on my eye and my conversational abilities and plane tickets to Miami and Basel the way that it worked on my body. I could see myself gliding through this sophisticated life, making the right choices about which art would stand the test of time.

A neat stand-up file perched on one edge of my desk. I grabbed a folder and opened it. A list of names, some of them wealthy collectors, some with check marks, then a tally below for RSVPs. The invitation list for the opening? I noticed Janis Rocque on it, but no check next to her name.

I shoved the folder back, grabbed the next. A gallery guide, marked PLEASE PROOF. Phew. Proofreading was familiar ground.

Hal Giroux's Shoe Cathedral

Longtime Los Angeles luminary Hal Giroux brings his monumental installation *Shoe Cathedral* to the Westing Gallery from November 2–December

> 22, 2003. An exclusive invitation-only reception on November 1 will be followed by open gallery hours Tuesday–Sunday, 11:00 a.m.–5:00 p.m.
>
> Known for interactive installations that question and refigure the quotidian in our lives, Giroux will juxtapose the heights of human architecture with earthbound human apparel to examine the connections between religion and commercialism in contemporary life. [Oh-kay. And the emperor's new clothes are smashing, too.] Giroux has been the director of the MFA program in visual arts at LAAC for twenty-two years.

The guide included a late-1970s picture of Hal slouched on his elbows on an airplane wing in an airplane graveyard. The young Hal was bearded and bushy-haired and grinned with impish glee. He looked only a few hours older than his students, who posed around him, all white, all sporting long locks and tight flared pants, their faces adoring. The guide listed Giroux's awards and a few earlier works and quoted an art critic who said, "Hal Giroux demands his viewers to reconsider their place in the world of objects. His made things are things made visible." Blurbs were often overblown, but this one made little sense. The installation itself seemed a bit perky and obvious. Shoe, cathedral. Let's take sacred iconography and smear it with the mundane or vulgar. It's *Piss Christ*! It's the Virgin Mary painted in elephant dung, only much less risky. I felt inclined to join Janis Rocque and Yegina in their scorn for Giroux, then reminded myself I had no real talent for scorn. I was much better at trusting the best in people. At being trustworthy. In two and a half hours, I'd leave for my interview and prove this. The suit made me feel like I could manage higher heels, though. I wondered if there were any in the heaps of shoes around the gallery, and if anyone would notice me borrowing them.

A white cup slid across the low wall that circled my desk.

"I got it extra frothy because that's what the other gallerina liked," said a husky voice. "I know you're not the same person. But you can have it anyway." I followed the French-tipped fingers holding the cup to a plump pale arm, a white sleeveless shirt, red hair. Layla smiled when I met her eyes, but it was a smile that splashed like salt, and it seasoned her words with sharpness.

I thanked her and took the cup, wincing at the heat, nearly dropping it. It thunked to my desk, making a tiny, creamy splash. I didn't know what to wipe it with.

"Oops, extra hot, too," Layla said. "My fingers aren't very sensitive."

"I'll let it cool," I said. The droplet glistened on the chrome.

Layla didn't leave. She looked over at Pearson and Erik and shook her head. "Two-thirds of the shoes got delivered to LAAC by accident," she said and sighed. "They should be on their way now."

"That's a shame," I said in what I hoped was a proper intonation. "Will it delay you much?"

Layla leaned against my desk.

"Do you know about the RSVPs?" she said. "Hal wants to see the final numbers."

I handed her the folder with the list in it. "I'm guessing the checkmarks are yeses."

Layla scrutinized it for an uncomfortably long time. I had the impression she was working up the right words to say to me.

"Have you temped in a gallery before?" said Layla, making a note on the list.

Yes? No? "I've just been interning," I said vaguely, wiping the droplet with my finger, noting that my emergency manicure was already chipping.

"Well, piece of advice," said Layla, returning the folder. "Never show anyone anything when they ask for it." She smiled that same assaulting smile. "I have to go help these oafs."

Layla walked away with a sway in her step. She had the body of a fifties starlet: busty, with hips that seem shocked at the smallness of her waist. Her long arms and her preening confidence were the only signs of her genetic relationship to her father, Steve Goetz.

Layla strolled into the installation, trailing her hands over shoes and wires. Pearson and Erik hadn't spoken for the last hour, and they greeted Layla with silent nods and kept working. No discussion. It was possible that they might not talk about Brenae or Hal the entire week. They might hardly talk at all, making my eavesdropping a waste of time.

The shoes were rising in columns, some already two feet high. The men had found a way to stack them, crisscross, and Erik was wiring them in. Pearson sorted for him. The columns, with their toes and heels, gave off a sense of wrong burial, of bodies stacked and piled. Layla joined the sorting. She seemed to dislike touching the shoes, holding them with her fingertips as she soldiered on, her face dutiful. Only when she handed things to Erik did her expression change, growing shadowed with doubt. According to Ray, Layla and Erik were the couple, together and apart since last year. I wondered how Erik liked dating the only child of a famous collector and a pharmaceutical fortune heiress, photography concentration at LAAC. I could see why Layla liked Erik. He was adorable, with that tumbling brown hair, nimble build, and ready smile; he had already landed his own solo show in Chinatown and had won a fellowship to Rome for next year. Yet in Layla's presence, Erik's shoulders hunched and his eyes were evasive. They flitted to Layla when she wasn't looking, and flicked away when she was.

As I pulled Layla's extra-frothy coffee closer, I noticed the guest list she had handed back to me. Scribbled in the margin, in tiny letters, were two words:

Quit now.

I took a sip of coffee and flinched. My tongue shorted out on the heat.

Across the room, Layla looked up and aimed a vacant smile at me. I returned it with a frosty, close-lipped version, and bent back to the press release, crossing out her note.

This day was growing new depths already. I took another sip, ignored the burning.

10

AN HOUR LATER, MY PHONE'S buzz pierced the quiet of the gallery. Kaye: *She's running late. 1:30 okay?*

Sure.

Great!! Sorry.

Across the room, Layla moved closer to Pearson and Erik. "'Of course your work has holes in it. You're a woman.' That's what that stupid aesthetics dude said to me," she told them, clearly continuing some previous conversation. "Can you believe it?"

Erik shrugged. "Sounds like a stupid aesthetics dude."

"And then for three hours we didn't get off whether you have to 'earn' the right to make protest art. Whether you have to be a 'true victim' in order to have a voice," said Layla. "I shouldn't have signed up for that slot. October is the worst. Everybody is sick of looking at art, and they just want to seethe about politics." She paused. "They just want to sound impressive to Hal."

Layla had to be talking about her crit. I had listened many times to my coworkers, LAAC graduates, gripe enjoyably about crits at the school. The crit was LAAC's principal way of teaching art, and generally meant an hours-long, in-class conversation with one student about his or her work. I'd heard that crits could go on for six or seven hours in Hal's courses, lasting late into the night with sleeping bags, but even Layla's three-plus hours sounded long to me. Still, there was a hint of neediness in her voice. She wanted to be heard.

"I'm just sensitive right now because open studios are coming up." Layla dabbed her forehead with her fingertips. "I'm not ready."

Another pause, during which neither man spoke.

"I was all set to show my nail-salon-worker series, but now I'm having second thoughts," Layla added.

"Crits got the best of you? Trouble with your oeuvre?" Pearson spoke in a honeyed tone to a men's penny loafer. "Drown your sorrows with a reality check at the No One Gives a Crap Saloon. Open 24/7. Locations everywhere."

"Shut up," Layla said blankly. It was hard to tell if his ribbing upset her.

Pearson tossed the loafer toward Erik. "Who were you expecting to appear at your 'open studio'?" he asked.

"Never you mind," Layla said. She tied the laces of a child's sneaker in a neat bow.

"Seriously, who did Daddy line up for you this time?" Pearson didn't wait for her answer but instead stomped around the room, flinging shoes aside, as if looking for something.

"Come on," said Erik, glancing at me. "We need to focus on this together."

"We need the shoes," grumbled Pearson, dredging a skein of wire from beneath a heap. "I wonder whose bright idea it was to send them to LAAC."

"It was Hal's idea," said Layla. "And I'm expecting Lynne Feldman at my open studio, okay? I told her myself, and she sounded really thrilled to be reminded. She said she loves the open studios."

Lynne Feldman sounding "really thrilled" about anything but her own museum shows and her cats was laughable to me, but I was impressed with

Layla's pulling power. From the way my LAAC friends had painted it, the open studios were less a chance for unknown students to get discovered than a big, raucous party celebrating the common tragedy of their anonymity. But Layla would never be anonymous. Not to a Rocque chief curator. Because of her father, she was a potential future donor.

Pearson studied the wire as if something important was written in its loops.

"Sorry, Layla," he said. His voice was gruff but penitent. "You should use any connections you've got. I hope it's a great visit."

"I wish I was back in my second year, prepping for open studios," Erik said, "and actually graduating on time."

"You will," Layla said with a force that verged on fury—only it wasn't against Erik; it was *for* him. "And you've already got two major collectors and a curator sniffing around. You just have to get it done."

Erik hung his head, sheepish, as if he had been chastised instead of praised, and gestured at the pile of shoes. "This is what we need to get done."

Another text from Kaye: *Bad news. Call me ASAP.*

"I know," said Layla. "We should work late," she added. "We should call off those interviews."

I didn't want to phone Kaye. It was obvious that the actress was canceling on me.

"Okay?" Layla said when neither of the men responded. "We shouldn't be doing them anyway."

"Okay, okay," interrupted Pearson, surveying a column. "That one's crooked."

Layla threw a blue sneaker toward Erik. "Okay?" she said in a despairing tone.

My phone started buzzing. I turned it off.

Erik didn't answer, just crouched low and shoved at a sandal sticking awkwardly from one side of the column. Now the three crew members made a triangle, Layla the tallest point, Pearson bending, Erik low to the ground.

A close silence rose between them, and suddenly they all seemed so young to me, clean and smooth as new candles.

"It's not going to bring her back," said Layla, her voice full of emotion.

Erik shrugged, stood. He walked over to another column and examined it from all sides, pushing, adjusting. His hands were so strong that their sinews popped when he squeezed. "It's not about bringing her back," he said, flushing.

Layla didn't react right away. She sorted a couple of shoes, then let her head fall forward, her red hair tumbling over her face. "Right," she muttered.

Pearson watched the exchange, his eyes gleaming as the tension rose.

"Look," said Erik, "the guy said he has something to show us, and I want to see it."

"Help me out, Pearson," said Layla, still kneeling, looking up. "You didn't want to do it, either."

Pearson straightened to his full height. "I don't recall having a personal reaction," he said coolly. "I just questioned the merits."

"Fine. Question the merits now. What can they possibly be?" Layla said.

Neither man answered.

"Are you asking me?" Pearson said after a moment. "Perhaps some of us would like closure." He inflected the last word with his usual mocking tone, but he pegged a shoe across the room with extra force.

A shadow appeared at the door, knocking, then clinking—the sound of rings on a fist hitting the glass. I spotted a thin, unsmiling face framed by a black, chin-length bob. Zania de Wilde, the last of the foursome. I let her in. She mumbled a thank-you and scurried past me.

Zania was slim and olive-skinned, with a high waist and small breasts, but her most noticeable feature was her expression. She wore the regal, overly patient face of someone who ruled a tiny, misunderstood country. As soon as she entered the gallery space, the men scrambled and shifted as if they'd been caught slacking, and Layla stood up, dusted her hands, and went to her friend.

Whatever distancing effect Zania had on the others, she drew Layla to her instantly. They spoke in low, intense tones, Layla slouching and gathering herself like dough around Zania's upright frame. According to Ray, Zania was Nelson's daughter from his former and only marriage. At eighteen, she'd trained as an anarchist and then disappeared into a maw of global protesting for three years before emerging to get her undergraduate degree at LAAC. Like Layla, Zania exuded wealth even though her jeans were deliberately ratty, her tank top tight and plain. She had the ripped abs that only a personal trainer can summon, and her bob looked expensive.

"The shoes," said Zania, her voice high and soft, "will be here any minute."

As the crew burst into talk about what they'd built so far and what they needed, I took a sip of Layla's latte. It had finally cooled and it tasted delicious, with caramel and hints of smoke.

I needed to call Kaye, but I didn't want to face the truth.

For a few more minutes, I watched the crew. Layla seemed like several people at once—the silent adorer of Erik, the eager subordinate to Zania, the sly one who'd told me (or warned me?) to quit. She also wanted to nix the interviews with Ray, which might have been ordinary caution, or a wish not to dredge up more grief. But maybe it was to protect Erik from further scrutiny. Clearly, he wanted to talk about Brenae. Why?

There was a charmed air about Erik; he had the harmless good looks and superficial ease that people used to call bonny. He'd also left the room three times for the bathroom and come back flushed. Whatever substance habit he had, he was barely hiding it, but in the orchestration of the artwork, the others treated him with deference, stepping aside to let his eyes and hands take over. It was clear he was their star.

I turned my phone back on and slipped out onto the palm-lined boulevard outside. After years of navigating downtown's skyscrapers and steep hills, the first thing that struck me about the Westing's block was its flatness and open sky. The street was wide enough and the buildings short enough to allow sun to flood the sidewalks all day. Restaurants greeted the brightness with patios, striped umbrellas, and lemon-ginger elixirs. Beside them, tiny, cave-like shops peddled army jackets and T-shirts so flimsy they were already shredding on their racks. Some pedestrians were clearly tourists, trudging along in capris, sucking in their inland waists. Others looked like they'd been posed there with their low-slung jeans, bone hips, and gleaming tans. The overall atmosphere didn't feel snobby, though, not exclusive at all—but insatiably splendid. There was so much light to go around. Venice reminded me of every beach town, and none of them.

I spotted Ray across the street and up a block, sitting in a parked gray sedan. His eyes were closed. Had he fallen asleep? I thought of his face in the coffee shop this morning. He looked different from when I'd first met him. There was something sunken about his face, especially around the eyes.

My phone thrummed. Kaye.

"Maggie, I'm sorry," she said. "I think you should go there at one thirty anyway, but she will likely not show up. She's got tons of calls with producers. She's gotten so hot all of a sudden. Like overnight."

"I understand," I said coolly, although my face felt numb and warm. My suit hung on me like a wet towel.

"But you should go just in case," she said. "You should definitely go."

I felt a nudge. Zania had somehow materialized beside me, along with a whiff of coconut shampoo.

"The shoe truck's coming. Supposedly there's a dolly in my father's office," she said. "Do you have a key?"

"Maggie?" Kaye sounded farther away. "Are you at work?"

"Are you leaving?" Zania said. She looked troubled by the idea.

"In an hour or so," I told her, and turned away, cupping the phone. "I'm sorry," I said to Kaye. "Can I call you back?"

"Of course. You should go. And let me know if she comes," said Kaye, already fading.

I hung up and turned to Zania. "It's really tight out here. For a truck,"

I said to her, gesturing at the wedge of curb space not already occupied by parked cars.

"There's a back door," Zania said. "The gallery has reserved spots back there. Where did you park?"

"I got dropped off," I lied.

"You should take a reserved spot next time," she insisted. "Don't pay the meters of this corrupt city."

The others glanced up as we entered. They were down to the last shoes, but they needed so many more. Instead of looking closer to finished, the elegant room looked violated by heaps of junk.

I told Zania I would search for the key, but she was already pulling open a desk drawer, handing me a gold one attached to a keychain that was a blank white cube.

"Ha-ha," I said. "Did he have this specially made?"

Zania shrugged. If she'd known where the key was, she could have gotten the dolly herself, so I wasn't sure why she'd followed me outside. Her face registered nothing but a slight impatience. As in, *Do your job, gallerina.* I walked down the hall to the only door and unlocked it. A murmur of conversation began behind me, and I paused, trying to catch it.

". . . and she's paranoid she did something to offend my dad," Zania said. "He won't say. He didn't fire her, though."

"Well, it's not an improvement," said Layla's voice, "so hopefully it is temporary."

Pearson muttered something indistinct.

"I thrive on judging," said Layla. "I mean, who would ever wear this sandal? It looks like a straitjacket for a hamster."

"Norwegian hippie hamster," said Erik. "With relatives in the mafia." Then, "Nelson's probably paying her more than Hal is paying us."

"I'm going to be so late for class today," said Zania. "Undergrad sucks. You can't fathom how oppressive my schedule is."

"Actually, we can," Pearson pointed out. "We already got our BAs."

"I blocked mine out," said Layla.

I pushed open the door to Nelson's office and slid through, leaving it open a crack. Beyond stretched a sitting area with a turquoise modernist couch and two chairs, an oval of orange carpet. This must have been where Nelson met his clients. Bright, clean, and a little too empty. This was your groomed future, complete with an artwork you just had to buy.

Nelson's desk posed in the far corner, bare except for a printer and a couple of files; the ribbed curve of his office chair aimed toward the spot where his laptop would sit. Three chrome file cabinets lined the other wall. A couple of wooden art crates stood nearby, a crowbar on top. The room was a replica of Nelson de Wilde—polished and immaculate—except for a lumpy bag of takeout containers in his trash that smelled faintly of rotting coconut.

There was no dolly here, but I walked around the room once anyway, peering behind the couch, possessed by the sudden intuition that there was something here to find. But what and why?

I didn't know much about Nelson beyond his power as a gallerist. Whenever he appeared at any opening, Nelson struck my artist friends speechless. They didn't see a forty-something man with sun-stained skin who rarely touched food or drink, whose only appetite appeared to be young women. They saw a kingmaker. Nelson specialized in showy, conceptual pieces, and he liked objects more than performances. He liked things he could sell. Kim Lord had fit his bill in every way. He had discovered her, supported her. And yet he had also betrayed her. He had to have betrayed her. For money. And now he was letting us spy on Hal for money. He needed a lot. Nelson was famous—revered—for his long-term support of artists. Once he signed someone, he never let them go, which was not true of many gallerists. He gave generous stipends and waited years for work.

The door opened, and Zania's frowning face poked through. I blurted, "I can't find a dolly," but she was fixated on the trash can.

"What is that smell?" Her small mouth crumpled inward. "Oh God. He forgot again."

I saw Pearson stride down the hall behind her.

"Incoming!" he shouted.

AS SOON AS THE RAMP went down, Layla vanished to make a phone call and Zania continued to loudly "search" the gallery for the dolly. As I watched the men struggle alone with the giant task of unloading crates of shoes, I had a lightning-fast internal debate about whether I wanted the crew to take me for a real gallerina or if I wanted them to trust me. Ray was right; I was more persuasive on sincerity than on sophistication. So I helped out. I lugged and staggered, truck to building and down the hall to the gallery. The hall was the worst—narrow and practically forty feet long. After a few chuffing trips, Pearson came up with the idea of sliding the crates on blankets from the truck and into the building, but it was still hard work, and I felt a third sweat soaking my suit and dripping my thin layer of foundation away. The two men didn't say anything to me, but I caught Pearson giving me an appraising glance when he thought I wasn't looking. He appeared less condescending as he flexed and strained, and more like the kind of sturdy, unflappable person you hoped would show up to fix your broken furnace. Erik pounced and sprang, as agile as ever, but he was laboring, too. His cheeks puffed with breath when he upended the crates into enormous piles in the gallery space. Hundreds and hundreds of shoes. The crew had their materials now.

When Zania and Layla reappeared, they ignored the unloading and waded straight into the shoes. "Let's get an all-suede pile," Erik told them. "All leather, too."

"We're fine," Pearson said to me when I walked back to the truck. "We can take it from here. Thanks, though."

By the curious way he said it, by the way we were suddenly alone and only a few feet apart, I felt compelled to explain. "I grew up in a rural state," I said. "We were raised to pitch in."

"You're from New England," he said.

I regarded him as calmly as I could, but he didn't look calculating, just curious.

"How'd you know?" I said.

He shrugged and moved toward another box. "Just a lucky guess."

"Come on. What was the clue?"

"Your accent and your crow's feet," he said, sounding resigned. "Long winters are hard on the face."

I tried not to touch the wrinkles I'd always hoped would wait to form until I was at least thirty-five and married, with a mortgage and a child on the way.

"How about you—Brooklyn?" I said.

I was wrong, I knew, but I suspected that Pearson preferred to fool people with his urban veneer.

"Hudson, actually." He wiped his brow with a blue handkerchief and gazed out to the truck. "It'll be Brooklyn in another ten years. But when I was a kid, Hudson was a train stop and a river. Latchkey kids wandering around the rust and brick."

"You sound like you miss it."

"No," he said with a frown. "I don't miss it. But at least we learned not to wait around for someone else to do things for us."

The reference was obvious, even though Layla and Zania, who'd acted so useless when the shoes came in, were out of sight. Pearson might have a country-club name, but, like Brenae, he saw himself as an outsider to the wealthier students.

"Why did you come to L.A.?" I said.

"Hal invited me," he said, pride in his voice.

"You met him in Hudson?"

"I did actually. Back when I was too much of an idiot to understand that you didn't just corner Hal Giroux and ask him to look at your art. Or to write to him repeatedly afterward. But he always wrote back. Sometimes just a couple of sentences, but always. Eventually . . . I applied to LAAC and here I am."

The pause after the *eventually*—I wondered if that was when Pearson had been arrested for assault. I'd have to check with Ray. "Ever look back?" I said.

He shrugged. "Why did you come here?" he asked instead, examining me.

"To L.A.? Oh, partly running away, partly following somebody," I said lightly. "You know."

Pearson's intense look did not waver, but his eyes grew softer and rounder. "Yeah," he said after a moment. "I do know. Thanks again."

Then he grabbed the box and started hauling it toward the gallery.

I stared after him, feeling as if I'd just run some difficult fitness test, my sweat-damp clothes sticking to me. I went to the restroom to salvage my makeup. When I spotted myself in the mirror, I recoiled at the redness of my cheeks. I looked like a kid at an August soccer practice again. But Pearson had revealed himself, just a crack, today. He noticed things about people. He was touchy about his working-class roots. He revered Hal. How had he felt about Brenae? I still couldn't quite tell, but he held some emotion for her that he didn't want known. He wasn't the man in the video, though. That was Erik; I'd known that from the first time I laid eyes on both men.

I RETURNED TO MY DESK and observed the crew out of the corner of my eye until it was time to leave. I told them I'd be back at 3:30 p.m. Ray's car was gone from the street, but I walked down the main strip, took a few turns, and heard a car pull up beside me. It was the gray sedan. We'd made plans for Ray to drive me home.

I hopped in, trying to appear confident and ready for my interview with Hollywood stardom.

"So?" he said.

I related everything I could remember from the morning, from Layla's note to the conversation with Pearson to the conversations about the interviews.

"*Quit now*," said Ray. "That's what she wrote?"

I nodded. "I don't know if she was being snide or if it was a real warning."

"Hard to say," Ray said in a pondering tone. "But she didn't say anything else?"

"No."

We were retracing the route I'd taken that morning, and passed the same palm frond I'd tripped on, its pink pelvis trailing a long wisp of beige. The walk seemed like a long time ago already. I felt tight and energized now, the loose dread of the early morning gone.

"Erik seems to want to talk with you," I said.

Ray's face was flushed from sitting in the warm car, but I could still see the keen look spread over his face.

"It's obvious why, isn't it?" he said. "Pretty sure he's the guy in the video."

I agreed. It didn't matter if the head in the video was blurred. The upper back and shoulders, the way the man moved—it all matched Erik's physique perfectly. On the chance it wasn't him, we'd find out this afternoon when he watched the footage.

"We'll see if he confirms it, but you gave me some good leverage," Ray added. "I called the desert festival people and found out who shot *Packing*. It was Erik Reidl."

"He also shot her undergraduate film *Camping*," I told him, working to suppress any triumph in my voice.

Very late last night, after I'd written my mother, I'd found online archives through the USC library of their student campus newspaper, and a 2002 feature on Brenae that revealed more about her campout project. For her undergraduate thesis, Brenae had camped in a foreclosed home in South Central, pitching her tent inside its living room and bedrooms, tucking herself in her sleeping bag, cooking marshmallows and hot dogs over a gas camping stove. According to the article, on the last day, Brenae had had a tattoo artist ink the words *This land is your land* onto her bare shoulder. A slow take of the inking, set to Freddie Tavares on steel guitar, had concluded the movie. Erik was named in the article as her cinematographer. I told Ray all this, watching his squint deepen.

"Do you think Erik has seen the sex video before?" I said.

Ray shrugged. "Hard to say. Seen it, heard about it."

I decided it was time to voice my main concern about our new findings: "But if it's not Hal in the video, then Janis has no—"

"If you and I recognized who it might be, why wouldn't Hal? And if he did, he failed to handle the situation properly." Ray turned on my street, toward my pink adobe apartment building.

"You think Hal warned Erik that Brenae wanted to expose him as a rapist," I said. I didn't like the last word in my mouth, and my saying it aloud made Ray blink, but it was what we had witnessed.

Instead of answering, Ray gazed at the pink building, slowing the car. "It's like a giant welt," he said. "Or a pox. What do you think, welt or pox?"

"I think we're talking pox," I said. "Pox doesn't work alone."

"Hal probably warned Erik. Protected his future prizewinner." Ray said the last word sardonically. "Even worse, I think Hal made sure anything incriminating on Brenae's laptop was erased. Someone knew how to shred data."

"Is that enough for Janis?" I said. "It's all speculative."

"She has ways to confidentially inform the school's board of trustees that she suspects something," he said. "She could start there."

"But what if the video dates back to Brenae's time at USC?" I added. "Then it's not even Hal's campus. And what if Erik claims it was consensual?"

Ray slid to a stop by the hydrant outside my front gate.

"Did it look consensual to you?" he said.

"No," I said. "But we don't know what they said to each other. He could claim she was using him. He could claim anything. She's dead. I could see the board turning a blind eye just to keep it all quiet. And then what would Janis do?"

"You should be thinking harder about what you want to do," Ray said. He leaned back against his headrest and looked over at me, at my suit and at the sweat dried in my hair, his gaze frank and assessing. "Find the real story and write it."

FIND THE REAL STORY AND write it.

I'd shaken off Ray's comment with a laugh and changed the subject. But he was right. The whole story was more complicated than a botched university response to a woman's complaint. Why did Brenae have to die? Why did a woman so talented have to shoot herself at night in a school that had nurtured generations of young artists?

Brenae's videos were the greatest puzzle to me. In *Packing*, Brenae's sensuality flowed through the entire work, the camera lingering on the lushness of her gestures, the way she cradled her gun. Beautiful and powerful, she ruled every frame. In *Lesson in Red*, Brenae's assailant pinned and obscured her body until the red filter soaked them both. Brenae's face was pained, her voice anxious. Her words hurt. Two women more different could not be imagined, and yet they were both Brenae: the radiant genius and the victim.

And instead of probing deeper, I was waiting, futilely, to meet the actress who would play young Françoise Gilot—also brilliant, and also physically and emotionally abused, first by her father and then by Picasso. Picasso admired young Gilot's intellect and poise, and his nightly talks with her were a master course on the artist's mind. He also shoved Gilot on a bridge over the Seine and threatened to toss her in. He held a burning cigarette against her cheek and offered to brand her. He mocked her body shape after she'd borne him a child. "Every time I change wives, I should burn the last one," he told her. "That way I'd be rid of them." Gilot stayed with Picasso for a decade anyway. I wanted to ask the actress what it felt like to embody such a heroine.

Kaye called me while I was finishing my salad, staring across the butcher-papered table at the empty blue plate that I had told the waiter not to clear. Just in case.

"She's on the way to the airport," she said glumly. "They want her in New York early for media now. There's a lot of buzz for the play. Everybody loves Picasso, I guess."

"Gilot's the one who's still alive," I grumbled. My notes on the artist, stuffed in my purse, were baking in the heat.

"Did you take a day off? I'm really sorry."

"I had it off already," I said. "I've been digging into some new ideas to pitch magazines."

Kaye sounded relieved as she hung up, and I clung to that as I paid the ridiculous bill and walked out in my ridiculously overpriced suit into a whole block spangled with posters for the next Harry Potter movie. I was lying to Kaye, or I thought so at the time—but long after that October afternoon, it struck me that if I hadn't come back early from that lunch break, I might not have seen what I saw next. And if I hadn't seen it, I might never have known the real story of Brenae Brasil.

11

THE PAIR OF THEM WERE sitting in his navy-blue coupe, in the shade of the little parking lot behind the gallery. I passed them while searching futilely for my own spot on the street. Despite Zania's insistence that I park my car at the Westing, I wasn't sure I wanted the crew to view my old station wagon. So I'd driven past the organic juicery and the small-batch ice cream shop, even down as far as the night club that hadn't changed its pugilist sign since the sixties and was open already, its rummy interior visible through a propped door. No luck. I'd cruised back by the Westing to start again, and there they were.

I pulled to the curb and peered in the rearview mirror.

Layla sat in the passenger seat, her arms not quite crossed. It was more like she was clutching her elbows, as if holding herself in to keep from flying apart. Her profile was to me, her long red hair obscuring her face.

Nelson's expression was easier to read. He looked patient and paternal, as if he were coaching her to understand some difficult lesson. She shook her head sharply, but he kept talking and eventually she sniffed and nodded. I couldn't tell if she was crying. I didn't think so. She didn't seem the type to cry often.

I didn't know what they were talking about, but everything in their manner suggested they knew each other well. Very well. When Nelson finished talking, he gently slipped a hand inside her shirt, and then Layla's red head dipped toward his lap until it disappeared.

12

WHEN I GOT BACK TO the gallery, the crew was listening to the local public radio station. PSAs and twangy indie pop looped through the air. Only Pearson and Zania seemed in the room, focused on the shoes. Erik kept checking the door, but when Layla returned, he frowned at her kiss in greeting, feigning intense concentration on an arch of red pumps. Layla went to work with her mouth parted, eyes far away, as if she hadn't left the car, was still back there, bent over Nelson's crotch.

Although it wasn't my place to judge, the thought of Layla and Nelson together made my skin crawl. And even more than the sex, their intimacy troubled me. What if Layla knew about the whole investigation? And if she did, why wouldn't she inform her friends and boyfriend that I was eavesdropping on them? Presumably because Nelson had asked her not to. If that was true, then Nelson meant more to Layla than Erik did. Or Zania. That was a funny fact. Not especially germane to Brenae, but funny nonetheless. I wondered what Ray would make of it.

—

"TIME TO GO," LAYLA SAID at 3:30, "or we'll be late."

Erik was the first to leap up but the last to leave, running to the restroom, misplacing his keys.

"I can drive," Layla said from the door. "I'll drive us."

"No, but I don't want to lose them," said Erik, rooting among the shoes. "They'll get lost."

Pearson and Zania were long gone by the time Layla found Erik's keys on the ladder and she and Erik departed. His usual boyish poise had crumbled, and he wore an expression of desperate benevolence, as if he were a prince about to give away his entire wealth. Layla followed him out with narrowed eyes. They promised me that someone on the crew would return by six, when I was supposed to lock up and go.

The Westing sank into quiet, the partially constructed artwork tumbling in all directions. One tilting column looked perpetually close to falling, but it never did. I checked my e-mail. Other than some messages from Rocque coworkers, my mother had written. She appreciated my note about James Compton and said she didn't know anything about London art, but that I was lucky I was around so much culture, and that I would take that with me wherever I went. (The lead was buried in that last phrase, of course. *Wherever I went.* She was still waiting, longing, for me to leave Los Angeles.)

A jingling and a slam at the front door, and there was Hal Giroux himself, holding a manila folder. He scowled when he saw the empty gallery.

"They getting lunch?" he said.

It was nearly five.

"I'm not sure," I hedged. "They just said they had to go out for a while."

The vital, bearded Hal from his 1970s heyday had faded beneath close-trimmed gray hair, an age-mottled complexion, and a stringy neck. Hal was a fretful version of his old self. The full cheeks that had made him look smug and satisfied now sagged low, dragging on his cheekbones. His eyebrows pinched close together as he examined the shoe towers. Then, without speaking any further, he wandered over to the installation and started making adjustments, pushing a shoe here and there. He shoved at the leaning column unsuccessfully. Shoved again, failed again.

He looked over at me.

"They were working hard until three thirty," I said. "I'm temping for the regular gallerina. I'm Mary."

Hal grunted a greeting and grabbed the gallery phone, opening his wallet and reading a card there, then punching in numbers. He dialed three and listened before hanging up. "What are they up to?" he muttered. "Next time they leave, get them to tell you where they're going, okay? The media could be coming through here as early as tomorrow."

"Okay," I said.

Hal glanced around the Westing. "It always feels so cramped in here. I told Nelson to buy on the East Side when he could have gotten a hangar for the price of this, and he didn't listen." His eyes landed on me again, his gaze hang-dog and sorrowful. "You always miss the L.A. you don't have, right?"

"You've helped make L.A. what it is," I said, prim and sincere. "For artists, anyway."

He dipped his chin, a little nod of acknowledgment. "Eh," he said, but he looked pleased.

"I just saw a lot of LAAC artists out in Wonder Valley," I added. "Amazing work."

"Did you?" he said. "I couldn't get there this year, but we always have a good showing."

"People could not stop talking about *Packing*. Such a tragedy."

Hal blinked. "Oh yes," he said in a reedy voice. "Brenae was a great loss for us. Terrible shame."

Hal didn't look sad. He didn't look afraid. He didn't look triumphant. It was as if part of him had completely drained out at the mention of Brenae's name, and the emptiness was talking instead of Hal.

"I couldn't believe it," I said. "She had so much going for her."

"A terrible shame," Hal repeated. He opened his folder, glanced at something inside, and then closed it again. "I'll give this to Nelson later. Will you tell them to ring me when they return?" He turned to leave, then took one last look at me. "Nice suit, by the way," he said, and pushed his way out the glass door.

PEARSON RETURNED, ALONE, ALMOST AN hour later, with a heavy mallet in his hand. He ignored me as he strode past to the shoes. With quick jerks of his body, he plucked a handful of shoes from the piles, set them on a patch of bare floor, and raised the mallet. *Slam. Slam.* The floorboards rang from the blows, the noise reverberating through the gallery, amplifying on the bare walls. Pearson's muscled arms rose high, and the mallet came down. The shoes split, seams popping, tongues sliding out. A clog snapped in two with a loud crack.

I sat at my desk, still and silent, my hands near my cell phone and the landline.

Pearson kept hammering until his first pile broke to pieces, and then found more, his face purpled and intent. The mallet swung. The floor thudded and echoed. The shoes shattered to chunks and shards.

When the pile of destruction rose knee-deep, he tossed the mallet down and grabbed the wire, lashing the pieces together into a column like the others, but misshapen, torn, distended. It took me a few minutes to interpret, and then my breath snagged in my throat. It was a genius move. It was typical Hal, to have one element in his architecture violent and distorted while the rest arched in harmony. But Hal had not done this, and the man with the mallet looked like he wanted to strangle someone. With his large, fisted hands.

Finally Pearson caught me staring and looked up. "What?" he snarled. "What? You want to take some pictures for publicity now?"

I let his voice ricochet through the gallery for an uncomfortable moment. I let my eyes fall to both phones, one and then the other. Then I answered.

"No," I said in my best civilized voice. "Could I get you a glass of water?"

With wooden movements, Pearson set down the wire and shoes he'd strung together. Then he picked up the mallet and tossed it toward the edge of the room. Sweat made his forehead shine, and when he met my eyes, he wore a ragged, disbelieving grin. It was the first time I'd seen him smile, and his stretched mouth made his head look larger, clownish. But the expression in his eyes was gouged and hurt.

"No, I don't want water," he protested. "You don't need to stay, though. Isn't it almost six?"

It was 5:50. "I'm heading out soon," I said. "Hal said to call him. He came through about an hour ago."

He looked alarmed. "Did you tell him where we were?"

"I didn't know," I said. "I assumed you were getting lunch?"

He nodded, but mistrust flickered in his face. "Right," he said, turning away. "I'll call him."

My phone hummed. Ray. *Anyone there?*

Only P, I texted back. *Angry. But calmer now.*

Pack up. I'm at same coffee shop.

Pearson was staring at the distorted column, his shoulder slumped, forehead dripping. "Are the others coming back?" I asked, wishing that I had an obvious motive to stay yet also relieved to flee.

He shrugged.

I gathered my few things. "I have to go. You'll lock up?" I called to him.

"If I ever go home," he muttered and walked up to the desk. His black shirt clung with sweat. "Hey, sorry for my performance."

"Seems like it was a breakthrough." I gestured at the distorted column. "It's so Hal."

Pearson regarded his own handiwork and blew out a breath. "We'll see." His voice was light, but his eyes did not hide his bitterness.

—

RAY WAS WAITING OUTSIDE THE coffee shop. "You okay?" he said when he saw my face.

"He didn't come anywhere near me," I said. "Thank God I'm not a stiletto, though. He smashed one until the heel broke through the sole. I'm guessing he didn't like what he saw in the video."

"No." Ray looked me over again. "You feel safe going back there tomorrow?"

"I don't know," I said truthfully. "I'm not on his bad side. But if I was—" An image of Pearson's hands holding a pummeled sneaker stopped me. "I won't be alone with him."

As Ray drove me to a taqueria in Mar Vista, I gave him the main details of my day, except for seeing Layla and Nelson, which I wanted to hold for later. The restaurant—with a cracked linoleum floor and the smells of grilled peppers, onions, and beef—was a recommendation by Alicia Ruiz. Before long, we were sitting in an orange booth with giant plates of *cochinita pibil* and carnitas tacos.

"So Pearson smashed some shoes, Layla told you to quit, and Erik looked guilty," said Ray.

"There's something else," I said. I started to launch into spotting Layla and Nelson together when Ray's phone buzzed.

He looked at the number and rubbed his head. "Sorry. I have to get this, and it might take a few minutes. Why don't you listen to the interviews while I'm out?"

Before heading outside, he slipped a recorder onto the table and pulled a set of headphones from his knapsack. I put them on, the leather cupping my ears. Zania went first. I listened to her for a little while. She denied recognizing the male in the video, but she didn't sound convincing. Instead, she wanted to make a point. Many points.

Zania: The thing is, you could see this video as art or you could see it as a call for help, but Brenae, she saw everything as art. She saw everything and everyone as a step higher. You know? She was on a ladder and every person she met, even friends, even men, was a rung. So this guy, whoever he is, was he really abusing her, or was she staging something to make a point? Maybe she wanted to show injustice for women . . . or maybe she just was over someone and had regret sex with him. I mean, who films their own sex life anyway, and then tries to build a career on it? Perverts. But she wasn't a pervert. She was self-obsessed.

People want to cast Brenae as a saint now, but she didn't want to be a saint. She wanted to be a star. That's different. And she was a star. This video is art. That's the problem. It's art, but it's a cry for help and it's for perverts. So what do you do with it? What does the school do with it? What do the police do with it? What does a gallery do with it? I need some water. My throat is getting dry.

Just beyond the window of the restaurant, Ray paced, his hand to his ear, the expression on his face amused and patient. My eyes fell on his knapsack, opened a crack, a slim black notebook inside. Without waiting for any reservations to kick in, I eased it out, eyes on Ray. As if he sensed my gaze, he looked back. I touched the headphones and gave him a thumbs-up. When he turned away, I flipped quickly through the notebook. His handwriting was tinier than a line of ants, but I saw a whole lot of e-mail addresses, some of which had an illicit ring—getsum@hotmail.com, icepartay@yahoo.com—and dozens of cell numbers. Then I saw a date and the names of people I recognized and some I didn't, including Layla Goetz-Middleton, Erik Reidl, Nelson de Wilde, Dee Rager, Phil and Spike Dingman, and someone named Genevieve, no last name, with a question mark after her.

I slipped the notebook into the bag.

The addresses looked like dealers of some kind. The names looked like a list of art-world people. The date was a year ago, around the time his brother Calvin died.

I went back to Zania's interview.

Ray: So you had no knowledge of this video before today.

Zania: No. I knew she was working on a couple of projects about LAAC, but she didn't say what they were. After London, she wasn't around much. We didn't hang together. The crew disbanded.

Ray: Someone erased this off her hard drive after she died.

Zania: That's gross.

Ray: Any guesses who?

Zania: No.

Ray: And you don't recognize the male in this?

Zania: His head is blurred out for a reason. We're not supposed to know who he is. We're supposed to see him for *what* he is.

Ray: What's that?

Zania: The patriarchy. The systems of oppression that start at birth, privileging boys over girls and men over women. This woman, Brenae, she can't leave the system. The only way she can participate is by letting it screw her.

Ray: Say someone shared this video with the press. Tomorrow. Whom would it affect the most?

Zania: Obviously, LAAC. The school would be exposed. And the guy, I guess, if people do figure out his name. But he walked into that. He should have known who Brenae was.

Ray: Would LAAC be exposed, though? There's no evidence this happened at the school.

Zania: Brenae told a lot of people that her next two projects were about LAAC. She told me. It's not a big leap of logic.

Ray: But there's nothing on here to suggest it's the school's fault that she's in this situation.

Zania: It's a metaphor. The school is the situation. And the art world. Male artists getting the praise. Male artists getting the scholarships and gallery shows and biggest price tags. Male artists getting into museum collections, two to one, sometimes three to one.

Ray: Has your experience at LAAC reflected this? Hal's crew once had three women and two men.

Zania: I'm an undergrad, as everyone loves to remind me. My opinion isn't that important.

Ray: Still, I'd like to hear about your experience.

Zania: My experience? It's busy. Really busy. And I'm afraid I can't spend any more time on this right now. I hope your client finds the answers they want.

I fast-forwarded and let it play on Layla.

Ray: I really appreciate you meeting with me. As I've explained, my client, as a former donor to LAAC, is concerned about Brenae Brasil's treatment at the school and wants to understand what happened leading up to her death.

Layla: To what end? I mean, what will you do with what we tell you?

Ray: If the school committed any wrongdoing, my client will encourage the board to investigate further.

Layla: Would I be called in to testify or something?

Ray: Not necessarily.

Layla: I don't want to be called in.

Ray: Fair enough. Can you tell me how long you knew Brenae Brasil and in what context?

Layla: I met her last fall when she started the program at LAAC and Hal put her on the crew.

Ray: What were your impressions of Brenae's time at LAAC?

Layla: I don't think she was ready for how hard it was. How hard it is.

Ray: What makes it hard?

Layla: I mean, college is about potential, but when you hit grad school you really have to become something. You can't just be someone's shining possibility. I think she was lonely, too. She didn't make friends that easily.

Ray: Were you friends?

Layla: We socialized. I would say we were strong acquaintances, but she wouldn't call me her friend.

Ray: Would you call her your friend?

Layla: No. I guess not.

Ray: Was her suicide a surprise to you?

Layla: Of course it was a surprise. We were all devastated.

Ray: Was she close with anyone on the crew—Pearson, Zania, Erik?

Layla: I don't know.

Ray: You couldn't tell?

Layla: I don't know. We all worked together. Ask them.

Ray: I'd like to show you a video that Brenae made before she died. It was erased from her laptop by someone after her death, but a copy remained and found its way to my client.

Layla: What do you mean someone erased her laptop? You mean the police?

Ray: No, not the police. It appears someone handled her laptop after she committed suicide but before the school found the body.

Layla: That's horrible.

Ray: Hard to imagine, isn't it?

[pause]

Layla: I'm ready for the video.

Ray: The material may be upsetting to you. You can tell me to turn it off at any time.

[Brenae's voice-over plays for an excruciatingly long time. Then there's a click and shuffling sound. Then a protracted silence.]

Layla: What do you want me to say?

Ray: Do you recognize the people?

Layla: I recognize Brenae.

Ray: Not the man?

Layla: No.

Ray: Do you have any thoughts as to why Brenae made this?

Layla: No.

Ray: How about who would destroy it?

Layla: I don't know.

Ray: I think you might.

Layla: I've never seen this in my life.

[Another silence.]

Layla: You think I could watch this and erase it? It's sickening.

Ray: What would you have done with this video if you saw it six months ago?

Layla: I didn't see it, okay? I'm done. You can talk to the next person.

[A door slam.]

Then Erik.

Ray: I really appreciate you meeting with me. As I've explained, I work for a client who is concerned about Brenae Brasil's treatment at LAAC and wants to understand what happened at the school leading up to her death.

Erik: Don't we all. I'm glad you're doing this. I really am. The police—they covered what they needed to cover—but it's not over. There are people still really wounded about her death.

Ray: What people?

Erik: Just like all the students who believed in her, you know? They just showed *Packing* out near Joshua Tree last weekend, and people were amazed. There were about thirty new art installations out there, and all anybody could talk about was if they had seen *Packing* or not. Brenae was a titanic talent. She should not be forgotten.

Ray: You shot *Packing*.

Erik: Yes, I did.

Ray: You were the cinematographer for Brenae's undergraduate films as well.

Erik: You did your homework.

Ray: How long did you know her?

Erik: Almost three years. And yes, because I know you're going to ask, we were in a consensual relationship for about eight months.

Ray: When?

Erik: It started in 2001. Lasted most of the school year at USC. Ended in the summer. Kind of badly, but I was going off to grad school and I wanted to focus. I wanted to cleave tight to my work. I was in a really ascetic phase for eight months, fasting and no sex, no drugs. Lots of walking in the desert.

Ray: Why?

Erik: Why what?

Ray: The fasting and the abstinence.

Erik: I wanted to purify myself.

Ray: From what?

Erik: *For* what. For my art.

Ray: Did your relationship with Layla end your phase?

Erik: Actually, it was the night I went to Fatburger and ate six cheeseburgers in a row. I couldn't stop. After I puked them up, I thought to myself, *This is BS*. I am twenty-two years old. I am supposed to taste life. And I was done with being a monk. [pause] You think I'm joking, but I'm dead serious.

Ray: When did you start dating Layla?

Erik: We got together around the last week of school—2002, I mean.

Ray: Was it monogamous?

Erik: Huh?

Ray: Did you engage in physical relationships with other people after you started dating Layla?

Erik: No. No.

Ray: Did Layla know about you and Brenae?

Erik: No one knew. We didn't tell anyone.

Ray: How did you meet Brenae at USC?

Erik: I was her TA. But before you ask any more questions, I swear that I didn't grade any of Brenae's work. There were a couple of teaching assistants in the class, and so I made sure that I never had any part in her academic record. If I had, I would have championed her too much. [laughs] I thought she was crazy brilliant.

Ray: And you chose to conceal your relationship.

Erik: We both thought it was better to keep it on the down low during the first semester, because of the TA thing, and then we just kept doing it that way.

Ray: Doing what?

Erik: You know. Making her videos. Hooking up. Honestly, it was a very sexual, passionate thing. But not boyfriend-girlfriend. We were both really, really committed to our work, really pure about it, and we didn't want the distraction of anything else.

Ray: Let's move on from USC. How often did you see each other once Brenae enrolled at LAAC?

Erik: At first, not much. Then she got on Hal's crew and it was hard not to be thrown together all the time, especially when we went to London. But I didn't give her any encouragement, and I didn't reject her. It was just neutral, you know? That made her mad.

Ray: How did she react?

Erik: She made a fucking mess for me. When we went to London, Brenae told Layla that we were still involved. Layla confronted me, and it led to this huge fight. I told Brenae off. Pretty forcefully. And I think that at the same time, Brenae's brother got arrested, and so she left campus for a while to fix that, and when she came back, she was in bad shape with her professors. Meanwhile, I don't know what happened, but Brenae was off Hal's crew and then her funding got cut. I should have defended her. I should have done something, but it was so sick when I left USC and broke things off. She started cutting herself, and she made screen prints with the blood and sent them to me. She could be so strong and fierce, and just dissolve like that. Like it was all someone else's fault that she was hurting so much.

Ray: Do you think she may have grown to view your relationship differently than you did?

Erik: It was always cool between us. It was all about the art. Her art. She needed me and I gave. The sex was a definite perk for both of us.

Ray: Did you see Brenae the last week she was alive?

Erik: I tried. I went to her studio, actually.

Ray: What day?

Erik: It was a Tuesday, I think.

Ray: Why did you go that day?

Erik: Don't recall. Best day for my schedule, I guess.

Ray: But what specifically prompted you to visit her? If you were "being neutral," as you say. If she'd been melting down for weeks.

Erik: I don't know.

Ray: You sure?

Erik: You know, I was stopping by someone else's studio, and I thought I should check on her because she'd kind of disappeared.

Ray: So what did you do?

Erik: I knocked on her door. She didn't answer. I walked away. That's it.

Ray: That's it?

Erik: Yes.

Ray: Did Hal Giroux ever talk with you about Brenae?

Erik: We all talked about each other. It's grad school. The conversation goes on 24/7.

Ray: What did Hal say to you regarding Brenae?

Erik: He thought she was really talented.

Ray: As talented as you?

Erik: I'm not comfortable with that question. Is there anything else? I thought you had something to show us.

Ray: Did Hal tell you anything about a video that Brenae made?

Erik: You mean the one she was making about parties?

Ray: A different one. A more intimate one.

Erik: Not sure what that means, but no.

Ray: You sure.

Erik: Yes.

Ray: Okay.

[a rustling sound, then Brenae's voice-over]

Erik [after a minute]: Jesus. This is so wrong. This is just crap. This is just the kind of crap she would do. Jesus.

Ray: You had no knowledge of this?

Erik: Turn it off. I've seen enough. I should have known.

Ray: Should have known what?

Erik: Listen. This kind of thing—it destroys people. You can quote me on that to whoever you want. The police. The board of trustees. This kind of thing destroys people. I never forced her to do anything.

Ray: Did Hal warn you that Brenae had filmed you forcing her into sex?

Erik: What? I never forced her.

Ray: But he did warn you, and you went to talk to Brenae at her studio. My guess is she told you off. Then what? You knew she had a gun.

Erik: You think I'm a killer?

Ray: Of course I don't. But I need to know what happened when you talked to her.

Erik: You're trying to trap me. Showing me this crap. I'm done here—

"How far did you get?" Ray was back.

"Just got to Erik accusing you of calling him a killer," I said. "I listened to most of Zania's and all of Layla's."

Ray sent a fork into one of his soft tacos. "Pearson monologued quite a bit on his position as an outsider to what he referred to as the 'student melodramas.' But he went beet red when he actually saw the video."

"He was furious tonight."

"Shocked, too," Ray said in a thoughtful tone.

"What about Erik? You think Hal warned him?"

"Erik flinched before I even pressed play," said Ray. "He was dreading it. Covering it up with his abstinence and Fatburger stories, but the whole time his leg was shaking."

"He knew what he did to her," I said, my mouth sour.

"He knew," confirmed Ray. "But I think he witnessed it today for the first time."

I disagreed, but I didn't articulate why. You know when you're hurting someone. Someone's body beneath your body. For a moment we sat together, in the steam of the grill, in the division this created between us.

"The heart can justify a wrong for a long time," Ray went on, "especially if you stop seeing a person and only see a cause."

"And his cause was . . . ?"

"Brenae, in Erik's mind, was his creation," said Ray. "Think of it. Everything he taught her about art. Every video he shot of her. Every door he opened for her at LAAC. He can't finish his own work, but he finished her." He paused. "Maybe she didn't need him anymore, and he wanted her back."

This version of Erik and Brenae's story hadn't occurred to me. "You mean he was jealous of her success," I said.

"Not exactly," Ray said. "He didn't want to lose his power over her. His power to make her."

"When you asked him about forcing her into sex, do you think he was lying to himself? Or to you?"

"Some combination."

I told him about Erik's frequent disappearances to the restroom. Ray said he'd noticed the burst blood vessels in Erik's face, had concluded that he was probably a drinker and that that contributed to his two different selves, the easygoing Erik and the manipulative one. This made sense to me. It all made sense, what Ray was saying. It should have felt satisfying, figuring out some things together, but I couldn't get Brenae's face out of my mind, or the chilling fact that someone—knowing she was dead—had erased the art she'd made.

"Killing her would make a spectacle," I said softly. "But staging a suicide and cleaning up after—it could end her life and career without pointing the finger at anyone."

"Very deliberate for someone like Erik," said Ray. "And flawless in its execution."

"Someone who wanted to protect him, then?"

"Maybe to protect him or LAAC."

I thought of Hal. Of Layla. Of Pearson, the heavy, methodical swing of his mallet.

"Thirty pages of notes and labs from one of the best homicide units in the country," I said. "They determine a suicide. What are they missing?"

I could see the doubt in Ray's face. It turned the corners of his mouth down and tightened his eyes. "You sound like a reporter," he reflected after a moment. His tone was not derisive, but there was a caution in it.

"So talk to me like a detective. What are they missing? You must have a theory."

"I don't have theories. Theories tend to obscure facts," said Ray. "I have a client who wants to know exactly how Hal Giroux responded to a cry for help and a death at his school so that she can force him to resign and he can't bounce and build a museum downtown. All I've ever really needed to find out is when *Lesson in Red* was shot, who erased the files, and why. Today brought me some steps closer, but it didn't clinch anything."

I thought about Janis, Ray's "client," wanting dirt so she could unseat Hal from his throne at LAAC and stop his plan downtown. It was an underhanded move, not her usual method. Janis had never been afraid to say anything to anyone's face. Why wouldn't she insist to the city that Hal find another location?

Almost as soon as I entertained this idea, I knew. The city wanted a big, shiny new museum, not the ragtag old Rocque, with its leaky, garage-like galleries, its bewildering and occasionally offensive art. Not with its recent murder. Janis couldn't take down Hal in this culture war without extra ammunition. Yet still. At the heart of all this was a young woman in pain, not a negotiation over territory.

I asked Ray what he'd found. As I listened to his answer, I stared at the grease on my empty plate, its dingy swirls.

"Three of them hadn't seen the video before," Ray said. "Harder to tell with Layla. She had a look on her face like she'd been expecting it all along. Her motivation to erase the file would be to shield Erik. Simple."

"Not that simple," I countered, remembering her outrage. "Why would she shield him? Why wouldn't she want him burned at the stake?"

"No idea." Ray chuckled. "So say it was one of the others—why would they erase something without watching it?"

"Maybe it wasn't one of the crew," I said. "Maybe it was someone else at LAAC. Maybe Hal."

"I don't think so. You need some software and know-how," said Ray. "Hal has a reputation for being a technophobe. He doesn't even own a cell phone." He paused. "I'm still puzzling over Layla's reaction." He crossed his arms and tightened them, buckling forward like he was sick to his stomach. "Like that. The whole video. She's keeping something back."

The body language reminded me of Layla in Nelson's coupe earlier, and I told Ray what I'd spotted between her and the gallerist.

Ray stopped chewing, pushed his plate away, and asked me to repeat everything I'd seen.

"It didn't look like the first time," I admitted, and wondered aloud if Layla was upgrading boyfriends from Erik to the gallerist, gamely overlooking the complication that Nelson was her best friend's dad.

"Maybe," said Ray. With what seemed like forced casualness, he pulled his plate back and began eating again. But his movements were robotic, and the meat didn't stay on his fork, so he balled up the tortilla with his hand

and bit into it. He caught me watching him, and his eyes went soft and lazy. "You should get another one," he said, gesturing at my plate.

He was trying to change the subject from Layla and Nelson. Something about them bothered him. Their age difference?

"You think Erik knows about them?" I said.

He swallowed. "No."

"Do you think Brenae did?"

"Hard to say," he said carefully. He asked me to give him an exact play-by-play of my day, from the moment I walked in, the latte from Layla, my conversations, to looking for the key in Nelson's office, to bringing in the shoes.

There was something else, I realized, as I related the whole day to Ray, some other detail of the morning that was bothering me, but I couldn't put my finger on it. I just had an intuition that what I had missed was obvious, and I ought to be pointing it out.

As Ray and I sat in the booth together, talking intently across a wreckage of plates and napkins, I wondered what we would look like to strangers. Coworkers? A couple? Despite the measured course of our conversation, I knew that Ray's eyes were on me a lot, and that I blushed at odd intervals, sensing his attention. This awareness built alongside my interest in the discussion, like a chord following a melody. I blinked it away, returning my mind to the task between us. We were coworkers, that was all. We had discovered much in one day, and yet Brenae's death seemed muddier than ever.

We agreed it was best for us to part ways at the restaurant and for me to walk alone to my car, lest we be seen together if any of the students or Hal returned to the Westing. Tomorrow I would continue observing at the gallery, and Ray said he would transcribe the interviews for Janis, and ask her about how he should proceed.

"I need to talk to her, too," I said. "If I want to write about this, I should tell her."

"Do you?" said Ray.

“I’m giving myself the week to decide,” I said. When the words came to my mouth, I intended them to be about the story, but with Ray looking at me so hard, they gathered a different weight, and I faltered before finishing the sentence.

We bused our plates, then I accompanied Ray to the door, chatting about something meaningless to cover up my embarrassment at the sudden intensity of the moment before.

“You sure you don’t mind walking three quarters of a mile?” Ray asked me, and then grinned, his face brightening. “I guess I’m asking the wrong person. Though I wish I could plant a few maple trees to shade you.”

“Maybe I should aspire to jacaranda these days,” I said.

“Should you?”

It was a stupid conversation, but we both were smiling. Both uneager to leave. From behind the counter, the prep cook nodded good-bye to us, then flipped a tortilla into a warming iron and pressed down.

“Sorry for the long phone call,” Ray said. “My nephew. My brother’s son. You know.”

I didn’t know much except that the boy lived in North Carolina and that Ray clearly cared for him, but I nodded.

“He needed help analyzing a recess game,” said Ray.

“Must have been a complicated game,” I said. I’d listened to more than ten minutes of interviews.

“Lots of rules. Lots of changes to the rules,” he said. “And some little twerp who always cheats anyway.”

We faced each other beside the door.

I laughed. “I guess nothing has changed.”

“No,” he said, holding my eyes for a beat too long before turning away. “It hasn’t.”

13

I'D DONE SOME DIGGING OVER my summer in Vermont into the death of Ray's half brother. Every time I searched online for information on Calvin Teicher, I felt like I was trespassing on a property that did not belong to me. I had to take breaks to pet the dogs or rip at the mint overtaking the garden or make iced tea. I made sure to erase my online history so that my mother didn't spy on what I was doing.

First, I found the small news report of Calvin's death. A Boyle Heights hotel. Evidence of sleeping pills in his system. The sink bloody where Calvin's head had smashed it, his body found fully clothed, prone, in an overflowing tub.

Then I found a picture of Calvin—a small and blurry snapshot for a college publication. He had the same blue eyes as Ray, but they looked out from a sharper face: His chin was pointy, his cheekbones high, his hair thin and cropped short. He wore tiny glasses. More keen argument and wit than absurd humor and tenderness. A brother to Ray, but a different make.

I even called the Boyle Heights hotel where he'd died, pretending I was delivering a pizza, to find out if there was a back entrance where someone might have sneaked in and out without being seen by the front desk. There was.

And I looked up Steve Goetz again, seeking a connection that Ray had hinted at during a conversation I had had with him last spring. But Steve Goetz and Calvin had attended Yates University in different years, and there was no obvious link between them. There was no apparent motivation for anyone to kill Calvin.

All roads led to the conference that Calvin had attended in Los Angeles. He had come to speak on a panel about Britain's nineties art scene, with a focus on the role of a young artist and dealer named James Compton. In his thesis, Calvin made the case that Compton's gallery, fueled by his edgy, egalitarian worldview, ultimately changed the map of London, spurring trendy resettlement of once abandoned areas and vast increases in real estate prices. He also wrote, "Compton liked dangerous friends, friends who smuggled ether from Poland for him, friends who sold him explosives. Friends who came looking for him after he died, claiming giant debts."

I copied that down when I read it. I copied it into a little blue notebook devoted to Calvin's death, my self-conscious attempt at documenting a case I'd had no business trying to puzzle out. But by the time I returned to L.A., almost three months had passed without any further word from Ray, and I left the notebook in a box I still hadn't managed to unpack. I unearthed it now and flipped through the pages, noting my self-consciously tight, readable hand. As if I had expected someone to find it someday, and that someone to see that I had tried to understand him.

I tossed the notebook back in the box and looked around my bedroom, with its one nightstand and one lamp, the obvious solo occupancy. Books spilled over every surface. A woman was supposed to know how to make a home, and I just wanted a place to think and read and sleep.

Prints of night-city skylines circled me on the walls. Bangkok, Cairo, London, Vancouver, their skyscrapers aglow with lights. Globetrotting dreams courtesy of the apartment's owner. What would I hang now? What images would tell people who I was inside? When I closed my eyes, I saw the case file, I saw the gallery, I saw the crew sorting shoes. I saw the proprietary way Nelson reached for Layla's breast, and the compliance in her face as she bent to him. I also saw Ray, wherever he was in L.A., staring into space, seeing these same things, trying to work the puzzle together into a picture.

When you're doing a puzzle, you often start with the edges. The frame. The frame dictates the composition: how far or close up you see the castle or horse in the picture and how it's arranged in relation to everything else. In the death report, the frame was Brenae's suicide—where she did it, how she did it, how she died. The detectives had looked closely, intently, at the series of actions that preceded her taking her life. They'd interviewed witnesses and found evidence that proved Brenae's death at her own hand.

Listening to the students today, however, the frame changed for me. How Brenae died didn't exactly matter. How she had lived mattered more: what she wanted, what she needed, whom and what she loved. In her last week alive, she had reached out to Janis Rocque for help. She had also contacted her brother. Why were Janis and Davi the only ones she'd sought, when she knew so many people at LAAC? Why did she distrust Layla so much? What had happened in London?

Wherever Ray was now, under the same smudged moon and orange sky, listening to the same police helicopter begin to ratchet through the night, he must have been muddling over the same questions. Or was he? I couldn't help thinking that his frame was different, that his picture of today's discoveries was different, and that somehow it also included his brother.

14

THE CREW WAS ALREADY WORKING when I arrived at the gallery the morning after the interviews. Pearson acknowledged me with a nod. The others ignored me. They were preoccupied with the shoes. Sorting, piling, stringing, each falling into a specific role. If the video had had an effect on them, they were endeavoring to hide it. The backlash was like a creature locked away in another room—invisible, except as a thousand tensions in the air.

Pearson resumed his role as their manager. All engineering questions went straight to him, and he answered with calm directives. His column of destroyed shoes rose in the gallery's center, exactly his height—he must have worked on it all night—but he avoided it studiously, as if it were an embarrassing friend who disclosed too much.

Layla was the chief communicator, moving between Zania, Erik, and Pearson, making sure everyone had the materials they needed. She often stood back and took in the whole scene, hands on her hips, and then, shaking her head, went about organizing new piles. She changed her demeanor for each interaction: with Pearson, she was polite and deferential; with Zania, prone to mutual disgust at the shoes; with Erik, contemptuous and confused. She disregarded everything Erik said, but I often caught her appraising him out of the corner of her eye and slowly tucking her red hair behind her ear.

Erik wore rumpled clothes and an aggrieved expression. He wrenched at the rising columns, chucked a shoe so hard it scuffed the wall, and, as he'd done the day before, disappeared frequently to the bathroom. And yet there was no doubt he was the master maker here, wiring and building with his sensuous, expert hands. No matter what Erik touched, it looked better after. The ugliest penny loafers he wrapped and layered like clusters of grapes. A huge scuffed basketball shoe sprouted a bouquet of smaller sneakers from its ankle hole. He moved fast from task to task, whistling tunelessly through his teeth, his curly hair tumbling in his eyes. He rarely stopped to evaluate his creations. Once his hands were empty, he hastened to fill them again.

Zania seemed the most engaged, even relieved, by her tasks. She was principal sorter of the unusual, pulling out her finds—a hot-pink pump, a Roman sandal. She did not immediately share her discoveries, but piled them up secretly, off in a corner, and went through them a second time, rejecting many before showing the chosen ones to others. The whole time Zania worked, she looked disdainful, her hawk-like face closed and her movements abrupt, except for the moment she found a rare shoe, and then her expression brightened like a child's spotting sea glass at the beach.

The gallery acted as a fifth character in their play. Though the white room was designed to become an unobtrusive stage to any kind of artwork, the height of the walls and ceiling mattered to the proportions of the cathedral. The light mattered, too, where it pooled. Pearson measured everything and paced, looking across the room from different vantage points. He even pulled out a light meter and stared at it, calculating. His primary ruminative state was splayed-leg stance, his palm coursing over his bald head.

The crew didn't talk much, so in the lull I turned to the computer and began digging into LAAC's history. If anyone asked, I would say I was thinking of applying to school there, but in reality, I was curious about Zania's claims about women's experiences as students and artists. I checked the school's press releases on its website, compiling a preliminary list of recipients for scholarships and awards. Ray was right. It appeared, from what I had so far, that more than two-thirds of the honorees were male.

I also found the archive of the LAAC campus newspaper and searched through it for pieces on campus sexual assault. There were several articles, mostly vague updates by the administration. Yet one described five cases of campus date rape, and the school's sluggish and incomplete response to them. A flurry of letters to the editor supported and denied the claims. A few letter writers shared their own stories.

> *My roommate got escorted back to her dorm room by a guy because she was nauseous from drinking too much. She started throwing up in her trash can, she felt so ill, and he stayed for a while. She thought he was being nice, making sure she was well enough to go to bed, but she LITERALLY had just SPIT OUT her last mouthful of BILE when he said, "So, uh, can I just have a blow job, then?"*

> *My friend woke up after a party with a guy on top of her and her pants down. She's too embarrassed to tell anyone, but I know she can't get it out of her head.*

> *The guy who raped me is still walking around our dorm. I'm won't report him because I don't want my parents finding out what happened to me. I have to leave the room as soon as he arrives.*

In short, LAAC didn't look especially worse than most colleges. It was the same story across the country. Earlier in the year, UMass Boston and Brown researchers had published a study of nearly 2,000 men at an unnamed midsized urban campus and found that, of the 120 who admitted to rape or attempted rape, over half had done it multiple times. Unless this anonymous campus had a particularly sadistic population, the conclusion was chilling: serial rapists prowled American universities. Why? Because the consequences for them had not arrived. Women were afraid to accuse, and if they did, they often suffered in the public eye. Especially if the male student had some campus prominence: basketball player, wrestler, football player. And then there was the issue of alcohol and drug abuse. Intoxication increased the likelihood of sexual assaults. It also blurred memory, creating a he-said, she-said dilemma for adjudicators. Often the victims were blamed.

Brenae did not appear to be intoxicated in *Lesson in Red.* She looked stone-cold sober, and prepared, as if she'd meant to film everything that happened. To show how she'd caved in to Erik's coercion, time and again. To trap him as she'd felt trapped.

He comes. He asks me. I say yes. What can I say? What will happen if I say no? Where will I go?

With her video, Brenae was documenting one of the hardest aspects of sexual crimes. What if the stakes of saying no feel too great? What happens to a yes, then?

I wasn't sure I knew.

Brenae could have refused him, but she didn't feel she could. So she hadn't.

Erik's openness and outrage in the interview with Ray seemed genuine. But then so did the distress on Brenae's face.

Nelson de Wilde interrupted my research that second afternoon. The moment he entered the gallery, the big open room seemed to flinch. Nelson barely cut his eyes sideways at me, and I sensed that I had a small stain on my collar and that my lips were chapped. The crew paused in their work, as if suddenly uncertain how to proceed.

Nelson passed me without comment. In profile, he had heavy shoulders, carefully diminished by the slim cut of his expensive suit. He moved like a big man, though he wasn't especially tall, and when he crossed the gallery his footsteps had a low, decisive beat. Layla waited. Erik waited. Nelson ignored them. He nodded to his daughter, Zania.

She tossed down a sneaker. "I hope we didn't take these from homeless people. Did we?"

"They were slated to go overseas," Nelson began.

"Oh great, from refugees," Zania said. "Even better."

"I paid for them with a generous donation," Nelson said smoothly, eyes holding hers until she gave a thorny little smile. Then he asked Pearson for an update. Pearson pinkened at the attention and effused about the Westing space. "If we had time, we could go a lot higher," he said. "But we're running low on time."

"It's not going to happen. The shoes came yesterday," Erik whined. "We're so freaking behind."

"We'll get there," said Pearson.

"Can we change the name to *Shoe Lean-to*?" said Erik.

Nelson regarded him. "I'll tell you a story," he said, turning to include me, to include all of us. His voice lowered but deepened in pitch. "One time, I was working with an artist who shall not be named, and her crew quit on her two days before the show. She was making a sculpture out of her own body fat mixed with makeup, and we couldn't get the temperature in the room right. Too cold, and it was too hard to mold; too hot, and it would melt. She just ragged and ragged on her crew and blamed them, and they got sick of it and they all walked out." He gave a humorless chuckle. "So there I was, with the media and collectors calling me. Do we cancel the show? Postpone it? I said to her, 'You give me twenty-four hours. I'll find you a new crew. You tell me what you want, make it really direct and easy to follow. You pay overtime and you let me talk to them and we'll get your shit done.' She throws up her hands and says okay," he said. "So I went to every butcher at every market in East L.A. and said, 'I have a job for you. Two days. Good pay.' And they came and they pulled it off, everything she wanted. They had real skill with meat, with fat. It was their craft. And she worked with those same guys for ten more years. Her best sculptures came through them. One of them got his own career, too." He nailed Erik with his eyes now. "You've got to recognize there's a craft here and you are the craftspeople. You are not the artists. Not yet. You make Hal shine, and you never know where it will take you. You don't, and guess what. He's still the artist. He'll go on without you."

Layla nodded at this, but her face was expressionless, as if she hadn't processed what he was saying. Erik turned away and went back to wiring shoes.

"Thank you for the lecture, Daddy," said Zania. "We really needed to be told how insignificant we are."

"Honey," Nelson said, but his attention was still on Erik, on the younger man's bowed, curly, oblivious head. The gallerist's mouth twisted with dislike.

Then Pearson asked Nelson something under his breath, and they fell into a conversation so quiet that even Layla was straining to hear. Pearson seemed to be troubled by its drift, but he nodded and looked more solid than ever, standing on his heels. Nelson reached out and patted his arm, then turned away. As soon as his back was turned, Pearson wiped his face with his hand, then shook his head and returned to the shoes.

I saw Layla watch the interaction and struggle to conceal the worry on her face. Unperturbed, Nelson went into his office and shut the door. I saw my desk phone light up with his extension—he was making a phone call. When he came out again, twenty minutes later, he complimented the crew on their progress in a tone that suggested they could work harder. He did not acknowledge me except to tap my desk when he passed and give me a wink. It was just a wink, but it said: *I know who you are and this ridiculous stunt you're pulling, and I'll get rid of you if you interfere with the crew finishing this installation, got it? Good. Nice neckline.* I felt my cheeks grow warm and then noticed Layla staring at me. It took a long time to stop blushing, and by then the blush had turned to something else, an uncomfortable burning.

FOR THE NEXT TWO NIGHTS, I met Ray after I left the gallery and we debriefed watching the boats in Marina del Rey while eating some kind of foil-wrapped food he'd brought. The air was cool off the gray-blue water, the city at our backs. The grass was spinning itself into straw after a rainless summer, but in the quiet air it looked more golden than dead. Ray talked less than I did. He claimed he was still working on transcribing the interviews, verifying for accuracy every statement that the crew had made. It was important, he told me, not to pass on any falsehoods to Janis.

"Like what?" I said.

"Like Pearson claiming that Brenae didn't attend one class in the spring semester."

I was certain that Ray had to be doing something else with his time, too, but I didn't ask on Wednesday, when he showed up with a sunburn on the left side of his face, clearly from sitting in a car somewhere for hours. *What'd you find out about Calvin today?* I was tempted to say. My pride kept me silent. This was a professional opportunity for me, and not an inquisition into Ray's private life. As if through an unspoken mutual pact, we veered from personal questions and kept our conversation focused on the crew, Brenae, and LAAC. I left the car quickly when Ray drove me home.

Back in my spare living room, I filled my notebook with other discoveries. I called Brenae's high school and paid for her senior yearbook to be overnighted to me: it featured a photo spread that Brenae had done of senior prom, showing only the dancers' feet. It was an evocative series, yet likely infuriating to the students who'd wanted a record of their pretty smiles and hairdos. On her own senior page, Brenae's "faves" included the color purple;

avocados, salted; and every Pavement and Dr. Dre album. She took part in debate, band, drama, and soccer.

I checked police records for the older brother: he had been booked twice for marijuana possession. With the third strike, dealing meth, it was probable that he'd get a jail sentence.

Davi Brasil was all over the budding social internet, cultivating his music career. He had three times as many friends on Friendster as Brenae, and a Myspace page full of moody photos he'd shot and sparkling praise from female fans.

Brenae's father had once signed a public petition about water rights, but otherwise Brenae's parents and eldest brother had no online presence at all.

Brenae's apartment had already been rented again.

I wrote to USC professors about Brenae, and one wrote back: *She was extraordinary, and she wanted everyone to know it. I probably wasn't her favorite teacher because I insisted that she master the fundamentals of painting, and painting was too slow a medium for Brenae. But I predicted a great career for her. I'm deeply saddened to have been proven wrong.*

Another professor told me she'd saved one of Brenae's video works and left me a copy with her department. It was from Brenae's *First-Generation College Student* series. I sat on the giant blue sofa and fed in the DVD, watching Brenae swim the length of a pool with her eyes and mouth taped. Two cameras, one underwater, one above, alternated footage of Brenae in a red swimsuit, her blind, even strokes. About halfway across the blue expanse, she ripped off the mouth tape to breathe, bubbles spewing. Then she paused and tried to put the tape back on, but it only stuck loosely, then flapped free. For the rest of the swim, Brenae struggled to replace her gag. The effort made her lose her sense of direction, and she splashed in zigs and zags, treading water, coming up for air, sticking the gag back on. Finally she gave up and pulled off one of the eye tapes, too, her lid beneath red, dented, and puffy. Sighted now, she swam the last feet to the edge. The final image showed her gasping through the dangling tape, her hair flattened to her skull, one eye tearing up, one still covered. Her light brown fingers clutched the edge. This was Erik's cinematography again, three years ago, when Brenae was just nineteen. I thought about what Ray said, that Brenae was Erik's creation and this was the reason he couldn't see her as a human being. I didn't know how anyone could watch this video, much less film it, without seeing the human being.

ON THURSDAY MORNING, I WAS running low on West Side outfits, so I picked a dress I rarely wore, a black one with cap sleeves and a slim cut. I hoped it said *unconscious sophistication* and not *holiday cocktail party.* Today was Thursday, and my decision loomed: tell Janis I wanted to continue this investigation my own way, as groundwork for an article, or hand over everything I'd found out and go back to the Rocque. My phone buzzed with an L.A. number.

"Good," said a brusque female voice when I answered. "You need to get ready. Ray is going to pick you up in fifteen minutes to go out to LAAC. We have our own personal tour. We'll be able to see the scene of her death."

Just as I realized that the caller was Janis Rocque, she hung up.

Exactly fifteen minutes later, Ray rolled up, dressed in a silver-gray suit. He told me he was playing the role of a potential donor ("Oil money, honey," he'd informed me), with intentions to renovate the school's crumbling 1970s-era studios and then plaster his name all over them. The early hour was to shave off traffic time and to beat Hal's possible arrival at LAAC.

In the warm morning light, I felt a little ridiculous in the black dress and heels. Ray glanced over my outfit with the same suppressed mirth as I greeted his suit, and then gestured at a sack of pastries and two full coffees. Hungry as I was, I was afraid of crumbs all over my dark lap, so I didn't eat. But the silence seemed like a waste. I floated a few stale topics—weather, time zones, traffic—before cutting to the chase.

"What are you looking for today?" I said.

Ray gave me an appraising look. "Timeline and location," he said. "First, I hope to prove the video was shot in her studio. Second, I hope to see how someone got in and out of it on Thursday, possibly with her laptop in hand. The medical examiner dates the time of her death to sometime before dawn on Thursday. Computer forensics show that the files were shredded on Thursday evening. On Friday, LAAC staff found her body." He paused. "Someone must have entered her studio and wiped the files, or took the laptop away then put it back. That had to happen on Thursday."

"Have you talked to the detectives at LASD? It seems like they must have pursued this," I said. "Can Alicia connect you to them?"

"One of them already stuck his neck out giving her the file," said Ray. "For now, that's all Alicia can do."

"She doesn't seem to want to get too involved."

"All this digging doesn't make sense to Alicia. She sees things in a criminal justice framework. Either it's illegal or it isn't. If it isn't, move on," said Ray. "But she feels for Janis. And she can't stand not keeping an eye on me."

He said this casually, as if the detective's interest in him was obvious.

My throat closed, and I cleared it, annoyed with myself. "How long have you known her?"

"Ten years, off and on," said Ray. "She's my ex-girlfriend's cousin."

For a moment, I was too surprised to ask another question.

Ray's voice went on: "Ynez lives in North Carolina. She's an emergency room nurse. We were together—lived together—for about eight years, but it's been—it hasn't been working for a while, and definitely not since Calvin died. I broke things off over the summer." He looked at me, then to the road. "Alicia originally connected me with Janis, back when I first came to L.A. I helped them both with Kim Lord's case, and Alicia promised to keep me abreast of developments in Calvin's. But then she got divorced, and the sole custody of her son has been too much for her to manage, so she took a desk job. She's not on homicide anymore. She can't help me much now, and I'm not sure she wants to. She's pretty tight with Ynez."

Ray looked to be in his early thirties: of course he'd have been in some significant relationships by now. The fact of Ynez didn't surprise me. It was his closeness with Alicia—apparently, they knew everything about each other, about her son, about Calvin. Why hadn't either of them mentioned this before? It would have been so easy to slip it into conversation months ago.

"So you are still investigating Calvin's case," I said.

"Actually, today, I'm getting paid to investigate Hal Giroux," said Ray.

"Really," I said.

"Really."

His little notebook said differently. But if I mentioned it, Ray would know that I'd snooped in his stuff. We passed a truck full of crates of apples, the fruits red in the shadows of the wooden slats.

"I guess I don't trust you in a suit," I said finally.

"You shouldn't. And I really am sorry. I could have been straight with you a long time ago—about—about everything." Ray gestured with his open hand, as if the traffic and the steep hills and the smog-white sky around us were included in his omissions. Then, without waiting for me to answer, he said, "There's another thing I was wanting to tell you, if you don't mind my changing the subject."

"Go for it."

Ray rummaged in the bakery bag with one hand and pulled loose a palmier, the light, golden, flaky pastry rolling toward itself in two big swirls. "You like these?" he said. "My stepmother, Willow, used to make these. She ruined my brother for whoopie pies, donuts, all that stuff. Drove our dad crazy. But really"—he bit into it, crumbs flying—"these things are not that good. And they make a huge mess. Cal thought he had one up on the whole neighborhood, though. He'd tasted the authentic Paris cookie." He held it out to me. "Want one?"

"Was he always like that?" I said, fishing for the other palmier. "Wanting to be superior?"

The pastry was mouthwatering. The coffee, too—a frothy latte. Ray had clearly gone out of his way to find a decent bakery, which was not always easy in L.A.

"His whole life," he said.

"It's really good," I said, trying hard not to sputter crumbs.

"Maybe Willow's recipe needed work," he admitted.

"I read Calvin's thesis," I confessed. "He was a beautiful writer—it must have been terrible to lose him."

Ray looked momentarily befuddled, forlorn. "How did you . . . ?"

"The librarian at the Rocque helped me get it from Yates," I said. "I'm really sorry, Ray. Were you close?"

Trucks passed on either side, casting us in a sudden valley of shade. Ray glanced at them and sped out of it.

"You rarely say or do what I expect," he said in a soft voice. "We were opposites," he added. "He loved art. I loved science. Spider-Man, Batman. He hated our vacations at the beach. I loved them."

He sank into silence.

"But we were close," he said after a while. "Especially after our father died."

And then, as if a tap had opened somewhere inside him, Ray began to talk. Calvin had been his only blood relative after their father died, other than a few second cousins. They had grown up together in their father's house. Ray's mother had died when Ray was very small. Ray's dad had married Willow Teicher when Ray was four, and Willow gave birth to Calvin when Ray was six. A self-described "women's libber," she'd insisted that her son carry on her last name, an unconventional choice that puzzled and rankled their neighbors, and subtly reinforced Calvin's destiny to abandon his hometown. The brothers had drifted when Cal left for graduate study at Yates, but they came together again after Cal went into rehab for addiction to snorting Adderall, courtesy of his high-pressure college life. In rehab Cal had met a borderline female patient with multiple addictions named

Katrina, who'd gotten pregnant and carried the baby to term but didn't want anything to do with motherhood. So Cal had brought his infant son, Nathaniel, home to North Carolina and raised him with Ray and Willow helping out, all the while working on his thesis.

"He had this sling he put Nathaniel in, and the kid would sleep while he typed," said Ray. "The kid was a prodigious sleeper, a really contented child. I'll give his mother credit for that. She stayed off everything while she was pregnant. It was the only advantage the kid got, though. And Willow." Ray sounded deeply fond of his stepmother.

I waited, pulling my seat belt loose from my shoulder, letting it slide back.

"Anyway. Paris cookies," he said, as if that summed things up.

"What do you think happened to Calvin in L.A.?" I said.

Ray tapped the steering wheel.

"My brother was brilliant, but he didn't have a lot of sense," he said. "A couple of months before he died, he took his last bit of Yates stipend and went to London to interview people who'd known James Compton. He came back excited. He claimed he had 'a whole new angle' on Compton, but he wouldn't tell me what it was. He said I'd be 'too much of a cop' about it."

Soon after, Ray said, Calvin had traveled to L.A. to present part of his thesis on James Compton at a conference.

"He called his son the first night, as promised," said Ray. "The second night, he didn't."

The third day Calvin was found dead in a hotel bathroom. "The forensics team couldn't make much progress because of all the water. Whoever killed him took his laptop, a pair of pants, a pair of shoes, and a pillowcase." Ray cleared his throat. "We think the pants and shoes were for the suspect to change into. The pillowcase to carry the killer's bloodied clothes out. That meant we were looking for someone Cal's size or smaller. He was five eleven, size ten in shoes. Narrows it down to over half of L.A.

"Cal disdained owning a cell phone, so no calls or texts," Ray continued. "He picked up his conference badge, did his panel, disappeared, and then died. You're probably the only one outside Yates who read his thesis, other than me and Alicia." He took another bite of the pastry. "Not sure that opened up any new lines of inquiry anyway. But it is pure Cal."

I told him I was impressed by Calvin's enthusiasm for the British art scene and James Compton's role in it.

"He was trying to turn it into a book," Ray said. "He could have done it. But he was also a dreamer, a dad who never made enough scratch for his kid. And he was still an addict." Cal had kept clean in North Carolina, but in L.A. he'd hoped to score again. "He tried to connect with a few dealers while he was out here. There are records in his webmail. As I said, Cal had no sense. And when he backslid, he slid hard. But LAPD followed up on all the dealers, and not one checked out. The only other clue in his hotel room was a little L.A. snow globe from a tourist shop, and the name 'Genevieve' written on a piece of paper." Ray had painstakingly traced the snow globe to a shop in Venice Beach, but the owner had no recollection of Calvin.

Ray still couldn't figure out who Genevieve was.

"I left L.A. last summer because I decided that finding Calvin's killer wouldn't help me. Or Willow. Or Nathaniel." He looked at me, not wary, not shuttered anymore, but dead certain. "I belong with him. The boy." *I belong with him.* Love and fear mixed in his voice, making the simple statement echo in the car. "And I need to bank the funds to support him, in case anything—" He turned away, a thin scar on his right cheek shining in the sunlight. "My line of work doesn't guarantee a long life, so when Janis offered me another well-paying gig, I took three weeks of vacation time to come here. I think I can stretch it a few more days, and then I have to go home again. And then this story—whatever it turns out to be—will be all yours." He paused, and his tone changed. "I'm happy to stay in touch, if it helps you. I won't be able to fetch your coffee anymore, but I can be a sounding board." He smiled, but his eyes were on the distance again, the dry hills and telephone wires, the white stripe of the aqueduct descending.

"Thanks," I said. "Does Janis know all this?"

"Most of it," said Ray, and then added in a mutter: "Enough to scold me for leaving you behind."

My stomach fluttered. "As if Janis doesn't have enough to do, she has to matchmake, too," I said, forcing a laugh.

I waited for a joking reply. When it didn't come, I had the sinking feeling that Ray had been referring to leaving the investigation. Not leaving me.

"Your nephew must miss you," I rushed to say. "I'll take you up on the sounding-board offer."

Ray remained silent, his face tense. He was reading the green freeway signs, the next exit in five miles. Another eleven to Valdivia. Then he looked at the steering wheel and the long lanes in front of us, as if somehow either could offer him another direction in which to turn. Finally he sighed and sank back in his seat. "You cool enough?" he said, glancing over. "I can turn up the AC. Let me turn up the AC." He cranked the knob and asked me about my latest research on Brenae, chill air spilling over both of us.

15

UNLIKE THE SPRAWLING VILLAGES OF most colleges, LAAC was a single, bulging hive. Centrality and connection defined the architecture. Our drive into the parking lot today revealed the college in glimpses—a long white walkway here, a shaded patio there, the wavy roof of the new music theater. At LAAC, you could stroll the entire campus without leaving a building, without breaking free of the school's humming activity. Along the way, the ghostly tracks of its illustrious alumni crisscrossed your path—this was a MacArthur Fellow's studio once; that was the stage where an Oscar winner had made his debut. Every doorknob on campus had been touched by someone famous.

LAAC was a pressure cooker, an incubator, and a chrysalis. Although my young alumni friends ranged in personality and background, they all had one thing in common: they questioned everything but the value of art. If they'd arrived at the school with faith in some other higher purpose—honoring God, their parents, their culture, money, love—they left the school with that certitude in tatters. Instead, art sewed their existence together. For this conversion, they'd gained a tremendous education and an ability to see into our culture, to dismantle it, to find the reasons behind the reasons. In conversation, they could unravel an average person like me. Yet the change came at a cost. An ordinary life—working at any dull or obligatory job, marrying, buying a house, raising kids, even wanting wealth at all—was, for an LAAC grad, no longer acceptable as a means for happiness. You could do it, but you might betray your true nature. Far better to starve and self-deny than to yield to a life of quiet desperation. This transformation was Hal's real legacy. His masterpiece. It's one thing to influence culture with your paintings or sculptures, but to transform hundreds of young men and women, one by one, into new creatures in your own image? That is the work of a Creator.

Janis was waiting in the parking lot with her driver. She hopped out as soon as we pulled up. She did not look ill. In fact, she looked like she was refusing to look ill, all wound up in her blue pantsuit and huge round sunglasses. Yet the sight of her stabbed me.

"We're late," she said, although we weren't. "Shall we go in? I'll brief Maggie on the way." With a nod at Ray, she put her hand on my arm and steered me over the asphalt. I realized I'd never walked beside Janis. Most of the time I'd stared up at her behind a podium. Her dark, curly head came to my shoulder now, and there were sparse patches of scalp that shone in the sun, but her grip was strong and her stride quick and forceful. She radiated energy and determination as she launched into telling me about Steve Goetz and Hal Giroux's secret plan to build a massive free museum for Goetz's contemporary art collection two blocks away from the Rocque. "They're already in negotiation with the city for building permits," she said. "I think Goetz has a grudge with me over the Kim Lord business."

"Two blocks away?" I said. "How did you find out?"

"I have my spies. They're much farther along than we expected," she said in a bitter voice. "Our lease comes up next year, and the city might pressure us to make our museum free, too. They might even decide not to renew the lease. We're in a race against time."

The hush-hush nature of the plan proved the men's animosity toward

Janis. They wanted to wipe her out. Sure, she would always get credit for being a downtown pioneer, but Goetz and Giroux would arrive as conquerors to replace her.

"Hal's done with this place," Janis said as we stepped onto LAAC's paved arcade, which led to the green main building, with its two blank glass doors. "He wants a grand exit to a better opportunity, but there aren't many for a guy his age. It's my belief that he tried to bury Brenae's suicide and her artwork so he could keep his reputation spotless and make this leap. Big-time director of the big-time Goetz Museum." She paused, her hold on my arm tightening. "I didn't want to share the news with anyone who worked at the Rocque until I was sure. But you still need to keep it—and this whole investigation—to yourself. We might find enough; we might find nothing." She jabbed her chin at Ray. "He's interested in seeing the layout here, thinks it might shed some light on who came and went after Brenae died. Today, you and I can just keep quiet and support him. He's a very good investigator," she added as if I were just meeting Ray. "Very thorough and discreet."

I was still processing all that Ray had relayed in the car, a veritable avalanche of personal information, followed by his intention to return home again. It was as if he'd been in a race to tell everything to me before it was too late. The past week had made us comrades, professional but true to each other. But after this morning, there were more dimensions to Ray—the grieving, frustrated brother, the loving uncle—to mix in to the image I'd constructed of him as the bottled-up detective who kept appearing in my life. I didn't like Ray suddenly evolving into a cocktail of confused selves, especially one who seemed to have feelings for me. I liked how he'd been the first night, when we'd gone to see Davi play, and he'd cruised through the whole evening with the certitude that he would get the information he wanted. Vulnerable Ray made me pity him. No, not pity. Ray was leaving L.A. behind for good reasons. I saw that. Pity meant charity, forced sympathy, and not this soft, achy, deflating sadness, like something I'd held taut inside me had sprung a tiny hole.

I dreaded the car ride home with him—what would we say to each other now?—but here, at LAAC, we had a job to do.

We entered the main building through the glass doors. Beyond was a cavernous chamber. The ceilings hung high over a two-story lobby lined with theater lights. Corridors stretched off in all directions. I could hear dim sounds of music and thumping feet, but I couldn't tell where they were coming from. The architects had designed the space so that students from all the different disciplines—art, music, dance, film, criticism, and more—would cross one another's paths, cross-pollinate, collaborate. Later in the day, the space would be bursting with commotion.

Empty this morning, however, the surfaces looked old: the paint faded, the tile worn, the room lacking the alabaster glow of newer Los Angeles locations. Hal had erected a castle, but after a couple of decades in this city, all castles eroded. You weren't supposed to erode with them, though. Not if you were a genius. You were supposed to go out and build another. I understood Hal's career motives. And why should he care about the Rocque's future? Bunker Hill was fair game to him. Not to me. It was irrational, I knew, but I hoped Ray would find exactly what we needed to nail Hal today. Some clue that Brenae had left behind.

The campus welcome office wasn't open yet, but Janis jabbed at her phone and spoke into it, then nodded at us. "Someone's coming."

Ray stood loosely beside me, examining the lobby. I tried to see what he would see, through the eyes of a trained professional. Was he looking at the objects and their locations now, imagining the timeline of the week Brenae died? I could only picture what was missing: the students. An image of Brenae popped into my mind, plunked on one of the couches by the window, hunched over a laptop screen. And then in my mind's eye, I saw Erik, sauntering in, spotting Brenae, then pivoting to avoid her.

Erik and Brenae. Mentor and student. Lovers. Hardly unusual in the history of art. Picasso and Gilot, Rivera and Kahlo, Pollock and Krasner, Rodin and Claudel, Stieglitz and O'Keeffe. The older ones gave the younger ones their knowledge and experience; the younger gave their inspiring energies. And usually their bodies. Their affairs, passionate at the outset, rarely ended well, yet such relationships happened in every generation, and sometimes the world benefited greatly.

I remember Erik's deft hands piling and twisting shoes; I could see him focusing a camera on Brenae's mouth as she lifted the dripping gun to it. What if she had inspired him? And what if he had given her the footage she needed?

As we waited for our LAAC guide, my mind played a romantic version of Brenae and Erik's first meeting: Here was the dusty, dim classroom at USC, a cluster of students in flip-flops and battered T-shirts, and there was Erik pacing back and forth in front of a slideshow, asking questions. The students, mostly freshmen, hung in silence. Erik captivated them with his freewheeling commentary, his curly-headed boyishness.

Finally, one student raised her hand. Brenae's voice was flat, declarative. She refuted the question he asked. Or she changed the question. She had barely outgrown her childhood body, but her face was burnished now by an intense lust—lust not for the young man directing them but for what he stood for: authority, skill, knowing. She wanted it so badly it sharpened her, making her profile cut the air. He softened to her interest. It was real interest, he realized, fresh and intelligent, an instructor's dream. The air grew vivid between them, and the other students fell away. After class, Brenae stayed. She challenged him again, and he faltered. She left the room first, her walk awkward, as if she knew he was watching. And he was. The light in her made him blink as he thought over her questions, as he drove home later, imagining better answers.

BUT THAT WAS THE EXPERIENCE I had longed for, once. It wasn't necessarily Brenae's experience. There she'd been, a first-generation college student, all alone, in a prestigious university in an enormous city. Had she concealed that her mother worked in an auto parts store, that her father managed milking protocols? Such lives weren't anything to be ashamed of where I'd grown up, but Los Angeles schools drew many worldly and monied students, coached all through their childhoods to secure a competitive college berth, to ensure they retained their social class. Had Brenae known how much she would change among them? She'd said in her bio for *Packing* that the day she'd entered her first art history course, she'd switched her major from premed to art. Erik must have been there.

What had Erik been like three years ago? I tried to conjure a younger, dewier version of his flop-haired charm, but all I saw was his power. Erik was Brenae's gateway. He was already an artist, he had department connections, and he held the camera as she began making her own work. He knew how to shoot her, and he made her ideas more real than ever before. Erik was a legitimizer. He belonged, and if he said Brenae belonged, too, then she did. She needed that, coming from nowhere, feeling like no one.

What else did she want from him? The lust, the sex, that was clear, at least according to him—but had she wanted love? Was it too old-fashioned or naïve these days to want love?

Say Brenae hadn't. She'd only wanted knowledge. Intellectual gains. What if their relationship had started as lessons—Erik had so much to show her, she wanted to learn everything—and then moved to manipulation, the way Picasso had manipulated the young Françoise Gilot, praising and pursuing, embracing, then later deriding, then making her admit his mastery over her, driving her out, begging her to come back?

It was impossible to know. Yet as I looked around the vaulting bunker, with its bulletin boards layered thick in posters, I realized that over the decades of LAAC's existence, this space would hold every version of the powerful story of mentor and student: both the generous and the cruelly indifferent ones, the one that ended at the classroom, and the one that began there; the one where they never touched; the one full of abiding trust; the one where they buoyed each other, gift of a lifetime—as well as the version where one held the other down, the version where they both drowned.

Gilot had refused to be a victim. After ten years, and numerous threats from Picasso, she'd left, taking what she'd gained and leaving the rest behind.

Brenae had left, too, but she had gained nothing.

A PALE, UNSMILING MAN MATERIALIZED beside us in the lobby. He was so thin that his hips could fit into the jeans of a twelve-year-old girl. He grimaced as we shook hands, his hairy wrists immediately retracting into their buttoned sleeves. "I'm Jim, the studio manager. Sorry, the director doesn't generally come in today," he told us. "Would you like to see the studios?" He held up a ring of keys and key cards. "I understand that's why you're here."

"We'd love to see the studios," said Janis. She glanced at Ray for confirmation, and he nodded.

"Anything else you'd like to show us along the way," Ray said in a thickened southern accent, "feel free."

Jim gave a little shrug, as if tour add-ons were not his bailiwick, and started toward a corridor on the far side of the lobby. Our footfalls made hollow sounds. I was glad to be here, glad to have some context to visualize Brenae's last days, but without talking to people, I couldn't imagine we'd find anything new at LAAC. Instead, the silent, vacant corridors reminded me of the interchangeability of the students. For a few years, LAAC was *theirs*, their paint-spattered studios, their dinky library, their cafeteria with the pork buns on Wednesdays. Then, abruptly and just as intensely, it became the possession of others. The constant flow through the school would have protected Hal, enabled him to side with whichever student he chose; in two years, few would have personally known Erik Reidl or Brenae Brasil.

Jim walked swiftly, occasionally naming a department, a lab, all marked by small signs. The building's windowless stretches, filled with aging 1970s tile and paneling, didn't help its eerie feeling of repetition and displacement. Only the library was open, empty except for a couple of students and the librarian at the desk. We passed it quickly, and then the Super Shop, where Brenae had worked. It was closed, the welding, sandblasting, and woodworking machines inside hulking and still. I stared in, wondering where the desk was where Brenae had stood, checking out tools to the students.

Janis seemed nettled by our silence. "What questions do you have for Jim? He's been working at LAAC for three years, he tells me. Former graduate. Sculpture major, am I right?"

Jim gave her a nervous smile. "I did some different installations."

"Sounds vague, Jim," Janis said with her stern good humor.

Jim looked startled, then laughed. "Didn't seem so at the time."

Were we supposed to ask about Brenae? I glanced at Ray. He shook his head.

"Did you like being a student here?" he asked Jim.

"It changed my life," Jim said.

"How so?" I said.

"A better question is 'How not?' The experience here is like nowhere else." There was no snobbery or admonition in his voice, but he seemed puzzled by my question, as if I didn't understand LAAC at all.

We approached a staircase. "Oh," Jim said, halting. "Would any of you prefer to use the elevator? We have an elevator."

"Does it go directly into the studio building?" said Ray.

"No, we still have to go outside for a minute." He jangled the keys. "But we can take it if you want."

"That's all right," said Ray. "Stairs are fine."

I guessed at Ray's line of questioning: he wanted to know if there were multiple ways to access the studio building. This might explain someone entering Brenae's studio on Thursday without being seen.

Outside, morning sunlight filled a truncated courtyard, flanked on all sides by snaking walls. It looked like a cross between a prison yard and a secret garden. The sky bloomed, open and blue above. The grass was sparse, broken by patches of gravel and steel benches, yet here against a wall, someone had artfully stacked a pile of dusty glass jars, and there, silver wire wound around a pole, twisting on itself in a complicated filigree. Mysterious symbols emblazoned a large hunk of pink rock, making it look antique and new at once, a contemporary Rosetta stone.

I paused over it.

"What's it mean?" I said.

Jim turned back. "It's a translation of the menu from Canter's Deli. Someone made up their own hieroglyphic language, and that's the key that unlocks it all."

The symbols—tiny cats, an umbrella, collections of dots—did not evoke matzo ball soup and pastrami to me, but the stone's pale pink luster did conjure California adobe, a solidity that also seemed fragile.

Jim stopped at a new steel door and held up his ring of keys, flipping through them.

"People prop this open most of the time, but not till later in the day," he muttered.

He turned the lock, and we entered a narrow, white-painted hallway, etched and stained with nameless substances, the tile floor cracked. Both sides of the corridor were lined with dented doors, some painted brightly, some stickered, some plain. One door had no handle at all, just a hammer hanging off a wire. For the first time since arriving, I felt the hive mystique of LAAC, the air of common industry and creative life that hung over these spaces. Behind each of these doors, all day and night, people were painting, etching, threading, sketching. The walls came as high as the thresholds, but the studios' ceilings were all connected, which meant you'd be able to hear your neighbor talking, not to mention sawing or pounding. And pounding. And pounding.

"These belong to the undergraduates," said Jim. He gestured weakly at the walls. "Obviously they could use an update."

"Might we look inside one?" Ray sounded exceptionally courtly.

"Um." Jim flapped his hand again. "They're all full. And people are a bit sensitive about . . ." He trailed off. "We can knock."

"That's all right," said Ray. "Don't want to wake anyone up." He sounded peeved, though, as if it were such a small request, after all, to peek into someone's empty studio.

"Lead on, then," said Janis.

We came to the end of the corridor and opened another creaking door. Every footfall we made was amplified by the bare walls and floor. The studios' lack of privacy struck me again. Why hadn't more people heard a gun go off?

"How do people deal with the noise?" I said.

"High-quality headphones," said Jim. "First thing they tell everyone at orientation: buy a pair of headphones or you'll lose your mind." He said this without amusement, beckoning us into a broader hall, with fewer doors, more light, walls that reached the ceiling.

"Big difference," Janis observed.

"These are the Shangri-la of studios," said Jim. "They all go to graduate students, and there's a lottery for them. It would be great if all the spaces looked like this."

"Any chance we can step inside one of these?" said Ray. "They're really impressive."

"Um," Jim said. He looked at the walls as if noting some new markings there. "There is an empty one in the next building. It's not as nice, but . . . Or you could come back when we have more time to arrange things. Ask permission."

He fiddled with his key ring, his fingers twisting.

"I'd like to see one of these now," Ray said firmly. "I don't have time in my schedule to come back."

I realized Ray knew that Brenae's studio was on this hall. He intended to see it. I wanted to see it, too, but ever since we'd left the main lobby, I'd had the distinct feeling that there was somewhere else on campus that I needed to go.

Jim shook his head. "I don't—"

"Show the gentleman what he wants," said Janis. "Your development director would do it. I know her, and she does anything for a buck."

The manager glanced at the hallway's entrance and exits, then scurried over to a door at the end of the hall. "You can't touch anything," he said. "It belonged to the student who passed away last spring, and the police asked us to leave it open for the rest of the year. It's clean, but I hope you're not squeamish."

Up until the instant Jim had said the word *squeamish*, I had intended to follow Ray and Janis into Brenae's studio, to see what Ray saw and try to discern as best I could what he was trying to find. But now another idea occurred to me. A very Brenae idea. If Brenae couldn't show her videos on the walls of LAAC, she might make them public another way.

"Sorry," I said. "You might have to excuse me." I clutched at my stomach.

It took some willpower not to look over at Ray and Janis, who were frowning at my sudden queasiness. Why wouldn't I want to see the scene of Brenae's suicide?

Let them ponder. I would explain later.

"Sorry," I said again. "I just need a breath of fresh air. I'll catch up with the tour."

"I know, right?" Jim said sympathetically. "Trust me, it was way worse when the forensics people were here. I saw some things that I want to scrub from my mind."

"Like what?" said Janis, sounding equal parts amazed and disgusted at the turn in conversation.

"They use putty knives," said Jim. "Anyway. A quick look, okay, please? I could really get in trouble." He followed them inside.

I wandered away, casually, my eyes on the ground, like I was fighting the urge to hurl. I'd lost my chance to scrutinize where Brenae died. But it couldn't be helped. I had to get back to the library.

I KEPT MY EXPRESSION BLANK as I entered the room, feeling out of place in my pseudo-fancy West Side getup. The students glanced at me and went back to their laptops. The librarian, who looked like our tour guide aged twenty years—skinny, blinking, with an obsessively trim beard—gave me a thorough stare. I returned it with a firm smile and ducked into the shelving. I looked in the books first, just in case, but the last names skipped straight from Bennio to Broncs. Then I went to the videos, lined up in their library sleeves, the colorful DVD cases replaced by plain white covers, the titles typed large. Like all lucky discoveries, it seemed like this should have been harder to find—that there would be a fake drawer or trick shelf hiding Brenae Brasil's *After-Parties*. But there it was. The video she'd supposedly destroyed, left in plain sight, for someone to discover.

I didn't pause long. I stood beyond the sight lines of the librarian. Within moments I'd slid the DVD into my purse, returned the jewel case, and made my way out.

I hurried back to the studio wing through the door I'd propped open and nodded to Jim, who stood in the hall, tugging at his shirt cuffs. I entered Brenae's studio as Ray and Janis were turning to leave. It was just an empty room, light-filled, with walls as soft as bulletin boards and punched with holes from hundreds of pushpins. The scene of Brenae's death existed only in notes and memories now. The acoustics amplified our slightest moves. Even our breath sawed in and out.

Ray was studying the window, opening and shutting it gently. It had a half pane that shoved out at the bottom, and the rest rose six feet high, with a view of a wood-chipped median, the parking lot, trees, and the sky. An unremarkable suburban view.

The room had been scoured by crime experts. I knew from their reports which corner Brenae had chosen, and what the dents and scuffs on the wall there meant. Technicians had scraped off pieces of her brain and skull to dislodge the bullet embedded inside. They'd bagged the bullet, the gun, and every other object in the studio, including the laptop, an empty pill bottle, a pair of slippers, a mug with dried coffee ringing the bottom, and lots of shredded paper that they diligently tried to tape back together to find a message. But the paper was blank. They'd bagged the mattress, too.

They'd also bagged Brenae, and, in another building in the county, a medical examiner had checked her thoroughly for bruises or signs of penetration (none), then examined the wound and took toxicology samples, while the detectives had spoken to students, faculty, and family about Brenae's last days. Everyone they interviewed had alibis, except Pearson and Davi, who'd both been home alone that night. Every expert on the case had come to the same conclusion: sometime between midnight and 4:00 a.m., Brenae had lain down, put a large, heavy pillow over her head, stuck the gun up under her chin, and pulled the trigger.

But as I stood there, in the room where it had happened, I still couldn't believe it. And I knew Ray couldn't, either. That's why he'd been checking the windows, and now the ceiling. We were unable to un-see murder. The violence of Brenae's death: it demanded an explanation other than isolation and desperation. And because we possessed the sex video, something that LASD hadn't seen, the case seemed different now from the one they had solved. Their detectives had located Brenae's suicidal motivations everywhere—in her financial situation, her precarious position at the school, her lack of medication. To me, they had a locus. Erik. Erik had gone to see her on Tuesday. He claimed that his attempt to talk to her had failed. But by Thursday, Brenae was dead and, by Friday morning, *Lesson in Red* erased.

"Anything?" I whispered.

Ray turned away and pointed at the skylight, to the plastic glow-in-the-dark galaxy that someone had glued up there.

"Fake stars," he said.

"NOT MUCH TO UNCOVER," RAY said as soon as Jim had left us in the parking lot. The students were starting to gather on campus, and perhaps Hal would be showing up soon, too. We hid in the shade of a sycamore behind Janis's car.

"I wouldn't think so," said Janis. "It was months ago."

I nearly announced my find in the library but noticed that Ray was looking off into the distance, hands in his pockets, his gaze dazed.

"What?" I said. "Just tell us."

"You have a minute?" Ray asked Janis.

"Of course," said Janis.

He went to his car and pulled out his laptop from the trunk. While it booted up, he glanced at me. "Why did you leave the room? You lose your stomach for this?"

Ray had walked close to me all the way back through the studios, the secret garden, down the tiled halls, out the glass doors. As if to catch me if I stumbled. I didn't want to lie to him or Janis, but I was afraid if I showed the DVD to Janis now, she would take possession of it, and it wouldn't be mine, my discovery.

I felt a grip on my arm. "It's all right," said Janis. "Grief works in strange ways. You didn't know Brenae personally, but you feel like you do now. It's all right to feel sick about it."

She kept her hand on me, wearing a concerned, maternal frown, and I almost confessed my discovery, but she swiveled back to Ray. "Go on, then. Show us what you've got."

Ray set the laptop on his trunk and lifted his screen. "Tell me what you see," he said. "On the floor, next to them."

Lesson in Red played again, the whole excruciating thing. It was getting harder and harder for me to view the man pushing into her. The more I knew about Brenae. The more I knew about Erik. Beside me, I felt Janis shifting from foot to foot.

"This footage is monstrous," she said. "I can't stand it."

"There," said Ray, hitting pause and pointing to something on the floor by the bed. "What does that look like?"

A tiny, pointed thing, white and shining.

A glue-on star.

My nerves prickled. The plastic star, if it was a star, wasn't proof that the video was from Brenae's studio. But it was close. If Brenae had shot the video at LAAC, and not while she was an undergraduate, it refuted everything Erik had said. Erik had claimed the relationship was over. Erik had claimed it was all about sex and that he'd ended it over a year ago. But it didn't look ended at all.

"And there," said Ray, touching a shadowed rectangle on the wall beside the mattress. "That's an outlet that matches one in the studio. It's right beneath a couple of screw holes in the ceiling where Brenae could have mounted a camera. She may have even knocked down the star, mounting it."

"Well," said Janis, satisfaction in her tone. "Isn't that something."

Cars were pulling into the parking lot now, and I looked over at LAAC, the scattering of students heading into the building with their knapsacks and instrument cases, ready for their classes.

"I want you to see the new museum site," Janis added to Ray. "My driver will take you to the Westing," she told me. "It's your last day there, honey. Nelson wants his old assistant back."

Janis's words hung in the air. My last day at the gallery? Then what?

"I'm going to show Ray's interview transcripts to a few people. Probably the video, too," said Janis, seeing the disbelief on my face. "Look, LAAC is by and large a marvelous place. I want it to thrive. Being here today makes me lean away from the public exposé. I'd rather use peer pressure through the right channels first. If the board gets wind that Hal protected one student at a horrendous price to another, especially a young woman of Brenae's background, they'll have to investigate. Hal will get distracted. These museum plans will be put on hold, and the damage won't happen to LAAC. It will happen to Hal. That's better in the long run."

Was it? I didn't think so. I looked at Ray for support. He ran a hand down his lapel.

"What you're saying is that you want to do this gradually," he said to Janis. "Say the board doesn't respond. We still—"

"They'll respond," Janis said curtly. "This is a scandal."

My purse weighed heavy on my shoulder. Maybe Janis would take down Hal, but she wasn't standing up for Brenae, for her story. Her full, real story, written in flesh and blood.

"I'll find you later," Ray said, giving me a loaded look.

"Sure," I said, but I didn't keep the anger from my voice.

Janis checked her watch. "And don't worry about the new museum, Maggie," she said warmly. "To Hal and Steve, it's business and glamour. To me, it's family. I won't let them win."

JANIS'S DRIVER PLAYED SOFT PAKISTANI music and kept to himself, which was fine with me. I pulled the silver DVD from my purse and stared at it, wondering what it contained. What had Hal said? It was footage of people leaving parties. He'd rejected it for being trite and uninteresting. But Brenae had stowed it in the LAAC library, perhaps because she wanted to belong to LAAC history. Now that I'd seen her vacant studio, once soaked in her blood, now that I'd heard even Janis Rocque giving up on her, I realized how inexorably Brenae's history could be wiped away.

It was up to me now to save it. I still wondered if I had the right. I wasn't an artist; I was middle class and white from a white state, and I'd never felt the precipice of economic insecurity or the cultural isolation that Brenae might have faced at the college. I'd never been reduced to her position, literally beneath a man who used her. Furthermore, I believed in the slip from attraction to lust in the face of power. I knew it could happen for a woman—even if rationally, politically, and personally she resisted seeing herself in that role. It had happened to me.

NOTHING HAD EVER KINDLED BETWEEN me and my beloved art history TA. But I had been more than an intern to Jay Eastman, the journalist who'd led me to Nikki Bolio and who'd protected me after our source's death.

It had sneaked up on us slowly. I was an eager, naïve college graduate who still wore wrinkly batik and drank chamomile tea from mason jars. Jay was in his forties, bearded and with a head of wavy gray hair that made him handsomer than he had probably been as a younger man. Distinguished. Always in crisp cotton and polished shoes. He had a New York accent that bored into his words, which were witty and emphatic.

In my first weeks, all I did was show up at Jay's rented office in Winooski and type up his interview transcripts for the day. I don't think I struck Jay as anything more than a dutiful rube, but he had no one else to talk to, so gradually we began to bond over our loud next-door office neighbors, a husband-and-wife team who were operating a dying nonprofit and a dying marriage at the same time. Jay was married, too, with one son, and he seemed to get a grim amusement from the couple's shouting matches. But he never confessed anything personal, and I never pressed him. Instead, our conversations evolved from mutual eyerolls and quips at the couple's spats into deep probes into the communities he was studying—and I helped him. I know I did. I helped him understand my impoverished rural neighbors and their choices. Jay was from a suburb of New York—to him, the desperation in the country was an abstraction that could be shaped to fit a theory.

To me, it was many individuals' hopes shattered, for different reasons. I challenged him to get to know us better.

Our dialogues became heated, flirtatious, and though we stayed on opposite sides of the room, seated at our cruddy rented desks, I could feel us connecting in ways I had never connected with anyone, not even the two-year boyfriend I'd just broken up with. I felt larger, expanded and buoyed by Jay's attention, and when he left the room, I missed who I was when he'd been in it. I began to think about Jay all the time, to joke with him in my head, to wonder what he'd thought of my last remark. He thought of me, too. When I left on a family vacation for a week, I returned to my apartment mailbox stuffed with a copy of his most recent book, just published, a postcard inside. "Maggie: I miss you inordinately," he wrote. "Please come home soon." I never said anything about the postcard, and I don't think he wanted me to, but I told him later that I loved the book. It was true. That summer, even Jay's sentences had a sensual effect on me—they were so exact, so introspective. Jay was no hack; he was a reporter who could make you feel like you were there.

Bit by bit, Jay also worked on me to push a source, another young woman, to open up. Nikki was a dealer's ex-girlfriend, a bashful, acne-pitted blonde with a dancer's body. I knew her from a restaurant where we both worked. (Jay didn't pay me enough to live on, so I supplemented with a few dinner shifts.) I had heard Nikki brag about her leather jacket's expensive price tag, then watched her sell it cheap to another waitress a few months later.

"Tell her how important she is," Jay counseled me, pacing our office with long strides. "Has she got a younger sibling?"

Nikki had two nieces and a nephew.

"Tell her she's making their future better. Ask her to remember how Vermont was when she was a kid."

In fact, Nikki's childhood with a single mother had been poor and hard, but that's how we hooked her eventually. Nikki loved her mother, was intensely loyal to her. And her mother had begun taking pain pills, then selling a few, then taking more.

I told Jay that I didn't want to keep pestering Nikki, in case what she said would incriminate her mom.

"Come on, Maggie. What kind of mother is she on drugs? She's killing herself," Jay said impatiently. "This book could get help for people like her. We're sounding the alarm in a national way. Funding and programs will follow."

Under pressure, I finally arranged for Nikki to meet us both, and for Jay to question her. First, he warned her for her safety and flattered her for her courage. I watched him work, also in his thrall: the wise, renowned, handsome author and the country girls. Nikki flushed and bit her nails, but she didn't leave.

"They're going to come after me," she said when she explained the dimensions of the drug ring and their use of snowmobile trails to ferry the drugs. "But I don't care. I just want my mom back."

When Nikki was found dead, and her mother lost her only daughter, Jay told me we'd be safer if we stayed apart. He then retreated to New York. My tutelage with him abruptly ended in a few strained e-mails. I moved home and started applying for teaching jobs in Asia, feeling dazed and grim, older than my age, and also like a child who had damaged herself playing with dangerous toys. After a couple of months, Jay returned to Vermont to tie up loose ends. He wrote that he knew I was angry and sad about Nikki, but he insisted on seeing me. *I don't like how this ended,* he wrote me. *Any of it.* I agreed to meet for lunch. Jay chose a dim, romantic alley restaurant, and, hating myself a little, I dressed like it was a date.

He was waiting at the table when I walked in, and his face brightened forcefully at the sight of me but then darkened when he saw my expression. For the first twenty minutes, it was a one-way interview. Familiar ground for Jay Eastman, famous reporter. What was I doing now. How would I like moving to a hot country like Thailand after growing up in freezing

Vermont. Was I learning the language. It was a tonal language, hard to pronounce, wasn't it. Jay had wanted to see me, but now that I was in front of him, his damage was evident. He speared his salad and gulped his drink. He was racing to be done.

"How's the book?" I said finally.

"It's coming together." Jay set down his club sandwich and apologized to me again for what happened to our young source. "It wasn't your fault. Ever," he said, his usually strident voice humble and broken. "You were working for me, and I'm sorry, okay? I'm so desperately sorry that this occurred." He also told me the police had subpoenaed him, but they wouldn't subpoena me because he had erased my tapes with Nikki and shredded all my notes. "I don't want you victimized by some idiotic law," he said. "It could put you in danger, not to mention ruin your career."

Jay looked middle-aged to me that day. Worn and paternal. And, for the first time, flawed. I didn't want to see it. As I sat across from him in the flattering light, I longed for the old flirtatious, conspiring Jay, the one who felt something more for me than just gratitude and protectiveness. I wanted the brilliant, powerful Jay I'd adored, who'd adored me back, when we both believed in our story, and in each other. The desire wove through my body like a steel fiber, so that when we rose after lunch and walked down the restaurant's alleyway toward the street, I was so tense, I sprang. I pulled Jay toward me and I threw my arms around him and kissed him on the lips.

He gave a little grunt of surprise. He didn't kiss me back, but his hands found their way to my waist, and for a moment we hung there, bodies pressed tight, the kiss finished but our eyes locked, staring into each other's.

He murmured my name and let me go. We strolled to the street together. He fumbled for conversation again, but I had nothing to say. I had said it with the kiss and the look.

It's still one of the most intimate moments of my life.

We parted at my car, and I never saw Jay Eastman again. To this day, I am sure that if we had met at night for drinks, if I had kissed Jay in our office instead of the alley, if I'd had my own place nearby to lead him to, my own bed, or if he'd been younger or more willing to take what I'd offered—then we would have slept together. It is just as possible as the alternative: the single kiss. Sex would have thrown my life into worse confusion. But I am haunted by what might have been, by the certitude that if I went back to that moment in the alley, I would still want it, the carnal release.

16

THE CREW MUST HAVE BEEN working all night. When I entered the Westing, I regretted that I hadn't gotten to watch them. The edifice was real now, an architecture to step into, to train the eye upward, toward the skylights. The columns rose into arches of shoes that extended to the ceiling, not in an exact string but in an arrangement that ribboned and dangled, exposing the sharp grace of the high heel, the loafer's comfort, the sturdy boot.

The scents of sweat, leather, and rubber had intensified, blending into something arid and sweet. The light in the gallery was alternately broken and open. Mundane, ethereal.

I didn't know how they'd done it, but the feeling of *cathedral* had arrived.

The students were so absorbed in stringing shoes that they were indifferent to my awe, and I watched them for a moment, knowing what I now knew, having stood in the empty room where Brenae had died. This was my last day as gallerina. While I was watching the crew make Hal look magnificent, Janis was calling her contacts at LAAC, spreading news that would bring him down as their director. By the time *Shoe Cathedral* opened, Hal might be out of a job, and the students would have lost their mentor. The truth would come out about Erik; the crew would disband. And this week—when they made something powerful and memorable together, despite their tensions—would become a ruin.

Pearson noticed me staring and gestured at me to walk inside the structure. As I did, my eyes landed on laces, straps, stilettoes, open gaps for sun. I wanted to sit down, to be still and low, with my chin raised. A supplicant.

"You should put a bench in here," I said. "Has Hal seen this?"

"He was here all night," said Pearson.

He moved aside, and I spotted the smashed column behind him, the gouged and flattened shapes. It stood just to the left of the apse. It undermined the flow of the architecture, and suggested collapse. Involuntarily I stepped back from it, but I couldn't tear my gaze away.

"This is unbelievable. Did any of you sleep?" I said.

My praise made Erik cast a wincing smile in my direction. "Not much," he said.

"Have you seen the espadrilles?" Layla asked Zania, and Zania pointed across the room. "Excuse me," Layla said, deliberately bumping me from her path.

"I think Nelson left you some work," Pearson said to me.

I took the hint and walked to my desk, now piled with stacks of paper, folders. There was a note: *Please collate media packets by 11:00 a.m. Thanks.*

Nelson's handwriting was cramped and dark, as if he pressed the pen hard. Its introverted appearance didn't quite match the tan, lean man who had reached so casually into Layla's blouse and cupped her breast. I made neat work of the packets, tapping the papers so their corners and sides aligned before I slid them into folders. All the overblown praise in the press release seemed merited now. Why did this make me wistful? I should be glad that Hal would resign, that Erik would be exposed. It was a victory, but some essential part of the battle remained unfought.

My phone buzzed. Yegina. I stepped outside to answer.

"How's gallerina life?"

The day after I heard about Janis's cancer, I had e-mailed Yegina, telling her what I knew, and saying that I'd decided to take the gallerina gig after all. Yegina had apologized for not informing me about Janis sooner. *I've only known a week, but I couldn't betray her trust. I hope you understand.* I understood. It was an unspoken rule that Janis traded in everyone's secrets, but no one knew hers.

"I can't get into details," I said, "but our fearless leader is arming herself with scandalous information to do a behind-the-scenes takedown."

"Is she?" Yegina said thoughtfully. "That doesn't sound like her."

"She wants to save the institution—well, both institutions—but not the man. Things were getting really heated up downtown, and she thought she had to act fast."

There was a silence. "Interesting. But then how would you write about Brenae? If it's all behind the scenes?"

"That's the complicated part. I'll have to tell you more after it's done. How's the conference today?"

"I just got to the main building. Hiro flew to D.C. this morning to meet me, and then he asked me to marry him," she announced. "I didn't say yes."

"You didn't?"

"He was so sweet about it." She sounded overwhelmed. "He told me that in Japanese conjunctions don't work exactly the same as in English, that *Hiro* and *Yegina* wouldn't have an *and* between them, we'd just be *HiroYegina*, and that's what he wants to be in any language, and then he rambled on about unity and proportion in symphonies and trees. I kind of lost him there, but he was so sweet, and I told him I'd have to think about it." She paused. "I feel awful."

Yegina's feelings about marriage were like a burn victim's about fire. After a long, painful divorce from Chad the jobless sitar player, she'd never wanted to get hitched again. But I also knew how much Hiro meant to her, how calming his influence had been on her usually frenetic existence. He liked taking care of my friend. He had fixed all her broken window screens. He had bought her a high-end blender. He made a killer cheesecake, Yegina's favorite dessert. I couldn't think of anything negative about Hiro, except that his proposal was a pretty fast move for someone who liked cultivating hundred-year-old shrubbery for a hobby. He and Yegina had only been dating six months.

"Don't feel awful," I said. "He should know you're coming to weddings from a different point of view."

"But that's the problem," said Yegina. "If I explain my objections to marriage, he'll probably agree with me. He won't want to get married. And then we never will."

"So say maybe," I said, glancing back into the gallery. The students were clustered, talking. What conversation was I missing?

"I wish," Yegina said glumly. "I'm not ready to make this decision. We were just supposed to have a sexy week together in the capital, and now there's this huge weight on us. Do I send him home?"

"Ask for time," I said. "Tell him you need a week to soul-search."

Yegina made a doubtful grunt. "I need a year," she said. "I know he wants kids. That was a discernible section of the tree speech." She hesitated. "There's something else. It's also complicated."

"It might need to wait, then," I said. "I've got to go back."

"It might not happen anyway. We'll talk later," she said, and then her voice retreated.

I hung up, suppressing a surge of nerves. It wasn't jealousy I felt. More like homesickness. Homesickness for a simpler time. A year ago, Yegina and I had been in the same place—heartbroken over crappy relationships, devoted to our jobs at a struggling museum and to our friendship. A grueling day at work meant we had to jump on the DASH and get mochi in Little Tokyo; a lonely night meant we'd meet for a silent movie on Fairfax. There were so many city pleasures to explore, to escape into, and put off the future for another day. But marriage and kids for her. A possible new career for me. The old days weren't coming back.

My black dress brushed the windowsill on the way back into the gallery, streaking it with dust. I rubbed the cloth, then grabbed for the door handle, but a hand reached ahead of me.

"After you," said a male voice. I look up into the close-shaven face of Nelson de Wilde.

"THE SHOEMAKER'S ELVES," NELSON MUTTERED as he observed the installation. If he was pleased, he didn't show it. He didn't look angry, either, just focused, as if he could let everything else fall away when he examined art. He thrust his hands in his pockets, peering at every inch of it.

Pearson, Erik, and Zania kept working. Layla slumped, stood erect, then wandered deep into a corner.

Nelson didn't acknowledge her. Instead he approached the desk, checking through the folders I'd made. "Any other calls?" he said in a low, intimate tone, as if he were speaking only to me.

"Uh, to the gallery? No."

Nelson watched me now, for another long moment, appraising. It wasn't like the way Ray and Alicia looked at people. They were sneaky and guarded about how sharply they observed you. Nelson turned on the full spotlight of his attention, and he seemed, with each passing moment, to be building a case study of who I was. After a while, he nodded and gave me a smile that was somehow also sexual, and not quite in a cheeky or predatory way, but just acknowledging his approval of me. It happened so fast, and with such possessiveness.

"I need you to keep Hal on task today," he said, running his fingers lightly on my desk. "He tends to let his interviews run over. We have five in a row this afternoon."

"Absolutely," I said. I felt like my friend Kaye when I said it—Kaye, who, until her doula phase, had made six figures as a personal assistant to Hollywood executives. *Absolutely* was one of Kaye's signature words—formal, flowing, with a touch of confidence. Fleetingly I wished I looked more like her now, perennially beautiful and pleasant, an impulse that surprised me. Two interactions, and Nelson had effortlessly manipulated me into a servile box. I didn't like it at all.

"Thirty minutes for each. Tops," said Nelson.

When our eyes met this time, I kept my own gaze deliberately blank, and Nelson kept staring until I had to blink.

"Got it." I tidied the already tidy folders on the desk.

Nelson turned to speak to the students. "This is very good. It's coming together magnificently," he said. "You can stop work at noon and be off until three, all right? You need a break."

"You should take a lunch break, too," he ordered me. "Be back at one, please."

I checked my watch. It was eleven thirty. Did Nelson mean I should leave now? He gave me a forceful little nod. He meant now.

"Does that work for you?" he said.

"Absolutely," I said again, and grabbed my phone, my purse. I could feel his eyes on me as I stalked to the door.

IN MY LAPTOP IN MY silent apartment, the DVD spun and began to play. Handheld nighttime footage of young people unspooled. They chatted and laughed outside galleries, on the LAAC campus, on sidewalks I didn't recognize. The cinematography wasn't as good as that in *Packing*. Brenae hadn't paid much attention to lighting or composition, and Hal was right, without Brenae herself in frame, defiant and charismatic, stealing the show, it lacked a certain flair. Perhaps she'd wanted to be as invisible as possible. This video was about everyone else.

I watched women with spiked hair and men with tattooed necks, and men with pageboy cuts and women with pageboy cuts, and jeans and flowing dresses and sleeves of roses and no jewelry and fists full of big rings and shaved heads and light brown skin and white skin and dark brown skin. Hands fluttering in the air and hands holding blue plastic cups of beer. People leaving in clumps, and one by one. I saw Erik, I saw Layla, I saw Lynne Feldman, I saw Zania and Hal, I saw my coworkers Phil and Spike, wearing cutoff overalls and combat boots, their legs long and hairy. I half expected to see myself. I'd probably been to one of these openings. The dirty, faded lanterns of Chinatown swung overhead. The traffic lights of Sunset blinked and shone. The partygoers were stuffing themselves into cars and climbing onto motorcycles and stumbling away on foot. The video was boring and endearing, in the way yearbooks and slide shows were boring and endearing. Hal was right. This wasn't great art. I felt my eyes grow tired, and wondered what I was missing at the gallery. Then on the screen I saw Nelson de Wilde walking away down the street, side by side with a young man it took me a moment to recognize. I knew him from somewhere. From a picture online. I paused the image and went to my search engine to make sure. I was sure. Brenae had captured Nelson de Wilde leaving a party with Ray's brother, Calvin.

IN 1993, JAMES COMPTON THREW a street fair called Ditchfest in East London that drew hundreds to a run-down area of the city. In 1994, he died. In 1995, a new venue opened half a mile away, operated by an East London native named Nelson de Wilde. It was a music club at night, but Nelson invited many of the Ditchfest artists to design the walls and spaces. Soon it became one of the hottest nightspots in the area. When he closed the club two years later, Nelson became a de facto dealer, unloading now valuable works in order to fund his emigration to Los Angeles. Then he opened the Westing, his golden nest for so many future art careers. Had Nelson known James Compton? How could he not? Had Calvin talked to him about Compton? Did Nelson know about Calvin's murder? What about his half brother, a detective, working for Janis? Ray and Calvin didn't share a last name, but still.

Nagging at me most of all: Did Ray know who Nelson was, and where he had been? It had taken me thumbing through Calvin's thesis bibliography and forty hasty minutes on an art history database to piece these bits of Nelson's past together, and potentially connect him to Calvin. So how could Ray not know all this?

And yet he had never said anything to me about it.

The white receiver of my apartment phone grew warm in my hand before I called Ray. The sight of Calvin and Nelson together deeply troubled me. I had no idea what it would do to Ray. At the same time, I feared I already knew. He suspected Nelson de Wilde. Of something.

I remembered the list in Ray's notebook, the names of people who might have run into his brother on his last night alive.

Brenae's footage held one answer.

Ray didn't pick up my call. "There's something you need to see," I said to his voicemail. "I have to go back to the gallery, but when you get this, call me and I'll come down the street and give it to you."

17

HAL GIROUX WAS EXCEEDING HIS thirty minutes with a New York reporter by thirty-five more, but every time I appeared in the doorway to Nelson's office, he shooed me away. Hal excelled at this—as soon as I materialized, he waved a gnarled hand at me and rolled his head back toward his guest in one fluid motion, the way a horse avoids a harness and ignores you at the same time.

I retreated with a polite face. Hal didn't know what he was in for. Let him have his last moment in the sun. Janis must have made some calls by now, and soon the school would have to act. The more I thought about the crew's interviews with Ray and their reactions to the video, the more I was sure who had erased the files from Brenae's laptop. It wouldn't take much, just one confession, to damn Hal to never work again.

The two waiting journalists had already roamed the installation twice and were sitting at opposite ends on the hard bench by the door, clutching their media packets and glaring at me. One of them had just made a loud, complaining phone call about her delay.

"Do you think he'll want to reschedule?" she said to me. Her voice was thick with ire. "I have to go in fifteen minutes."

I told her I'd check on Hal, and walked all the way into Nelson's office this time, and up to Hal, who was lounging on the turquoise couch, legs crossed, grinning at the New York reporter, a skeletal young guy with huge, gorgeous brown eyes. It was clear Hal was loving the interview and wanted something from it.

I told Hal that two people were now waiting for him. "Should I ask them to reschedule?"

"Yes, do," Hal said, but the reporter leaped up.

"Don't let me limit your coverage," he said.

"Oh, they can wait," Hal replied in a caressing tone, but the reporter was already thrusting his notes into a satchel and slinging it over his shoulder. The young man's chest was concave, his limbs long and his fingers thin and white. His physique reminded me of a piano prodigy's, but I knew who he was—the architecture critic from a major art magazine. Hal wasn't making a building with *Shoe Cathedral*, though. So why the huge fascination?

And then I knew: architecture. The new museum.

"You'll talk to Vera, then?" Hal said as he followed the critic out. "I mean, just mention it. I can't spread myself too thin with these matters, but I'd love to know her interest level."

"I'll talk to Vera," the critic said, and held out his hand. "Great to meet you, finally. The legend in person."

Hal gave a pleased chuckle. "Mary will show you out."

"No need. I can find my way," said the critic, moving off with alarming speed.

Just as I was about to follow him away, Hal motioned me back inside the office. He shut the door softly before whipping around to me. His eyes were hard, and his slumped cheeks wagged with his words.

"Are you out of your freaking mind?" he said. "Who gave you the authority to interrupt me like that?"

"Nelson told me to keep you on time," I said. "I'm sorry—"

"Nelson has no idea what it takes to talk to these people," said Hal. "Time." He snorted. "It's not time."

He stared into the office with its tangerine carpet and modernist couch, the chrome cabinets. "Look at this crap," he said. "It's like an intern picked it out. People are so good at playing like they care, but only some of us really care, you know?"

I nodded automatically. I said, "Absolutely."

"And even fewer of us would stake our lives on it," Hal said with a little catch in his voice. "The rest just want money."

I fought to keep my expression sympathetic. "He's supported artists for forever, though," I said carefully. "Hasn't he?"

"Of course he has," Hal said. "Why, are you an aspiring artist, too?" His tone was sly.

"No," I said.

"Good. What else needs to be done out there?" he said, and pointed in the direction of the gallery. "Does it look finished to you?"

It took me a moment to realize what he was asking. Me, the gallerina.

"The damaged column," I said finally. "I wonder if there should be echoes of it elsewhere."

"Echoes," mused Hal. "Tell me more."

"A broken shoe here and there. So your eye might catch them, but not your mind."

Hal peered at me, the steel in his gaze softened by curiosity.

"Hiding in plain sight," I couldn't resist adding.

"Thank you, Mary," he said, and walked over to the blue couches. "Bring in the next one, okay?"

This time he took the couch the critic had been sitting in. His back faced the door, his bald patch showing. He ran a hand over the bare spot as if he knew I was watching him, and then dropped the hand to his lap.

WHEN HAL LEFT LATER THAT afternoon, he conferred with his assistants first, speaking in a low, intense, praising voice, gesturing at what they'd done. I couldn't hear his words, but I saw the effect, how they nodded and sat straighter, basking in the light of his scrutiny. Then Hal began grilling each student as he gestured at the columns and arches, and they answered, one by one. By the time their conversation ended, it was clear whose artwork *Shoe Cathedral* was. Even if he hadn't personally made much of it.

Afterward, Hal came by my desk. "I'm sorry about my outburst," he said to me, not sounding sorry. "But if you want to get ahead in this business, the first thing you need to learn is tact. You were tactless to interrupt us. Who cares if those buzzy little bloggers had to wait? Time doesn't matter. Power matters. Influence matters. Time is just—" He made a sprinkling motion with his fingers, and his face went suddenly kind. "It's the most expendable thing you have."

Then he strolled toward the door before I had a chance to respond.

"We're getting there. Go celebrate tonight," he shouted back to the assistants. "I owe you all . . ." He paused, opened his arms. "Everything."

The assistants waved. In three faces was the same thirst for Hal's approval. In the fourth, a shrouded mutiny. The door shut behind him.

Zania noticed me watching her and walked over. "Did you get hell from Hal?" she said.

"Oh no," I said. "I was just trying to do what Nelson asked."

"We came in while Hal was chewing you out," Zania said, holding her slim body erect and looking down at me over her long nose. "But don't mind him. Tomorrow he'll tell you that your organized mind is exactly what he's missing and thank you for keeping him on task. Chastising you is the first sign that he likes you."

"I'll be okay," I said, embarrassed. "This is my last shift."

"Then you should come celebrate with us," said Zania. "We're having people over at my father's house. Pearson says we owe you because you carried all those shoes."

"I'll take some payback," I said, hiding my surprise. Though I'd wanted a chance to observe the crew longer, I hadn't expected it to happen. Mentally I'd been preparing to return home to my notes, pondering how to pursue Brenae's story without Janis's endorsement.

"You look like you need a good time." Layla smiled at me, but her head shook *no* at the same time.

"And we're completely sick of one another. You're fresh blood," Pearson added.

They were conspiratorial again, their divisions buried under shallow cheer. I didn't understand how that was possible. Unless. Unless they had decided to band together to protect someone they still admired. Or most of them still admired.

"We're going to jump in the pool before everyone gets there," said Zania, "and order a disgusting amount of . . . of what?" She turned.

"Pizza and wings," said Erik.

"Sashimi?" said Layla.

"We had sushi yesterday," said Pearson. "I vote wings. Dripping with fat and buffalo sauce."

A look of revulsion crossed Zania's face.

"I'm no carbs," said Layla. "I could do steaks."

"Wings don't have carbs," said Pearson.

"But they have bones," protested Layla.

"Steaks have bones, too," said Pearson.

"Not filet."

"I don't even have to try," said Pearson.

"Filet and pizza and wings," Zania said to me with a grisly smile. "Coming?"

18

WHEN I WALKED HOME TO change clothes for the pool party, the breeze switched. West wind to east wind. I'd experienced alternations in the air currents all my life. Everyone does. But they'd never tasted to me the way they tasted in L.A.: the soft, clear salt wind from the ocean suddenly washed back by the grit and heat from the city, the desert beyond. Sunlight streamed through both winds, my body strode through both, but every time I crossed through east wind to west wind, or back again, I inhabited a different state of being, as if someone had replaced a lilting piano soundtrack with crashing noise rock.

West wind: What if the crew had found out that Hal was being investigated by LAAC? I wanted to see their reactions.

East wind: A foreboding filled me. Layla shaking her head at me as she smiled. *Quit now.*

East wind: Why foreboding? Because the party was at Nelson's house?

West wind: It was a party. What could happen with so many people around?

East wind: What did Nelson's connection to Calvin mean?

East wind: Ray still had not responded to my call.

East wind: Ray was concealing something.

East wind: He was protecting himself. Or maybe he was protecting me.

YEGINA PHONED AFTER I'D STRIPPED off the black dress and was rummaging in one of the dressers for my swimsuit. A calm had settled over me, and I answered on the first ring.

"Are we still going out tomorrow night?" she asked. "I'll be in by mid-afternoon. And what are you wearing?"

Yegina and I had planned to attend Dee's gig at a British-themed bar in West Hollywood on Friday. It was the week before Halloween on Melrose, costumes encouraged. "I have that red wig."

"The same red wig you wear every year?" said Yegina.

I was too embarrassed to admit that I liked the wig's simple transformation. Punk, redheaded Maggie was disguise enough for me. "I could go as you. I have an old dress of yours."

"Ha. Too scary."

"Do they sell fake British teeth?" I said. "I could dress up as Johnny Rotten."

Her silence spoke more than a comeback.

"Maybe you should go with Hiro," I said.

"I can't go with Hiro," said Yegina. "He hates loud music. And anyway, I told him I wasn't ready to answer the proposal. He flew out this morning."

"I'm sorry," I said. I felt both disappointed and relieved. I wanted Yegina to be happy, but I didn't want to face months of conversation about wedding plans. Yet. "Do you want to talk about it?"

"What I want is a real night out."

"I'll find something to wear," I promised, wanting to relate everything we'd discovered at LAAC, and Janis's decision, wanting to breach the confidentiality I'd promised to Detective Ruiz and kept breaking for Yegina, but I held back.

"How was Janis today?" she asked.

I thought of Janis speeding around LAAC, her determination and grim cheer. "She's coping." My voice wavered.

"The first time I met her, she came into my office and asked to use my phone," reminisced Yegina. "She called some board member and chewed him out, right in front of me, for voting down the budget because of growing exhibition expenses. 'We're here to uphold art and artists,' she told him. 'Not to mind our personal collections.'"

"That sounds just like her," I said, laughing.

"By the end of the call, he agreed to donate another five hundred thousand dollars. It was amazing."

"She's never given up on the Rocque," I said. For the first time, that troubled me. I said as much to Yegina but kept the details vague.

"It's like Hal wins or she does, and there's no in-between," I said. I told her about the pool party, my last chance to observe the crew who built his show. "It's clear they worship him the way we worship Janis. What if his museum is good for downtown? Should we destroy the vision because the man behind it is flawed?"

"He's not the only one who can dream it," said Yegina.

I CHECKED MY INBOX BEFORE leaving. The only nonwork transmission was from my mother, who was still pressing me about coming home for Thanksgiving. *We'll buy you the ticket,* she wrote. *Just name your days.*

I saw my mother sitting at the keyboard in our wooden house, her blond hair pulled back, her hands slightly chapped from the new cold. The last dry October leaves were stripping themselves from the trees outside. I saw the bareness that was coming for her and my father, their three children grown, their careers winding down, and the slow grip of age tightening around them. Listening to Ray describe Cal's loss had made me appreciate my family. What luck to be harbored by my steady, generous parents and brothers for all my childhood, to be unmistakably loved.

I thanked my mom and named my days. It felt like an insurance policy. Whatever happened to me that night, the ticket would be waiting for me when I got home. My mother wouldn't hesitate to buy it, to cement my return.

THEN RAY CALLED. "WHERE ARE you? I went by the gallery."

I told him I was heading to Nelson's house, at Pearson's invitation. "We bonded while I helped him and Erik carry the shoes," I said. "I think my willingness to do grunt work disarmed him." Then I added, "I'm not done, Ray. I don't care if Janis fires me."

"I know," he said.

A silence fell between us.

"I ever tell you what Pearson's felony was for?" he said.

"You said he assaulted someone."

"He was at a party. A guy spiked his soda with acid. A prank. When Pearson came down from the trip, he found out and beat the guy within an inch of his life. With his bare fists."

"That's awful," I said. "Why are you telling me now?"

"Just be on your toes," he said, then hesitated. "What did you want to give me, anyway?"

I told Ray about finding the DVD, watching it, and seeing Nelson and Calvin together in it, and said that I had the DVD with me.

"You took it from the library?"

"I wanted you to see it."

"You should always put things back," he muttered. "You never know who is watching."

It took me a moment to understand.

"You've already seen the video," I said slowly. "You already found it there."

"I spent a couple of days at LAAC last week," he admitted. "That's how I knew where Brenae's studio was."

"So you know that your brother met Nelson de Wilde. On the night before he died."

"I do."

"But then what are you—"

"Waiting for? I was looking for someone named Genevieve, but I don't know who she is."

I paced my apartment, watching time tick toward evening as Ray told me how he'd spent months studying the evidence in Calvin's murder: a brutal beating that looked unpremeditated, and hadn't quite killed its victim. Drowning was the cause of death, but his attacker had left him unconscious in the rising water. It could have been a drug dealer. But Calvin had bought drugs before without incident, and drug dealers were careful about homicides. It was likely someone Calvin had angered. But who? And why? Did it have to do with the conference? Murderers didn't usually lurk at art history conferences. And yet James Compton himself had been a wild card, a figure of unpredictable violence, with some criminal associations. What new angle had Calvin found about James Compton, and why wouldn't someone want it known?

Ray had spent last winter digging into the Los Angeles art world. By the time Ray had met me in the spring, Nelson de Wilde had become his main suspect. Nelson was from London, and he had burst onto the same cultural scene a year after James Compton's death, with a club and money and connections that no one seemed able to explain. The man was a superstar supporter of artists, and he'd had no criminal record in England.

Desperate to find some crack in the gallerist's armor, Ray began to look into the financial side of the gallery business and concluded that Nelson must have had a significant source of undisclosed income in order to run the Westing. Where was the cash coming from?

A gallerist's most obvious source of revenue was art commissions. Sell an artwork, get a percentage of its cost. After Kim Lord's case practically dropped into his lap, Ray had concluded that one of Nelson's secret sources of cash was Steve Goetz buying and rebuying Kim's paintings—not honestly earned money, but not technically illegal.

Soon after the Kim Lord case had been solved, Ray had gone back to North Carolina for a couple of months to maintain his job there and take care of his nephew. During that time, he and Ynez broke up. He told her he didn't have romantic feelings for her anymore. She told him that he was dangerously obsessed with his brother. He'd been planning a trip to London to retrace Calvin's steps.

Ray related all this information in the same cordial tone that he'd discussed Calvin's potential killer, but his voice strained on the word *obsessed.*

"She was right," he admitted. "Because when the opportunity arose to orbit Nelson and the Westing again, I leaped at it. I'm closer than ever. This video is one clue. And you walking on foot to the gallery that day made me realize something else about my brother. He could have easily walked from the Westing to Venice Beach and bought that snow globe for Nathaniel. But that is just speculation. I can't prove he ever went to the Westing at all. So I started digging into *Genevieve* again. The name that Calvin had scrawled on a piece of paper. A person? The name of something? And who or what is now funneling Nelson's gallery the money to survive?"

"You could have told me about Nelson and Calvin," I said.

"I was about to, on the drive to LAAC," Ray said evasively. "But then I thought it might distract you from your own work."

"You were right," I said. "I am distracted. Does Nelson know who you are?"

"That's unclear," he admitted. "Janis never gave him my last name."

"But you think it might be dangerous for me to go to his house," I said.

"I wouldn't advise it," said Ray.

Yet even as he spoke, I knew I would go.

"Okay," he sighed. "Give me a definite time that you're leaving the party, and I'll park down the street and meet you."

"Nine," I said.

There was a short hesitation. "I'll be there," he promised.

"You sure?" I said.

"I'm flying home on a red-eye," he said. "Tonight. My boss—my real boss, not Janis—nixed my request for an extension today. I'm out of time for now. I'll see you later, though."

Maybe he was telling the truth about his boss, but after everything he'd confessed that night, Ray's departure seemed like yet another secret that he had been keeping from me. It was getting late, and I didn't want to dwell on it, though. I sped through our good-bye. I drove to the Palisades. My beat-up station wagon climbed the curving, hilly, gate-lined streets that led to Nelson's house, and I tried to picture myself exiting my car's stale, safe air and donning my department-store bathing suit to swim in a pool at a home that had cost more than my father and mother had made in their whole lives combined, all while on the alert for the man who might be involved in Ray's brother's death.

I topped a rise and saw a number flash, indicating Nelson's address, and the silver intercom box at the gate. The car glided past it all, and I pulled to a stop by a sycamore tree and stared at its patchy peeling bark, silhouetted before the tumble of hills, the sprawling city and sea beyond. My breath began to quicken.

It was a beautiful name, *sycamore*. This city was full of beautiful names. Pacific Palisades. Mar Vista. I remember how La Cienega had run through me like a voltage whenever I'd said it aloud, my tongue sparking on the consonants and vowels. I thought *cienega* must mean something grand and otherworldly like "castle" or "star." I found out that it translates from Spanish as "swamp," and that was even more wonderful, in a way, envisioning a wet, murky, secretive place in this arid basin.

I knew I couldn't save anyone. Brenae's death could not be undone. But

I could keep searching for the truth. I filled three pages of my notebook with my impressions of the day. Then I rolled down my windows, heard helicopters in the distance, and tasted the west wind. Clear, sweet. I rolled the window up again.

19

EVEN THE WATER IN NELSON de Wilde's curving pool felt enhanced by wealth: silky, prickly, and a little more buoyant. "It's salt water," Zania said when I asked. Then she dived under in her lovely, superbly impractical maroon velvet suit and swam for the other end, emerging by the tiled wall.

Nelson's house was a glassy, wood-paneled modernist shoebox with a second-floor expansion. The pool looked crammed into the lot, undersized, a pool-ette, but every feature—the intricate tile, the shape, even the ceramic ladders—looked expensive. Where had the money for this extravagance come from?

Pearson was inside, changing clothes. It appeared to be a lengthy process for him. Erik appeared in his swim trunks, bare-chested, staggering, cheeks blotchy. He was holding a large bottle of bourbon by the neck, the brown liquid sloshing. "Your dad has such a killer wine cellar," he told Zania. "It's earthquake central here, and he's got a wine cellar. That's values."

Zania looked at him blankly.

"I love your dad," he said. "When's he coming?"

"Sometime after ten," she said. "He's got an opening to go to."

Erik swayed from foot to foot, contemplating the pool. "He thinks I'm full of shit, and I respect that," he said. "I'm not the artist. I'm the craftsman."

"You're more than that," Zania said with a note of passion in her voice. "We all are."

"Where's Layla?" he asked. "She keeps disappearing on me."

"Kitchen," said Zania. "She's ordering food."

Erik rubbed his face with his arm and took a swig.

"She's in the kitchen," repeated Zania.

"You're here to celebrate, aren't you?" Erik slurred at me. "This isn't going to be much of a fucking party if no one is celebrating."

Layla called Erik's name. "Come help me order."

Erik stumbled across the patio, toward the back door. Zania watched him retreat with her nose scrunched. She appeared to have forgotten about me. I thought of her interview with Ray, how she had expressed both resentment and admiration of Brenae, but also exonerated Erik. *It's a metaphor.* To her, the man in the video was a symbol alone. I wondered why Zania made excuses for Erik, when she was so quick to judge the system that made him.

"How long have you lived in L.A.?" I asked.

"Seven years," said Zania.

"Do you like it?"

She made a face. "Not really. I didn't want to leave London, but I didn't want to stay with my mum there, either."

The crew's trip to London had changed everything for them, especially Layla and Brenae.

"London," I said dreamily. "Do you ever go back?"

Zania scooped the water with one hand and poured it into the pool. "Last spring," she said. "It's changed. I grew up in a big old broken-down flat that would cost a fortune now. The crew, we stopped in Shoreditch. It's packed with pretentious people. And their designer dogs." A faint British accent cropped up as she talked about the past. I hadn't heard it before.

"Must have been fun, though, traveling together."

She snorted and looked off to the kitchen, where Layla and Erik were. Then she plunged underwater and rose out again, her hair slicked to a dark rope. Clearly not a conversation she wanted to continue. I tried another tack.

"I saw somewhere that your father used to own a club there."

"Local bartender makes good," she said with pride. "His place was all the rage in the nineties."

"I love the nineties art scene there," I gushed. "I'm crazy about its stories. I was reading that Ditchfest's ten-year anniversary is coming up. Did you go?"

"I helped out at the kissing booth." She seemed pleased by the question.

"You must have met some people who are really famous now."

"Yeah." She dropped a few names and shrugged. "Should have saved up my allowance and bought their artwork then."

"What about that guy who organized it? James Compton? He seemed like a trip."

She bobbed in the water. "He was all right. He wore white suits and talked posh, like he was better than everyone, but he made things happen."

"It's a shame he died. I never heard of anyone overdosing on ether before."

"Well, James did," she said shortly.

Something sensitive there. I decided to leave off my prying, and just shook my head.

"Idiotic way to go, if you ask me," she added.

"Yeah, pretty stupid," I echoed, and waited.

"Not that I knew the truth at the time," Zania said. "My parents told me he had a heart attack, and I believed them."

She swam a few strokes, then stood at the edge of the pool, dripping, as Layla's and Erik's voices rose inside. We couldn't hear what they were saying, but Zania listened intently nonetheless, tilting her head and swiping over her ears with her palms so her wet hair fell back and away. She looked troubled, then the slightest bit satisfied.

Abruptly the voices stopped, and Zania's face turned blank again. She gazed at me, as if astonished to see me there.

"Do you think your dad's excited about Hal's show?" I said.

"He needs to make money on it," she said. "But no one makes money on Hal's shows." Seeing my inquisitive look, she added, "Hal won't sell his work. He never sells anything. Dad keeps trying, but Hal refuses."

Mentally I calibrated what this meant for Nelson's business. A month-long show for no profit? Why would he do it to himself?

"What happens to the art?" I said instead.

"Depends. This time, Hal wants viewers to take shoes home with them. He wants us to rip them out in the last week until the cathedral falls apart. He's going to announce it at the opening. The whole thing will collapse while it's on view. Everything we made. My dad gets nothing from this but press." She sounded proud. Then she shivered. "I need to jump back in or get dressed. I hate this pool. He keeps it too hot." Then she shouted to Layla and Erik, "How long till the food?"

"Half an hour!" Layla said, her voice muffled.

As I digested the new information about Nelson's finances and his patronage of Hal, a large male figure in a black rash guard and navy board shorts appeared, strolling under the pool lights. "That means an hour, then," Pearson said, and sat on a lounge chair. His body-hugging shirt reminded me of his considerable size. He could beat any of us to a pulp.

"You're swimming?" Zania said. She sounded alarmed.

"Maybe. I like to warm up first," said Pearson.

"The water is warmer than the air," she said, and jumped back in, sending a spray of water in my face. I edged back to the far wall, away from her.

Pearson looked over to me, his eyes widening as if he had just noticed me for the first time. "You look different with wet hair," he observed.

"She looks less mysterious," said Layla, appearing behind him. Her voice was welcoming, but she didn't smile. "How long have you lived in L.A., Mary?"

"Four years," I said truthfully.

"Four years and still temping?" She made a face. "I'm so sorry."

Layla was wearing a white bathing suit with white cutoffs, her pale, freckled chest and arms exposed. She came to the edge of the pool, sat down, and lowered her legs in the water, sinking them up to her knees.

"I'm trying to change careers," I said.

"From what to what?" Layla said.

"I was in retail," I said. "Eventually I'd like to work at an auction house, but I want to understand how the art market works." I swam a few strokes, hoping to end the conversation. When I raised my head again, Layla was still watching me. Pearson had switched to a straight-backed chair. His calves were thick and muscled. He seemed in no rush to enter the water.

"Take it from a collector's daughter," Layla said after a moment, "the art market doesn't work. It's the most dysfunctional economy on the planet. There's no rhyme or reason to why one painting makes a thousand and another ten million. People do make money, though, gobs of it."

"That would be the very definition of a functioning economy," said Pearson.

"You know what I mean," Layla said.

Zania dived to the pool bottom again. I could feel the vibrations of her body underwater. No sounds came from the house. Where was Erik? When were the other partygoers coming?

"Art-making is not an economically viable career," said Pearson. "But the art market is booming. People like our wonderful host can afford hilltop pools on what they earn extorting people."

"Nelson supports artists," Layla retorted. "Name someone who has done more than he has."

"Incoming!" Erik sprinted onto the deck and jumped in over Layla's head, soaking her. After a moment, she shrieked and leaped after him. The center of the pool shimmered and tossed, Erik careening about with a lunging, desperate joy, as if he were trying to splash away his drunken dread. Layla laughed, but covered her mouth like she was frightened. I retreated to the edge.

"You should come in," I said to Pearson.

"I dislike pools," he said agreeably. "Prefer oceans."

"Where do you swim?"

"Anywhere in the Atlantic," he said, then shifted in his chair. "There I go again, whining about the West Coast. I'm the worst kind of transplant."

I asked who else was coming that night.

"A lot of LAAC people," Pearson said. "Maybe a couple of other gallerists. Maybe even Janis Rocque. The grande dame herself. What do you bet she shows up rocking a navy pantsuit?"

I swallowed my irritation.

"Wow, Janis Rocque," I said. "Do you go to parties like this a lot?"

He laughed. "You're too sweet for this business. Look at them." He gestured at Zania and Layla now both tackling Erik, snickering, dragging him under. "You want to be like them?"

I WAITED UNTIL BOTH DOWNSTAIRS bathrooms were occupied with people changing from their swimsuits to find Zania and get directions to the bathroom upstairs. "There's only one hall, three rooms. Bathroom's the first left. Can't miss it," she told me, digging her small fingers through the paper sacks of takeout.

In fact, the swimming had made me ravenous. I wanted to eat, but instead I fled the room and slipped up the smooth wood steps to the second floor.

I wasn't going to be stupid and reckless tonight. I knew I shouldn't try to help Ray. But Zania's comments about her father and his past had made me curious. He had known James Compton well. He wasn't coming home until later. As long as I didn't spot a surveillance camera, I might wander into the wrong room, momentarily confused, or maybe a little nosy about a famous guy's digs, on my way back downstairs. I would stick to my timeline, and my timeline would keep me safe.

The bathroom smelled faintly of sage. I turned on the light and fan and closed the door, to signify occupancy, and tucked my dry clothes in the linen closet. Anyone coming upstairs would assume I was inside, changing. Then I tiptoed down the hall, entering a cloud of acrid maleness and dust, the scent of a bachelor's house. There were two other doors. At the end of the corridor, one was ajar enough to allow me to spot the edge of a bed.

I peered in at the bedroom, sweeping the ceilings and corners first. No cameras. The decor looked like it had been designed by the same eye as Nelson's gallery office—it had a geometric black-and-white theme, understated but masculine, tasteful enough but yielding no clues to the owner's true personality. A light fur of dust coated two photos, one of Nelson holding baby Zania, and another of overlapping shadows on a rocky beach, a taller and smaller figure. Father and daughter.

I scanned the ceiling corners again, then stepped in and slid open the door of the closet, cringing at the whooshing noise. The scent of dry cleaning gusted from a neat row of suit jackets, white and pastel shirts, ties dangling from a special hanger. The man had his wardrobe hyperorganized. Or maybe he had a house cleaner who liked taking garments to the cleaners and hated dusting. At any rate, the lack of clutter intrigued me. Everyone has a bit of junk they overlook or stash away, but this closet held only essentials, each one in its place. I was about to peek behind the suits when there was a noise in the hall.

I froze, hand extended, breathing the chemical odor of Nelson's clean clothes.

What would I say if someone came in?

I waited. Each goose bump on my still-damp body multiplied by dozens, and my nose began to itch. I wondered if my feet would leave footprints in the plush rug. *I was just looking for an extra towel,* I mouthed. It sounded weak to me, especially when I imagined uttering it to Layla's sly, glittering gaze. Better to hide. I counted to sixty. The noise did not repeat. Turning, feeling every inch of my exposed spine, I reached my hand into the back of the closet (blank wall), shut the door again, checked under the bed (more dust bunnies), then peered into the hall. It was empty.

Nothing about Nelson's bedroom suggested secrets, just the life of a meticulous bachelor who didn't have a very good house cleaner. There was one more door on the hall besides the bathroom, and I paused there, wondering if I should risk it. How long had I been gone?

A doorbell rang downstairs. "More delivery," shouted Zania.

I tested the knob. Unlocked. The door opened soundlessly. I stood on the threshold, stunned.

Glass cases lined every wall but the far one, each lit inside, each holding objects. In the closest case was a red guitar, propped on a stand, and a punk leather suit zipped up over a mannequin. A handwritten note from a rock star cheerily thanked Nelson for repping him. In the next case, a crumpled metal sculpture and a stained pillow also came with thank-you notes. In the next, a chunk of wall, splashed with bright graffiti, perched next to a clock made out of some pastel foreign currency. More notes, presumably from other famous artists.

It looked like one of those restaurants where the owner hangs up hundreds of photos of himself shaking the hands of celebrities. A trophy room.

No, that wasn't quite it.

The lighting was too dim. The vitrines both illuminated and shrouded. More like a place of worship. A shrine.

And there were cameras here. Two. Aimed from the ceiling at the cases. I looked around for Kim Lord. A portrait, a signature. Nelson would have something of hers.

As I stood, unmoving, I felt Brenae's eyes across the room before I saw them. There she was, in a framed print, staring. It was a video still from

Packing, the cereal-eating scene, the gun in Brenae's hand, raised just below her parted mouth, its silver tip dripping white milk. Brenae's eyes were half shut, as if she had just looked up from her private hunger to see the viewer watching her. The image was so sexual and intimate that it made a wave of heat spread through me. At the bottom, a white space had a block of type on it, and a quick handwritten scrawl below, but I couldn't read either from across the room.

I don't know how long I waited, staring at the print, before I remembered where I was. It might have been mere seconds, but it felt like ages, the act of seeing Brenae here, mounted in Nelson's collection. Of course the two of them would have crossed paths, and Brenae would have been just the type of rising star to interest him. But nowhere, in anything I'd read or heard since her death, had I learned that she had ever signed with his gallery.

I calmed myself by observing the rest of the room. The desk had no papers on it. The computer was off. The bookshelves held a predictable arrangement of monographs on major artists like Kandinsky, Matta, O'Keeffe. There appeared to be a number of books on antiquities as well: cuneiform tablets, Babylonian sculpture, cities from the Old Testament.

If I stayed away from the cases, I could remain off camera. I had a clear line to the trash can. It had a mess of papers in it.

I hesitated. I was running out of time.

I wrapped my towel around my head, obscuring my face and shoulders, and slunk to the wire receptacle, sifting silently through it. British chocolate bar wrappers. A W-9 form. A crumpled, printed page from the web, the URL etched on the top margin. It was a petition for a police order of protection against stalking and/or harassment. *I believe I am a victim of* and then there were checkboxes for *stalking* and *harassment*. Some of it had been filled in, but a dark hand had slashed all over the words, making the letters impossible to read.

I felt Brenae's gaze on me again. I was too close now not to look. I stepped over to her photo, a glossy print. Underneath was a typeset list of student names, including Brenae's, for a semester show at LAAC. It was a gallery guide, Brenae's artwork chosen for the honor of visually representing all the rest. Over the names, she had scribbled a message: *Thank you for coming! Can't wait to meet.*

Heart slamming, I shoved the papers back in the trash and retreated, my head still encased in terrycloth, only the eyes showing. I twisted the knob, opened the door a crack. The hall was still empty. Thank God. I reorganized my towel situation and crept toward the stairs. The carpet was so soft it tickled. I had almost reached the steps when the bathroom door opened and Pearson walked out. He was dressed in a T-shirt and cargo shorts again. The chlorine had roughened his pale cheeks, and his size once again struck me. His arms were like cudgels.

"Oops," he said, staring at me.

"Oops," I repeated hoarsely.

"Were you waiting to change?"

"Uh, yeah," I said. "But I can go downstairs."

"No, please," he said. "I'm all done."

I took a step back to let him out.

"It was nice of you to come," he said, drawing nearer. "Are you glad you did?"

"Yes," I said faintly.

His wide palms grazed my bare shoulders, then pulled me toward him. The kiss happened before I registered it, his lips parting mine, his tongue in my mouth. It wasn't a bad kiss, and it wasn't what I wanted, but I let it go on for a moment, weighing my options, before I pushed him back.

"Sorry," he said, still holding my shoulders. "Couldn't resist."

"Me, neither," I said, smiling a little, playing the part. I pushed him again, and this time he released me. "But I'm starving. Let me change, okay?"

I HID IN THE SAGE-SCENTED bathroom, hunched over my knees on the closed toilet seat, long enough to slow my breathing. The bathroom sink was not wet. Pearson had not been carrying his swimsuit. If he had come upstairs to pee, he had not washed his hands. This was not unheard of for a dude, but Pearson was about to eat. Wouldn't he wash his hands if he were about to eat? And yet why would he follow me up here and hide in the bathroom? To ambush me and kiss me?

I had to go back downstairs and face them. I dropped the damp towel on the floor and peeled off my swimsuit, my naked body flashing in the mirror. I kept my head down, avoiding my reflection, as I tugged on dry clothes over my sticky damp skin. I knew my eyes were red-rimmed from the pool water, my hair lank and wet. My makeup had washed off and I had nothing to reapply, my crow's feet visible. Pearson had noticed them, too. Pearson was noticing a lot about me.

I didn't want to pursue that thought further, so as I tried to finger-comb out my tangles, my mind jumped to the petition for protection against stalking and harassment. Who was it for, Zania or Nelson? Or was it against Nelson? Either way, the last five minutes, starting with Brenae's picture and ending with Pearson's kiss, made my spine crawl. I didn't need to see anything more. I needed to leave.

AS I SLIPPED BAREFOOT DOWN the shiny wood stairs, Layla, Zania, and Erik were munching from a chaos of white containers and arguing about something in low, intense tones. It was dark out, and the pool shimmered beyond, looking bluer and deeper than ever.

Layla set down her fork as I appeared. "Want some takeout, Mary?" she said to me with controlled warmth.

"Thank you." I put a couple of wings on my plate. "I have to go soon, though."

The women watched me silently. Erik's drunkenness had deepened to a leaden focus on his food. He kept trying to pin a red slice of sashimi with his chopsticks. "Get over here," he muttered to it.

"Where's Pearson?" I said.

"He went for more wine. Or to smoke his ciggies." Zania made a face. "He likes to pretend we don't know."

"He smokes in the wine cellar?"

"There's a door out to the yard," said Erik. The sashimi slipped from his chopstick, and he slammed the table with his fist. "I can't do this," he muttered.

"Erik," said Layla. "Calm down."

"Stay," Zania said to me. "We ordered too much. Besides, if you're looking for a real job in L.A., there will be tons of networking tonight."

"Great." I sat and tried to chew through the chicken, but it tasted too salty, too wet. I had twenty-five minutes left before I was supposed to meet Ray. I listened to Layla talk about her portraits of nail salon workers and how she was eye-dropping chemicals the salons used on the photos, melting holes. "The problem is, I can't stop the holes once I start them. They keep spreading." Beside her, Erik ate savagely. None of the three would look at one another. It all seemed like a stage set. Unreal. Fixed for an audience. My T-shirt clung to my damp skin and I tugged it loose, struggling to keep even breaths.

Erik's phone buzzed and he looked at it.

"Hal," he said. "I'm answering it." He stumbled up and pressed a button, holding it to his ear. "Here," he said, walking out of the room, out of earshot.

Layla and Zania watched after him. After a few minutes, he came back and slumped down, hanging his head.

"What did he want?" Layla asked.

Erik's curls fell in his face and his white teeth flashed. "He said he hopes we're having fun. He says I shouldn't worry. The board can't prove anything. It's all going to blow over. Because no one"—his open palm slammed the table—"did"—*slam*—"anything"—*slam*—"wrong." He looked at Layla. "I can't do this. I can't let him fall on his sword for me and my career."

Layla gaped at him as if unsure she'd heard him right. "You think they'll spare you?" she said distantly. "That you'll have a career?"

The phone slid from Erik's hand onto the table. "I can't do this," he repeated.

"Can you excuse us three for a minute?" Zania was talking to me, her eyes hard points.

I checked the clock. It was 8:47. "I'm going for a cigarette," I mumbled, then grabbed my purse and scooted down the steps to the wine cellar.

Behind me, I heard Zania say, "Everyone's going to be here in an hour. You need to get it together, or you're going to embarrass my dad."

The staircase was narrow and led down a single flight to a dim room lined with shelves and bottles. Red clips held the bottles in. A nod to earthquake security, I supposed, but they looked like claws. A wall of claws. Each set gripped a cylinder of dark liquid.

Most L.A. homes I knew did not have basements, and the dense, close atmosphere felt foreign, oppressive. The air tasted gritty, like it had been carved out of a packed, ancient mud. The light shining behind me ended in lakes of shadow. The room had two doors. In the dimness their outlines blurred. Neither appeared to lead outside. Instead they seemed like entrances to somewhere deeper.

Upstairs, a chair scraped across the floor, and there was an explosion of voices. Then I heard footsteps. The door to the upstairs shut, casting the wine cellar into darkness. I couldn't see my own hand in front of me.

I hadn't turned on the cellar light. The switch must have been at the top of the stairs. I could climb back up the steps and flip it on, but the voices above had gone silent. As if they were waiting. The darkness pounded around me. I wanted away from this house. I walked forward and felt for the doors, my fingers touching cool glass oblongs, then the rough gloss of varnished wood. Voices erupted again.

My fingers traveled down the wood, knocked something metal. I almost cried out when I realized it was a doorknob. I groped for a grip, twisted it. It did not give. Locked. What was it hiding?

Upstairs, they were talking loudly. Arguing. Footsteps back and forth. A bottle touched my cheek as I felt around for the other door. I shrank back, losing my bearings in the darkness. The next step was a stumble into the wall of hooks and glass, and then I found the other flat opening.

This knob turned. I pushed the door and stumbled through.

The corridor beyond stretched for ten feet, ending with a wall and another threshold leading off it. Evening light purpled the air. I strode down it, trying not to make a sound, palm flat on the smooth cement. A shadow on the far wall twitched. I froze. It wavered again, then I heard a groaning sigh. I crept forward and peered around the edge of the turn. It was a hatch to the night outside, filled with faint cigarette smoke and Pearson, his broad back toward me.

I braced my shoulders and stalked toward him.

"I heard you were smoking," I said calmly before I emerged.

Pearson tilted his head at me and blew out a puff. "I am," he said, sounding surprised. "Are they getting anxious for wine?"

I shrugged. "I'm anxious for a smoke," I said.

"No doubt," he said, and tilted his pack at me.

"But the rest of them are definitely anxious for wine," I said, taking one.

Pearson whipped something from his pocket. I flinched.

"Jesus," he said. "It's just a lighter."

He held the flame for me. My hands shook, but finally I pulled in a long tug, suppressing a cough.

"I like the evening here," Pearson said, leaning back, taking another puff. "I try to get outside to see it. So I can forget the parts of L.A. that I don't like."

"I like both," I said. "The evening and L.A." The nicotine hit my adrenaline panic, swirled in my skull. My mind swam. "You think Hal's show will go over well?" I asked.

"Well enough," said Pearson. "It's his best work in a while."

"Because of you."

"Because of Hal."

Ask him, I thought. I was almost free now. The house had not held me.

"You sound like you would do anything for him," I said.

"Do I?" said Pearson, his voice going hollow.

I waited. The little lawn before us had darkened to silk, and I couldn't quite see Pearson's face, just the red glow of his embers.

"You talking about Brenae?" he said.

"Actually, yes." I ignored the spike of fear down my spine. "You're the one who wiped the files from her laptop."

He didn't move.

"You never watched them," I said. "You just did what Hal asked. No questions. You knew she was dead, and you were shredding her work."

"Do you always go by Mary?" Pearson said. "Your license says Maggie."

He loomed beside me, rigid as stone. The air from the wine cellar felt cold on my spine.

"I never liked Maggie," I said. "Why were you looking at my license?"

"I was curious," said Pearson. "The private investigator. The new gallerina. All on the same day. All the questions your guy asked me." He stamped out his cigarette. "You both find what you need?"

His face drew closer to mine, his brows low, his lips pressed. This time he wasn't about to kiss me.

I took another tug on my smoke and blew it out, hoping Pearson would step back. He didn't. "Not enough," I said. "I want to hear your version. All of it."

I met his livid gaze and didn't wince.

"Erik's not a killer," said Pearson. "Neither is Hal. Maybe he warned Erik about that video. Maybe Erik said something to Brenae that hurt her deep. But she took her own life, and that is a terrible, cowardly choice. For anyone. They didn't pull the trigger. She did." A frowning grin broke his face. "LAAC gave Brenae a full ride, and she squandered it. I got the whole bill. Sixty thousand dollars in loans. I'm still paying them off, and Hal's the only reason I can, and still be making art for a living. So am I going to protect him and the school, and not some tragic narcissistic bitch? Yes. Did I know what was on the videos? No. I thought they were just some protest message. Brenae whining about the system that obviously doted on her. I never guessed it was that." He looked away, his neck pulsing. "I could bash Erik's face in for what he did."

I waited.

"Anything else?" said Pearson. He folded his arms.

"Do the others know?"

"About you?" he said. "I think Layla suspects something. She's the one who wanted to invite you tonight."

Pearson swung away and lunged through the doorway, into the inky dark of the cellar. "You ask me again, I'll deny everything. You quote me, I'll sue you."

20

WHEN I CRUISED FROM NELSON'S driveway at precisely 9:00 p.m., Ray appeared in his sedan and motioned me to keep driving, so I took a number of twisty turns until I reached the Pacific Coast Highway. I skimmed south along the edge of the continent, watching the steel-gray ocean stretch westward on my right. Ordinarily, I would have been relieved to see the sea, but I felt taut and sick. The surface looked impenetrable and unimaginably powerful, barely suppressing a violence that could sweep over us all.

When I hit a standstill, my phone rang and Ray told me to pull into the next beach parking lot. His car slid in beside mine, facing the water, and we both got out and leaned on the hood of his sedan, arms crossed.

"How much time do we have?" I said.

Ray checked his watch. "About twenty minutes."

Pulse racing, I told him about the party, the trophy room upstairs, Brenae's photo and message, the stalking petition, leaving through the wine cellar, and Pearson's confession. I left out the kiss. As usual, Ray didn't interrupt me once, and I wondered what his mind was fastening on.

"So there it is," I concluded. "Hal asked Pearson to do it. I don't know if he'd ever go on the record, though."

"Might not matter," said Ray. He was looking far out to sea, his eyes on a shipping vessel close to the horizon. "At least for Janis."

"What's her update?"

"There's a special meeting of the LAAC board of trustees tomorrow with Hal. Closed session," said Ray.

"He'll resign in exchange for them keeping it quiet," I predicted. "Erik will be expelled." I paused, shifting my feet on the sandy pavement. "Except I'm still not letting this go, Ray. I'm not going to let her be buried twice."

"Good," he said in an approving tone.

"I'm going to have to quit the Rocque."

"Give it a week or two," he advised. "Janis might change her mind and want to help you."

Ray's body was tense beside mine. The streetlight sharpened the lines of his face, reminding me of the night in Wonder Valley.

"What about you?" I said. "What do you think about what I saw in Nelson's office?"

"I think you shouldn't have gone in there," he said.

"I wouldn't have if I hadn't seen Brenae on the wall." I shuddered at the memory of the dim chamber and Brenae with her sexy, parted lips, her hopeful message. "And then the stalking petition. That was strange."

"Best not to dwell on it," he said. "Whatever it is, it's not your fight. Likely Nelson led Brenae along and then dumped her like everyone else when she started to crack up."

"What about her footage of Nelson and your brother?"

"What about it? Even if she knew who my brother was, she wouldn't have connected his death with Nelson." He sounded sure. "And even if she did, she wasn't fool enough to pursue it. Brenae's fight was with Hal. She thought he was blind, and she was going to make him see. *Watch me.* Remember?"

"How could I forget?"

Brenae hadn't asked to hang in that dim shrine, hidden away, an artifact. She'd asked the world to see her.

"You're shaking." As if by instinct, Ray put an arm around my shoulders.

His touch jolted me. I wanted to lean into it. I wanted him to pull us tight together. "I'm mad," I admitted. "I'm also glad you're here." I raised my face to his, meeting his eyes. A moment passed, during which neither of us moved, and I didn't breathe.

Ray sighed regretfully and pulled away. "I wouldn't have missed you," he said, and stood up, brushing his arms as if to remove the sensation of my skin against his. He took a step away from me, spun back. "How early do you get to LAX, when you fly?"

"At least an hour. More since 9/11," I said, also springing up. I refused to ask him now if he was returning to L.A. I took out my keys. "You should go." *I couldn't have wished for a more banal parting,* I added internally. "Have a safe trip."

Ray held out a hand to me and then let it drop, his expression cloudy. There was something else he needed to tell, or was hiding. I waited. He owed me the whole truth, and as the quiet dragged on and he didn't leave, I hoped he might stay. But then a parking cop came up and told us we had to pay or move on, and the chance was lost. While the cop watched, we gave each other a businesslike hug good-bye and got in our separate cars and drove off. I told myself not to, but I looked back for Ray. The night had sealed his face away, and all I saw were two bright headlights falling behind me as the traffic thickened and the exits came.

21

THE NEXT MORNING, I IGNORED my phone's silence and plunged into Rocque business, checking proofs, copyediting, attending a planning meeting. Janis was not there, but our director, Bas Terrant, shared the happy announcement that our curators' efforts to bring a show of new Cuban artists had finally paid off. A familiar buzz filled the room as everyone chimed in with ideas—this was the Rocque at its best—and beyond us, the building seemed to expand with our plans, from the carpentry room to the galleries, to the office tower where we typed and talked. After a while, Bas cleared his throat, flashed a shiny, uncomfortable smile, and got to the bad news. Our latest box office numbers were still high, courtesy of the notoriety of Kim Lord's murder, but not high enough to get the museum out of debt. We might have to face layoffs down the road. This year. A ten percent reduction in staff. No one looked surprised, but many looked frustrated and resistant, including our chief curator, Lynne Feldman. I cornered her afterward and relayed my pleasure at seeing her in Wonder Valley.

"It was quite the weekend," she said, tucking in her chair. "But *Packing* was the highlight."

I asked her to clarify what she'd said that night, about LAAC brushing Brenae under the rug, and what that might do to her legacy.

"I don't know if a twenty-two-year-old has a *legacy*," said Lynne, frowning at my choice of words. "But I'm surprised by Hal's response. When I contacted him about the work I'd heard Brenae had done at school, he said most of it was destroyed by her, and good riddance. He acted like she'd suddenly started making rubbish."

Today was the meeting between Hal and his bosses at LAAC. I wondered how he would talk to them about Brenae now. I bet he would be singing a different tune.

Lynne gathered up her notes from the meeting with her red-painted nails. "Why the interest?"

"Just a fan," I said.

"I've seen too many careers snuffed out too soon," said Lynne. She looked at me soberly, and I knew we were both thinking of Kim Lord and the little office far below us where her body had been struck down. "I stay sane by focusing on the living. And this place." She patted the plain, off-white wall of our conference room. "Well, maybe not this room," she added. "It needs something, doesn't it? It's needed something for years . . ." She trailed off, but her valedictory tone was clear.

"Do you think the Rocque will survive?" I said.

"The more important question is: Will the art survive? And who will continue to shape its meaning?" said Lynne. She clasped her notes to her chest and swept past me, trailing the faint smell of bergamot. "Good to see you back. I can't stand this crackpot place without a few sane people."

YEGINA'S BOYFRIEND, HIRO, CAME BY my office at the end of the day, his clothes rumpled, his eyes caved in by jet lag, and perhaps by tears. I motioned for him to sit down. His appearance worried me. With his broad shoulders and slow smile, Hiro was handsome in a warm, reassuring way. But today he exuded edginess and discontent.

"Don't tell her I was here," he said. "But I just want to understand: Is it me? She would tell you if it was me, wouldn't she?"

"It's not you," I said. "It's the timing. You rushed her."

How could I explain—if Yegina hadn't already—all the ways she'd tried to keep her last marriage alive: therapists, retreats, partial separations, even an open relationship, and that her ex-husband had taken advantage of every one, and her bank account, until exhaustion had finally broken her.

Hiro stood up and began flipping through a catalog of Warhol screen prints on my windowsill. "I thought she would be happy. Now that she's not—I don't know."

"Give her some space. Let her decide what her happiness is."

His hand on the open book, Hiro gazed out my window to the concert hall that was titanium-paneled now, almost finished. The sides gleamed, curving and whitening the sunlight. "What's that movie where the guy decides to wait outside a girl's window for a hundred days and if she doesn't come out to him, he's gone forever?" he said to the view. "And it rains on him and everything, and she doesn't come out. She just watches him suffer. Finally, one night, he goes. I didn't like him leaving. I always thought true love shouldn't have a condition. One hundred days. What kind of love expires in one hundred days?" He paused for a long time, so long that I thought he was done speaking.

"Maybe—"

"Now I don't know," he finished. "Would she believe him if he didn't show his limits? He would have no self-respect."

I knew the movie's name. I remembered the scene where the dark-haired boy gave up and walked alone and heartbroken down the alley, the town's fireworks exploding above him, and later when the girl in the pink coat came to him, solemn with her desire. But the name of the movie didn't matter. What mattered was that my friend was falling for Hiro, and it frightened her. She was afraid she'd mess up again.

"I always liked that he left. He finally let her decide," I said. "On her own."

Hiro looked down at the open catalog, the bright colors of the screen prints, studying them for another lengthy interval.

"You liked that he left?" he said, shutting the book with a thump.

"I liked that she went and found him," I said. "Maybe let yourself be found."

Hiro nodded thoughtfully and turned from the window. "Have fun tonight. She really wants to be with you. She says you're her wisest friend, even though you don't think you are."

"Doubtful," I said, smiling. "But it's nice to be missed."

"Right," Hiro said, slapping my doorjamb. "I'm going to try that."

LET YOURSELF BE FOUND.

In the movie, the young woman goes in search of her admirer. She enters the projection room where he works, where he stands in blue-white light, feeding reels into the machine.

He stares. She has found him, and this answers the question of his love. *Yes.* But for a few seconds, they stare, disbelieving. Then her hands flicker to his shoulders; his arms go around her; he lifts her, spins her, all the way to another room, for a kiss. On the projector behind them, the reel flutters to its end. Its soft whisper stops.

Time stops for love.

And yet. What if she had not come? What would that have done to him, and to her?

Brenae was last seen entering her studio on Tuesday. As far as we knew, she had spent the entirety of Wednesday alone and killed herself before the next day dawned. What had she been waiting for, all that time? For someone to find her? If not Erik, then Layla or Zania, or Janis or Nelson or Hal, someone, anyone who had pretended to be her lover, her friend, her supporter? How long would she sit in that room, her body hollowing, becoming a lack of self, becoming no one?

At the end of the day, I drove home, west into blinding sun, my eyes aching all the way into their sockets. I was seeing Brenae's last full day not as a retreat from her world, but a test of it, hour after hour ticking by, the studio lightening and then darkening, the clatter and voices outside and the stillness and silence within. The replaceability of everything in the room, her art most of all. What was her art worth? What was her life worth?

The gun waited for her choice.

Watch me.

BY THE TIME I TOOK the stairs to my apartment to change for my costume date with Yegina, I thought I had done an excellent job forcing the two cases and Ray from my mind. At least I did in five-minute bursts, and then the series of impressions would return: Erik and Brenae on the mattress; Layla sitting at the edge of the pool, legs submerged to her knees; Brenae and her gun on Nelson's wall; Nelson and Calvin leaving the party; Ray holding the palmier cookie. It was evening and no call from Ray or Alicia or Janis. I didn't know what I'd expected, but not this.

I sat down at my laptop and scanned the local papers' websites. Nothing about LAAC or Hal resigning. It was too soon.

The sublet felt less like my home than ever. There was my heap of books and printouts on Françoise Gilot, and there was my little pile of dishes in the drain—one plate, one cup, one pan, a cluster of silverware. My sheets, my toothbrush, my dresses in the closet. Still, the rooms felt alien. I turned on the radio while I got dressed, listening to the report of the fire consuming the hills to the east of the city, and the sudden promise of rain. I drank a glass of wine. It tasted sour. I stared around at the dining room set, the rocket lamps. Nothing looked out of place, but everything seemed jarred and different. Something had happened to Ray. Or was happening.

Frowning in the mirror, I donned the red wig, a cloak, and bright lipstick. I didn't look like anything or anybody, and I would be going to a neighborhood where almost everyone had a flair for appearances. But I was tired of appearances tonight. I just wanted to be invisible.

My intercom buzzed.

"I'm Raggedy-Gon Jinn," I said downstairs to Yegina's look of wry shock, which was enhanced by her black lips and eyeliner, all black clothes, black gloves. "What are you, a goth?"

"Goth Moth." She gestured to gauzy pale green wings in her back seat.

"Nice," I said. "That's effort."

"So tell me what's happening with Hal Giroux," she said.

"I can't," I said. "But his days might be numbered."

A shadow crossed her face.

"What?" I said. "What's wrong with that?"

"It's about a new museum," she said. "I'm being recruited."

THE TRAFFIC ON THE WAY to the bar was congested enough to review Yegina's story twice, once for hopes and once for worries. We lurched to a stop seven or eight times behind the same white van, and each time I couldn't help thinking that the motion of our car, in this line of cars, echoed my worries tonight, revving and slamming over and over, but never going anywhere.

A few days ago, Yegina had gotten a call from Hal Giroux. He wanted to gauge her interest in applying to be the exhibitions manager for a new downtown museum. A museum bigger and newer than the Rocque, free to all visitors, eclipsing us in every way—programming, architecture, and events. She and Hal talked about the scope of the museum, its funding, potential architects. ("Vera Trudeau is one of the architects on his list. Can you imagine? So dreamy.") Then Yegina asked about the fate of the Rocque under such a development, and Hal was evasive. "Institutions age," he told her. "Some fade. New leadership can't always save them."

"What should I do?" Yegina said. "I can't betray Janis. I never liked Hal. Then again, he built LAAC. Can you imagine the city without it? He raised so many generations of talented students."

I could hear the real reason beneath Yegina's indecision: if she passed up this chance, she might never get such a big break again.

"Wait," I suggested. "Don't say no or yes. Yet."

"Ha. That strategy went over really well with Hiro." Yegina sighed. "We're on hiatus right now. Goth Moth is a free spirit."

"What does that mean?" I said. "Hooking up with other people?"

Yegina answered by careening around a corner, narrowly missing three pedestrians and an entire strip mall.

"I guess not," I said, laughing.

She glanced over, her thick makeup hollowing her eyes. I didn't want to betray Hiro's visit to my office, but the moment demanded something.

"He cares about you so much," I ventured. "He's going to wait for you."

We were on Melrose now, with its glib store names and fetching, two-story buildings lined up as bright as magnets on a refrigerator.

"Have your night out," I added. "That's what you wanted."

22

YEGINA DONNED HER WINGS, AND I helped her tie the slippery sea-green ribbons. Before we even finished securing them, several people had passed on the crowded sidewalk and made appreciative comments. "Go, Luna," said one.

"Fairy freaking godmother," said another, "grant my wish."

"Ready or not, here's Goth Moth," Yegina said, and I took a step back to regard her.

In the twilight, under the shine of street lamps, she looked beautiful, more beautiful than I had ever seen her. The tight black costume and black makeup contrasted sharply with the wings that floated behind her, transparent, ethereal. Her black hair spilled; her high cheekbones angled up with the wings.

"Is it crooked?" she said. "You're frowning."

"It's fantastic," I said, unexpectedly breathless. Yegina's costume wasn't just a disguise; it was an oracle. And it was predicting that Yegina would rise, she'd fly, but she'd stay herself, too. "You look amazing."

You're going to work for a major new museum, I thought. *You're going to marry Hiro. You're going to have kids in a few years, and Hiro will cut back on his career so yours can flourish. You'll become another wonder of this city, the daughter of an immigrant fleeing war, reshaping your America. You might even finally start listening to decent music.*

"Thank you," Yegina said, then added with a kind tone, "You sure you want to wear that cape? You could just go in the wig."

My phone rang. It was Alicia Ruiz.

I held up a hand and turned from my friend. "Hello, Detective," I said cautiously.

"Sorry to bother you," she said. "I was wondering if you'd heard from Ray."

"Not since last night," I said, my mouth going dry. "He was flying home."

"What time did you see him last?"

"Around ten. Is he not in North Carolina?"

"He told his family—and me—that he was taking a midnight red-eye last night. He never showed up."

"Maybe he had to do stand-by?"

"Without his suitcase or wallet? I checked his apartment. I need to reach him. This afternoon, Erik Reidl confessed to his involvement in the death of Brenae Brasil."

"What?"

Yegina saw my face and gave me a questioning look. I touched her arm and took a few steps away, cupping my ear.

"My reaction, too," said Alicia. "Apparently he described the scene pretty accurately. He said Brenae opened the safe where she kept her gun and asked him to take the weapon. Away from her. He refused. Then he panicked and left."

"So he didn't shoot her."

"He claims he 'murdered' her by pressuring her. He's full of himself. Anyway—" She stopped short, as if remembering our roles. "I wanted to get

Ray's interviews with Erik to the LASD to catch any discrepancies. Tell me if you hear from him."

"Wait," I said, sensing Alicia was about to hang up. "Did you contact Janis?"

"She hasn't heard from him, either."

I swallowed. If Ray hadn't contacted me, it meant he was distancing himself. But if he hadn't contacted either of them, it meant something was wrong.

"What did Ray tell you about Nelson de Wilde?" I said.

"Why?" she said after a beat.

"There's another video by Brenae," I said, and told her about my conversation with Ray, and finding *After-Parties*, and the footage of Nelson and Calvin leaving a party together. "Zania de Wilde told me that her father knew James Compton. If Ray has disappeared, is that enough evidence to follow up?"

"You're sure it's Nelson and Calvin in the video."

"Positive."

"I'd like a copy of that video," she said. "As soon as possible. Where are you?"

I told her.

"Wait there. I'll get there as soon as I can," she said.

"That's great," I said. "Thank you."

"You let me know if you hear from Ray, okay?" the detective said. "And just stay put."

She hung up. I wedged my phone into my jeans.

"What's up?" said Yegina.

"Some developments with one of Hal's students. And Ray's missing. Maybe," I said. "Or maybe he's just being Ray."

I told her that Detective Ruiz wanted to pick me up.

"Really?" Yegina sounded disappointed.

"It won't be for a while. Let's have fun now," I urged her. I turned and started walking in the direction of the bar, which was a half-dozen black scalloped awnings down the block, glowing with studded-leather lights. "You got a great parking spot," I said, feeling like part of me had been swept high above, ripped and tossed by a rising storm, while below my normal bantering self carried on with her normal evening. "Next Friday night you wouldn't get within two miles of here."

"What was the bit about James somebody?" said Yegina, following me.

"Some investigating I did about Ray's brother," I said. "It's probably not credible, though."

"You're starting to talk like them," said Yegina. Her wing gently poked my shoulder.

"Not for long," I said.

We threaded through other pedestrians, mostly groups of wealthy older women, and men in jeans and crisply ironed button-downs or tight T-shirts. They all smiled at Yegina and slid their eyes over me.

"Hey—weren't you going to ditch the cloak?" she said. "It looks itchy."

"I need the sackcloth tonight," I said. "I need to stay awake."

THE BAR WAS CALLED CAMDEN, and like many L.A. tribute venues, it was the embodiment of *esque*. The violent, chaotic joy of British punk had been massaged to a design theme here—rather than a dirty grotto with bad lights and cheap beer, Camden flattered its patrons with well-placed luster, each lamp circled in a studded leather shade, mahogany walls wearing discreet bands of red and blue. Black-and-white photos of snarling bands were labeled with cheerful handwritten comments, and the drink menu opened with a silver zipper. Dee started apologizing for the place as soon as we spotted her, her hair deranged to spikes and her eyes inked with sharp corners. She looked slightly more gorgeous than insane. A typical Dee appearance.

"Did you come as a vampire strawberry?" she asked me with dubious delight.

"Something like that," I said.

"Right on," said Dee. "Unsexiest costume in West Hollywood is actually a distinction when you think about it."

"I'm trying not to," Yegina said as she gazed around the decor with a puzzled frown.

"It's bloody offensive, isn't it?" Dee whispered. "Turning Johnny Rotten into a cocktail," she said. "But the drinks. Are. Amazing. Try a Captain Sensible."

"Any updates from Janis about the crisis in Valdivia?" I said.

Dee's face hardened.

"Oh no," I said.

"The crisis in Valdivia has been settled," she told us, her voice icy. "No further investigation by the school. Early retirement for Hal. A golden parachute. A certain student banned from campus but allowed to finish his degree. Apparently, Hal was very persuasive, especially with the collectors he's helped to get bargain prices on the artwork of future stars." She made air quotes with her hands. "'We don't want to take down a giant over one simple error of judgment,'" she said in a mocking tone. "That's what the chair told her. And they were all thrilled about the new museum downtown."

"What a crock," I said.

Yegina was frowning and picking at her gauzy sleeves. She had fallen for Hal's persuasion, too. And his vision. It was hard not to.

"This isn't Janis's scene," said Dee, gesturing around the dim bar. "Or I wouldn't have left her alone tonight. She was going to tuck in and read her biography of Georgia O'Keeffe, but when I left, she was just staring at the blank wall."

There wouldn't be any investigation. No news reports. *Shoe Cathedral* would open, to strong reviews. The school year would unfold, Erik would graduate, Layla would have her open studio, Zania would gripe her way through undergrad life, and in March, a year from the night Brenae shot herself, Hal would announce that it was time for him to step down. The tributes and venerations would start. The great director. Decades of mentorship. Hundreds of protégés expressing their gratitude and praise. And then a second tide of press would rise about the Goetz Museum, lofting Hal once again. Meanwhile, where would Janis be? Finishing her chemo, or getting sicker. Facing another budget shortfall. Listening to Bas propose layoffs and cuts. She had lost. I could not think of what to say.

"How are you holding up?" Yegina slid her arm around Dee, giving her a squeeze.

"I'm all right." Dee blinked. "Getting used to gossiping about radiation and lymph nodes instead of exhibitions and openings."

Her inked eyes began to glisten.

"Listen," Yegina ordered her, "this is your night. Enjoy yourself for all of us." She gestured around the crowded bar, her wing bobbing. "Look at everyone here for you."

Dee gave a stiff nod. "That's what she said. I better get lit now, or she'll be pissed with me." She widened her fake smile and sauntered off to talk to someone else.

"Thank you," I said to Yegina, impressed. "That was the right thing to do."

Yegina nodded and scanned the bar. "Not what you hoped would happen."

"I didn't think he'd be patted on the back and congratulated," I said. "You did?"

Yegina continued to watch the room. She seemed taller and more rooted at once. In the dimness, her black makeup transformed her face to a stark mask. "Hal was their biggest fund-raiser for twenty years," she said to the distance. "LAAC is the house that Hal built. But once he leaves it—" She shrugged and focused on me. "Janis hired you for a reason. She wanted someone to find out Brenae's story. You did. Or you started to. Just because Janis made her move doesn't mean that yours is over."

I pictured Janis in the LAAC parking lot, staring at the main building, the sloping green shaded by eucalyptus trees. *LAAC is by and large a marvelous place. I want it to thrive. Being here today makes me lean away from the public exposé.* Janis believed in institutions. She'd been certain that LAAC would do the right thing.

"Drink?" said Yegina, gesturing to the already crowded bar. "I'll buy one for you."

"How about three," I said bitterly. "I can get them."

"Might take a while, Strawberry." She smiled, eyeing my wig.

"Fine," I said. "Thank you."

As Yegina moved off to order us a Minor Threat and a Voidoid, I searched for a corner to hide in. I dialed Ray, expecting no answer. The phone went to voicemail.

Five minutes passed, and Yegina had made no headway with the bartender. I plunged through the bar's packed other side and thrust my red-wigged head into the bartender's eyesight. Red had a tried-and-true effect that Yegina had overlooked in her pitying dismissal of my outfit. People noticed a color they habitually stopped for. Within moments, I had two martinis myself. Forget the cute cocktails. It wasn't that kind of night. I waved to Yegina to give up and checked my phone again. No calls or texts.

"Thank you, blokes, for coming tonight," said Dee, her accent thicker than usual. "Show's about to start." She'd taken the small stage and was standing in that swaying, long-legged way that rock stars stand, as if they are hanging from their mics. Dee gestured at a pianist and drummer joining her and launched into her first song. It was not punk at all. She had an airy, nocturnal voice that slid from octave to octave, then abruptly darkened and deepened. Dee was the aural manifestation of Goth Moth, part shadow, part winged creature.

I felt a tug on my cloak.

"It's you," I said to Yegina. "You're the music."

She smiled, took the drink, and swayed beside me as Dee sang three songs. I wished fleetingly that Yegina and I were having a night like old times, would go home late to her house with some spicy takeout, gossiping about everyone and everything we'd seen.

Instead, Yegina nodded at someone across the room. It was Bas Terrant, our director, and a fling of Yegina's that had quickly ended in professional friendship. He'd become a big supporter of hers. He would be devastated if she left the Rocque.

"I may have to go outside for just a teeny-tiny bit," she said to me.

"You mean outside with Bas?"

"It's to talk about the new museum," she said. "He knows. He e-mailed me this afternoon to tell me he has some ideas about how I could negotiate for myself and for the Rocque."

At this point, I wondered who in L.A. *wasn't* aware of Hal's "secret" plans.

"You should go," I said, resigned.

"Come with us," said Yegina.

"I need to be here when the detective shows up."

"I'll wait, then." Yegina squeezed my arm and gave me her whole attention. In her look, I saw the specter we were fighting together that night—not Hal's future or Brenae's story, or Hiro hurt and Ray missing—but a simpler, plainer ghost. We were both older now. The last eight months had altered us, and the once-sought consolations of a perfect cocktail and an attractive, mingling crowd no longer suited us. We didn't want a carefree, forgettable evening. We wanted responsibility and change. Yegina was seeing her chance, and she deserved to seize it.

I shoved her. "Go."

She fluttered away, her wings glittering. The room was filling with more people: Dee's crew from the Rocque shuffled in all at once, casting their skeptical, amused looks at the decor. But their faces shone when they looked at Dee. She pranced and crooned, her long legs slamming in sharp boots. She was not an impeccable singer—her voice went flat on every fifth note—but she threw herself into it, her usual stylish charm deepened by grief.

I swayed a little, trying to let the music pull me out of my mounting anxiety. Janis defeated. Ray missing. Yegina leaving the Rocque. Too much for one night.

Several songs later, Dee took an intermission, and I decided to go outside to wait for the detective. As I maneuvered past some woman's squishy front, apologizing, I heard a squeak. "Mary." My head was spinning from the martini and the noise in the bar, and it took me a moment to piece together the red hair, the freckles, the big hips. A curtain-like, pink paisley dress.

"You're here," I shouted to Layla and her astonished gaze. "Why are you here?"

"Why are *you*?" she shouted back.

"I'm friends with—" I shouldn't mention Dee. "One of the bartenders. You?"

"I know the guitar player. From LAAC."

The light in the bar cast Layla's face blue, and deepened the haunted look in her eyes.

"Are you okay?" I said.

She cupped her hand to my ear. "Erik's at the Valdivia police station. He's claiming he murdered Brenae Brasil—remember, the suicide at LAAC last March? It's freaking sick. I couldn't stay, and I can't go home to our apartment."

I opened my eyes wide. "Erik killed someone?"

She gestured at me to follow her to a nook, against a mural where the boy hooligans of The Damned grinned through layers of disintegrating cream pie. The noise lessened.

"He didn't pull the trigger," she said. "It's so complicated. I hate him right now. I hate Hal, too."

She looked genuinely hurt and confused. And vulnerable and pretty, in a way I hadn't appreciated before. Layla's presence was a shock to me, but she seemed untroubled by our encounter, as if it were natural to bump into another person from the art world, and more particularly me, who had so closely witnessed her past few days.

"Don't mind me, gallerina," she said, pushing my arm. "I shouldn't have told you. You barely know me. You should go have a fun night."

"What happened with Brenae Brasil? What did Erik do?" I said.

"He saw her that week. He used to hook up with her sometimes, back in undergrad," she said. "He went to see her because Hal sent him. Hal told Erik that Brenae was threatening to—"

Dee took the stage again, and there was a roar of approval, interrupting our conversation.

The band smashed and strummed, and Layla leaned closer to me to be heard, but I still only caught phrases: "list of demands . . . video projection . . . victimized women . . . if he didn't meet her demands . . . she would do a performance artwork called *Gun-Shot* . . . Hal didn't think she was serious. He thought she was being ridiculous, actually." Dee began singing, and the instruments quieted. Layla kept talking. "Hal knew that Erik and Brenae had been close. He thought Erik could tone her down. So Erik went to her studio, and then two days later she was dead. But he told me all along that he didn't do anything to her. He just left." She closed her eyes and shuddered. "Now he's changed his story. Because suddenly he feels so guilty that she killed herself."

None of this was in the police report. Hal had claimed to be completely blindsided by Brenae's suicide. Not fed a list of demands about women's rights on campus, or else Brenae might shoot herself, as an artwork and a protest. *Watch me.* What else had he erased from her computer?

"You look totally confused," said Layla.

"I am," I said. "I didn't know any of this. I was just excited to see Hal's show come together."

"Me too," said Layla. "Welcome to my screwed-up life."

Dee's song got to the bridge, and the music hit peak volume. Layla and I stood together, facing it all until the song ended.

"Nice hair color, by the way," Layla said dryly.

"It looks better on you."

To my surprise, her eyes glistened. "Come with me," she said. "Pearson, Zania, and I are going to meet at Nelson's place," she said. "We need to hash out what we can do."

"I don't think so," I yelled back. "I'd be barging in."

Layla shook her head. "You could shed new light. I already know what Pearson is going to say. What Zania will say."

I didn't trust any of it. Ray missing. Layla's sudden appearance at the same bar. This invitation.

"I've got to find my friend," I said. "I'm riding home with her."

"Okay," she said, looking disappointed. "I'll be here if you change your mind."

The air in the bar had thickened with breath and shouts, and the farther I got from Dee, the better she sounded, all the flaws in her voice erased by the volume of the audience. Outside, streetlights soaked the avenue, and the sidewalks filled with glittering people. I looked up and down for the detective but didn't see her.

Yegina wouldn't go far. I texted her. *Where r u?*

Waiting for drinks at Sink. Come!

I looked around for Sink. I walked up and down the street, staring into windows, accidentally body-checking a young woman in a group heading in the other direction.

"Ouch," she said, treading on my foot with a very high heel. Pain shot up my ankle. I yelped and staggered sideways, leaning into a cool wall for balance. She didn't turn around.

Layla wasn't here by accident. Her offer wasn't spontaneous. It was a lure or, at the very least, a dare. For me. *Come with me.* Why? Because I knew something. Because I knew what Ray knew.

Whoever had beaten Ray's brother had not quite killed him, but left him to die. Calvin's killer was not a murderer by nature. He couldn't bring himself over the brink of it. But he was a planner. He'd left the Boyle Heights hotel room in the clothes of his victim. He'd left no trace. And if pushed again, he would plan again, attack again, and leave no trace. This time with help.

The night air had a heaviness I rarely felt in Los Angeles. A storm was coming. I breathed it in, still hesitating. Go on to Yegina, or stay here and wait outside for my ride. I called the detective and got her voicemail. Called again. Voicemail again. I stared down the avenue of headlights, thinking of all the mountains ringing this city that I couldn't see. Then I thought of Ray and the car ride with the fado music, the heartbreak inside it, heartbreak that went beyond logic or explanation, which was Ray's grief over his brother. You couldn't just let that kind of heartbreak go. It had to consume you first, with rage or vengeance or self-destruction. Ray hadn't gotten on a plane last night. Whichever acts he had done in the past twenty-four hours, he had known they would be mistakes. Now I had to make my own. I had a hunch about where Ray was, running out of time. I left Alicia a long message, limped back into Camden, and wove through the crowd. Layla was leaning against a wall with two martinis in her hand, her head tipped back, her long lashes shuttered. She looked like she was preparing for a séance.

"Hey," I said.

She opened her eyes, gave a sharp, humorless laugh. "Want a drink?"

I stared at the clear liquid in the glass. The sunken green oblong of the olive. I saw Nelson's hand slipping into Layla's shirt, holding her breast.

Be yourself, Ray said. Play the part. Play impulsive, innocent Maggie.

"Want to share my cab home?" I said, taking the martini. "They can drop me off first and you can keep going to the Palisades. I can't handle this place for much longer."

"Good call," she said. "One last drink. Then we'll go."

THE EFFORT OF SPEECH WAS too much. Everything was too much for my body: the night air, the sidewalk. My legs. My legs couldn't recall how to walk. They fumbled and jellied, and I stumbled against Layla. She held me up by looping my arm over her shoulder and we lurched along. "You don't drink much, do you?" she said through clenched teeth.

"Only. Had. One," I said. In truth, I had tasted two sips of her martini because she was watching me, and then sloshed the rest into a napkin holder when she turned to the stage to clap for Dee. Two sips. She must have put enough sedative in the drink to knock me out.

"I valeted at the French restaurant down the street because they're always faster," she says. "It's just one more block."

"Cab," I said.

"I forgot. I drove."

My phone started buzzing in my jeans pocket.

"Friend," I said.

Layla muscled a hand into my pocket and I felt the buzzing stop. "You can call her when we're in the car," she said, hauling me faster.

"My friend," I said again. If I could somehow alarm Yegina. If I could somehow warn her.

"I can't take you back there," Layla said. "You can't even stand up. You can call her from the car, and she can come get you."

I balked and we almost tumbled to the ground. The cars passing seemed to brighten their headlights, blinding me.

Layla tightened her hold. "Mary. People are staring," she hissed in my ear. "Let me get you somewhere safe."

When we reached the restaurant, she snapped open her purse and handed the man a tag and a twenty. The attendant grabbed a set of keys and motioned for another valet. "Lucky you have a good pal," he said to me.

"She's just a total lightweight," said Layla.

I am not a lightweight, I thought through the fog. I'd drunk a couple sips to convince her I was a fool. Then we'd started talking about Erik, and how Brenae had worshipped him, and how that worship had fueled him, and he hadn't wanted to give it up, no matter the cost to him or her, no matter if they both wanted their relationship to be over. How Layla had tried to understand this, even though it drove her mad. At that point, I started to lose feeling in my legs and told her so. And she told me we should go.

Now she was holding me so tight my wrist hurt.

"Cab," I slurred to the attendant, my eyes blurring to black. But I leaned on Layla because I couldn't help it, and then I passed out.

WHEN I WOKE, MY WHOLE body felt numb, but my head was slightly clearer. A seat belt had been pulled across my T-shirt and clicked. The edge of it bit into my neck, but I couldn't lift a hand to adjust it. My wig and cloak were on the seat.

Layla was alone in the front, driving, her white hands on the wheel.

"Where. We going?"

"Told you," she said softly. "Nelson's place. The Westing."

The Westing. Why the Westing? In my voicemail to Alicia, I'd told her all about Nelson's wine cellar, the second locked door.

"You. Drug me?" I said.

"You had too many drinks," she said.

There was a pattering sound, and tiny silver stars burst on the windshield. It was raining. The first rain in months. Layla cursed and fumbled for the wiper switch. Black rods creaked over the stars, smearing and erasing them.

"There's a plastic bag in your lap if you need to throw up."

The roof of the car began to drum, then pound.

AND THEN WE WERE ON the 10 freeway, in a flow of headlights. Wet signs flashed above me, the white letters of exits. La Cienega. Swamp.

The rain had stopped, but everything had a misty halo. I had feeling back in my feet and hands, and I was stretching them, clenching them quietly, but my torso still felt like a sack of mud. I was not sure I would be able to stand.

Layla must have sensed me waking because she cranked her neck and looked back at me.

"Why me?" My tongue was still thick, and the words slurred.

There was a buzzing sound in the front seat, and Layla picked up my phone, reading the tiny screen. "Oh," she says. "Two people are looking for you. I'll just tell them you called a cab home."

She tried texting with her thumb, still driving, swerving.

I fought to keep my eyes open.

"I still don't know why—"

"Sure you do," said Layla. "You didn't snoop around Nelson's house for no reason."

My phone buzzed again, but she ignored it.

"You don't have to do this," I said.

"Just shut up, gallerina. I tried to warn you. You should have quit on your first day."

I worked my muscles, clenching, bending. My thighs, hips, and belly still felt leaden. I wouldn't be able to fight her when the car stopped. I wasn't even sure I could stand. But the effects couldn't last forever—I'd only ingested a fraction of what she'd intended for me.

Layla drove faster, slamming the gas, then the brakes, as she wove through the busy lanes. The ocean was ahead of us, the open water. Even if I couldn't see it, I could always sense the end of the land, the big blackness where the lights stopped and the long emptiness took over. Once we got off the 10, we would be at the Westing in minutes.

"How did you find me tonight?" I said.

"Nelson knew you worked at the Rocque. I took a chance and waited outside the museum until you left. You're not hard to follow. You never look behind you."

"Where's Ray?" I asked.

"I can't help him," she said. "Shut up so I can drive, okay?"

23

"SO WE'RE GOING TO PLAY a game," Layla said in my ear as she helped me from the car. We were parked in the back of the gallery, where the truck of shoes had pulled up days ago. "If you shout for help, I'll stick this knife in your side. Right under the ribs. And then I'll twist." I felt the cool edge of a blade against my belly.

I complied by standing up and stumbling forward over the wet pavement. The sudden change in position made my head faint. Layla pulled me along, the knife tip jabbing. My legs still felt like they had been pounded into rubber and reattached to my hips.

When we reached the back door, she lowered the knife and dredged a key from her purse. I lurched away from her and tried to run, but fell after two steps. My shoulder, then my cheek, slammed the soaked asphalt. The pavement scraped my skin. The door swung open. It was dim inside. I felt Layla's hands dig under me and pull me into the hallway, then slam the steel to shut us in.

Afterward, she sat there for a moment, breathing hard, her dress darkened with rain. I couldn't hear anyone else in the gallery, and down the long hall, the spectral arches of *Shoe Cathedral* rose, looking from a distance like a giant spider crouched and waiting for us. I rubbed the wet grit from my cheek. It stung.

Layla stood up and walked down the hall to my old gallerina desk, dialing a number. "She's here," she said, then listened for a moment. "About two milligrams. I guess."

There was another silence.

"How do I know he's—" She sounded worried. "I don't want to do this by myself."

Another silence. Layla looked at the ceiling, her knuckles whitening where they clutched the receiver.

"I'm not doing this," she said in a smaller voice.

She waited.

"Okay, but you're coming, right?"

WHEN LAYLA CAME BACK TO me, she wore a different face. I had seen many Layla faces by now—her tender, insecure awe toward Erik, her protectiveness toward Zania, her cool scorn toward me—but this face was different. Her eyes did not seem to be looking outward at all, but focused on some inner landscape that was cold and barren, and she saw far into it, into that vast, bleak plateau. It was a terrifying face, and the hands that lifted me, yanked me toward Nelson's office, felt as merciless as claws. I tried to speak, but she told me to be quiet, and in such a voice that I feared what she would do if I disobeyed.

I let Layla pull me down the hall, into the orange-carpeted room. Layla's bare legs, the tiniest stubble on them, shone in the fluorescent light. Her sandaled foot accidentally kicked my ear. The whiff of the rotting coconut takeout still drifted from the trash can. Nelson's bookcase slid aside, revealing a panel in the wall, a keypad.

An intuition, faint but certain now. All along I had sensed that the dimensions of this room were wrong. The hallway too long. The office too short. A hidden room here. Not in Nelson's wine cellar. Alicia would be arriving at his house soon. Maybe even finding the gallerist there alone, looking puzzled at the intrusion.

When Layla had slung me all the way to the wall panel, she stopped, breathing heavily.

"Well, this is what you both were looking for, isn't it?" she said to me.

Layla sat down at Nelson's desk, propping her chin in her hands. My head felt clearer, but my muscles were still weak. I found if I lay very still, I could think better, but I wanted to run. I must have made a noise because she looked over at me.

"It will be easier if you sleep through this," she said in a tone that bordered on pity.

"Please," I said, keeping my skull pinned to the ground. "You don't have to do anything. It's all his fault. Not yours."

"I know," she said. She smoothed her hair back in swift, automatic gestures. "I could leave this whole disgusting mess."

I fought against the fog in my head. I had to press her. "You tried to leave once," I said. "You got scared by what happened to Calvin. You left for grad school. You found Erik. You were free."

A tremor crossed Layla's face, and then it went blank again. I needed to push for that tremor to return.

"Any person would take your side," I said sleepily. "Nelson manipulated you. The age gap. Your father's friend. No one guessed, so no one helped you."

Layla's face was still glassy and blank. I thought through the timeline: how she'd started dating Erik at LAAC, how the London trip had exposed him cheating on her, how she must have run back to Nelson. Then Brenae's death came, then Kim Lord's murder and Nelson's financial crash.

"You knew getting back together was a bad idea," I said. "But *Still Lives* went down and Nelson lost everything. You couldn't abandon him. Not even if you had started to believe he might have killed someone. Maybe two people."

Layla blinked. "He did not touch Brenae," she said. "Never."

"I meant James Compton."

"James Compton choked on his own vomit," Layla said. "Nelson adored him. He was devastated that James died."

"If Nelson didn't do anything wrong," I said, "how could Calvin blackmail him?"

She shrugged.

"Nelson stole something from James," I guessed.

"No, he kept some of James's money after James died, so he could carry on his work. That's all. But that guy, Calvin, claimed he wanted to tell the true story of Shoreditch. He wanted a stipend for a couple of years, he said. To make sure he got 'the facts' right. Ha."

"So what happened?"

"I don't know. I thought Nelson sent him away. I didn't know the guy would turn up dead."

"You didn't know any of it," I said. "Just leave me here and I'll call the police. I'll back you up. *Quit now.* You warned me, remember?"

Layla gave the smallest nod and sat up straighter. For a moment, I thought I had her.

"Go," I said. "Erik needs you."

Layla's face sagged into something that should have been a smile, but it was ghoulish and melancholy. "He doesn't need me. He never needed me. He needs Brenae."

The office phone rang and Layla answered. She listened, nodding, shrinking into herself. Then she hung up and strode to the door with her old full-hipped sway, the soaked dress clinging to her. At the threshold, she snapped off the light, casting herself in silhouette.

"You don't seem like a bad person," she said. "But you let yourself get used."

WHEN I WOKE AGAIN, THE light was still out in the office, but not in the hall. A wedge of glow hit the floor by the threshold, faintly illuminating the rest of the room. I felt someone else's presence, someone sitting where Layla had sat, before I turned and saw him, slumped, heavy shouldered. Without his deep tan and cap of silver hair, his form looked thug-like and heavy. There was something misshapen about his head. He did not move as I pushed myself up, but I felt him watching.

"Where's Layla?" Despite everything, I was alarmed for her. "What did you do to her?"

He remained silent, regarding me. Then his hand reached up to gently touch the side of his head, and I saw now that his ear was dangling, as if ripped from the side of his skull. His fingers dropped, covered in dark smears.

I scrambled toward the door, my weak limbs flailing. He rose and strode past me, the bloody, mutilated ear catching the light, trickles of red down the side of his neck. With a flick, he slammed the door, casting us in darkness. The only source of light was a thermostat on the wall beside the hidden door, which read thirty-eight degrees. My head slurred at this information. I couldn't imagine what it meant.

"I wanted you to be awake, that's all." Nelson's voice fumbled, as if he couldn't remember what he wished to say. He stood over me. "To see what was done to me. Do you see it?"

I crawled for the door again, my hands slapping the floor. I hadn't heard him lock it. There was still a chance. But my limbs refused to coordinate and then his hands were on me, shoving though my armpits, so that he was holding me up from behind, dangling like a doll. I could feel his chest against my spine, his thighs shoving mine across the room. "Do you see it?"

Crying out, I tried to kick at him and he cursed, but he kept his grip, pushing me toward the hidden door, punching at buttons.

"Do you see it?" he demanded again, lower this time, because now he'd pulled me in tight from behind, our heads were close, and then I could feel it, the warm slickness of his ruined ear against my hair, the back of my neck, and for a single instant, as he groaned, its deep, gouging pain.

"Yes, I see it." I wanted to be free of his grip. I didn't care what came next.

The cold blasted over us, then the lightlessness inside.

"Good," he said, and threw me forward, hard, into the freezing room, so that I staggered and fell facedown on the concrete floor.

Behind me, the wall closed. Then came a second, heavy sliding sound: the bookcase sealing me in.

24

THE COLD MIXED WITH THE dark, and the air chafed. The floor grated my cheek and the palms of my hands. As my adrenaline faded, I could feel the sleep pulling at me again, keeping me from breaking the surface. I wanted to sleep instead of remembering Nelson's ruined ear touching me, its pulpy caress.

I forced myself up. Faintness flooded my skull. I reached for a wall and found a shelf instead, covered in objects. Stone. Small shapes and large shapes, smooth and old.

Bones, my mind told me.

A cemetery, my mind told me.

Then: Art. Sculptures.

"Ray?" I said.

The air was still. I was alone in the room. It was frigid. Winter cold. Winter cold with no coat or hat. The thermostat on the wall said thirty-five now. The climate control settings would be for the artwork. Nelson had turned them down to their lowest temp. Near freezing. I would not survive two days at thirty-five degrees. I might not survive a day, not if I kept falling asleep.

I needed to get out. First, I needed to see. First, I needed to move.

I counted to twenty, and for every count I contracted my muscles, pushed myself to feel the objects around me (cool, hard, dust whispering on my hands), to crawl toward the door. At twenty, I collapsed, exhausted. Another twenty. I felt the whole door, every smooth edge of it, and around the edges for a light switch, but nothing. A lone blue glow from the thermostat on the wall. Thirty-four degrees now. I felt everywhere on the instrument for a button or switch, but it had none.

I sank to the ground and folded into a ball, blinking to stay awake, trying to keep the warmth in.

The rustle was so soft at first, I thought my ears were playing tricks on me. Then I heard it again: the smallest scraping sound off to my right.

"Hello?" I said.

There was a faint moan, but I recognized the voice, even broken to pieces like this. I scrambled in its direction, saying Ray's name, and smashed into his cold, limp body before I could stop myself. The groan lengthened, and I pattered my hands over his shoulders and chest, finding his face. Recoiled. It felt so much like Nelson's ear. Cold and soft-slick. Like the inside of a pumpkin before you dig it out. I smelled blood on my fingers.

"I didn't know you were here," I croaked. "What happened to you? I can't see anything."

Ray said a word a few times before I realized it was *pockets*. My hands fumbled their way down his damp chest until I found the rim of denim on either side of his hips, and I blushed in the dark, plunging my hand against his thigh. Nothing but lint in the first pocket. In the other, sharp hard teeth. A key ring. I pulled it loose, jingling.

"Keys?" I said, but then my hand felt the tiny metal tube. I groped at it until it clicked and light spilled into the room, over Ray. His face was a mask of pain, one eye blackened and swollen shut, lips huge and bloodied. The left side of his head aimed toward his shoulder, and his shoulder bent at an unnatural angle, his arm extending, fingers blue.

His open eye met mine.

"You should see his ear," I said.

"Maggie," Ray said from far away. "Did he . . ." A long pause. "Hurt you?"

"No." It sounded like I was lying, and I was. "Just tell me how we're getting out of here."

"Get . . . something hard," he whispered.

The words were costing him, and he closed his eyes, his breath rattling.

"Break. See-ing," he slurred.

"I don't understand."

He nodded as if to say, *Just do it.*

I crawled to the shelf and pulled something down. It was shrink-wrapped and so heavy that it clunked on the floor, bruising my fingers. The plastic refused to tear, and I bit it, savage with fear, until I got a piece to peel free. Underneath: old, smooth beige stone, carved with ancient, faded symbols.

"See-ing," he said again, softer this time.

"Seeing what? What am I supposed to see?" I tried to keep the panic from my voice.

After another shudder, he opened his eyes. He looked at me, his pupils so dilated that the black centers were huge and the blue was almost gone, and then he looked beyond me, above me.

"Ceiling. Only way." He barely uttered the words. "Out."

"The ceiling?" I said, catching on. "But how?"

"Climb. Save light," he said.

Then his lids fluttered shut.

Before I clicked the tiny flashlight off, I looked around the room. In the startled dimness of the single beam, I saw a shelf that rose all the way to the ceiling, stacked with engraved and sculpted stones. I didn't know enough about antiquities to recognize what they were. But it was clear they had originated from centuries ago, made and touched by people whose bones had long since turned to dust. There was a crate by the wall, a shipping label in plastic. I knelt to read the return address: 41 Genevieve Street in London.

25

SHIVERING, I GRABBED THE SHELF and pulled myself to standing, slowly, stumbling, the drug sludging my muscles. My hands probed the edges of the structure, reaching just higher than my head before my fingers touched open air. About six feet high. I jiggled the metal. Sturdy but loose. If I climbed it, I could send the whole thing toppling down. Exhaustion spread through me again, and I fought it off by blinking hard and flexing my hands.

First, I would need some kind of hammer. When I ascended the shelf, it might only be once, given my strength, and I needed a tool up there to smash the ceiling. I felt among the objects. Gravestones, tablets. I couldn't tell what any one was. The darkness, the drug, and the freezing air had muted shape and recognition. I needed something heavy. But not so heavy that I couldn't swing it. Not so light that it wouldn't break drywall.

My fingers closed on a smooth oblong with some kind of pointy tip. Whatever it was, I hoped it was solid. I tapped it experimentally on the wooden floor.

The pinging made Ray stir, but when I crawled over and checked him, he was motionless, his flesh clammy. "I'm going to try now," I said.

He didn't answer.

I shoved myself upright, my head spinning, and carried my hammer to the shelf, setting it down on the top. My huffing breaths filled the silence of the room as I strained up my makeshift ladder. One shelf. Two shelves. The structure swayed. I clung halfway, trying not to imagine where the shelf and its contents would fall, if they fell.

A noise came from outside the room. A whooshing sound, like water through pipes.

Was someone else inside the Westing?

Pearson? Hal? Could they have come back to check on the installation?

Alicia?

I shouted for help. I almost lost my perch and clambered higher, buoyed by the thought of rescue. By the time I reached the top of the shelf, my voice was hoarse and there were no answering footsteps. Nothing from Ray, either.

The dizziness hit. Not like a spinning feeling, but like a tide, black and full. My stomach heaved, and I nearly lost my balance. My scalp brushed the ceiling. I clung, crouched, waiting for the sensation to pass.

The pipes were quiet. No one was there to rescue us.

I felt around for the oblong and slammed the ceiling with it. The impact made my frozen fist ache. It was like wielding a baseball bat at cinder block. All the energy of my swing lashed backward into my body. I swung again, back aching from my crouch. *Wham, wham.* My shoulder recoiled in pain. I felt the ceiling. Nothing. *Wham!* A tiny dent.

I sagged over, exhausted, the hammer clunking on top of the shelf. How long would this take? Was it already too late? I looked down at the blackness. I spoke to Ray, but there was no answer, and my voice sounded echoed and strange, like I was speaking into a culvert.

I lifted the hammer. *Wham.* Sand kissed my hands. *Wham.* A bigger chunk tumbled, landing on the shelf. In the dark I felt for it. A crumbly, jagged piece. It was all I had. All we had. I closed my fist around it.

AFTER I MADE A HOLE in the ceiling the size of my fist, I started pulling down the drywall by hand, cringing when it tumbled to the floor, but unable to stop. The energy I had left could have filled a teaspoon, and the nausea was worsening. If I ceased moving, I would throw up or faint.

The hole widened to the diameter of a dinner plate. I pulled Ray's tiny flashlight from my pocket and clicked it on again. It shone into foam insulation. I punched at the insulation and felt it give. My knuckles stung. I punched again.

The insulation broke free, and through the hole I saw a gap beyond.

Holding my breath and closing my eyes, I pulled at the hole until it grew, and then stuck my head and shoulders through, pushing the foam apart with my skull. It tumbled off me, gusting dust all over my face. When I opened my eyes and breathed again, the cloud made me cough and retch, and I almost dropped the flashlight. Then, warm air settled in its place, and my caked, freezing face ached from its own thawing.

There was a gap between the ceiling and roof that extended all the way toward the gallery. Boards interrupted the sheetrock in a network of lines. The light didn't reach the far end, but I could crawl to Nelson's office and punch through the ceiling there and get us out. For the first time since he tossed me into the room, I felt a splinter of hope.

I shone the light down on Ray, who looked pale and sunken, his eyes closed. His arm angled wrong, as if he had fallen from a far height. The blood from his busted face was jellied on the floor by cold. I'd seen blood like this beneath animals that'd died in the winter woods, so thickened it looked solid. The dizziness swept over me again, and my legs trembled. I put the flashlight in my mouth. It made me gag, but I clenched my teeth and rose and pushed myself through the hole, grabbing for a two-by-four board crisscrossing the drywall.

Huge chunks of ceiling fell as I tried to hoist myself on the board. My body plunged, I slumped, almost lost my grip. In movies, this was the moment when action heroines would slide, smooth as spandex, into their own stunt rescue, but even sober and clear-headed, I would have struggled with the effort. It was like trying to clamber onto the highest rung of a monkey bar with all the other rungs removed. My arms would not do the job. I had to use my legs. I had to jump.

If I jumped, the shelf might tip and fall on Ray.

I looked down at him again. He opened his good eye. I didn't know if he could see me or the hole in the ceiling. He looked both like a ghost and like a beaten child, remote and uncomprehending.

I scanned the shelf below me, laden with stone tablets and pieces of statues. It was heavy. It would crush a man. But it also might not budge easily. Staying here would not save us.

Creeping as close to the hole as I could get, I bunched my legs and leaped. The shelf swayed and rattled behind me, loud in my ears as I lurched, gasping, onto the beam, scrambling for balance. Something long and sharp scraped my elbow. I held on, righting myself. But I couldn't stop from crying out, and the flashlight fell from my mouth, tumbling end over end, to the concrete beside Ray, glowing toward his empty, outstretched hand. I couldn't go back for it. I couldn't see the ceiling or the crawlspace anymore, or tell if my elbow was bleeding. I would have to feel my way, board by board, until I broke through.

I'D LIKE TO SAY THAT I spent the next minutes in brave motion, certain that I could rescue Ray and myself, that Calvin's death would be solved and his killer held for questioning, but the whole time I crawled, trying not to vomit, I wanted to give up. So I forced my mind to lemons. California lemons. Big, yellow, thick-rinded, and tart with juice. Sawing into them with a serrated knife. Making wedges for gin and tonics. Sucking on the sour, bright taste and swallowing. I thought about lemon trees. Lemon trees on my old block in Hollywood, draped in so many fruits no one would ever eat them all. The green of their leaves, their branches hung with gold ornaments.

Lemons were California to me. Condensed sunlight. Sharp, stinging hope.

I crawled in the dark toward where I thought Nelson's office would be, slipping several times, my knee cracking the drywall. By then, my eyes had adjusted to the dimness and I could make out shapes: where the eaves crossed, the soft peaks of foam.

I kept looking back at the hole to the secret room, to measure distance. The thought of Ray lying there, waiting or dying, paralyzed me each time, and I had to shake myself free. Finally, I estimated I might be above the office, but what if the office was locked, too? I had to get to the gallery.

The change in temperature was turning my muscles to jelly. The nausea was cresting again.

Lemons, I thought again, but it wasn't working now.

I was close. I knew it. The dust in my mouth and lungs made it hard to breathe. Sweat prickled my forehead, my once-cold face trickling with warm salt. My belly heaved. I was so tired.

Lemons. Lemon trees. Ray. Calvin. Brenae. Kim. Nikki.

None could lift me.

I shut my eyes and felt a new presence like a rush of wind. She was there—here—for me, as she had been one long-ago day in Vermont when she'd stormed into my apartment in her mud-season boots and stood over my body curled with fear and grief on my futon and told me that she was taking me home. My mother. Only it wasn't my mother alone. It was also Janis, summoning me back to Los Angeles, gripping my arm in the LAAC parking lot. It was Yegina, urging me to write Brenae's story anyway. It was Brenae, standing at the blue pool edge, her face wet, tape ripped away from her mouth, gasping for breath. Brenae was also inside me, mothering me. Picking me up, setting me forward. Insisting I go on. Saying *Just up there, it's right up there, just twenty, then nineteen, then eighteen, seventeen, sixteen breaths. Go on. You'll make it.* I fumbled over the foam, no longer caring about my cut hands, my aching lungs, my streaming eyes. I halted a dozen feet later and began ripping at the insulation below me, then kicking my foot through, frantic, pummeling. The sheetrock dented, dented, broke, and I fell into an arch, into a nave of shoes, tearing the arch down with me, sneakers, sandals, loafers, and pumps, flying apart as they tumbled, as if their hundreds of invisible owners were bursting away in all directions. I hit the floor. The cathedral above sagged and broke. Clattering, the shoes fell after me, around me; they rained.

26

TWO DAYS LATER, I SAT with Alicia Ruiz in the garden courtyard of the hospital. Sprays of palmetto and thick succulents surrounded us. The garden was tucked on the fifth floor between two towering wards. It didn't feel like a garden. It felt more like a secret, airlifted jungle with a concrete floor. There was nothing to do out here but sit in the shallow shade and slightly fresh air, trying to pretend that waiting through Ray's surgery was restful instead of nerve-racking. A smog-white sky spread above us.

Ray had a broken clavicle, a fractured scapula, cracked ribs, and lacerations to his right lung. For forty-eight hours, the doctors had stabilized him with IV fluids, a sling for his shoulder, and a tube to help him breathe. He looked like a car-crash victim being slowly strangled by translucent vines. Ray's "high injury severity" score made two surgeons recommend surgery for his scapula, to put pins in, helping the damage heal faster and easier. A third countered the idea, citing potential long-term nerve damage to Ray's arm. Ray chose the majority view, and now he was under anesthesia and we were waiting.

I still didn't understand how Nelson had gotten the best of him in a fight, even in an ambush at night in Ray's apartment. Nelson had had no gun, only a billy club. A strike from behind crippled Ray's shoulder. Then he fought back, nearly ripping an ear off Nelson's head, but he lost. Where was Ray's gun, where was his training at disarming opponents? It was almost as if he had intended to surrender. He couldn't have known that I would come looking for him, that Layla, an hour after leaving us, would call her father, Steve Goetz, and use the safe word he had once given her as a teenager, and her father would alert the police to stop Nelson's car. Ray must have expected to die. Yet here he was, alive.

As for me, I was fine. Hollowed but fine. I had already recovered from the drugging, my right hand was badly bruised but not broken, and the other cuts were superficial. A boring, easily resolved case for the ER, but not for the LAPD. Even with Alicia and a lawyer's intercession, I had answered the same questions dozens of times. *What happened at the bar? What happened when you exited the bar? What happened when you exited the vehicle? What were Layla's words exactly? Who lifted you into the room? Who shut the door? Did Ray Hendricks tell you anything about how he received his injuries?* Nelson and Layla had been arrested outside San Diego, and the police needed an airtight case against Nelson. The case was ours: attempted murder of me and Ray. Proving anything about Calvin's death would be hard. No evidence linking Nelson to his murder had been found.

The warehouse on Genevieve Street in London had been searched, and the police uncovered illegal Iraqi antiquities hidden in the packaging of contemporary artwork, headed for the United States. The pieces were all small and lightweight, and they fit into cleverly concealed hollows in the plastic foam that kept the contemporary art in place. According to a British employee, who offered information in exchange for police protection, the business had been running for seven years, ever since Nelson had bought the property. The same witness had also known James Compton, and knew that Compton had used the back room of the bar where Nelson worked to purchase looted items from college students who traveled to Turkey for spring break. It was "a popular racket for a while," the witness said. Free vacations, great pay, and the "added ethical bonus of supporting the funding of contemporary artists" while rescuing Iraqi treasures. He was sure that Nelson de Wilde had gotten his start watching Compton. The witness promised he would name international players in exchange for a plea.

All in all, illegal art smuggling and attempted murder were enough to put Nelson in jail, but not to convict him of a life-threatening assault on Calvin. An ongoing search of Nelson's properties had not yet turned up any other proof. Why would it? Who would keep evidence of beating someone nearly to death?

"Do you think there's any possibility at all that Nelson killed Brenae?" I asked Alicia. "What if she had connected him to Calvin's death?"

"Not his usual method." Her voice deepened. "Her body was unmarked. The location was too public. And he wasn't that skilled. If he had killed her, he would have slipped up somewhere and the police would have found it. They spent weeks. Ray didn't see any holes in her case, either."

She wore an uncharacteristic T-shirt and jeans, her feet in strappy gold sandals. This was off-work Alicia, and I could imagine her lounging back, a magazine on her lap, but she sat stiffly upright beside me. She was worried about Ray, but she was also still wary of me. I wished I knew how to signal my gratitude to her without insinuating that I expected to be pals. Alicia sipped coffee from a paper cup and checked her watch, until her phone buzzed. She looked at the number, frowned, then held it to her ear.

"Yes," she said. "Yes." She listened for a while. "That's great." She rose and walked to the corner of the garden, standing under an angel's trumpet tree, looking up at the dangling yellow flowers as she spoke. After an intense conversation, she hung up and strode back, sitting down again. "That was Layla's lawyer," she said. "She will cooperate with us fully as part of a plea bargain. And Erik's been released," she said. "Hal Giroux went to the station and spoke on his behalf. He said that he personally had requested that Erik talk Brenae out of sharing her video. He claimed he was worried Erik's visa status might get threatened if the school took action against him."

So Hal had finally publicly admitted it: He'd always taken Erik's side and not Brenae's. Even after he'd watched *Lesson in Red*, after he'd witnessed Erik's body pin her body and her stricken face stare back at him, demanding to be seen, even after hearing her agonized words, Hal had decided that Erik's acts were not real and that Brenae's outrage was a performance. He had seen all the evidence before him, and still had not believed.

"Erik says now that he did enter her studio on Tuesday," said Alicia. "He asked to see the video. Brenae refused to show it to him. She told Erik that he had to confess to Hal first that he'd coerced her into sex last fall, in exchange for him helping her get on Hal's crew. Erik said he denied coercing her. He claimed the sex was always consensual."

Alicia paused on this and rolled her eyes.

"Brenae also begged Erik to take her gun away," she said, "saying she didn't know what she would do if she kept it. He refused."

"He didn't take her seriously," I said.

"He didn't have to. He had his idol's support," said Alicia.

When Erik heard that Hal had come to the police station to defend him, the student broke down and retracted his confession of aiding in a murder. Of course he did. It was an empty drama. And Hal had rescued him again.

I tried to imagine that first, long-ago conversation between Hal and Erik about the video, two men sorting through the accusations of a woman they'd both held power over. I could see them sitting across from each other in Hal's office, the posters and accolades all over the wall, celebrating the success of the school. LAAC didn't need a scandal. It didn't need a young woman claiming she'd said yes but meant no, and showing her shocking footage. Maybe Hal had told Erik to apologize, to settle things privately. Maybe he'd even reprimanded Erik. But whatever he said, he defended him as innocent. He gave Erik permission to ignore Brenae's pain as oversized, hysterical.

Hal's lack of self-protectiveness surprised me. He should have seen how this could blow up. All he had to do was contact his student services office about Brenae's video, and they would have descended on her immediately with the appropriate counsel and resources. He could have let Erik burn, washing his hands of the whole matter with a single phone call.

"You'd think Hal would have covered himself, wouldn't you?" I said. "I mean, he's been the director of an MFA program for years. Why wouldn't he just call in professional campus help? Brenae couldn't have been the first traumatized student he'd met."

Alicia cocked one leg on the other knee and tugged at her jean cuff. "Yeah," she said. "He could have 'covered' himself. So why didn't he?"

I thought she was going to answer her own question, but she didn't. Instead she examined me, her expression both thoughtful and cynical.

"I guess he thought it was a bluff," I said.

She gave a small, tight smile. "I guess he didn't give a crap either way. He didn't think of her as a person. He thought of her as a problem. A bomb. Just like you said. Something to 'cover himself' from."

At her words, I felt my face stiffen, like someone had thrown cold water on it. The feeling spread to my chest, my gut. Deep down, was this how I really saw Brenae—not as a person, but as a problem? Was this how Alicia saw me seeing her? Alicia's motivation to advise on Janis's private investigation—was it really to keep things "legal," or because she didn't trust how we'd perceive the information we found?

All I knew was that Alicia had been there for us that night, no matter her own reservations.

She had gone to Nelson's house to find me. The lights were all off. With her son in the car, she wouldn't go down the driveway, so she called for backup. Two squad cars speeding for the Palisades while I was trying to climb through the gallery ceiling. When I dialed 911 from the Westing phone, I told them to contact Alicia. She was parked on the road above Nelson's property, waiting for a search warrant. She immediately alerted dispatch to be on the lookout for anyone resembling Nelson and Layla.

The pair were caught at a gas station off the freeway, seventy miles from the Mexican border. Without Layla's call to her father and the speed of Alicia's response, they might have made it out of the country. Without me being locked with Ray in the hidden room at the Westing, Ray might have died. We had both fulfilled our missions that night. But I was lucky. Rash and lucky. I knew that. I was lucky there had been a way out for me. I bowed my head.

"I'm sorry," I said finally. "You're absolutely right."

I felt Alicia tense, then sigh. Something nudged against my ribs, and I looked down to see her pushing her arm through mine, looping us together. She was actually much smaller than I was, and it was the first time I realized it, the way our ribs met, the bottom ridge of hers touching my waist.

"I know," she said in such a bored tone that I had to laugh. She laughed, too.

After that, we relaxed and leaned into each other, listening to the honks of traffic and gazing together into the little jungle garden, waiting for news of Ray.

HE RESTED ON A WHITE bed, IV in one hand, other arm in a sling, the tube still in his mouth. The bruises on his face and neck had purpled, making a garish map on his handsome features, but he looked glad to see us. The nurse stood by, fiddling with his monitors.

Alicia and I took our places on either side of him. She had the side with the IV, and she took his hand gently. I had the one with the sling, so I didn't touch him at all.

"Layla wants to cooperate," she said. "London, too. They raided the office on Genevieve Street, and found other illegal antiquities. Nelson de Wilde was shipping his clients' work through there and picking up some very expensive stowaways on the way."

Ray blinked.

"You got something to tell me, you can do it tomorrow," she said. "I'll be back with my notebook."

There was a pause.

"We made it," I said, trying to sound encouraging.

Ray tilted toward me, his blue eyes resting on my face. I had more to say, but it didn't come. My breath stuck in my throat. Across the bed, I saw Alicia slowly release Ray's hand.

"Willow and Nathaniel want to come out here, but I told them no," she said. "Because you said no. Are you sure?" She hesitated. "To be frank, they're out of their minds with worry."

Ray shook his head, his IV hand rising to pull out the tube.

"Sir," said the nurse. "Sir, you can't do that." She swept in, and Ray's hand fell.

"It's all right. Don't talk," said Alicia. "I'll calm them down."

In her face, I saw a quick, guilty evasiveness and I knew: Willow and Nathaniel weren't communicating directly with her. They were talking to Ynez, Ray's old girlfriend, and she was talking to Alicia. Cousin to cousin. *I belong with him,* Ray had said. He belonged with Nathaniel. What about with Ynez?

There was a moaning noise, and a stretcher sped by in the hall, propelled by a nurse and an orderly. The body on it, covered by a sheet, looked scarcely larger than a child's. The moaning switched to hoarse, agonized yelps.

I wanted to rip Ray out of this place. I knew it was just a room like any other room, and that all the tubes and monitors and nurses were there to keep him and others safe, to help them heal. I knew I should be grateful that he had such good care. But a restless anger engulfed me anyway, watching him gagged and threaded with needles, his brown hair matted to his head, his thin cotton johnny wrapping his bruised chest. I wanted his old sleepy gaze back, his courtliness and his absurd questions. I wanted him through with this. Through the damage and healing. Through the raw hurt of Calvin's death. I wanted him home, wherever home was. I wanted him whole. Just standing there motionless above him took enormous effort. It felt like someone was stripping pieces of me from the inside.

"We should go," Alicia said quietly.

I reached out and brushed Ray's forehead, above his uninjured eye, smoothing his brown hair back. "Do whatever they tell you, so they'll let you go," I whispered, and turned away before he could reply.

The corridor outside the ICU was so clean, the walls shone with faint reflections.

"Thank God, right?" said Alicia beside me. "He looks good."

I nodded, still unable to speak.

"You don't think so?" she said, and shook her head. "He'll be up and gone the first chance he gets."

27

"YOU MUST BE DYING TO get back into your bungalow," Yegina said, staring at my sublet's jumble of furniture, the photos of empty sidewalks. She had come over with two towering bags of premade meals, convinced that my battered right hand had made me incapable of shopping or cooking.

"It hasn't been that bad here. Just lonely." I cleared my table of a bouquet of orange lilies from Janis Rocque so that Yegina could set her parcels down. The bouquet had appeared the day after Nelson's arrest and was already almost a week old, but I couldn't throw it out. Petals and pollen scattered over the counter.

Yegina stood close to me, swiping up the petals with her long-fingered open hand. "I'm so sorry," she said. "I've been so caught up with my job and Hiro, I just let you drift."

"I think I needed to drift," I said. "Not from you, but from who I was."

Yegina stopped swiping and looked at me. "And now?"

I sat down on the huge blue couch. Yegina dropped the petals in the trash and perched beside me, her black-trousered knees beside my jeans. She put a hand on my arm.

“Don’t make me call your mother,” she said. “She’ll pry it out of you.”

I hadn’t called my mother at all yet. I didn’t want to tell my parents what had happened in the past two weeks. They would fly out, the two of them this time, and demand I choose a different life.

“I’m quitting the Rocque,” I said. “I want to work full-time on the story of Brenae Brasil. I have so much reporting to do, and I need to find an editor who will work with me.” I faced her. “Janis paid me enough for my gallerina gig that I can live for three or four months. And then, who knows. I’ll find other freelance work.”

“Does Janis know?”

“I’m going to meet her tomorrow.”

Janis was scheduled for a double mastectomy, to be followed by chemo and radiation. For a private person, she’d been surprisingly open about this to everyone. She had declared that she was stepping away from all her duties at the Rocque in order to address her health. (“You won’t miss me scowling at your staff meetings unless you’re a total suck-up,” she’d told the museum’s executive committee.) I’d worked up the courage to ask to see her, and she’d invited me to her estate.

“Lucky you,” said Yegina. “Was that all, though?”

That wasn’t all. I also wanted to say how different I felt now. Not different exactly, but deeper into the self I wanted to be. The self with a purpose.

“I’m happy,” I said cautiously. “Not the giddy kind, but the real kind.”

“I can tell.” By the fragile, pained pleasure on Yegina’s face, I could see how much she’d worried for me. “What about Ray?”

Ray had left the hospital the day after his surgery, arm in a sling, and requested a medical leave from his job in North Carolina to recuperate and follow the investigation of Nelson de Wilde. We’d made a plan to catch up next week when he was in less pain; he promised he had somewhere to take me. I explained all this to Yegina.

“Anyway, we’re even now. He saved my life. I saved his.” I shrugged to cover up the waver in my voice.

"Actually, I think that makes you in enormous debt to each other," she said with a knowing smile.

"I'd rather hear about you and Hiro," I said.

"I said yes," she said.

"You did?" I whooped.

The smile grew on her face.

"You set a date?" I said.

"Next December," she said. "After the groundbreaking of the new museum." She rose, too, and went back to the bouquet, plucking out the most wilted stems and putting the vase in the sink.

"Congratulations," I said, trying to keep anything but joy from my voice. "I'm so thrilled for you," I added truthfully.

I expected details, but instead she pulled the remaining lilies loose from the vase. She let water rush into the silt and dried leaves at its bottom, pushing them up, brimming over, then ran the faucet until the vase filled clear. Then she dropped the lilies gracefully back in.

"You're waiting for the real news, aren't you?" she said.

"Getting married is real news," I said, then grinned. "Okay, yes."

She put the vase back on my counter but stayed standing, like she was pitching me at a board meeting. "Promise you'll listen to the whole thing?"

I promised.

Yegina had been conferencing all week with Janis, Bas, Hal, and Steve Goetz. She, Janis, and Bas had proffered the idea that the Rocque could be annexed into the new museum but keep its experimental performance programming ("which was always Janis's first love"). Rather than being a single institution, the museum could become a downtown complex, eventually incorporating more buildings around it. One day it would rival the Smithsonian, but with an L.A. angle on the art of the present and future. Steve Goetz told her he wanted to think about it, but he called back the next day and said he liked all of it. Everything Yegina said. And that he wanted to phase Hal Giroux out by the time the museum opened and replace Hal's presence with hers. As assistant director of the whole complex.

"Hal represents the past," Goetz had told her. "You represent the future."

"Get that in writing," I told her.

"That's what Janis said. She told me Steve Goetz is a hustler with a gold purse who thinks he's a grandee." Yegina laughed at the phrasing. "I don't like him," she admitted. "I don't like how he talks about artists, or art. But he owns gobs of it, and he's right. I am the future." She pulled a tissue from her pocket and dusted my counter. "We both are. It's the end of an era." Her voice was triumphant, but her eyes were wistful. It was the end of an era for Janis, too. The last time I'd left the Rocque, I'd looked back at its long bank of windows, wondering how I would begin my mornings without seeing my own reflection stride across them—on my way to the realm where Janis ruled.

"She'll be with you in spirit, if not on the phone at all hours," I predicted.

"It's weird that the leaders are going to become us eventually." Yegina looked at me. "Our generation."

"Hal won't give up that easily," I said. "He'll go into private consulting and make pots of money."

"The way you wrecked *Shoe Cathedral* when you fell, he actually loved it," she said. "He was bragging about it on the *Art News* blog. He said it's more complete than ever. The Westing's closed, of course, but Hal already got a photographer in there, and they're planning to sell high-end prints of the wrecked installation to raise money to mount a retrospective tribute to Brenae Brasil."

I knew all this already, but hearing it from Yegina, cast in her new hopefulness, it seemed like a genuine attempt at reparations, and not a cheap publicity move.

"About time," I said. Yegina continued to swoop her makeshift cloth over my furniture. "Would you please stop dusting?"

Yegina folded up the tissue.

"You do know who Steve Goetz is," I said.

"I know that he's Layla Goetz-Middleton's father," she said. "But honestly, Maggie, I think he was so frantic when he found out."

Steve Goetz had claimed complete ignorance of his daughter's affair with the gallerist—an affair that dated back to when she was fifteen years old. "I regarded Nelson as a sharp guy, my daughter's friend's father. Not a dirtbag predator," he'd told Alicia. "I'm heartbroken and sick." Now Layla's father just wanted his daughter home. With his excellent lawyer by her side.

"That's not the only thing wrong with him," I said.

"And I know he was obsessively collecting Kim Lord's work before she died," she said. "But so what? I think he's just a completist."

"A completist."

"He'll get this done," said Yegina. "This museum will happen. And it can kill the Rocque or it can save it. I actually think he wants to save it. He's very deferential to Janis. He's even agreed to put 'Goetz' on his building, but not on the whole complex. For now, we're calling it the Next Museum."

"Until an even richer person comes along and pays for naming rights," I said.

But as I gazed at my proud friend, who'd worked for years without proper acknowledgment and now was getting the break she deserved, I felt my resistance fading. After all, I was moving on, too. The run-down, shoestring, risk-taking Rocque as I'd known it had to end, and maybe this way was the best way.

"Tell me how you said yes to Hiro," I said.

She smiled big again. "With lots of conditions."

THE NEXT DAY, JANIS LED me out to a patio that looked down on her sculpture garden. On the slope below, I could see the Richard Serra ellipse, like a giant, tilted rusting paddock for exceptionally tall horses, and beyond it, the grove of trees where I'd almost died last spring. I was glad the hole in the earth was hidden from me.

My boss was altered. The navy suit was gone. She wore jeans and a collared white shirt that gaped on her, her dark eyes peering from a face that seemed glossier and more worn at once. I avoided looking at her chest. No matter how she downplayed the impending loss with sardonic humor, I couldn't imagine losing my own breasts.

Janis lowered herself to her chair as if any moment she expected the furniture to fly out from under her. "Gigi will bring us some lemonade and cookies," she said. "I hope that's appealing. I actually don't know what you like to eat. You abandoned that lunch I ordered for you at Café Francesca."

"I love them both." I couldn't keep the choke from my voice. "And I'm really sorry."

"Oh, please don't cry," she said. "If you survive two murder attempts, you're not allowed to weep at the cancer lady serving you lemonade. Did they get him?"

"He's been indicted on attempted murder and illegal art trafficking," I said. "But it will be a long time before the trial."

She looked out over her garden of grass and flowers and million-dollar sculptures.

"I always knew Nelson de Wilde was a crook," she said with a satisfied air. "I always knew he had secrets. An expensive suit and a yacht-ready tan don't hide the real man. But the thing is"—she nestled deeper in her chair—"he was our kind of crook. He knew what we wanted, and he got it for us. Not always great art," she said, giving me a shrewd look. "Exclusivity. We wanted to have what no one else had, but everyone else wanted. That's a long, complicated, expensive game. Some gallerists and dealers have their own money to lose on it. Nelson didn't. Doesn't justify his brutality when he got trapped, but I understand its root. I tried to destroy the possibility of a brand-new art museum in downtown L.A. because I felt cornered. And cheated. Despair makes people ugly." She paused to watch a bee veer near us, then fly off again. "Fortunately, I'm used to being ugly, and I've learned it's far better to wear it kindly." She gave me a haggard smile. "No condolences now. For anything. We'll win in the end."

"I agree," I said, swallowing both my grief and my admiration, and I told her my plan. I summarized everything I'd learned about Brenae Brasil that week—how she'd faced increasing isolation this year, as her family contracted to cope with her older brother's arrest, as the school cut her off from the opportunities it had offered, as she lost friends to careerism. I told her about the fateful trip to London to install Hal's show, and the confessions that Layla and Brenae must have traded about their secret lovers: Layla and Nelson, Brenae and Erik. Brenae must have told Layla that Erik still came to her, demanding sex, and Layla hadn't believed her. Neither had Hal. Hal had taken Erik's side, because he was worried about his favorite student losing his visa status, and future opportunities to stay in the States.

I told Janis that I thought there was a real story in Brenae's death about the American dream gone sour and that I was going to quit my job in order to tell it. But not in the ordinary way. I wanted to record people talking about Brenae, and to piece together a tale from their impressions—her family's, her crewmates', her instructors'. Radio was probing into American life this way, and web versions of audio stories couldn't be far behind. I wouldn't be a Gay Talese or a Tom Wolfe, a man with crisp lapels and elegant manner, revealing America to Americans in language that was glossy, witty, discerning, and entirely his own. Instead, I wanted to organize a conversation, one that might be raw and inconclusive, but more authentically Brenae's. And all of ours.

Janis watched me with a closed expression, her eyes glinting from time to time. "And you want me to pay you to do this," she said.

"No," I said. "I want permission to interview you, too."

"Me." She hitched backward in her chair.

"If you hadn't asked me to look, I wouldn't have seen," I said. "If Brenae hadn't written to you, we wouldn't have the video. You're part of this story." I was having a difficult time not choking up again. Fortunately, a friendly woman with choppy auburn hair arrived then with lemonade in frosty glasses and a plate of blond, sugary discs.

"Thank you, Gigi," said Janis. "Please." She gestured to the drinks.

I took a glass, a cold, sour, sweet swallow. A lemon taste. "You're essential to it. To leave you out would mean leaving out one of the greatest champions of art this city has ever had—"

I broke off because, over the years, I had seen Janis tired, angry, and even vengeful, but I had never seen this expression on her face: her right hand rising to cover her mouth and her eyes blinking fast. It was remorse. At my silence, she slowly lowered her hand to her lap and faced me, her chin set. Then the pieces clicked into place—why Janis had never confronted Hal directly, why she'd rigged this entire covert investigation before acting on Brenae's behalf, and then only in the most tactical way.

"You watched *Lesson in Red* before she died," I said. "The whole story about the assistant you fired and the closet full of mail, it wasn't true. You got the video before she died, and you didn't believe it, either."

"I called Hal immediately," she said in a scratchy voice. "He told me that Brenae was unhinged, and he was handling it. Hal and I never got along, but I respected him, and the school was his domain. I believed he was telling the truth. And to be honest, I didn't like Brenae's project. It was tawdry. I didn't think it would serve a young artist's future to expose herself like that. No one would see her talent. All anyone would ever see was her being . . . subjugated." She paused, her lips a thin line. "But when Brenae died, I felt like I had failed her. I did fail her. I ignored my regret, because I was embarrassed. Then *Still Lives* started heating up, and Kim Lord went missing, and I got distracted. For months. Running a museum that became a murder site." She spoke the next words with her old certitude. "I was wrong. You may interview me, and I promise to tell the whole truth."

I almost excused Janis then. I didn't want her confession; it shadowed my reverence for her. But then I saw myself clawing those last lengths through the Westing ceiling, how Brenae had come to me, last of all my mentors. I had never wanted someone so broken and desperate to lead me, then or now, but she was my guide into her story. She had to be. "Thank you," I said. "I know how much it costs you to say that."

"Speaking of cost, how are you going to afford to do this research?" From the tone of Janis's voice, it was clear that she would be grateful to salary me, but I couldn't take it. I needed autonomy.

"I'll find a way," I said. "I can freelance as a copy editor. I'll have a good reference."

Janis's eyes moved over me, and I had the strange impression she was taking me in, really taking me in, for the first time, not my carefully chosen linen dress, not my blushing face and pinned hair, but the steadiness of my eyes, the set of my mouth, the tilt of my shoulders toward her, the way a queen would examine her newest knight, wondering how much courage he would bring, how much suffering he could bear, when suffering eventually came. And then her face contracted with an expression of approval, the deepest affirming nod.

We sipped at our lemonades. The tart and sweet blended perfectly, but Janis grimaced. "Nothing tastes the same these days," she said. "The flavor's off, but I can't remember what the right flavor is supposed to be."

Sadness for her flooded me. Her long reign was ending, or changing in inexorable ways. For a moment she seemed to shrink farther into the folds of her white blouse, but she shook her head when I started to speak. "You going to miss it?" she said. "The Rocque?"

I tried to picture the museum without me in my little office on the fourth floor, overlooking the concert hall that was finished now, and the Next Museum that would rise between, filled with art. The very streets around us would change, day by day, as more people poured in to see the new cultural destination, and the Rocque would become smaller, less visible. An annex instead of a fortress. Its old, defiant outlier spirit would fade, too, no matter how vital and exciting Yegina kept its programming.

"I'll miss what it was," I said honestly. "I think everyone will."

Janis made an appreciative noise. She took another sip of lemonade and winced.

"My father never thought his museum would last," she said. "He called it a stepping-stone, for someone else to reach the other shore. I always thought that person would be me." She gazed down over the green expanse of lawn, the sculptures casting their shadows across it. "But maybe there is no other shore here. Our downtown's potential is that vast."

"Can you say that on record?" I said.

"I'm not finished," she said. "Maybe the point is that we're always seeking. And it, whatever it is—hope? greatness?—is always retreating." She coughed. "There I go, sounding like I'm about to die. And like I haven't spent a lick of time in the tent cities east of Main. Watch out," she warned, her eyes crinkling. "I might only talk to you about the Dodgers."

28

THE CAR RIDE TO SAN Pedro was strange and long. I knew Ray, but I didn't. His body in the seat beside me seemed profoundly familiar yet foreign, like something I'd read about before but never seen. He was driving one-armed, his black eye faded to a jaundiced bruise. The afternoon I'd met with Janis, he'd called and asked me if we could postpone our meeting for one more week, and then a few days more. But finally we were riding together down the Harbor Freeway, flanked by massive trucks heading to the port. The picnic he'd brought filled the car with a salty, roasted scent, and I saw the top of a bottle of wine peeking from one bag. It was a real date.

Oddly, this fact eradicated my confidence. I was not sure we were meant for dates, Ray and I, that somehow we'd already gone far past them and yet would never get to them, either. For his part, at first, he barely looked at me, and our conversation circled awkwardly around Nelson and Layla. It would take some time to gather the evidence necessary to convict Nelson of Calvin's death, as well as his attempts on our lives. Layla's testimony was key to this, and she was insisting she'd been manipulated by Nelson since she was a minor and should be prosecuted differently. It was all very complicated, and I sensed that Ray was obsessing over the details on a daily basis.

"I still don't understand how you lost a fight with him," I said.

"I didn't lose. I made him mad enough to kill me," Ray said, his tone matter-of-fact. At my inquiring silence, he went on. "When he left my brother, Calvin was still alive. Calvin drowned in the bathtub later. So the whole time, I knew I was looking for an almost murderer—someone who would mess up, somehow. Someone who was afraid to strike again. I had to force him to strike, and then I had to fight back enough to make him want me dead."

I tried to picture the blow that shattered Ray's shoulder, but the image that came was Nelson's bloody, dangling ear. Ray had ripped it from his skull with his bare hand. The force it must have taken.

"How did you know he wouldn't just kill you then, in your own apartment?" I said.

"Because he needed to be rid of me. I knew about his secret room," Ray told me. "I guessed he was hiding black market goods somewhere. He owns no properties except the house and the gallery. When you mentioned the wine cellar entrance to Nelson's house, I went and looked there. I left behind enough hints of my presence to rattle him. By then, I figured it had to be the Westing. Something about that long hallway you said you had to drag the shoes down, and only one door. It didn't add up."

Then his tone dropped its pride and turned formal, humble, as if he were arguing a losing case. "The thing is, because he saw you digging in his trash on the surveillance camera, he connected me and you, and that put you at risk," Ray said. "When I pushed him, he went after both of us."

"You didn't make me do anything."

"I should have recognized that you would become a target," said Ray. "Though if you hadn't, I might not be alive. I'm caught between apologizing and thanking you, and both seem too weak to be appropriate. In this circumstance."

Did I want an apology? Or gratitude? Why was the conversation about what Ray needed to give me? The word *circumstance* bothered me, too. I did not feel like Ray and I were a circumstance, but I did not know what we were, riding together today, only that it felt far distant from the night I agreed to go with him to watch Davi play, certain I would never see Ray again.

Finally, we exited the freeway and cruised through commercial blocks to the neat adobe neighborhoods of San Pedro. As the city petered out to a few streets and an open horizon, I tasted the sea air seeping into the car. A picnic at the beach. For us.

"Don't worry," he said. "It's your kind of place, where I'm taking you. It'd get an A-plus for historical value and decrepitude."

He parked in a block of pastel ranches punctuated by palm trees, hopped out, grabbed the paper bag awkwardly with his free arm. There was green space beyond, blocked by a tall black fence, and beyond that, the glittering Pacific.

"Let me carry it," I said.

He shook his head. "We just have to follow the fence a ways," he said, and walked off into the weeds, as if eager to put distance between us. "Hey, there's Catalina Island." He gestured out to the smoky gray shape of land in the distance.

The tall weeds slapped at my calves. I'd chosen a simple cotton dress and practical sandals. My bare legs felt whispery warm and smooth beneath the dress, my body free. I noted a NO TRESPASSING sign.

Ray stopped at a spot in the fence where the bars had been bent to the side, making a larger gap. "I think there's a better one farther down," he said, and tramped off.

"We *are* trespassing," I said.

After another futile march down the fence, we looped back. During that interval, I kept sniffing the lunch. It smelled so good.

Too good.

I stopped in my tracks, aware of what was happening. What I should have expected would happen.

Ray didn't notice. He was preoccupied with the gap. "I did this a few weeks ago, before all this—" He patted his sling. "Well. Here goes."

He stepped through the fence sideways, with his good arm first, his hips smushing against the bars, then his sling. A look of pain crossed his face.

"We can just go to the beach," I said. "We can just sit in the car."

He kept straining, the pain in his face deepening.

"I don't even need this picnic," I said, hefting the bag, with its white-wrapped parcels, its bottle of wine. "I know you brought me here to say good-bye. The real good-bye, the one we've both rehearsed in our minds since the moment we met. Your good-bye is 'Here's the beautiful ocean and the cliffs and some tasty caprese sandwiches and wine,' and you saying how much you're attracted to me, maybe more than anyone you've ever met, but you're going home, because you're not trustworthy, and because I deserve a good life, not one dating a rural cop with a kid who needs him, and blah, blah, blah. And my good-bye is saying, 'You're right. I can't leave L.A., or my new career. So go. You're free.' Maybe you'll kiss me. Maybe you won't. Maybe we'll have great sex a few times. It's all up to how we take the news, I guess. Maybe if I start crying, you'll just hold me."

Ray stared at me, stuck in the stupid black fence, his legs bent.

"Well, I'm not crying," I said, setting the bag down. "But I might eat one of your sandwiches before I go."

Ray gave a big push and staggered through to the other side. "Just come see it. I really want you to see it."

Through the bars, I saw his good shoulder slumping and his face looking anxious.

"It's called the Sunken City," he said. "It's a neighborhood that fell into the sea in 1929. Big chunks of road are still there. Old foundations. You love ruins," he said. "You won't want to miss it."

I peered past him to a fat palm rising from some juts of square rock. Not rock. Walls. Someone's former home, broken to pieces.

"You came all this way," he said.

"I see it," I muttered.

"See it with me," he said, and he wasn't begging, but I'd never heard such emotion in his voice, and the look in his eyes was unbearably open and true.

I knew what would happen if I went through the gap, I knew even then, and the prospect sent a tide of dread and hope through me. I nearly buckled under its force, and it felt like something temporarily wiped the backs of my eyes, making the ocean and island flicker in the distance. I circled a bar with one hand, feeling the hard, thick rod of it, wondering who had been strong enough to bend such a thing. I looked back to Ray's car, an ordinary gray sedan perched on an ordinary California street.

Ray didn't say anything more. He just wiped his forehead and waited, watching me.

A siren went off in the distance, an urgent sound. Another emergency somewhere. Maybe another death.

I silently dipped to the paper bag and passed the picnic, piece by piece, through the gap. There were big sandwiches, a bag of cookies, fruit, and wine. Ray repacked the bag and set it down.

A second siren joined the first, then the long, gouging call of a fire engine.

I took a breath and mashed myself into the gap, feeling the bars crush my breasts and my hips, feeling myself wedge deeper, unable to go forward and back. My chest and pelvis hurt.

"Where am I going?" I mumbled. I felt Ray's hand take mine, warm and strong.

I shoved again and tumbled though, staggering to my knees in the long grass and dandelions. Ray caught me, one-armed, and lifted me, and I want to say I kissed him first, because I did—I found his lips before he found mine, the rightness and the heat crushing through me. His good arm closed around my waist, he held me hard against him, his mouth urgent, and for a few long moments, even the ocean beyond us vanished. Then he raised his head and whispered something into my hair, and it was all back, the smog-white sky, the crumbling cliffs, the barred fence behind us, the sling across his chest.

"What did you say?" I asked as Ray's fingers rose and brushed my collarbone then slid behind my head, twining there.

He smiled. "You'll have to find out."

And this time, he kissed me.

29

Seven Months Later

AT NIGHT, CAST IN AN upward glow by lights from below, the central LAAC complex looked less like a hive and more like a space station set in a hilly grove, surrounded by silver miles of parking lot. I drove around for a long time before finding a space, reluctant to go in. Around me, a pilgrimage of young and old Angelenos made its way to the graduation projects on view in the buildings and studios.

Brenae would have been twenty-three this month. Erik was twenty-seven. Hal, fifty-eight. Of the three of them, only Hal would be here to see Brenae's vision come to fruition. He'd been working the personal-redemption angle all winter and spring, fund-raising and advocating with his former employer for Brenae's art to appear in a posthumous exhibition at LAAC during the May week that the second-year MFA students showed their final work. Janis had helped with promotion and even privately invited Erik. *While I know the video will embarrass you to view, I hope you will con-*

sider the message this might send to other young men. Erik had responded from his fellowship in Rome with a letter about his regret for Brenae's death. But he refused to attend.

As I entered the streaming crowd, I couldn't decide if I despised Hal for using his position to manufacture a grand apology that might inflict further pain on Brenae's family, or grudgingly admired him for owning up to his mistake and honoring Brenae's wishes to make the statement she wanted to make. I wondered if people were here to see the apology even more than the art.

When I reached the central room where Ray, Janis, and I had once waited for a tour of LAAC's studios, there, in the hub of it all, a giant projection flickered, showing a younger, scrawnier Brenae sitting cross-legged in front of a tent in a living room with graffiti tags and dirt streaks on the walls. She was holding a stick over a tiny camp stove, a marshmallow on the end of it. With slow, deliberate motions, she turned the stick, then raised it and blew. The camera zoomed in: a close-up, as Brenae bit and burned herself, flinching. Then she kept eating anyway, the thick white goo clotting her mouth. It was as mesmerizing as it was hard to watch. This was the first film she'd made with Erik Reidl, and already he had packaged her: the tempted virgin consuming the forbidden fruit, the pain and pleasure in her face.

A placard announced that *Camping* would run on a loop with *After-Parties*, while *Packing* and *Lesson in Red* would only show once, at 8:00 p.m., introduced by the new LAAC director, and then Lynne Feldman and Hal Giroux. I had nearly an hour to kill before the main event.

A clanging noise interrupted my thoughts, and I turned to see a stream of dancers, a dozen of them, wearing fatigues and holding mirrors, swaying in tandem as they threaded their way through the crowd. They followed a woman in all white, her face covered with green makeup, pounding an army helmet with a hammer. *Clang, clang.* As the dancers passed out of sight, no one in the crowd actually responded to the performance; no one paused to remark on its meaning. There was so much art at LAAC, all around you, it was like leaves in the autumn wind.

A quick survey of the crowd didn't reveal my friends. I was sure that Yegina and Hiro, and Janis and Dee were here, but I didn't mind exploring on my own. I needed to be open and ready tonight; I had my recorder, my handheld boom, extra batteries. At the posted studio map, I paused and read through the graduates. One name popped out, and I froze. The noise of the room flattened to an incomprehensible babble. A crowd began to grow behind me.

Finally, I stepped aside and dialed a contact on my phone. Ray answered on the first ring.

"Are you home already?" He paused. "It's only ten here."

So he remembered. I'd e-mailed Ray the invitation to Brenae's memorial screening at LAAC. I thought he'd want to know. Part of me hoped he might fly out to see it, but only the part of me that wanted to hurt as I lay awake at night, missing his body with mine. We'd made no promises or plans, by mutual agreement. We steered away from long phone calls. It was the rational choice for now. Ray couldn't leave North Carolina, and I couldn't leave California. But it wasn't easy.

"The screening is in an hour," I said. "Layla's got an open studio, though. Should I go?"

"Does she?" He sounded disappointed, as if he'd hoped I'd called for another reason.

"I wonder if she'll actually be there."

"Hard to say," he said. "Doubt it."

The rumor was that Layla had gone to some expensive rehab retreat and now didn't leave her parents' house.

"Are you afraid of her?" Ray asked.

"No," I said. I missed his voice, its warm reassurance. "Well, maybe I am."

"It's your call," he said. "Though technically, neither of us should talk to her without lawyers present."

"Since when did we let that stop us?" I said, plucking a map. "Come with me."

LIGHTS FESTOONED THE LITTLE COURTYARD to the studios, outlining the benches and the Canter's Deli stone. The glow and the crowds made the place festive, but as I described them for Ray, I could also see the starkness of the buildings beyond, how the night exposed the dinginess and the worn paint, how the lit hallway could look long and scoured and vacant when all the doors were closed.

Layla Goetz-Middleton's studio was not on the same wing as Brenae's—how could it have been? How could Erik have sneaked around between them without being seen? But it wasn't far, either: less than fifty yards apart, just another room in LAAC's maze of rooms. I tried to explain to Ray what I saw through the doorways as I passed—pink prongs extended from three walls, and an urn at the center bubbled over with red cloth; a black-and-white projection showed a diver jumping into an empty pool; a giant hair dryer, the size of a bear, blew on the hair of a blond doll figure posed on the floor. Ray's befuddled responses made me grin and almost forget my destination until I reached Layla's studio.

"I'm here," I whispered in the hall outside the door. "It sounds like it's empty."

"Go in," Ray said. "You've got nothing to be afraid of."

I leaned on the corridor wall instead.

"Maggie?"

"I'm imagining you here. With me."

Ray was silent, and then: "That could go many ways."

I laughed sadly and pushed myself through the doorway.

A simple line of photos circled the studio, most of them close-ups: of hands, of bent heads, of crumpled gloves, of pans full of cotton swabs. At first it looked medical—nurses and patients—but this was Layla's series on nail salon workers. Accompanying the images was a timeline of a single worker getting her job, getting paid low wages for long hours, getting pregnant, getting sick, losing her baby. Nothing shouted outrage or injustice—but the chronology and its visual juxtaposition were painful to read. Layla didn't have the flair of Erik or Brenae, but she could drive home a point, and she had.

A small sign read, DUE TO PERSONAL CIRCUMSTANCES THE ARTIST CANNOT BE IN ATTENDANCE TONIGHT, BUT PLEASE USE THIS PHONE TO ASK HER QUESTIONS. A flip phone sat beside it. I related the scene to Ray.

"Do you think anyone's called?" I said.

"Doesn't seem too popular a spot," said Ray. "But you're there."

I was there, and I felt like I needed to do something, to confront something.

"Stay on the line." I took in a breath, and then picked up the phone, holding it to my other ear, dialing the only number in Contacts.

Layla answered on the third ring. The sound of her voice made my cheek go cold, as if the phone was made of ice.

"This is the artist speaking," she said after a moment.

"Hi, I'm a visitor in your studio, and I just wanted to say how moving your show is." My heart was pounding and my throat almost choked, but I forced the words to come out. "Really."

"Thank you," she said. "That means a lot."

She didn't recognize me. I lowered her phone. My thumb drifted over the end button, but I didn't hang up.

"Do you have any questions about it?" came her voice.

I raised the phone again. Hearing Layla brought me back to her scorn in the car to the Westing, back to the dead look in her face when she dragged me into Nelson's office. Maybe she had called the police that night. But it had been to save her life, not mine or Ray's. And yet I felt I owed her something. Not forgiveness. Not pity, either. I steeled myself to talk without hesitation or emotion.

"Who or what inspired your work?" I said.

"Great question," she said. "I like to see what's invisible. Nail artisans wait on people all day, all over L.A., literally at our feet, breathing toxic chemicals, and we don't think about them at all, or what we're doing to them—"

I interrupted her: "I mean, was there one person or moment that made you want to be an artist?"

"My father," she said automatically. "He loves art more than anything."

The phone felt small in my hand. There it was, the note I was looking for. Not forgiveness. Not pity. Layla's truth. She had never astonished or dazzled her father, not in the way Erik or Brenae had, not in the way she wanted to. He didn't believe in her talent, had never hungered for it to prove itself. But then one day Layla herself, as a young girl in the arms of another knowing and powerful older man—had become an artwork of his making, desired by him, shaped and defined by him. How could she let that go?

I thanked her and hung up. Two men drifted into the room, gazing at the photos, but too fast. Seeing and not looking. "Steve Goetz's daughter," commented one. "They're letting her graduate."

"What happened with her again?" said the other.

I listened to them diminish Layla to a crude item of gossip before I realized Ray was still on the line, waiting for me.

"Did you get the answers you wanted?" he said in my ear as I joined the flow of traffic into the next wing of the studios.

"I don't know," I said. "But I have nothing more to ask her."

"You tell me how it all goes," said Ray, his voice softer and more distant. "Or maybe one day, I'll listen to it on your show."

"That could be a long time yet," I said, struggling to sound hopeful.

"I'll wait," he said. "Good night, Maggie."

BRENAE'S STUDIO WAS AS EMPTY as the day we'd visited. The scuffs on the floor. The fake stars on the ceiling. The pushpin holes in the walls. A sign outside read, IN HONOR OF BRENAE BRASIL, and inside, people pivoted in silence before wandering out again. As I hung back in the hall to watch, I wondered how many of them were thinking not of Brenae's art, but of her death, here, in this very space. Putting the gun to her mouth and pulling the trigger. To know these walls as the walls that had absorbed the sound of the shot—this floor as the floor where the mattress lay, her corpse upon it—was to see a still chamber of death amid the life and creative force of the rest of the campus.

It was also to hear a silence. A silenced voice.

The morning of the screening I had been listening to my interview with Nancy Brasil, Brenae's mother, marking the best quotes. I had earned Davi's trust over several sessions, and their mother had warmed to the idea of my visiting Brenae's hometown and talking with her. Nancy bore an eerie likeness to Brenae, with a rounder, older, less expressive face. It was clear she wanted to speak, but the act unraveled her. Long pauses trailed into unfinished sentences. I was about to excuse myself out of compassion when a dog barked loudly on the street outside and Nancy burst into a story about the girl her daughter had been.

One day, teenage Brenae had chased a growling dog away from a child, and then adopted the dog when its negligent owners wanted to get rid of it. She trained it herself. "The dog became a sweetheart, a real pal to the whole town," said Nancy, "and Brenae was the one who'd given him the chance. She saw that his circumstances were not who he was, you know? And she changed them."

She was smiling at the memory, but then her face quaked and she covered her eyes.

What does anyone say in those moments that's of any use? I told her how sorry I was, my own voice breaking. Her hand fell away, and she raised her chin.

"The problem is that courage can look like anger to people," she said, holding me in her full gaze, "until they actually understand the pain you're feeling."

At the threshold to Brenae's studio, I listened to the quiet for a long time. Then I pulled out my recorder to capture it.

At quarter to eight, I clicked off my machine and was stowing it back in my purse when I heard someone say my name. I turned to see Zania de Wilde standing across from me, her arms folded, her head tilted back to regard my face. She wore a black suit with a high collar, and black boots that laced up her narrow calves.

"You've moved on, I hear," she said, as if she'd researched a few things about me.

"In some ways," I said. "How about you?"

She shrugged. "Still at LAAC."

"How are your classes?" I said, hand on my recorder. Softly I clicked it on. I couldn't use anything she said, but maybe I would want to hear it again.

"Like you actually care," she said.

I asked if she was helping with Nelson's case. He claimed he was not guilty of any assaults, only the illegal art trafficking.

"No," she said. "But I believe him."

My gut twisted as I fought the urge to contradict her. Zania stood at the threshold to Brenae's studio, then brushed her hair back from her cheeks. "My dad had a reputation in London. He came from rough places. Nobody messed with him. He could have kept James Compton's money and made himself huge." Her chest swelled with a defiant breath. "But he moved away so he could become someone new, and devote his life to helping artists."

I wondered if Zania would defend her father if she'd seen pictures of Calvin's body, of Ray's fractured shoulder. Maybe she *had* seen pictures. Maybe Layla had told her about how Nelson had seduced her and controlled her for years. Regardless, I didn't want to hear Zania's thoughts on her father. I already knew who he was.

"If you ever want to talk about Brenae, let me know," I said. "You have a rare perspective on her."

Her hand went to her neck, tugging at the tight collar. "I hope I never see you again," she said, looking into the empty room beyond us.

I left her there. It was almost time for the screening.

THE LOBBY WAS SO CROWDED when I arrived that the only space left was at the left edge of the projection, opposite the podium where Hal Giroux was now speaking, extolling the talent of Brenae Brasil, and "humbly asserting" his own regret at not celebrating it sooner.

"What you are about to see will shock and pain you, as it did me," Hal said. "But shock and pain should not be avoided for the sake of partial truths. I learned this the hard way. In art, as in life, we are always mastering this lesson, mastering our own understanding of the suffering of others and extending our compassion to them. I failed Brenae Brasil. I cannot make up for that." He paused, letting the confession sink in. I looked around for Janis's reaction, but her height made her hard to spot in a crowd. Hal went for a few more minutes, repeating himself and soaking in the spotlight, his voice rich and full, his collar parted at the neck, his forehead glistening with sweat. He did not look like a man ashamed, but a man grateful to relieve himself of his burden, and I was pretty sure that Hal thought that, once this night was over, he would be exonerated, privately and publicly. Maybe he would be. Maybe he was doing all he could. I could tell by the tense look on Lynne Feldman's face that she didn't buy it one bit, but when she got up to the podium, she simply introduced Brenae's biography and both films, and when they were made.

Packing played: Brenae shopping and eating with her weapon, sleeping with her cheek cradled against the barrel. As much as I understood about her now, she still seemed larger than life in the film—not a person, but an emblem, a figure, writ as large as any Hollywood movie character. A woman with her gun: her child and her defender and her killer in one. My eye sockets hurt from seeing her up there, so vibrant and full of life, but I didn't cry. I was bracing myself for *Lesson in Red*, and I could feel the tension in the crowd shift as the white title text displayed, and the voice-over began.

He comes. He asks me. I say yes. What can I say? What will happen if I say no? Where will I go?

There was an audible gasp as the film cut to twenty-foot-high Erik, head still blurred, lying on top of Brenae, pushing into her while her face turned away. The voice-over repeated. The blanket shuddered and slipped from her breast. The scale of the video made the sequence a thousand times worse, and I turned away from the screen. That's when I saw them in the crowd, Yegina and Hiro, staring at the video with pained eyes, and not far from them, Dee, looking queasy, and Janis, her head raised and shoulders back, as if braced for a blow. Janis had almost finished her treatment, but she'd lost weight and her frame looked thin, her complexion waxy in the flickering light. Somehow, she sensed my gaze and met it gravely.

He comes. He asks me. I say yes. What can I say? What will happen if I say no? Where will I go? The voice-over grew louder and more desperate as all of us in the crowd listened and watched and did nothing. When the screen washed red, our faces washed red, too; for a moment, each of us wore the same stained color, and then the film ended and we wore plain light again.

The silence after the video finished was long and deep. It was as if no one knew what to do with their bodies, and we just stood there, some heads bowed, some people furtively looking around, as if hoping to find a friendly face to free them from the tension. Finally, Lynne Feldman took the mic and encouraged everyone to see "all that LAAC has to offer tonight, and all the talented young artists who have brought their work to you. Let's honor their spirit and inquiry. Let's make them feel seen."

The crowd began to nudge apart. Out of the corner of my eye, I saw Yegina waving to me. And beyond her, Janis and Dee, roped together by their arms, Janis's face calm and resolute, her wig slightly askew. They paraded across the room. I felt a rush of affection for Janis, mixed with the old awe, and wondered what she would tell me now.

But before I could reach her, a hand grabbed my elbow. It was the shaved-headed manager of the Super Shop where Brenae had worked. Dee had pointed me out to her, and she wanted to be interviewed. That conversation led me to one of Brenae's coworkers, who rhapsodized about Brenae's skills with the woodworking tools, and then to someone who'd known Brenae since USC.

As I filled my recorder with their words, I barely heard what Janis leaned over to say in passing, thronged as she was by her crowd of admirers and collector friends. Later, when I walked to my car alone, the school retreating behind me, the last few students still clustered and talking on the damp lawns, her comment registered.

I reached into my purse for my phone. I knew it was too late to call anyone, and still I wanted to share all the stories I'd learned that night about Brenae, and to feel the release of knowing her, imagining her. Alive again. Here.

She'll be remembered now was what Janis said to me.

Acknowledgments

WHEN I SET OUT TO expand the *Still Lives* fiction project into new areas of the Los Angeles art culture, I knew I would need to cut out far more than I could include. All fiction about Los Angeles is an oversimplification. A city of four million people is four million cities, each filled with stories and points of view. And L.A.'s rich, multifoliate world of artists, dealers, curators, critics, professors, and students would be impossible to capture in its entirety, even in a slice.

Instead, I have created fictional institutions and characters in place of real ones, and a tighter web of relationships, in order to demonstrate some of the fundamental issues in American art-making in the early twenty-first century: the "hot" market for contemporary work and its rapid commodification; varying ideals about what a museum should be; the charged mentor-mentee relationships in expensive, reputation-building art schools; and the challenges of being a pioneering artist for a historically under-included race, gender, or class. Death, via suicide or murder, is also a heightened reality in this fictional world, emblematic of the extremes of Los Angeles and the way that young and vibrant hopes are often executed by power.

I owe a debt to The Museum of Contemporary Art, Los Angeles, for teaching me firsthand about the tremendous complexity and history of L.A. art. The following books were instrumental in further research: *Seven Days in the Art World* by Sarah Thornton; *It Happened at Pomona: Art at the Edge of Los Angeles 1969–1973* by Sarah Lehrer-Graiwer; *Jack Goldstein and the CalArts Mafia* and *The Beat and the Buzz: Inside the L.A. Art World*, both by Richard Hertz; and *Creating the Future: Art and Los Angeles in the 1970s* by Michael Fallon. The art documentary films *The Cool School* (director Morgan Neville) and *The Price of Everything* (director Nathaniel Kahn) were also illuminating. The study that Maggie Richter uncovers on campus rape and repeat offenders is a real study by David Lisak and Paul M. Miller; it can be found in *Violence and Victims* 17, no.1 (2002). The stories of assaults that Maggie read in the LAAC campus news are based on stories that victims related to me throughout my own undergraduate and graduate life.

A novel is a dream wishing its way toward completion without its first readers. Rita Mae Reese, Sara Houghteling, Elizabeth Fenton, Sarah Frisch, Miciah Bay Gault, Liz Powell, Angie Palm, and Mirra Schwartz, thank you for reading and helping me shape my early drafts. Thank you, Gail Hochman, my wise and ever-supportive agent, for asking all the right questions next.

To Dan Smetanka, my editor, thank you for always seeing the book inside the book, and for being its brilliant, generous, exacting champion.

To the Counterpoint-Catapult family—which is just large enough and dear enough to make me panic that I am forgetting someone—in my mind, you all won the Halloween contest. Thank you, Andy Hunter, for your pioneering energy and warm leadership; Megan Fishmann and Lena Moses-Schmitt, for your blazing publicity skills; Nicole Caputo, for your artistry; Dan López, for your many talents in the L.A. office; Rachel Fershleiser, in marketing; Wah-Ming Chang and Jordan Koluch in production; Janet Renard, for your eye; Katie Boland and Miyako Singer for the many details you arrange.

Thank you, Jaya Miceli, for your breathtaking covers. They teach me.

A huge thanks goes to Reese Witherspoon and Hello Sunshine for the deep impact you are making for women authors, as well as the passionate readers I've met through your book club. Thank you, Marianne Merola at Brandt & Hochman for bringing my books to audiences around the world. My gratitude also goes to my savvy TV/film agent, Mary Pender at UTA, and Temple Hill and NBC/Universal, especially Julie Waters, Adam Fishbach, and Jess Goldberg, for working to take this project to the screen.

To the University of Vermont, thank you for the grant to support this book, and for my inspiring English department colleagues and students. Dan Fogel, Major Jackson, Didi Jackson, Val Rohy, Huck Gutman, Greg Bottoms, Sarah Turner, Tony Magistrale, Chris Vaccaro, Philip Baruth, Holly Painter, David Huddle, Chloe Knapp, Margaret Edwards, and Angela Patten deserve special thanks.

Finally, thank you to my mother for your strength, generosity, and integrity—a daughter could not have a more powerful role model. Thank you to my brothers for your abiding support and for occasionally running the vacuum cleaner during my overbearing childhood performances. To everyone in the Parmelee clan and to my in-laws, you've taught me that caring for people means raising one another up, and I'm grateful.

To Bowie and Bruce, you are the light I wake for every morning. To Kyle, I don't know where to begin except that test in Fred Chappell's Modern Poetry class, where you answered the question wrong but you got a point for humor anyway. I loved you then, I love you now, and I'm still learning from you. Thank you for always believing in this work.

© Karen Pike

MARIA HUMMEL is a novelist and poet. Her most recent novel, *Still Lives*, was a Reese's Book Club x Hello Sunshine pick, Book of the Month pick, and BBC Culture Best Book of 2018, and has been optioned for television and translated into multiple languages. She is also the author of the novel *Motherland*, a *San Francisco Chronicle* Book of the Year, and *House and Fire*, winner of the American Poetry Review/Honickman First Book Prize for Poetry. She has worked and taught at the Museum of Contemporary Art, Los Angeles, Stanford University, and the University of Vermont. She lives in Vermont with her husband and sons.